MURDER IS A BEACH

ROSE PRESSEY

MURDER IS A BEACH

A MAGGIE, P.I. MYSTERY

This is a work of fiction. Names, characters, organizations, places, events, and incidents are either products of the author's imagination or are used fictitiously.

Published by Thomas & Mercer, Seattle

www.apub.com

ISBN-13: 9781477819913
ISBN-10: 1477819916

Cover design by Inkd

Library of Congress Control Number: 2013920363

Printed in the United States of America

This is to you and you know who you are.

Chapter One

A crime was the last thing I'd expected to witness while relaxing on the beach, but that was exactly what had just happened.

Being a private eye had always seemed like a thrilling career choice. Now that my dream had become a reality, I was having second thoughts on whether the excitement was such a good thing after all. Things had gone from mundane and boring to chaotic in a nanosecond.

When my Uncle Griffin Thomas passed, I took over his private investigation agency. Maggie Thomas, P.I., had a great ring to it, but as exciting as it seemed initially, it would be a miracle if I could keep the business going. Not only did he *not* use a computer, he'd had an assistant who was now *my* assistant, Dorothy Raye. She carried her knitting needles and crossword puzzle books with her everywhere she went, not to mention that she had a strange obsession with peppermint candies.

It didn't take much to persuade me to get my concealed carry permit and private investigator license, pack my bags, and head south. Being fired from my telemarketer job made the decision quite easy actually. After losing that job I couldn't be too picky, so I jumped at the chance to take over the agency. I hated that job selling burial plots anyway. I'd studied criminal justice in college until I'd changed my major to fashion.

Uncle Griffin's investigations had focused on catching a cheating spouse or finding long lost relatives. I'd grown up on the other side of Florida, in the Panhandle. After tossing my clothing into my Ford, I headed south to Miami Beach to make a new start. I added highlights to my dark hair and even bought a sexy red dress just in case I ever got the chance to enjoy the nightlife. So far it didn't look as if that were going to happen. My wardrobe mostly consisted of shorts and T-shirts, so it had been a daring venture for me to buy the dress.

It had been quite some time since I'd had a date, but I hadn't given up on the idea entirely. The red dress had definitely been an impulse buy. Dorothy wanted me to go out with Jake, but I wasn't so sure that would be a good idea. Our personalities seemed to mix like oil and water.

Based on my past relationship, I should have just given up. After I'd dated someone for over a year, he'd broken up with me for someone else. He'd tried some lame excuse, but in reality he was just a dirtbag. In hindsight I was glad that he'd called it off.

Moving to Miami wasn't as easy as I'd thought. It took a while to find an affordable place to live. I finally rented a tiny studio apartment. The best amenity was that it had running water and air conditioning that worked over 50 percent of the time. Luckily, it was just a short drive to my office and a couple blocks from the beach.

After finding a tiny apartment that near the beach and not far from my new office, I was ready for my new adventure. Little did I know that I'd get my first case on my first day as a private eye. I was even more shocked when my client was murdered. Jake Jackson was equally shocked when I solved the murder. I'd planned on taking it easy for at least a day after I wrapped up that case, but now it looked as if my mind would be occupied with thoughts of this mysterious woman.

My fun day at the beach had turned into witnessing a potentially serious crime. The smell of salt air mixed with coconut-scented sun lotion surrounded me as I'd relaxed on the beach with a tantalizing book. I was soaking up the warm sunshine when I spotted the woman on the boat off in the distance, with the aid of my binoculars. A brute of a man was dragging her across the deck, and then they disappeared below.

I was looking through my binoculars when I noticed the boat moving along the coastline. Detective Jake Jackson had just walked up when I spotted the woman on the boat. Jake was easy on the eyes, as Dorothy said. He had thick dark hair, compelling blue eyes, and classically handsome features. However, I pushed his fine physical attributes to the back of my mind.

Jake had entered my life when I discovered my first client murdered. After that, it seemed like he popped up almost everywhere I went. He was convinced that either I would accidentally be killed, or I'd accidentally kill someone else. Actually, he probably figured on both of those scenarios playing out. As far as he was concerned, my investigative skills were seriously lacking.

My assistant, Dorothy, was certain that I'd been trying to check out hot guys at the beach, but that was her hobby, not mine. Not that I hadn't glanced a few times. It was hard to resist when the men were out there without shirts, flexing their muscles right in front of me.

Jake called for backup officers, and then the Coast Guard was called right away. After hours of searching, no boat matching the description that I provided had been found. Now I looked like a complete lunatic.

"There's nothing else we can do," Jake said, running his hand through his dark hair. His tall, athletic physique gave him an air of confidence.

"I know what I saw," I said, crossing my arms in front of my chest.

"We'll just have to hope that if the woman was really in danger, she gets help."

It wasn't a question of *if* she was in trouble—it was a question of *how much* trouble she was in. No matter how hard I tried, I couldn't get her off my mind. Seeing something like that was disturbing. And it was even worse that I couldn't help her. But Jake Jackson was right... there was nothing I could do to help her, so I had to let it go.

"It's been a long day. Why don't you get some rest?" Jake's grin flashed briefly, dazzling against his olive skin.

I glanced over at Dorothy. She pretended not to listen to our conversation as she sat under a bright red umbrella, feverishly moving her knitting needles and taking in all the police action. She had been knitting the whole time while she watched the good-looking detectives.

The law enforcement officials had gathered in a nearby parking lot after Jake called, but now Jake and I had returned to the beach. Thank goodness, I had a cover-up for my red polka dot bikini because it would have been even harder for law enforcement to take me seriously as a private eye if I were half-naked.

Steady waves rhythmically hit the shore as I stared out at the spot where I'd seen the boat. The other detectives were all leaving, and it was just the three of us now. Even the people on the beach were clearing out, as the sun had already set and darkness was just minutes away.

Jake was now staring at me, waiting for a response.

I nodded. "Yeah, I guess I should get some sleep."

Dorothy stuffed her knitting needles into her bag. "I'm out of here. I hope you don't cause any more search parties while you're at dinner." She laughed and walked away toward her Cadillac.

"Do you need a ride home?" Jake raised his brow questioningly.

"I can drive," I said, motioning toward my car.

Jake flashed a smile as I climbed into my Ford. I'd been in his police car more than once, but luckily I'd never been taken to jail. Well, other than to report the bullets whizzing past my head.

Chapter Two

The next day I took off to grab dinner for Dorothy and me. After weaving through traffic and following her directions, I pulled up to the parking lot of the Captain's Quarters. The place looked like an abandoned building, with weather-beaten shutters and an aged wood façade. Palm trees surrounded the back of the building, and the front overlooked the water. The parking lot was mostly full, and I had to circle a couple times before I found a spot. Since it seemed so crowded, I assumed the food was good.

I opened the door and stepped into the air-conditioned space. The cool air felt good against my hot skin. The space was decorated with all things nautical. Fish were mounted on the walls, and they seemed to follow my every move with their eyes.

Floor-to-ceiling windows lined the back of the restaurant, overlooking the water. An outside deck surrounded the restaurant, and there was also a dock for boats to pull up and enjoy the food. Of course, looking out at the boats didn't help me forget about what had happened the day before. I was still shaken by what I'd seen and wasn't sure if I would be able to eat much of my dinner.

After checking out the menu, I placed my order for two fish sandwiches, coleslaw, and Diet Cokes, and then headed over to the bar to wait. Just as I approached, I spotted a familiar face. I thought about backing up before Jake noticed me, but it was too late. He turned around and our eyes met. He grinned, then turned around on the stool for a better view of me. I hurried over to the stool and sat down. Jake moved over a couple stools closer to me but didn't speak. Figuring this Jake Jackson out was no easy task. Sure, I'd done a little online search of him. I'd peeked at his Facebook page and saw that his relationship status was single. After that, I'd quickly closed the page. I didn't want to be considered a Facebook stalker.

"Can I get you something?" the bartender asked.

"I'll have water, thanks," I said, not glancing over at Jake.

Once the bartender walked away, I watched Jake out of the corner of my eye.

He took a sip of his bourbon, then said, "All you're going to drink is water?"

"It's a little early to drink." I glanced down at his glass and then at him, studying the clear-cut lines of his profile.

He took another sip, then said, "It looks like you're following me now." The corners of his mouth tilted up.

"Something on your mind?" I asked.

He looked straight ahead. "Nope."

I turned around and looked past the crowded restaurant onto the back deck. I froze when I spotted it—a white boat with blue letters on the side. The last word written on the back was *Vita*. I'd spotted that with my binoculars yesterday. There was no doubt in my mind that this was the boat.

"That's it," I said, pointing at the boat.

Jake set his drink down and focused his attention on the boat I'd pointed at. "That's what?"

"It's the boat where I saw the woman." My voice was reaching panic mode.

I knew by the look on his face that he didn't believe me, but that was his problem, because I was more confident than ever.

I set my water on the counter and jumped up. "Come on. We have to see if she's there."

Jake hurried after me as I ran out to the deck. I didn't even notice whether people were watching me. Of course, I was sure they wondered what the heck I was doing. I marched toward the boat, on a mission.

Jake grabbed my arm, and I stopped. "Don't do anything crazy, Maggie. Let me talk with them."

I sucked in a deep breath, then said, "Fine. But you'll have to check the boat."

"I can't do that without a search warrant," he said with compassion in his voice.

"Well, I guess you'll have to get one." I tossed my arms up.

"Did you ever happen to think that maybe you imagined what you saw? Maybe they were just playing around." Jake studied my face.

My brow furrowed. "I think I know the difference between just playing around and a woman being attacked."

"I didn't say that you don't know the difference, but you have to admit you were far away. Not to mention you were viewing the scene through binoculars." We exchanged a long look.

What Jake said about how I'd witnessed the crime was obviously true, but I was confident in what I'd seen. I wasn't changing my mind, and I wouldn't back down.

I followed Jake over to the boat. No one was standing around, and it looked as if no one was on the boat.

"Maybe they went inside to eat," I said, looking over my shoulder at the crowded restaurant. The deck buzzed with activity. People sat at tables, chatting and eating their lobster, while the servers moved about with trays of food and drinks.

A waiter walked past, and Jake stepped out in front of him. "Did you see anyone get off this boat?" Jake asked, flashing his badge.

The waiter's eyes widened as he looked at the badge and then at Jake. He shook his head. "No, I just came out here."

Jake nodded and the waiter hurried away as if he didn't want to be handcuffed.

"Why don't you wait here, and I'll check out the boat to see if anyone is on it," Jake said.

I nodded, but I knew that as soon as Jake was on that boat, I'd probably follow him. I couldn't let him handle this alone. Yeah ... as if he needed my help to handle anything. In reality, I just wanted to know what was going on, and I didn't want the information secondhand and after the fact.

I tried to control myself and wait for Jake to return, but after a minute I gave up on waiting and climbed onto the gently moving boat. I tried to calm my nerves as I looked around. It was eerie knowing that I was in the exact spot where the woman had been.

Jake had just stepped onto the main area of the boat when a man popped around from the back. His thick chestnut-colored hair reached to his mile-wide shoulders. He was a solid man and looked as if he could snap someone like a twig if that person provoked him. Obviously, he'd been on the boat the whole time. He must have heard us climb aboard. My stomach sank. I knew this was the man I'd seen on the boat yesterday. He scowled and stared at Jake and then at me. Jake was in front of me and didn't know that I was behind him.

"Who the hell are you?" the man asked with a scowl.

Jake flashed his badge again. "I'm Detective Jake Jackson with the Dade County Police."

The man glared at Jake, then asked, "Who is she?"

Jake whipped around. He quirked a brow when he saw me, then said, "She's with me."

"What do you want?" the man asked.

This was a tricky situation. Would Jake tell him that I'd seen a woman with my binoculars? It sounded kind of crazy now that I thought about it, but it was the truth.

"We have reason to believe that a woman may have been injured on this boat," Jake said.

I suppose that was a legitimate statement. Not the full story, but it was probably all that Jake wanted to tell this man. I looked at the man to gauge his reaction.

He frowned and then shook his head. "I'm the only one on the boat."

"Was someone else on here with you earlier?" I asked, not giving Jake a chance to question the man.

He looked away and then said, "No, it's just me."

I knew he was lying, but how would I be able to prove it?

"Do you mind if I look around?" Jake asked.

The man stared for a moment, then finally nodded. "Yeah, sure, take a look, but like I said, I'm the only one on the boat."

Nothing seemed out of place on the boat. But if there had been a struggle, he'd probably cleaned it up by now. There was white leather seating at the back and a couple more seats behind the front wheel.

Jake nodded and moved toward the door that led below deck. I rushed over to follow him.

He turned to me and whispered, "Stay up here and keep an eye on that guy, okay?"

I wasn't sure if Jake was just saying that to keep me from snooping down there with him or if he really thought the guy would take off. But did Jake really trust me alone with this guy? I mean, he'd obviously done something to the woman. Of course, I had a gun and I wasn't afraid to use the thing to defend myself against a murderer.

I waited by the door for Jake and kept my eyes on the man the whole time. The sun was going down, but the lights from the restaurant illuminated the entire area, so I had a good view of his face. By his glaring, I knew he wasn't happy that we were there. "Do you always search people's property at random?" he asked.

I looked him up and down. He wore tight dark blue shorts and a white-and-blue striped shirt. A gold chain was around his neck, and a matching gold bracelet on his right wrist. The less I engaged with this man, the better.

"Only when it's necessary," I said, returning his glare.

After a minute, Jake returned. I was thankful that my stare down with this guy was over.

He shook his head. "We're sorry we bothered you."

The man gestured with a tilt of his head. "No problem."

I glared at Jake, and he motioned for me to follow him off the boat. I hesitated but then followed him back to the restaurant's deck.

"What happened?" I asked as I walked along beside him.

"There was nothing down there. No woman and no signs of anything out of the ordinary. I'm sorry, Maggie; if there's nothing there, then I can't arrest the man just because you thought you saw something." Jake held the door open for me.

"I told you I *know* I saw something," I said, stepping back into the air-conditioned restaurant.

He nodded. "I believe you, Maggie—really, I do."

I definitely wasn't in the mood for food now. I needed a long bath and an episode of *Magnum, P.I.* right away. Jake paid his bill, and I picked up my food; then we headed out toward my car. This wasn't how I'd thought my evening would end. To be honest, I'd thought my evening would end with me eating a fish sandwich while watching TV. But my new job was throwing a few curve balls into my routine.

Chapter Three

I placed the food in my car and turned around to face Jake. "Thanks for checking out that guy's boat for me," I said.

Jake stared at me. "I'm sorry that I didn't find anything."

I shook my head. "You did all you could. Maybe I'm overreacting, but it was just disturbing to see the woman in distress and not be able to help her."

"I completely understand." He reached for my hand, giving it a squeeze.

I met his gaze, and his hand lingered on mine. His skin was warm against mine. It had been a long time since I'd had butterflies in my stomach.

"I guess I'd better go. I have to be up early in the morning," he said, motioning toward his car.

"Me too." I watched him walk a few spaces over to his car.

Jake got behind the wheel of his car. He paused for a beat before starting the engine, as if he wanted to say more. I watched as he pulled out onto the street.

As I sat there in my car, I took in a deep breath and relished the sea air. I needed to clear my head, so I figured one of the best ways to do that was to take a walk along the beach. Dorothy had already sent multiple text messages—she wanted her fish sandwich. First, I had to take Dorothy her food, but right after that I was heading back to the scene of the possible crime.

After driving back to the location where I'd seen the boat yesterday, I locked my car door and made my way out onto the sand. The beach wasn't as hot underneath my feet, now that the sun had set. I hoped that a crab wouldn't dash across my feet, though. I could deal with big tough guys, but not with one of those little scurrying things.

I walked out to the shore and let the water splash against my legs. The moon was bright and reflected on the ocean. It was a romantic scene, so why had I sent the one guy who had shown any interest in me home?

I took off down the shore, thinking I was the only one on the beach. It was peaceful and a little scary at the same time. I made it a short distance down the shore when I noticed a group of people gathered up ahead. It looked as if they were standing over something.

When I got closer, I realized that something was definitely lying on the shore. The waves lapped up against it. My stomach turned, and my heart rate sped up. I prayed that what I thought I saw wasn't really what was there.

It looked as if a body was lying on the beach. And since the body was face down, I didn't think this person was relaxing in the sand.

I hurried my steps, but once I got close to the group, I stopped. There were three women and two men. They all appeared to be about my age. A dark-haired woman turned to look at me with a terrified look in her eyes.

"She's dead," the woman said matter-of-factly.

"Are you sure?" I asked.

She nodded. "Yes, we're positive. There's no pulse."

There was definitely a woman lying face down in the sand on the shore. She was wearing a white bikini. My legs went weak when I realized that the woman who had been on the boat had also been wearing a white bikini. It couldn't be her, right? Unfortunately, I knew that not only could it be her, it was more than likely her.

"Are you okay?" the woman beside me asked.

I didn't know what to say. First thing I needed to do was call Jake, but I'd left my phone in the car.

"You're sure they checked the body?" I asked. "What if she's still alive?"

"Yes, he checked." She pointed at the blond man.

Either way, I needed to get help there right away. I stepped closer to the body and knew immediately that they'd been telling the truth. She was no longer alive. Her body had already started to take on a bloated appearance.

Without saying another word to the woman, I ran back to my car to get my phone. This whole thing seemed surreal. My hands were shaking so badly that I couldn't even get the door open. Finally, I grabbed my phone from my purse and punched in Jake's number. I wasn't looking forward to explaining how I'd stumbled on yet another body. What were the odds? At least I hadn't been the one who found her first. I should have just gone home instead of taking a walk.

Jake answered on the second ring. "I didn't expect to hear from you so soon," he said.

There was no need to sugarcoat this for him. "I have a problem," I said matter-of-factly.

It seemed as if that was the only reason I ever called Jake, and I felt bad about that now, but there was nothing I could do about it at the moment.

"What's wrong?" he asked with anxiety in his voice.

"I was walking on the beach, and there's a woman on the shore. I know she's dead," I said breathlessly.

"What?" His voice was beyond shocked.

"It's the woman I saw on the boat." I spoke the words but still couldn't quite believe it.

"What were you doing on the beach?" he asked. "I thought you were having dinner with Dorothy."

"I decided to go for a walk on the beach," I said, not hiding my annoyance.

"I'll be right there," he said, and then the phone went dead.

I stayed by my car while I waited. I could have gone back out there with the people, but honestly, I wanted time to wrap my mind around what I'd seen. Or at least attempt to wrap my mind around what I'd seen. How had this woman gotten there? Had the man just tossed her overboard?

Chapter Four

Time dragged on forever until Jake showed up. Just when I thought he wasn't coming, his car turned in and sped across the lot. The light on the top of it flashed, and the siren was blasting. Other police cars were right behind him, with their lights flashing and sirens sounding too.

"What happened?" Jake asked as he ran over to me.

I gestured toward the beach. "She's out there on the shore. At least she was when I left her. There's a group of people who found her."

He took off toward the water with the other officers following him. I stepped over to the beach access and watched from afar. I'd been around too many dead bodies and crime scenes recently; I didn't need to see another one. But curiosity finally got the best of me, and I ventured closer to the scene.

I'd only barely made it back to the beach when I spotted the reporters headed our way. I recognized one of them from the nightly news. She held a microphone in her hand. They saw me looking at them, and we made eye contact. I hoped they wouldn't come over to me, but as the reporter stepped closer, with a laser-like focus on me, I knew she was headed my way. I looked around for somewhere to escape, but there was nowhere to go other than jumping into the water. Since that wasn't an option, I was stuck.

They would pretty much just be wasting their time by talking to me because I didn't have anything to tell them. I scanned the area for Jake, thinking maybe if I spoke with him, they'd leave me alone, but he was talking to the other officers.

A crowd of people had gathered nearby. They were my only chance to escape because I could hide among them. Why hadn't the reporters decided to talk with someone else? As I ran toward the crowd of people, a reporter called out to me.

"Excuse me," she said.

I stood next to the crowd, not looking over my shoulder. Someone else could talk to the reporters, although now that I thought about it, I could just tell them I didn't want to talk with anyone. "No comment." I could explain that I was camera shy. But knowing me, I would have started talking even if I hadn't wanted to. I had a tendency to get chatty when I was nervous. Avoiding them altogether was a much better idea. The crowd was discussing the grisly discovery, all speculating about what had happened to the poor woman.

After a couple seconds, I felt someone behind me. I made the mistake of turning around only to find the reporter was standing right behind me.

She brushed a lock of her blonde hair from her shoulder and smiled. "Do you know what's going on here?"

Just as I'd expected, I couldn't keep my mouth shut and said, "They found a dead woman on the beach." I pointed toward the body.

Her eyes widened. "Did you find the body? Are you a witness?" she asked.

I nodded. "Well, I saw the body and I walked up to the other people who had found her first."

"Do you know which of these people found her first?" She gestured.

I shrugged. "Not really. It's dark, and I was more focused on the dead body."

"Would you mind if we interview you?" she asked with little enthusiasm, as if I weren't her first choice.

I found myself nodding without even realizing it. Before I knew it, I'd stepped away from the group of people, and she was shoving the microphone in front of my face. The man with her had a light shining on me, and I knew when the police saw them, they'd probably tell them to get lost.

"So you found the body?" she asked.

I shook my head. "No, I was here when a group of people found the woman. The police weren't here yet."

"Do you know the woman?" she asked.

I shook my head again. "No, I don't know her."

"How long do you think she's been here?" she asked with a little too much fervor.

I glanced over my shoulder, looking for Jake. "Well, I don't know, but I'd say not long considering this is a public area. I was here earlier today."

"You were here earlier today?" She frowned as if totally confused by what I'd said.

"They were looking for a woman earlier today, and we were at this spot." I gestured over my shoulder.

Her eyes widened. "So this is a woman they'd been looking for?"

I'd already said too much. "I don't know." I wanted to add "No comment" to my last statement.

"And who are you?" she asked.

"My name is Maggie Thomas. I'm a private investigator here in Miami."

What was I doing, a commercial? She hadn't even asked that question. I should have kept my mouth shut.

She smiled widely, apparently happy with the info she'd gotten from me. "Thank you." Finally, she motioned for her film crew to follow her. I assumed she was off to find the next interview victim.

Jake approached after what seemed like forever. But he wasn't alone. A man in a gray suit walked beside him. Their focus was fixed on me. Jake's expression was much softer than the other man's, though. When they stopped in front of me, the other guy looked at me with a scowl. Now that he was standing in front of me, I recognized him. He was the detective who had questioned me when my client's killer had fallen off a balcony in a struggle with Jake.

"Can you tell us what you were doing when they found her, Maggie?" Jake asked.

I nodded and then recounted the whole scene. Their expressions were stoic through the entire story. I knew it was pretty crazy, but it was the truth.

When the other detective got a phone call, Jake leaned in close to me. "I thought you were going home," he whispered.

The other officer raised his brow and clicked off his call. I looked from the detective back to Jake.

"I already told you that I decided to take a walk along the beach. It's relaxing," I said.

Jake stared for a moment, then nodded. "We're trying to find out who she is."

"I know it's the woman who I saw on the boat," I repeated as if he hadn't heard me the first time.

"You've got really bad luck," the other detective said. "I mean, finding these dead bodies." His gaze was locked on my face.

"My luck isn't nearly as bad as the luck of the people I found," I said.

When I returned his stare, he looked away from me. I was good at staring too and could match his intensity.

After a moment, he looked at me again. "You have to admit that it's suspicious that you made the call about the woman and now she shows up on the beach."

I ran my hand through my hair. "Is it okay if I go home now? It's been a long day."

Without another question, the detective walked away. Now it was just Jake and me. He leaned close. "Are you okay?"

I nodded. "I'll be fine. I'm getting used to this now."

He stared at me as if trying to tell whether I was being completely honest with him. Finally it worked, and I said, "Oh, who am I kidding? I could never get used to it."

He grabbed my hand and his hold lingered for a moment. I let go and got into my car.

"I'll call you later," he said softly.

I waved as I took off. I was glad to be away from that scene. That man on the boat had to have known we were looking for the woman he'd probably pushed overboard. I had no way of knowing that he'd pushed her for sure, but it was the first thought that had popped into my mind when I'd seen her lying there on the beach.

Chapter Five

I didn't think of going back to the restaurant until my car was pointed in that direction. It was as if, subconsciously, I just took off on that course without even being aware of it.

The odds of the boat still being at the restaurant were slim, but if I didn't go check it out, I would always wonder. Within a few minutes I pulled up to the now empty parking lot. It looked as if even the employees had already gone home. I knew this was a pointless trip, so why was I getting out of my car and walking across the empty tarmac? The answer to that question: because my curiosity always won.

If the restaurant was closed, then the boats would be gone now too, but I'd driven all the way there—I supposed there was no harm in just taking a look. Besides, maybe being back to the location where I'd seen the boat up close would spark something in my memory. Maybe I'd seen something that I hadn't thought was important at the time.

I took my time walking up to the restaurant. It felt strange to be back there by myself so soon after having such an odd evening with Jake. I'd made it to the side of the restaurant when my phone dinged, indicating that I had a text message. I stopped and pulled it out of my pocket.

I've been thinking that maybe you should ask Jake out on a date.

The text was from Dorothy. How had she figured out how to send a text on her giant old lady phone?

I typed back. *No.*

I stuffed the phone back into my pocket. It immediately dinged again, but I ignored it. Dorothy would have to wait until tomorrow to continue her matchmaking games. Obviously, I didn't want to mention the little detail that I'd stumbled on another dead body. I'd ruin her night's sleep if I told her now, and she'd find out soon enough.

I made my way around the deck and to the back of the restaurant. Unfortunately, there was a small iron fence around the boat dock area. My eyes were adjusting to the darkness, but as far as I could tell, there were no boats there now. I should have just turned around right then, but no—I always had to push things.

I stepped closer to the fence and gauged the height. It was waist high, so I was pretty sure I could get across without killing myself, although it had been only a short time ago that I'd gotten my shorts caught while trying to climb someone's gate. On that occasion, I'd almost thought I'd have to call Jake to rescue me. Luckily, that hadn't been the case, because it would have been more than a little embarrassing.

The sign on the area specifically stated that there was no entering when the restaurant was closed, but I had to ignore that warning. I prayed that I wouldn't get caught and that no one would call the police if they saw me.

Just as I suspected, there were no boats at the dock. I walked over to where the boat had been just a few hours ago and stared out into the darkness. Water lapped up against the wood, and stars dotted the immense black sky. The wind blew my hair, and the salt air tickled my nose.

After standing there for a couple minutes, lost in thought, I figured it was time to go home. I turned to leave, and that was when I spotted something shiny on the deck. The object was just lying there as if someone had dropped it. I looked around, but of course, as far as I could tell, no one was watching me.

There was only a faint glow from the restaurant, and I assumed it was a light that they kept on all the time. I stepped closer and realized that the object was a gold bracelet. I reached down and picked it up. It was large, so I figured it was a man's. Could the man from the boat have lost it?

I'd noticed him wearing a gold bracelet. It had to be his, right? There had been a lot of people on the deck, although he had been one of the last out there tonight. If the bracelet had been lost earlier in the evening, someone would have found it before now. I studied the bracelet more closely, flipping it over. That was when I noticed the name "Sam" engraved on the back. I stuffed the bracelet into my pocket and headed across the empty parking lot toward my car.

The palm fronds rustled in the breeze. The faint sound was slightly spooky as it whispered through the air. It was probably my nerves playing tricks on me, but all the way to my car, I had the distinct sense of someone watching me.

This day had been so bad that not even an episode of *Magnum, P.I.* would make me feel better. Moving away from the city, I left the flashing lights behind and turned onto my slightly less noisy street. By some miracle, I found a space next to my apartment building and parked the car at the curb. I grabbed my purse and made my way to my front door. The surrounding buildings looked similar to my own. I was surprised that I hadn't accidentally walked into someone's apartment, thinking it was mine. The neighbors were rarely out and about. I'd only seen the man in the apartment next to mine for the first time yesterday. He'd flashed a tiny grin and nodded as he hurried into his place.

Kicking off my sandals, I tossed my purse onto the bed and then curled up on my tiny sofa. I watched a couple of my favorite episodes of *Magnum* and finished off the jar of peanut butter. I tried to focus on the show, but my mind was distracted.

It was times like this, when everything was quiet, that I wondered about what had really happened to my father. Dylan Thomas had been murdered in the line of duty when I was young. His murder was still unsolved. Would my life have been different if he were still alive? My mother was still in Vegas with her most recent husband. Sure, Stan wore too much cologne and had a serious comb-over, but he was a nice enough guy. Heck, I kind of even hoped that my mother kept him around. At least I hoped she kept him around longer than she had the others.

My mother had begged me not to take over my uncle's agency. But I'd needed a change, and nothing she could have said would have stopped me.

I stood up from the sofa, stretched, and then sat at the tiny desk on the other side of the room. While I waited for my laptop to turn on, I jotted down notes for my father's case. I'd been researching it for some time now.

I was working with names of people my father had arrested when he'd been a police officer back in the small town in Kentucky where I'd been born. It was a long shot, but I wanted to research every name on my list. Maybe something small, no matter how minute, might give me a clue that would lead to the killer.

A gang of men had claimed they'd killed my father, but the police had looked into it and ruled them out. I'd found a couple of them were now in prison for burglary and attempted murder, and the other two were still living in that small town. Maybe I'd get a chance to pay them a visit. That would be risky, and if my father were alive, he probably wouldn't want me to do it, but I usually didn't follow people's advice, even if I knew they are more than likely right.

After about an hour, I shut off the computer and climbed between the sheets. The air conditioner hummed noisily in my ear. I couldn't stop thinking about the woman on the boat. If only I'd seen her sooner—maybe then the police could have found her in time.

It took a while, but I eventually drifted off to sleep while making a mental list of things I needed to do the next day. The very last thought in my mind when I fell asleep was Jake Jackson.

Chapter Six

The next morning my phone woke me up. It wasn't the text message this time, but a full-on loud ring in my ear. I had a feeling it was Dorothy when I looked at the clock and realized that I'd overslept yet again. Could anyone blame me though? I'd had nightmares about all the dead bodies and had a hard time staying asleep.

I grabbed the phone mostly just to make the annoying noise stop.

"What in the hell is going on? Are you a magnet to dead people? I'm beginning to wonder if I should hang around you, Maggie Thomas."

Uh-oh. How had she found out about last night? "Did you call Jake?" I asked.

Dorothy scoffed. "No, I most certainly did not, and I am offended that you think I would do such a thing."

Dorothy didn't need to give me that fake offended thing, because I knew that given the opportunity, she would definitely call Jake. "I don't know what you're talking about," I said.

She wiggled her finger in my direction. "That's not what the morning paper says."

I shot up in bed. "What does the paper say?"

"It has the story about the young woman found on the beach. It says right here in black and white that a private eye named Maggie Thomas found the body while out for a stroll along the beach. You were alone on the beach? I thought I told you to ask Jake out last night. What did you do to him?"

I fell back on the bed. "I didn't discover another dead body. I just happened to walk up when a group of people found her. The newspaper has it all wrong. Plus, you thought I discovered a body and all you're worried about is my date?"

"Well, of course not, but the thought did cross my mind. What were you doing out there?" she asked.

"Just like the article said, I was taking a walk," I said with exasperation. Why did everyone keep asking me that?

Dorothy released a heavy sigh. I couldn't believe that they'd written my name in the paper. I definitely didn't want to be involved, and having my name listed in black and white as finding the body was not the way to do that.

"I'll be there soon, Dorothy," I said, hanging up the phone.

After jumping out of the shower, I slipped on a pair of khaki shorts and a green shirt. Green is my favorite color because someone told me that it brought out the green in my hazel eyes. I slid into my flip-flops and rushed out the door. I was in a hurry to get to the office, but I was in an even bigger hurry to get coffee—a large cinnamon vanilla latte, actually.

There was a coffee shop close to the office, and it wouldn't take long to pop in and grab a cup. What was another few minutes when Dorothy had waited this long? I was standing in line, ready to place my order, when I felt eyes on me.

"Looks like you're a celebrity." Jake was staring right at me, with a copy of the morning paper in his hands.

I groaned. Luckily, the man behind the counter took my order and gave me a few seconds' reprieve before I had to respond to Jake.

"I take it you've seen the newspaper," he said.

I stepped to the side so that the person behind me could place her order. "Yes, I saw it," I said in a hushed tone, taking the paper from his hands. "Do you have to wave it around for everyone to see?"

"You're lucky they didn't put your picture in there. No one will recognize you without the photo." His lips parted in a dazzling smile.

"Yeah, lucky me, but my name is in there, and that's bad enough." I grabbed my coffee.

Jake touched my arm. "Listen, I just wanted to tell you that it was nice to see you last night before all the craziness started."

A grin spread across my face, and I said, "It was nice seeing you too."

Lately, there had been a little too much craziness though. Jake ordered his coffee and then turned to face me.

"Did you find out who she is yet?" I asked, taking a sip from my cup.

After receiving his order, Jake and I were at the front of the store. He looked as if he was about to tell me something when he stopped and looked over at the man at the counter. I wasn't sure how Jake had known, but the man suddenly pulled out a gun and then pointed it at the person behind the register. It was as if Jake had sensed what was about to happen. The young man behind the counter put his hands in the air. I couldn't believe the place was being robbed right there in front of us. I had a feeling this criminal was about to realize what a stupid mistake he'd made.

Jake pressed his arm in front of me and pulled his gun out of its holster with his other hand.

"Get down, Maggie," he whispered.

I crouched down behind the table that we'd been standing beside. It wouldn't provide much protection if bullets started flying. I looked around at the other terrified faces. Everyone had already taken cover behind tables and chairs. Some people had been lucky enough to escape. I prayed that no one got hurt in this situation. The poor guy at the register was struggling to get the thing open and hand over the cash.

Jake jumped up and moved over to the counter where the gunman stood. He aimed his gun at the perp. The man must have noticed the change of expression from the guy behind the counter because he started to turn around.

"Put your hands up," Jake yelled.

The man slowly raised his hands above his head and then turned around to face Jake. His eyes widened when he saw Jake behind him with the gun aimed right at him. I bet he didn't expect that to happen. Like I said, he'd picked the wrong shop to rob today.

"Don't make another move," Jake ordered.

I was close to the door and noticed an older woman approaching. I didn't want her to walk in on this situation. I eased up from the spot behind the table and moved over toward the door. When I thought she was close enough to see me, I waved my arms through the air to try to get her attention. She scowled at me and opened the door anyway.

Jake turned around to see what the commotion was. That was when the thug took the opportunity to try to get the gun from Jake. The woman screamed when she realized what was happening. I'd tried to warn her, but she'd probably just thought I was crazy.

The lady froze on the spot. She had a deathly hold on her pocketbook. Her eyes were focused on Jake and the would-be robber. I was worried that the gun would go off, and she'd be in the line of fire, so I reached over and grabbed her. She screamed out again. This time she probably thought I was actually attacking her instead of trying to keep her safe. The woman struggled with me, but I eventually got her safely behind the table.

"Don't worry. The policeman is taking care of it," I said.

When I looked up and saw Jake still struggling with the guy, I wasn't sure what to think. They'd moved to the ground, and I knew they were in a battle for the gun. I had to do something before Jake was hurt.

I'd just placed my hand on my gun to pull it out when Jake snatched the guy up from the floor and slammed him into the counter. It looked like Jake was able to take care of the situation after all. Jake pulled the man's hands behind his back and secured his wrists with the handcuffs. Thank goodness, this situation hadn't ended badly.

Jake had looked as if he wanted to tell me something, but now it seemed as if that would have to wait.

"Are you okay?" I asked the woman whom I'd pulled to the floor.

She released a deep breath and nodded. "I guess I'm okay."

I took hold of her arm and helped her to her feet. "I'm sorry that I grabbed you like that."

She adjusted her purse and smoothed down her gray hair. "Oh, that's okay. You were trying to keep me safe, and I appreciate that, so thank you."

I smiled. "You're welcome."

The next thing I knew, police officers had descended on the area. The customers were quickly filing out of the shop. I guided the woman over to an officer and then turned my attention to Jake.

He was still holding the guy and hadn't noticed my eyes on him. Finally, an officer approached Jake and took the perp by the arm. He walked him across the room and toward the door. Of course, I couldn't help but glare at the guy as he walked past. He'd terrified a bunch of people, and that made me furious. Our eyes met for a moment, but he quickly looked away. There was something in his eyes that looked familiar, but I wasn't sure why. I knew I'd never seen him before, though. I watched as the officer escorted him out the door and toward the police car.

Someone touched my arm, and I jumped. Jake was standing next to me. I'd been so consumed by watching the criminal that I hadn't heard him approach. My jumpiness wasn't a great private eye move. I needed to be aware of my surroundings all the time.

"Are you okay?" Jake asked.

I nodded and offered a grin. "I'm fine. What about you?"

He ran his hand through his hair. "Much better now."

"How did you know what that guy was doing?" I asked.

Jake shrugged. "Sometimes you can just pick up on the vibes. He looked nervous. I figured it wasn't from drinking too much coffee."

People stared at us as we stepped out of the shop. I was thankful that Jake had been in the place at just the right time. The situation could have ended tragically.

Jake walked with me outside to my car.

"About what I said before, did you find out who the woman is?" I asked.

He shook his head. "We don't have a positive identification, but we are looking for the boat."

"I'm glad to see that you finally believe me." Satisfaction was evident in my voice.

He touched my chin with his finger. "I always believed you."

I couldn't hide my smile.

"I know what you're thinking," he warned.

My eyebrows rose. "What are you talking about?"

"Maggie, I don't think you should get involved with this case. It could be dangerous."

"You know more than you're telling me."

He took a drink of coffee, avoiding my gaze, and then said, "I didn't say that…"

His phone rang, which got him off the hook for the moment. "I'll call you later," he said as he grabbed his phone and headed toward his car.

I wouldn't let Jake Jackson remain silent for long. We would definitely revisit this topic soon.

Chapter Seven

Dorothy was knitting when I stepped into the office. She didn't bother to hide the needles anymore. If you looked from just the right angle, my office had a view of the ocean. I'd banged my knees more than a few times on my desk because of the cramped space, but other than that, I liked the cozy space. I still hadn't found the time to change the stenciling on the front door. Soon I'd replace the name Griffin Thomas with the name Maggie Thomas, Private Investigator. I really liked the sound of that.

Dorothy kept knitting and didn't look at me. I could tell that she wasn't happy. Today she wore a white blouse with a large yellow tropical flower print and coordinating yellow capri pants. Yellow bangles and big hot earrings accessorized the outfit. "It's about time you showed up," she said.

"I had to stop for coffee." I waved my cup in her direction.

She placed the needles on the desk and looked at me. "Well, you actually got a call this morning from someone other than the reporters who wanted to talk with you." She pushed to her feet, grabbed the little slips of paper with the phone messages, and placed them on my desk. She tapped them with her bright red painted fingernail. "You have an appointment today."

"I do?" I asked as I picked up the papers.

"Yes, he'll be here in an hour," she said as she walked back to her desk.

I had to recount last night's events several times in that hour before my appointment arrived. Mostly Dorothy just wanted to hear about seeing Jake at the restaurant. She was convinced we'd had some secret rendezvous. I'd also read the news article several times while I sat at my tiny desk. When my phone rang, Dorothy and I exchanged a look. After another ring, I answered, thinking it was probably my appointment calling to cancel. I couldn't have been more wrong.

"I've got information that I thought you'd want to know," Jake said.

"Oh yeah? What's that?" I asked.

"We have a positive identification on the woman. Now, Maggie, I'm sharing this with you because I believe you won't tell anyone else."

"I'm listening." I leaned back in my chair.

"Her name was Kristin Grant."

I jotted down the name. At least this was a start, and I was shocked that he'd shared the information. Right on time there was a knock at the door.

"Thanks for the info, Jake. I have to go." I rushed my words.

After hanging up, I hurried over and eased the door open. An older man stood in front of me.

"Are you Maggie Thomas?" he asked.

I looked down and noticed the newspaper in the man's hand. Dorothy hadn't asked what this man wanted, so I now became instantly suspicious. Was he some kind of crazy? Maybe he was a reporter, and he'd tricked Dorothy into an interview. There was nothing left for me to say about what had happened, so I hoped he wasn't expecting any answers.

"Yes, I'm Maggie Thomas. May I help you?" I asked.

He wore a beige button-down shirt and brown pants. He looked to be about Dorothy's age, with gray hair and bright blue eyes. "I'm in need of your services."

I stepped out of the way and gestured for him to enter. "Please come in and have a seat at my desk."

Dorothy looked at the man and gave a bashful grin, which was completely unlike her.

I gestured. "This is my assistant, Dorothy Raye."

He tilted his head. "Nice to meet you, ma'am."

"The pleasure is mine," she said softly.

The man sat in front of my desk and placed the newspaper down in front of me. It was face up to the article about my discovery the evening before. I glanced down and then back up at him. What kind of game was he playing?

"My name is Morton Grant. That was my granddaughter," he said in a weak voice. "The police informed me of what happened this morning."

My stomach turned. "I am so sorry."

"We hadn't spoken in a while. She'd cut off contact with the family, but I love her and want to know what happened. She had her demons, but I loved her just the same," he said.

I nodded. "I understand."

"When I saw your name and that you're a private investigator, that was when I knew I had to ask you to help." He pleaded with his eyes.

"Why not let the police find out what happened?" I asked.

He shook his head. "They have too much going on. If they don't find something right away, they'll give up. I need someone to focus all their attention on finding out what happened. I won't rest until I have answers. Will you help me?" he asked.

I didn't know what to think. Did he know that I'd seen his granddaughter alive on that boat? There was no way he could have known.

"Will you help me?" he asked again.

"Of course she'll help you," Dorothy said with a huge smile.

Maybe it was my imagination, but I thought Dorothy batted her eyelashes at the man. Was she flirting with him?

I nodded. "Okay, yes, of course I'd love to help you."

"Thank you," he said.

He pulled a card from his wallet and handed it to me. A gold bracelet was around his wrist. That was strange because it looked like the one I'd found the night before, which was still in my purse, as far as I knew. I looked down at the card he'd given me. "Grant Jewelers" was written at the top. His name was in the middle with "Owner" written under that. Well, that explained why he wore so much jewelry. Besides the bracelet on his wrist, he had several gold rings.

"You can reach me at that number any time. If I don't answer, please leave a message and I'll call you right back." He pointed toward the card.

"Can you tell me a little more about your granddaughter?" I asked.

"Like I said, she didn't talk to her family much. I tried to keep in contact, but she kept her distance." He twisted his hands in his lap.

"Why is that?" I asked. If I was going to take on this case, I had to know as much about her as possible.

"She always had a turbulent relationship with her parents. She just didn't want to talk to anyone." He shrugged. "We never really understood why. I will admit that her parents have always been strict and a bit cold."

Basic information about the victim would be useful. I hated to push him for details when he was in such an emotional state of mind. "How old was your granddaughter?"

"She was thirty-five," he answered.

Did she have any children or a husband? I asked.

"No. Here's a current picture of her." He handed me a glossy photo.

It was eerie to look at her beautiful face after seeing her on the beach. There was something haunting in her eyes.

I nodded. "Where did she work?"

"She was quite successful. She owns the Captain's Quarters Restaurant," he said softly.

I almost choked. What were the odds? There had to be a connection because I'd seen the man with the boat at the restaurant.

"I was just at the restaurant last night," I said.

He frowned. "Really?"

"Yes, Dorothy suggested it for dinner. We heard wonderful things about the food."

He nodded. "She had a partner in the business," he said.

"Who was her partner?" I asked.

"I don't know anything about him really. His name is Justin Mack."

I wrote down the name. "Okay. I'll look into it. I'll find out everything I can."

Morton Grant handed me another piece of paper and a key. "That paper has a few details about her, just general info. The key is to her apartment. You'll find the address on the paper as well. I came to you right away because I know the first forty-eight hours are crucial in finding the killer."

"We don't know that she was murdered," I said in a comforting tone.

"I know she would never go for a swim, and I don't think she would willingly get onto a boat. How else did she get into the water?" he asked.

Somehow that man had gotten her on his boat. He'd probably forced her against her will.

"I'll do everything I can," I said. "Let me ask you. Did she have a boat?"

He shook his head. "Not that I know of. She was always terrified to go into the water. She loved the beach but hated the water. I know that's strange . . . and terrible that that was how she ultimately died." He looked down at his hands for a moment.

"I know how hard this is for you. I'm here to help." I gave a sympathetic smile.

He looked at his watch. "If you'll excuse me, I have another important meeting."

Morton Grant stood and walked toward the door. He smiled at Dorothy, and she beamed.

When he walked out the door, she shook her head. "That poor man. You have to help him. It just breaks my heart."

I stared at her. "You like him, don't you?"

"Oh, don't be silly." She waved off my question.

Jake had wanted me not to get involved in this case, but it looked as if it were too late now. Maybe I could keep my involvement from him?

"How old was Kristin Grant?" Dorothy asked.

I picked up the newspaper. "It says she was thirty-five."

"Still so young." Dorothy shook her head. "So what do we do now?"

"We?" I asked with a raised eyebrow.

"Yes, 'we.' I am your assistant." She motioned from me to her. "You'll need my help."

"I need your help to answer the phone." I pointed toward my sad little desk with the silent phone sitting in the middle.

"Are you still on that kick?" she snorted. "Your phone's not ringing off the hook."

"You just want to help so you can be next to Morton Grant." I wiggled my eyebrows.

She scoffed. "I don't know what you're talking about. That is ridiculous. I am not interested. I haven't been on a date in years."

"And you were complaining because *I* haven't been on a date?" I asked.

"We should go to the restaurant," Dorothy said, changing the subject.

"I doubt the place is open today. Wouldn't they close since one of the owners died yesterday?" I asked.

Dorothy pondered the thought. "Maybe so, but we have to check it out. Besides, do you have any other ideas?"

Well, she had me there. "No, I don't have any other ideas. But I'm driving this time." I was convinced that Dorothy had never driven under the speed limit a day in her life. And I wouldn't even get started on her abrupt lane changing.

She shrugged and stuffed her knitting needles and crossword puzzles into her purse. She really never went anywhere without them. "I'm ready," she said as she made her way toward the door. "By the way, do you still have his card? I'd like to take a look, if you don't mind."

I suppressed a smile and handed her the card. "He's a nice-looking man. I wonder if he's married," I said.

She stared at me for a moment, then said, "He probably is taken. A man like that wouldn't have a problem finding a wife."

I shrugged. "I don't know; maybe he doesn't have anyone special in his life."

"Well, he just lost a granddaughter. I hardly doubt he would be worried about going out with anyone," Dorothy said, flipping the card around in her hand.

"That's true. But maybe you could be friends. After all, friends help friends through a lot of tough times. I bet he could always use another friend."

She bit back a smile. "We have work to do."

Chapter Eight

Thank goodness, Dorothy didn't insist on driving her Cadillac. Her driving resulted in me having repeated panic attacks. I climbed behind the wheel of my own car, and Dorothy got in on the passenger side. She immediately whipped out the knitting needles.

"If I'm not driving, then I have to be doing something with my hands," she said when I glanced over at her.

"I didn't say anything," I said, turning the ignition.

"You didn't have to. I know you better than you think I do." She pointed with one of her needles.

We made our way down Biscayne Boulevard toward the Captain's Quarters. Luckily, the traffic wasn't bad. Within a few minutes I'd pulled into the parking lot.

"I almost expected to see the police here. Won't they want to question the people she worked with?" I asked.

"Maybe you just hoped to see Jake." Dorothy didn't look up from her knitting project.

The parking lot was mostly empty, but then it was still early, and the lunch crowd hadn't gotten there yet. It did indeed look as if the restaurant was open, which surprised me.

"Looks like they're open after all," I said.

"Maybe she wasn't a very nice boss," Dorothy said as we got out of the car.

We made our way up the deck and to the restaurant's entrance. It seemed like forever since I'd been there with Jake, yet it had been less than twenty-four hours ago. I had no idea what I would even say to these people.

"We should just have lunch and try to act casual," I said.

"Something tells me that we will act anything but casual." Dorothy shook her head.

That was exactly what I was afraid of.

When we reached the door, Dorothy stopped. I looked back to see what she was doing.

"There's a sign in the window." Dorothy tapped the glass. "Look at this."

I stepped closer. "Help wanted?"

"Yeah." She looked at me. "We should apply."

I stared at her as if she'd spoken a foreign language.

"Don't look at me like I'm nuts. If we worked here, then we could probably find out a lot more. Heck, maybe we could pick up a few extra bucks. The sign says they're seeking a server and a bartender." She pointed at the small sign.

"That's hard work, Dorothy. Who would be the bartender, and who would be the server?"

"Do you have any experience in mixing drinks?" she asked. I shook my head. "Good, then I can be the bartender." She adjusted the pocketbook on her arm.

"How will we know if they'd even hire us?" I asked.

"We don't, but we can apply. It's worth a shot," she said.

I nodded. "Okay. I guess we can give it a shot."

"Do we know each other?" she asked.

"I think it's best if we act like we don't," I said.

I opened the heavy door and we stepped inside the restaurant. I immediately looked over at the bar where Jake and I had sat the night before. I focused my attention on the man standing behind the bar. He was wiping off glasses, but he didn't look up at us.

"We'll ask him for applications," I said, motioning for Dorothy to follow me. Dorothy hurried along behind me. "You know, they're probably going to guess that we're together, so I think acting as if we don't know each other is pointless," I whispered.

"You're probably right about that," she said.

Once we'd reached the bar, the dark-haired man looked us up and down. He continued to wipe a glass. He wore a white shirt and black pants. The restaurant's uniform, I remembered from yesterday.

"We'd like to apply for the positions you have posted on the window outside," I said in my most professional tone.

He nodded and sat the glass and towel down. "Sure. Wait right here, and I'll get the manager."

"It's been a long time since I've applied for a job," Dorothy said.

"You'll be fine." I patted her hand.

A man with salt-and-pepper hair approached and stuck out his hand. "You'd like to apply for the jobs?"

"Yes . . ." I looked at Dorothy. "My friend and I would like to apply."

His gaze traveled from me to Dorothy. "Great. If you'd like to have a seat at the table over there, I'll get applications for you."

I nodded. "Thank you."

After a couple minutes he came back and handed us the applications. "I'll be back in just a bit. Take your time filling them out."

"Thank you," I said with a smile.

Dorothy had already pulled a couple pens from her purse before I even had a chance to touch my bag. I wondered exactly what she kept in that thing. A little bit of everything, I suspected.

"Do we give them our real names?" Dorothy asked.

"That's a good question," I said, tapping my pen against the table. "I guess we have to, but I doubt we'll be working here long enough for it to really make a difference. We'll find out all the details we need and then quit."

"Who knows, maybe I'll like this job so much that I'll want to stay," she said with a devilish smile.

I stared for a second, then said, "Just fill out the application before he gets back. We don't even know if he'll hire us yet, and you're making a career at this place."

Dorothy waved her hand. "Oh, he'll love me … and you too."

Who knew last night when I was here that today I would be applying for a job? Things had been crazy since I'd moved to Miami, so I shouldn't have been surprised.

The application was pretty straightforward, so I had no problems completing it. I listed my last employment as a telemarketer, but I didn't mention that I was working as a private investigator now.

"I really don't have anything to list as experience," Dorothy whispered. "I've been working for your uncle for years. That will give our cover away."

She had a point. When I spotted the man looking at us from across the room, I said, "Just make up something. Tell them you were a bartender at TGI Fridays."

Chapter Nine

We'd just finished the applications when the manager approached our table. He pulled out the chair and sat across from us. For what seemed like a drawn-out length of time, he looked from Dorothy to me. In reality it was probably just a couple seconds.

"Are you grandmother and granddaughter?" he asked.

I knew I'd hear about his comment later from Dorothy. She preferred that I pretend she was my sister, or at the very least an aunt.

I glanced at Dorothy and noticed she was suppressing a scowl. "We're just friends. We happened to notice the sign in your window and thought we'd apply. My name is …" I paused. I had written my name on the application, but this was it; I had to tell him now. "My name is Maggie Thomas," I said, offering my hand for him to shake.

"My name is Dorothy Raye," she said, shaking his hand.

"My name is Art Butler. I'm one of the managers here."

"Nice to meet you, Mr. Butler," I said.

"Please call me Art." He collected the papers and looked at each one. "Well, ladies, thanks for stopping by today. I'll take your applications."

That was it? Wasn't he even going to ask us any questions? I'd seen the strange look that had crossed his face when he'd looked at Dorothy's application. What had Dorothy written down?

"It says here, Dorothy, that you graduated bartending school and that you've worked as a bartender for the past twenty years." His eyes widened.

Dorothy flashed a wide smile. "Yes, the restaurant I worked at recently went out of business."

He studied her for a moment and then looked down at the paper again. "You're certainly qualified."

I leaned over to look at what she'd written. Something told me that she hadn't listed knitting and crossword puzzles as her hobbies. I noticed that she had listed that she was fluent in Spanish and French. Was that true?

"Okay, thank you, ladies, for stopping by. I'll give you a call and let you know," he repeated.

Why hadn't he asked me any questions? He'd barely looked at my application. It didn't look as if this was going our way. Well, maybe it was going Dorothy's way, because she'd padded her skill level.

Art shook our hands again and then walked away.

"That didn't go well," I whispered.

"What are we going to do now?" Dorothy asked as she collected her pens from the table.

I sighed. "I'll think of something. Let's get out of here."

Dorothy and I walked toward the door. We definitely had less bounce in our step now. It felt as if we were being watched, but I didn't look back to see if that was the case.

"I can't believe you wrote all that stuff about bartending." I shook my head.

"Hey, I have made drinks for the Bunco women for many years. That's the same thing as far as I'm concerned." She waved her finger in my direction.

"What about that stuff you wrote about speaking other languages?"

"Parlez-vous français?" She spoke the words with a little lilt in her voice.

I rolled my eyes. "No, I don't, and neither do you."

"Sí, sí." She wiggled her eyebrows.

I still felt eyes on us as we moved across the room. Finally, I couldn't stand it anymore and had to look. When I glanced over my shoulder, a blonde woman stood at the back of the room watching us. Because she was wearing the restaurant's uniform, I knew that she worked there too. She looked to be about my age, but maybe a few years younger.

The scowl on her face was a little disturbing. It was as if she didn't want us there. There was no way she could know who I was—and then the thought hit me. How could I have been so stupid? My name was in the newspaper article as being the private eye who had been on the scene when Kristin's body was found. Someone might have noticed and connected the two. Maybe it was for the best that they didn't hire us after all.

"I wonder if the other owner is here." I scanned the area, but I had no idea who I was looking for.

"Kristin's grandfather should have given you a description," Dorothy said.

"I guess he figured the man's name was enough, but I should have asked."

A group of lunchtime customers had entered the restaurant, and we tried to maneuver around the crowd. I just wanted to get out of there at this point. I needed time to figure out my next move. I'd made a mistake, and I hoped that it wouldn't cost me the case. I was sure that Mr. Grant didn't want anyone to know that he'd hired me. If the manager read the article and put two and two together, our covers would be blown.

Chapter Ten

We had to stop and wait for the people to move away from the door. I looked over my shoulder and noticed the manager talking to another man. They were both watching us. That was it. I knew that they'd realized who I was. Would they call the police? I mean, we hadn't done anything wrong. Failing to list my current employment on the application wasn't a criminal offense. At least, I didn't think it was illegal.

Their eyes met mine, and there was no way that I could pretend that I hadn't noticed that they were watching us. As soon as I could get through the crowd of people, I was out of there. Dorothy had stopped and was playing with a baby.

I grabbed her arm. "We have to go, Grandma."

If looks could kill, I'd be dead and buried. I'd just perpetrated the ultimate offense as far as Dorothy was concerned. "What is wrong with you?" She scowled.

"The manager and the other man are watching us. I think they're on to us. I shouldn't have listed my real name. They probably saw my name in the paper," I said.

"Excuse me, young lady, but can we please be seated now?" the tall man asked.

The group of people looked at me expectantly. Oh, great. Now they thought I worked here. I just wanted to get out of the Captain's

Quarters. It didn't matter to me that they claimed to have the best seafood in Miami.

The woman holding the baby said, "Daddy, I don't think they work here."

He looked me up and down, waiting for an answer.

"I'm sorry, but I don't work here," I said.

He shrugged and stepped to the side. "Oh, well, I'm terribly sorry."

I glanced back and noticed that the men weren't there anymore. Thank goodness. Maybe now I could get out of there. I motioned for Dorothy to follow me.

We'd made it to the door, and my hand was on the handle when someone grabbed my arm from behind. I gasped and spun around. The manager was standing directly behind me. I had to think quickly.

"I'm glad I caught you," he said with a wide smile.

Yeah, I bet he was. I plastered a fake smile on my face. "Oh, is there something we forgot?" I asked sweetly.

"I was wondering when y'all can start working?"

I looked at him for a moment and didn't say a word. His words weren't registering.

Dorothy finally answered for me. "We can start right away."

"Can you work tonight?" he asked.

"Sure," I finally managed to squeak out.

"Great. Be here at five and we can go over a few things." He smiled and held out his hand.

I grasped it, but I was still suspicious. It seemed odd that he'd changed his demeanor so quickly.

He must have sensed my skepticism because he said, "We just had someone else quit, so we really don't have time to go through the usual hiring process." He smiled again widely.

Dorothy nodded. "We understand. Thanks again for opportunity."

He nodded, then turned and walked away.

Dorothy studied me for a second, before saying, "What's the matter with you?"

I shrugged. "I just think something is up."

"Well, he probably is up to something, but we still have to find out what is going on around here. Come on. I have a few things to do before I start my new job." She motioned for me to follow.

"You seem a little too excited about this," I said as I walked across the parking lot.

"It's an adventure. What's not to be excited about?" She tossed her hands up.

When I looked back, the manager and the other woman who had been watching us were standing at the door.

"The manager and that woman are watching us," I said. Dorothy started to turn around. "Don't look back," I warned her.

"Oh, you're just being paranoid." Dorothy waved her hand.

"Maybe, but I intend on finding out what they're up to," I replied.

Chapter Eleven

I wasn't sure I was prepared for my new job at the restaurant, but it looked as if I was about to find out whether I could keep from dropping food on someone's lap.

After I picked up Dorothy, we headed inside to report for our first shift. The place was already full of customers. The manager spotted us right away. It wasn't the same man who had hired us, but the word "Manager" was written on his name tag.

"You must be the new staff. Come on to the back, and we'll find you a uniform." He headed toward the back kitchen at a quick pace. Dorothy and I rushed to keep up with him.

He looked me up and down, then shoved a pair of pants and a shirt at me. "Here. This should work."

I held up the clothing. "They're a little big, don't you think?"

He stared.

"I'll make it work," I said.

Dorothy grabbed the shirt and pants from him with a frown. He didn't notice or didn't care—I wasn't sure which. After finding clothing for us, he left us in the dressing area.

"Can you believe this?" Dorothy said, holding up my shirt. "How am I supposed to fit my chest in here?"

"My pants are too big and my shirt is too small," I said, tugging on my sleeves.

Dorothy and I dressed and headed back toward the front. The manager looked up and motioned for us to come closer.

"Okay, you've got section four," he said as he shoved a tray into my hands.

"Where is section four?" I asked.

He glared at me as if I'd asked the dumbest question he'd ever heard. "In the middle. From that table over there to that table." He pointed.

I nodded, still not entirely sure which tables he meant. He grabbed Dorothy's arm and herded her behind the bar.

That was the last I saw of her for several hours. I was almost positive she was behind the bar because I caught glimpses of her as I zoomed past the counter with food in my hands.

All of my food orders consisted of at least six plates. It seemed as if every table was at full capacity. I gathered the food from the order window and shuffled it around on my tray. The thing was full of food, and there was barely any room to fit another thing on that tray. I knew that people were waiting on the food, and no doubt they expected it to be hot when it arrived. The chef was repeatedly yelling at me, but what he failed to realize was that his yelling only slowed me down. I was so nervous that I didn't know if I was coming or going. How did he expect me to get that food out there with all the shouting?

"Are you going to pick up this food or not?" he roared again.

I rushed back over. "Right away," I said with a fake smile.

"You took so long that the food is probably already cold. And if the food is cold, the customers will blame me," he said.

I didn't know why he was so worried. His cooking skills didn't seem to be too great, in my opinion anyway. I grabbed up the food and carried it across the room, with the tray on my shoulder. The thing was painful, but at least I hadn't dropped it yet.

As I made my way across the dining room floor, people yelled at me. I tried to ignore it and continued across the room. Unfortunately,

I had tables on each side of the room and in the middle. I didn't know where to start first, so I decided to take food to the corner on the left and then figured I'd make my way to the other corner of the room. After that, I'd hit the middle. But the customers shrieked at me from one side as I hurried over to the other. It was like having surround sound. I couldn't make these people happy. They all wanted me to help them first, before the other guests. I only had two feet and two hands. I could only move so fast. This was a lot harder than it looked.

I lowered the tray of food and was doing a nice job of balancing it, I thought. I grabbed plates from the tray and placed them on the table in front of a customer. He frowned and didn't even thank me. But I didn't have time for a thank you anyway because the next table was waiting for me. I rushed away so that I could get to the next customers before they started yelling again.

Once I was in front of the next table, I set the plate down, but before I knew it, the other table was hollering at me again. I was ready to cry or scream—maybe both. I ran back over to the man at the first table.

"Yes, sir? Is everything okay?" I asked with a sweet voice.

He looked at me and said, "This is the wrong food. I want you to bring the right stuff."

I looked down at the plate. "But you've already eaten some of it."

"Well, how do you think I knew it was the wrong food?" he asked.

I had no other choice but to take the food back. The customer was always right, right? The chef was going to kill me. I had to pick the plate up and take it back.

"I'll be right back with your food," I said as I grabbed the plate and put it back on the tray.

Even though I needed to get this plate back to the kitchen, I knew I had to take the other food to the waiting customers. There was no way they would wait while I went back to the kitchen. As fast as I could run with a tray in my hands, I moved over to the table and placed the food down. The man scowled at me. I looked down. Apparently, I had given him the half-eaten fish from the other table.

"It's got a bite taken out of it," he said with a frown.

Actually the food had several bites taken out of it, but I didn't want to press the issue. I knew I wasn't getting a tip from them anyway.

"Sorry," I said, grabbing the plate.

I'd suspected I would be terrible at this job, but I'd had no idea I would be this bad.

So now I only had one plate of food left. Surely I could handle that. This was going to the man staring at me from the middle of the room. *I can do this,* I told myself. If only I had a clear shot at him, there was no way I would mess this order up; but unfortunately, that wasn't the case.

There was a crowd in the middle of the room, so I had to maneuver around the floor. I looked down at the plate. Yes, I was pretty sure this was what he had ordered. Things were going well as I wove around the room. My focus was fixed on the man. I reached the table with success. I leaned forward to place the plate down in front of him. But I somehow lost my balance, the plate went forward, and all of the shrimp fell onto his lap.

The man jumped up. "What the hell is wrong with you?"

"I'm so sorry." I bent down to the floor and feverishly began picking up the shrimp, piece by piece, and placing them back on the plate. "I can get you more food. I'm really sorry."

"Don't bother," he snapped, tossing down the napkin that he'd been using to clean his pants.

He stormed off across the room. I knew he was going to talk to the manager, and I would be in even bigger trouble. I had been worried about Dorothy blowing our cover, but it looked like that job was reserved for me. I needed to get my act together before it was too late.

When I looked up, I felt eyes on me. The manager was glaring at me. He motioned for me to come over, and I knew this was not good. The man I'd dumped food on had just walked out of the restaurant. I made my way across the room like I was being sent to the principal's office.

Luckily, his lecture wasn't as bad as I'd expected. He wanted to know what the heck was wrong with me, of course, and if I had really ever waited tables before. "I was just having an off day," I told him.

Chapter Twelve

After several more hours, my feet hurt, and I wanted nothing more than to collapse into bed. Well, after I'd showered the seafood smell from my hair and skin. I'd known waiting tables was hard work, but there were muscles in my body aching that I'd never even known I had.

I finally served the last table for the evening, and I spotted Dorothy behind the bar. She was still talking and laughing with a few customers. How was it that she still looked as fresh as when she'd started the evening? I made my way to the bar and collapsed onto one of the stools.

"You look exhausted. Long night?" she asked with a wink.

"You could say that," I said, sighing.

"It was a long night, but the tips were good." Dorothy shook her full jar of money.

Maybe tips were good for her, but they had been lousy for me. "I can't wait to get out of these clothes and get home," I said.

The young man and woman at the bar got up. "It was nice talking to you, Dorothy. We'll see you soon."

She smiled. "Thank you for the cookie recipe."

I stared at her as they walked away. "Well, I'm glad to see you had such a wonderful evening." I frowned.

"Did you find out anything?" she asked as she wiped down the counter.

"No, I was too busy serving lobster and shrimp. What about you?" I asked.

She shook her head. "No, nothing."

"Let's change and get out of here. I think my days of working undercover at a seafood joint are over." I brushed the hair out of my eyes. I imagined I must look like hell.

"Well, you didn't give it much of a chance," she said.

"I gave it all I could," I said.

We gathered our clothing from the lockers in the back and stepped into the back room to change. I had my shirt over my head when the sound of footsteps made me pause. Someone stopped just right outside the doorway.

"Did you read about it in the papers?" a woman's voice asked.

"Yeah, it said they think she died from natural causes," a man answered.

I pulled the shirt the rest of the way over my head and then looked at Dorothy. "Did you hear that?" I whispered.

Dorothy nodded.

"How much longer are you working here? I was told as soon as the deal goes through, I'll have my money. As soon as I do, I'm out of here," the woman said.

My eyes widened as I looked at Dorothy again. I eased closer to the entrance, hoping that the couple wouldn't notice me. Dorothy released a little cough, and they stopped talking. I glared at Dorothy. She needed to eat one of her peppermints to stop that tickle in her throat before she got both of us in trouble.

I eased away from the entrance. There was a sound of footfalls pausing by the door, and I knew the people out there were listening for another movement. Did they know we were in here and that we'd overheard their conversation? I held my breathing, waiting for the confrontation.

Finally, the couple walked away without knowing of our presence.

"Couldn't you hold in that cough?" I asked when they were gone.

"No, I could not. I need a peppermint," Dorothy said, digging around in her purse.

"What do you think *that* was all about?" I asked.

"I don't know. We don't even know who was talking." Dorothy draped her purse over her arm.

She was right, of course. What we'd overheard was just one of the many strange things that had occurred at this restaurant. The place just had an odd vibe about it. The feeling came mainly from the people who worked here. We still hadn't met the co-owner of the Captain's Quarters, Justin Mack. If he didn't show up soon, I'd have to start asking around about him.

"Come on. Let's see who's still here. Maybe I'll recognize their voices," I said as I motioned over my shoulder.

Dorothy and I stepped back into the main area of the restaurant. There were a couple of servers sitting at a table in the corner of the room. The customers had all cleared out. The blonde woman who had been watching me earlier in the day walked up to the table to join the others. She had been working in the prep area and hadn't noticed that we had stepped out from the back room. The manager and another man I'd never seen before were standing on the deck.

"It looks like we'll have to come back to work tomorrow if we want to figure out which one of them was back there." I tossed my dirty uniform in my bag and marched toward the door.

I didn't look back to see if anyone watched us this time. I wasn't sure that I wanted to know.

Chapter Thirteen

The next day Dorothy and I decided to check out Kristin's place. After all, I had a key—why not use it? I pulled up in front of Dorothy's house. When she emerged out the front door, she was wearing white capri pants and a bright red blouse. Red bangles were on her wrist, and big silver earrings dangled from her ears. Her sandals were the same shade of red as the bangles. I felt a little underdressed in my blue shorts and white tank. The only jewelry I'd worn today was a delicate gold chain with a tiny heart pendant.

Dorothy climbed in and plopped her giant white purse down on her lap. "Let's roll."

"You look bright and cheerful today," I said as I turned out onto the street.

"Well, you never know who you might run into," Dorothy said with a smile.

"Like Mr. Grant?" I glanced over to get her reaction.

She waved off my comment but didn't refute it.

As I continued to navigate the streets toward Kristin's home, Dorothy asked, "Have you told Jake that you're investigating this woman's death?"

"Nope. Why should I?" I asked as I turned onto the street my GPS was indicating.

"Oh, I don't know; maybe because he might be able to help," Dorothy said.

"He would just tell me to stay out of it," I said.

Dorothy shook her head disapprovingly.

Kristin lived in a beautiful white stucco home with two giant palm trees in the front yard. The surrounding homes were similar in style, and the only noise was the faint chirping of birds. Instead of pulling into the driveway, I parked the car at the curb in front.

Dorothy and I hopped out of the car and made our way up the flower-lined sidewalk. I glanced around the neighborhood to make sure no one was watching us. Had the police already been by Kristin's house? They still hadn't said if there was any foul play involved in her death, but I knew that was the case. It was just a matter of time until I found out the truth. I didn't know whether Kristin had been pushed off the boat and drowned, or if she'd been killed before and then thrown off the boat, but the police couldn't keep that a secret forever.

I was glad that Kristin's grandfather had given me a key. Now I could say that I hadn't broken in if I were caught. But what was I looking for? I knew nothing about Kristin, so I wouldn't know if something was out of place. I guess I just wanted to know more about her life. That was the only way I'd be able to piece anything together.

Dorothy and I reached the door, and I paused when I took the key out of my pocket.

"Maybe this isn't such a good idea," I said.

"Well, of course it isn't a good idea, but we have to do it anyway," Dorothy retorted.

After pausing for a couple more seconds, I turned the key and slowly opened the door.

"Is anyone here?" I called out.

Dorothy stepped around me. "There's no one here. Let's go inside. I'd rather be in there than have someone see us standing out here."

Dorothy's sandals clicked against the marble foyer. Other than that, it was eerily silent. Kristin's place was clean and neat, but there were a few things lying around as if she'd completely expected to be home that evening. A pair of flip-flops had been kicked off by the front door. Mail lay on the small table in the foyer. I picked up the envelopes. There was a Visa card bill and an advertisement for a local shopping mall—nothing out of the ordinary there.

Dorothy and I moved through the house, coming first to the kitchen and then to the living room.

"I don't like being in here," I whispered.

"I don't either, so let's hurry up. What are you looking for?" Dorothy asked.

"I'm looking for something that will give me a clue as to why she was on that boat."

"Don't you need to find out who owns the boat?" Dorothy asked.

"Well, yeah, but that will take some time." I walked over to the desk at the other side of the living room and opened a few drawers.

There was nothing out of the ordinary, and just like the rest of the house, everything was neat and orderly. Stamps, blank paper, and pens were in the middle drawer. On the side of the desk were other drawers filled with papers from the restaurant. At least I had her business partner's name, so if there was something here concerning him, I'd know right away. In the other drawer was a daily agenda, so I pulled it out and opened it to the page for the date Kristin had died.

"What does it say?" Dorothy asked as she looked over my shoulder. I smelled peppermint candy.

"Well, apparently the police haven't been here yet, because I think this is something they would have found." I showed Dorothy the agenda. "It says she had an appointment with someone by the name of Sam James." That name immediately set me on alert.

"That's odd. That's the second time I've seen the name 'Sam' in the past twenty-four hours."

"It's a common name," Dorothy said.

I placed the book down and looked around the rest of the room. The item on the table next to the sofa caught my attention.

"Yeah, but it's not common to see in a picture a bracelet just like the one I found." I walked over to the table and picked up the framed picture.

The photo was of Kristin and two other women smiling for the camera. In the background was a table full of people. The face of the man behind the women wasn't visible, because other people blocked him, but I definitely spotted his arm. He was wearing a gold bracelet just like the one I'd found. It couldn't be a coincidence. Had the man on the boat dropped the bracelet from his wrist? Was he the person in the photo—the Sam whom Kristin was supposed to meet?

Dorothy was flipping through the pages of the agenda. "That name is listed as an appointment on a different date, and there's an address here."

"Well, what are we waiting for? Let's pay Sam a visit," I said.

A noise caught my attention, and I jumped. It was too late to get out of the house because someone was coming through the front door.

"We have to hide," I whispered.

Dorothy wasn't behind me. She'd already taken off down the hallway.

I ran after her. "Where are you going?"

"I'm finding a closet to hide in, and you'd do well to join me," she snapped.

Dorothy pulled open the first door in the hallway that she came to. Luckily, it was in fact a closet. She stepped in, shoved the hangers out of the way, turned around, and then pulled my arm. I quickly closed the door behind us.

"What if we can't get out?" I asked.

"Then we're screwed," she said.

Whoever had been outside had now entered the house through the front door. The footsteps echoed through the foyer as the person walked farther into the house, then stopped.

I heard nothing. Well, I heard Dorothy breathing in my ear, but other than that, there was silence. I was definitely shaking in my sandals. It was a good thing I'd brought my gun with me. If this was the killer, then I wasn't going down without a fight. Footsteps sounded again as the person continued down the hallway in our direction. Had the person seen us hide in here? There was no way. Who was in Kristin's home? Unless it was the killer and now it was our turn.

The footsteps sounded again and then stopped. I knew the person was right in front of the door. Dorothy grabbed my arm and held on tight as I gripped my gun. Another second, and the door swung open and Dorothy screamed.

Jake Jackson stood in front of us. "What in the hell are you all doing in there?"

I clutched my chest. "What in the hell are *you* doing out *there*?"

He looked at me questioningly, and I knew he didn't want to be the first to answer.

I released a deep breath and then said, "We came here for clues."

He stepped out of the way and motioned for us to come out. "Clues for what?" he asked as I brushed past.

Dorothy and I walked single file down the narrow hallway and back to the foyer. I turned around and faced Jake. "If you must know, I'm looking for clues to Kristin's death."

"Why would you want to do that?" He crossed his muscular arms in front of his chest.

"Because I was hired by her grandfather to get to the bottom of what happened," I said casually.

Jake ran his hand through his thick hair and sighed. "You shouldn't be involved."

"Well, it's too late for that. Why shouldn't I get involved?" I matched his stance and glared at him.

He looked the other way.

"Jake Jackson?" I asked in a stern voice.

I needed to find out his middle name, so I could use his full name.

Finally, he said, "She was shot before she went into the water."

Chapter Fourteen

I pointed. "I knew it. That man forced her on the boat and then shot her. I just have to find out why."

"You didn't hear that from me," Jake warned.

I shook my head. "Of course, I didn't hear it from you."

"This is a crime scene now, Maggie. We're going to be searching everything. What did you touch?" he asked.

I shrugged. "Not much … the door. Oh, and the desk. Things in the desk."

He shook his head. "What were you looking for—and did you find anything?"

I stared at him for a moment, and then said, "I just wanted to know more about Kristin Grant, and no, I didn't find a thing."

He looked at me suspiciously, but apparently he had no choice but to accept my response.

"Okay, well, Dorothy and I have to go now. I'll talk to you later." I waved over my shoulder as I walked out the door.

Dorothy shuffled along beside me. "Jake is adorable, and I think he loves that you're involved."

"Well, it's a good thing," I said with a click of my tongue. "Because I'm not stopping now."

So now we were headed to the address in Kristin's agenda book. With any luck, I'd find out who this person was. If it was the killer, then I prayed that things didn't get ugly quickly.

"Maybe I should go to the address alone," I said, glancing over at Dorothy. "I don't want to get you into sketchy situations with me."

"I think it's a little too late for that, don't you?" Dorothy asked as she pulled out her needles.

I nodded. "I suppose you're right, but that doesn't mean I have to continue to put you in these situations."

"I can't let you go alone," she said firmly.

It looked as if I wasn't going to win this argument.

Within a few minutes, we'd pulled up to the condo. There were probably about ten units in this building. The number we were looking for was at the end. The white stucco structure was flanked by palm trees on each side—other than that, there wasn't too much to make the place memorable.

"I hope this is the right place," I said.

Dorothy and I headed up to the door, and I knocked. I'd almost given up on anyone answering when it finally opened, and a man stood in front of us. It wasn't the same man who'd been on the boat, but they looked a lot alike, and now I wasn't sure which of them I'd seen with Kristin. He looked us up and down, and then glanced around; I guessed, to see if we were alone.

"What can I do for you?" he asked.

"We're here to ask about Kristin Grant," I said.

He stared at us for a second, then said, "I have no idea who you're talking about."

Then he slammed the door in our faces. I looked over at Dorothy. Her mouth hung open.

"Well, I didn't expect that to happen," I said.

"That man is just plain rude. I've half a mind to knock on the door and tell him to apologize." She wagged her finger.

"Obviously, he's not being truthful. We'll have to think of something else. I'll find out who he is one way or the other."

I glanced back as we headed back to the car. The man was watching us from a window. As soon as I got back to the office,

I'd have to do a little research on this guy. But also, who were the women in the picture with Kristin? They might be able to tell me who the man sitting behind them was. I wondered if Kristin had had a lot of friends. How would I find the women? If only I'd taken the picture when I'd had the chance. Now I'd have to go back and get it after the police were gone. But how long would they be there, and would I be able to get in if Jake was there? Would I even be able to get the picture if I did get in? I had to give it a shot.

"Don't forget, we have to go back to work," Dorothy said, breaking me from my reverie.

There would be no time to look for the women now. I had to find out something during this shift, or I would have to give up.

As I walked down the driveway, I spotted a small piece of paper on the curb. It was near my car. Had it fallen out when Dorothy had gotten out of the car? I wanted to pick it up, but with the man staring at us, I didn't want to risk it. My stopping to pick up something might be the little event that would finally set him off. He looked as if he was ready to lose it at any second. "A little unhinged," as my mother always said. No matter though, one way or the other, I had to have that piece of paper.

Curiosity would get the best of me until I knew what it was. A voice in my head said to just let it go, that it was probably nothing, but the other voice telling me to get the paper was louder. That voice would definitely win.

I'd have to come back for it. My plan was to drive around the block and park a couple houses away, then I would swoop in and grab the paper. As long as the man wasn't watching, I would be fine. He would never know that I'd returned.

"Do you see that paper on the ground?" I asked.

Dorothy glanced around.

"Over beside the car," I said under my breath, as if he might hear me.

Finally Dorothy looked in the right direction. "It looks like a receipt."

"Whatever it is, I have to take a look at it," I said.

Dorothy shook her head. "He's watching us. I can feel his stare on my back. You don't want to risk setting that guy off. He'll lunge out the front door and attack us."

"I know. I figured I'd just drive around the block and come back for it."

Dorothy frowned. "You're going to get us killed for a receipt."

"Of course, I'm not going to get us killed for a receipt. You have to have a little bit of faith in my abilities."

"I have plenty of faith in you, Maggie, but this is not one of those times."

After starting the car and taking off away from the house, I made a couple of turns and headed back down the street toward the house again. I tapped my fingers against the steering wheel.

"Will you stop doing that? You're making me nervous." Dorothy said as she dug around in her purse.

I ignored her, but Dorothy's previous words echoed through my mind. Maybe I was putting us in danger for a silly piece of paper that meant nothing. Actually, there was no "maybe" to it... I was definitely putting us in a precarious situation.

Easing the car to a stop, I shifted it into park and turned off the ignition. I'd pulled up in front of a house a couple doors down from the man's house.

"You really shouldn't do this." Dorothy pulled a peppermint from her purse and popped it into her mouth.

"I can run fast."

She snorted. "With those short legs? Are you kidding me? A turtle could outrun you."

I frowned. "Don't you have knitting to catch up on?"

She waved her finger at me. "Sassy."

I shook my head. "I know. I'm being sassy again."

Dorothy pulled out her needles. "Exactly."

I climbed out from behind the wheel and looked around. No one seemed to be out around the neighborhood. If anyone was watching me from inside one of these homes, I wouldn't know about it. I took off at a brisk pace down the street. After a bit, I'd reached the man's home again. Unfortunately, there was nowhere for me to hide—no trees by the sidewalk and no cars. I was out in the open and felt vulnerable. It would have helped if I'd had a place to retreat to if he popped up. I guess if he saw me, that would be the least of my worries.

When I looked toward his house, I didn't notice him at the door or looking out the windows. He probably thought we'd gone for good. I didn't want to take that for granted, though, and give myself a false sense of security.

I neared the paper and causally strolled up, trying not to act suspicious. Reaching down, I slowly picked up the paper and then placed it in my pocket. I glanced up at the house again, expecting the worst. The man wasn't watching me as far as I knew, but my stomach was still in knots.

After I got a few steps away from the house, I took off at a sprint. My car seemed a lot farther away now than I remembered. I could see Dorothy's head sticking up. Her gray bun on the top of her head was like a beacon. She shook her head as she watched me. The faster I ran, the longer it seemed, though. I'd halfway made it to the car when a dog popped up from a house next to me. His bark echoed across the neighborhood. He would surely alert everyone. Soon people would look out to see what all the commotion was.

It seemed to take forever, but I finally reached the car. I yanked the door open and jumped in.

"I got it," I said breathlessly as I cranked the ignition.

Dorothy shook her head. "You are making me nervous."

"Yeah, you said that already."

The dog was still at the fence, watching me. But at least he'd stopped barking now. I drove a couple of streets over and pulled to the side of the road.

"What are you doing now?" Dorothy asked.

"I have to know what the paper is."

Dorothy placed her needles on her lap. "All of this over a receipt."

I reached down in my pocket and pulled out the paper. Dorothy had been right. It was a receipt. But it was where the receipt was from that it made it interesting.

Even more exciting was the date on the receipt. "Captain's Quarters" was printed at the top, and underneath was the date of Kristin Grant's murder.

"Had you ever been to Captain's Quarters before the day we went together?" I asked.

"Why do you ask?"

I showed Dorothy the receipt. "Because the date on top is the date Kristin was killed." That meant that Dorothy couldn't have accidentally dropped the receipt. The owner of this receipt had obviously been at the restaurant the day of her murder, but was the owner of the receipt responsible for her death? According to Jake, Kristin had been at work at the time this receipt had been given. But did she make her boyfriend pay for his purchases? Was it his receipt?

Reluctantly, I pulled into the Captain's Quarters parking lot. It was time for our shift.

It looked like business as usual around the place. Customers were starting to arrive for dinner. After changing into my uniform, I got right to work waiting on the tables. There was no time to do any spying. The wait staff seriously deserved big tips for all this work. Thank goodness, I'd get a break, and I planned on using that time to snoop around.

Because most everyone would still be working when I took my break, it was going to be hard to speak with anyone. So I really had no choice but to snoop around in the lockers. Not that I thought I would discover anything, but what other options did I have?

I grabbed something to drink and headed back to the break room. Unfortunately, I wasn't alone in the room. The waitress I'd thought I'd overheard talking to the male employee was sitting at a table reading a magazine. This was a good and a bad thing. It was good because now maybe I'd learn something, but bad because I didn't know what to ask her. Clearly, I hadn't thought out this plan.

She didn't look up when I stepped closer to the table.

"Do you mind if I sit here?" I asked.

She shrugged her shoulders but didn't look at me, and she still didn't answer. I pulled the chair out and sat down. She still didn't respond. If someone were sitting at a table with me, I wouldn't be able to stop myself from looking to see who it was.

I took a sip of my soda and then asked, "So, do you like working here?"

She didn't answer. Well, this was going well.

"It's very busy here. I like it, though," I said.

She didn't look up as she flipped a page.

I leaned in closer. "I heard that one of the owners recently died."

She looked up at me. Without speaking, she pushed to her feet, grabbed the magazine, and left the room.

Why had she been so quiet? Why hadn't she spoken to me? At least now I was alone, though. I didn't know how long that would last, so I had to take a look around quickly. What the heck was I looking for anyway? Any sign of what she might have been talking about last night? I opened the first locker and saw nothing but clothing. I opened a couple more, but they contained the same types of items.

Finally, I opened another one and spotted a purse. Was it hers? I really didn't want to look inside. There was just something creepy about looking through another woman's purse. It was just wrong. I moved on to the next locker—I couldn't make up my mind if I had the nerve to look in her purse. The next locker contained clothing, but that wasn't all. There was a bag of what I assumed were pills. A lot of pills. Footsteps sounded in the hallway. Hurriedly I closed the locker.

I grabbed my drink and headed for the door, but stopped in my tracks when a man entered the room. He looked me up and down. I couldn't gauge his expression, but finally he smiled at me.

"Hello. My name is Justin Mack." He stuck out his hand. He wore black pants, a white shirt, and a tie.

I shook his hand. "I'm Maggie Thomas. I'm a new waitress here."

"Nice to meet you, Maggie. I'm the owner of this place," he said.

I wondered if he noticed my shocked expression. "Oh, it's nice to meet you. I wondered if we'd meet."

He looked quizzical. "What makes you say that? You wanted to meet me?"

I chuckled. "No, I just heard about you, and I thought maybe you weren't real."

He frowned. I realized I wasn't really making sense.

"Well, I'd better get back to work," I said, gesturing toward the door.

"Your name sounds familiar. Do I know you from somewhere?" He frowned.

"No, I don't think so." I looked at the door and wished that I could leave now before he figured out that my name had been in the newspaper article about Kristen's death.

"You don't look familiar, but your name ..." He stared at me.

I decided I would use this time to gauge his reaction to the mention of his partner's name, as it didn't seem like I would get away from him anytime soon. “Do you run this restaurant all by yourself? That’s a lot of work.” I eyed him for his reaction.

He frowned. “No—well, I do now, but I had a partner. She died recently.”

“I’m sorry,” I said softly. Did he have a connection to the boat that I’d seen? “You must really like boats since you have the restaurant right at the marina.” I stared at him.

He looked at me with a long pause, then said, “Yes, I do like boats.”

“Do you have a boat?” I asked.

He nodded. “Yes, I have a boat. You ask a lot of questions.”

I chuckled. “Oh, I’m just too talkative, I guess. My father had a boat too.”

He didn’t respond—well, not with words at least. But his expression indicated he felt the conversation was finished.

“I guess I’d better get back to work.” I gestured over my shoulder.

Once he nodded, I hurried out of the room. I was pretty sure he was still staring at me.

Chapter Fifteen

I'd been back at work for only a few minutes when I spotted Jake coming in the restaurant. How did he know I was there? He looked handsome, as usual, in a pair of beige pants and a white shirt. It appeared that he was alone, and I was thankful that he hadn't brought a date to the restaurant. I knew I looked like hell and smelled like shrimp. He was standing by the door, and I didn't think he'd noticed me yet. He looked around when the hostess asked him a question.

To my chagrin, the hostess was now bringing Jake in my direction. I had to hide. Grabbing a nearby tray, I raised it to hide my face and hurried across the room. I wove my way around a couple tables and almost tripped over a chair. Thank goodness, I didn't fall face first onto the floor. The thought had barely slipped from my mind when I stumbled over my own clumsy feet and dropped the tray.

A loud clang rang out as I steadied myself. I hadn't fallen, but the tray had hit the edge of the table on its way down and had knocked over a glass of water. I was afraid to look over because I knew everyone, including Jake, would be watching me.

Avoiding him was no longer an option, and I glanced over. Sure enough, Jake's gaze was fixed on me. He frowned and then hurried over to me. "What are you doing here?"

He looked me up and down. There was no way to hide the fact that I was wearing the uniform. I instinctively looked over at the bar and noticed Dorothy watching us. She was shaking her head at my obvious blunder. Jake followed my gaze and noticed Dorothy. His eyes widened. She waved at him.

"What's Dorothy doing behind the bar?" he asked.

I grabbed Jake's arm and pulled him to the side. "We're undercover," I whispered.

His expression didn't change for a moment, and then he burst out laughing.

I scowled. "What's so funny?"

When he finally stopped laughing, he said, "The fact that you're undercover."

I glared at him. "I don't think it's funny. I'm trying to get to the bottom of this crime and help my client."

He nodded and regained his composure. "Okay, you're right, it's not funny. I just want you to know that I don't approve of what you're doing, but since I know you're hardheaded, I won't tell you to stop."

"Well, it's a good thing because I wouldn't have stopped anyway. So what are you doing here?" I asked.

"I came for dinner," he said, smiling.

I looked at him quizzically. Now that I thought about it, Jake had been here the night I saw the boat. Maybe he wasn't being completely honest with me.

The manager was shooting dirty looks at me from across the room. "I guess I have to go back to work." I gestured over my shoulder.

"I hope I get to sit in your section," he said with a smile.

That was the last thing I wanted.

"Is everything okay over here?" the manager asked when he approached.

"Yes, I was just telling him about the specials for the day," I explained with a grin.

Jake held back a laugh.

"I think your customers are waiting for refills," the manager said, frowning.

He walked away, and Jake gave me a pitying look.

"It's all in a day's work," I said.

"Just stay out of trouble, okay?" He searched my eyes.

"You know I will," I said over my shoulder as I walked away.

While I filled my tray with sodas, Jake went back to the hostess, and thank goodness, she didn't put him in my section. I'd have to thank her for that later. The whole time I waited on the tables, I felt Jake's eyes on me.

When the crowd began to thin out, Jake came over to me. "You'll call me if you need anything?"

I nodded as I picked up dirty dishes from a table. "Yeah, I'll call you. Everything will be fine, Jake."

He ran his hand through his hair and nodded.

"Did you find out anything else about Kristin's murder?"

He looked around the room and then back at me, but he didn't answer my question.

"You didn't come here for dinner, did you?" I asked.

He shook his head. "No, I didn't."

"Are you going to tell me why you came here?"

"Well, Ms. Grant was co-owner of this place." He folded his arms across his chest and leaned back against the table.

"Yeah, I know. But there's more to your visit than that. You're not telling me everything," I said as I picked up a plate from the table next to us.

"I can't tell some things." Jake frowned.

"'Can't' or 'won't'?" I asked.

"What time do you get off?" he asked.

I glanced at the clock on the wall. "In an hour."

"I'll call you, okay?" He touched my hand softly.

I nodded and watched as Jake walked out of the restaurant.

Chapter Sixteen

After finishing up the last table, I couldn't wait to get out of there. Not just because I wanted to talk with Jake either.

I'd just changed out of my uniform when the waitress walked into the room. I'd finally found out that her name was Megan Cass. I had to get this woman to talk with me so that I could confirm that she was the one I'd overheard.

"It was busy tonight, huh?" I asked as I shoved my uniform in my bag.

She looked at me and nodded. I knew she could talk, so why was she refusing to speak to me?

"My name is Maggie, by the way." I stuck out my hand. I wasn't going to stop until she spoke.

She stared at me, then finally took my hand. "My name is Megan."

When she spoke, I knew it was the woman I'd overheard. I recognized her voice. This was my chance to ask questions.

I tossed my bag onto my shoulder. "So have you worked here long?"

"Um, yeah, a little while." She opened a locker and didn't look at me.

Okay, so that question hadn't gone over as well as I'd hoped. I'd try again. "Are you from around here?"

That was a stupid question, but her icy demeanor was throwing me off. Just as I was about to ask yet another question, her cell phone rang. She picked it up at record speed. Yeah, I knew she was relieved that she'd been saved by the ring.

"Hi, Mom," she said.

I knew when I'd been defeated, so I headed out into the dining room area again. Dorothy was still talking to people at the bar, so I decided to step outside. I'd almost made it to the door when I saw him. It was the man from the boat, outside on the deck again. I hurried to the door and rushed outside.

When I rounded the corner, he had vanished. He couldn't have gotten very far. I glanced back to see if his boat was there, but I only saw one small boat at the dock. If he'd come here on a boat, it wasn't the one I'd seen him on before. Why was he back here again?

One thing was for sure: I had to go after him. I raced down the sidewalk and made my way out to the parking lot. I scanned the area, but he was nowhere in sight. How could he have gotten away so quickly? Had he gotten into a car? I hadn't seen one drive away. I moved over behind the building and looked around. There was nothing back there but a dumpster. It looked as if he'd gotten away.

When I moved back around to the sidewalk, I spotted him. He was sitting inside a car, talking with another man. The man had his back to me, so I couldn't tell who it was.

I inched my way down the sidewalk so that I could get a better look. The last thing I needed was for the men to spot me, so I moved behind a car. I had a nice view from there and could watch the men. That was when I got a look at the other man's face. It was one of the other employees. So the man from the boat did know someone at the restaurant. And this was the guy who had been talking to Megan. This wasn't a coincidence. I had to find out who the man was and why he was talking to the employees.

My attention was so focused on the two men in the car that I didn't notice the manager when he popped out from the restaurant.

"What are you doing?" he asked with a scowl.

I hurried over to him. "Did you need something?"

"You forgot to close out your tickets," he said.

Now I wouldn't get the chance to find out what the men were talking about. Reluctantly, I followed the manager back into the restaurant. Just before I headed through the door, I glanced back at the men. They were still engrossed in their conversation. Maybe if I hurried, I could get back out there before they left. Should I have called Jake?

After closing out the tickets in record time, I rushed back outside onto the sidewalk. Neither of the men was in the car, although the car was still in the same spot in the parking lot. I'd have to find the employee tomorrow and uncover what his connection was with that man, plus figure out who that man was.

Dorothy was still inside, so I'd have to drag her away from the customers who liked to hang around the bar too long after we closed. Of course, she loved to entertain them with her stories, and they seemed to love to hear them.

I stepped over to the bar and noticed another employee. It wasn't the waiter who'd been talking to the man outside, but I knew this guy seemed to be friends with everyone in the restaurant.

I gestured over my shoulder. "Did you happen to see a man outside? He's tall with dark hair, and one of the other servers was out there talking to him."

He looked at me with a scowl. "Sorry, I don't know who you're talking about. There are a lot of men who fit that description."

Yeah, he was telling me. The employee walked away, and I turned back to the door. I ran my hand through my hair and contemplated my next move. It seemed as if my investigation was going nowhere. I'd better come up with something soon if I wanted to help Mr. Grant. Speaking of which, I needed to pay him a visit. Would he know the women in the photo?

The sound of footsteps walking up behind caught my attention, and I whipped around. Another male employee had stepped up behind me. He was probably around twenty-one years old and had shoulder-length blond hair.

"How are things going since you started working here?" He gave me a big grin.

I was shocked that he'd taken the time to speak to me. Everyone seemed to think of Dorothy and me as strangers. I mean, we were, but still... Dorothy's laughter carried across the room. She was laughing with some of the employees, and I realized that I was the only one they were treating as a stranger. I hoped that she was getting some useful information out of them. I shrugged. "It's been a little stressful, but I guess I'm getting the hang of it."

"Have you waited tables before?" he asked with a frown.

It was probably obvious that I hadn't. "A little," I answered vaguely. "Hey, by the way, I noticed some of the boats out there. Did you happen to notice one with *Vida* written on the back?"

His eyes widened. "Yeah, I've seen that one." He looked around. "I've heard rumors about that boat."

I leaned in closer. "Really? Like what?" This might be the break I'd been waiting for.

"I heard that the boat carries drugs," he whispered.

My eyes widened. Now that was something. "Does it come by here often?" I asked.

"Yeah, a lot. I think the owner is friends with a couple of the employees."

Immediately, Megan and the male employee came to mind. I suspected as much since the man from the boat had been talking to him. I couldn't ask too many questions because this guy would be suspicious. Plus, when I glanced up, I noticed that Megan was watching us. Did she suspect what we were talking about?

He glanced over his shoulder and then said, "I think the guy keeps his boat over at the marina. But you didn't hear that from me."

I met his gaze. Why was he giving me this information? "Are you working tomorrow?" I asked.

He nodded. "Yeah. Listen, I think my ride is waiting for me. I'll see you tomorrow?" he asked with a big smile.

"Sure, I'll see you then."

Megan continued to watch me as I walked over to the bar, but I pretended not to notice her. Dorothy and I needed to get out of there. If only I could get her away from her captive audience long enough.

"Oh, hi, Maggie. How were your tips tonight?" she asked with a giggle. The other employees looked at me.

"Are you ready to go?" I asked. When the others weren't watching me, I motioned with a tilt of my head toward the door.

Dorothy scowled, and then she finally realized what I was trying to tell her. "Oh, well, it's getting late and I have knitting to catch up on. I'll see you youngsters later. Don't do anything I wouldn't do."

"See you later, Dorothy. Thanks for the drinking game," one of the guys said.

"I don't think we should get too friendly with everyone," I said as I walked toward the door.

"How else do you think I'll get any information out of them?" She placed her hands on her hips.

"I know, but if we get too friendly they'll start asking a lot of questions, then you'll have to answer those questions. The more we tell them the harder it is to keep track," I said.

Actually, the harder it would be for *her* to keep track, but I didn't tell Dorothy that.

"I found out that the boat comes here a lot. Apparently, it has something to do with drugs. The man is friends with those two we overheard in the break room. I have to find this guy and go to him," I said.

"You can't see a drug dealer," she said.

Dorothy and I made our way across the parking lot. "I have to go," I said. "Besides, just because I go doesn't mean I'll talk with him. It just means that I'll snoop around."

"That's even worse. It's an easy way to get yourself hurt."

I waved off her concern. "I'll be just fine."

"Have you shared any of this info with Jake?" she asked.

"No, and I don't intend to."

"This isn't a competition. Maybe if you share with him, he'll share with you."

I frowned. "I doubt it."

"I thought he said he would help you."

"Yeah, well, just the same, I'm not telling him just yet. I want to see what I can find out first."

She shook her head. "I just hope you don't get yourself into a pickle. What did he mean when he said drugs were involved?"

"I don't know. I guess selling them?" I pulled my car keys from my purse.

"How would Kristin have been involved in that?"

"I don't know. Do you think she was buying the drugs from him?" I asked.

"Anything is possible, I'm afraid. That poor Mr. Grant. I wish there was a way we could shield him from all of this," Dorothy said with a frown.

As I neared my car, I noticed a black shadow at the front of the car.

"Someone is messing around with my car," I said as I took off across the parking lot. The sound of Dorothy's shoes clicking behind me echoed across the night. "Hey, you! Get away from my car!" I yelled.

Was this person trying to steal my car? I knew I should have parked it under a light. Everything was dark, but I guessed that this was a man. The person looked up and noticed us running toward him. I looked back and noticed that Dorothy was swinging her pocketbook through the air. I guess that was her warning signal that this person had better run for his life.

The man took off across the lot so quickly that there was no way I would catch up with him. When I made it to my car, I looked around, but everything seemed to be okay … for now.

Chapter Seventeen

"What do you think that was about?" I asked when Dorothy stepped up behind me.

"I don't know, but I'm too old for this running stuff." Dorothy waved her hands through the air.

I unlocked the car. "Dorothy, you shouldn't be running."

She climbed into the car. "Well, it was more of a shuffle and not really a run."

"You shouldn't be shuffling either." I scanned the area one more time but didn't see the person, so I climbed behind the wheel. I planned on spending the next day researching, but tonight after I dropped off Dorothy, I would go to the marina and look for that boat.

I pulled into the marina parking lot and finally found a spot. Dorothy would be angry when she found out that I had gone without her. She'd probably give me the silent treatment for at least ten minutes. Tomorrow night was her weekly Bunco game, though, and she would be busy getting ready for the big event. More than likely, I'd be forced into attending that game as well. If I won again, the Bunco ladies, or Bunco Friends Forever as they called themselves, might not invite me back.

The marina was full of boats that all looked a lot alike. Of course, it was dark, and not everything was visible, but I figured coming at night would mean the boat would more than likely be there. Lights from the boats twinkled like rhinestones against the black backdrop of night. Water lapped against the hulls as I made my way down the dock, looking from boat to boat. I made it all the way to the end and didn't see it. This was the closest marina to the restaurant, so I'd assumed this would be the place, but maybe it was one of the other marinas in the city.

When I turned around to head back toward my car, I noticed a man walking around his boat. He had been watching me, but looked away when I turned my attention on him. It was too late, though, because I'd already noticed him.

"Are you looking for something?" he asked with a bright smile.

I looked around, then back at him. "Yes, as a matter of fact, I am," I said.

He stepped to the edge of his boat. "Oh yeah, what's that?"

"A boat," I offered.

He slowly looked to his left and then his right, then stared at me like I was crazy.

"What I meant to say is I am looking for a boat with the word *Vida* on the back," I said.

He shook his head. "There are a lot of boats with that word."

Hmm. I supposed he did have a point. I released a deep breath. I guess this had turned out to be a wasted trip.

"Is there anything else about the boat?" he asked.

I knew very little about boats, so there was nothing else I could say about it. "Not really," I said.

"Where have you seen the boat before? Was it here?" He pointed.

"The boat was actually at the place where I work. The Captain's Quarters. There was a man driving the boat. He was a large man with dark hair. Wears a lot of jewelry." I gestured toward my neck and wrist.

He shook his head again, but then his eyes widened. "Wait. There was a guy here the other day who matched that description. I remember him because he had a good-looking woman with him. She wore a white bikini."

My stomach flipped. "That's him. Does he keep his boat here?"

He shook his head. "I don't think so. I'd never seen him before. He may have been using someone's slip without permission."

That didn't help me much. This guy probably moved around from place to place. It would be hard to find him if that were the case.

"Sorry I couldn't help more," he said as he began wiping down his boat again.

"Thanks anyway," I said. More than anything I wanted a long shower and then sleep. There would be no time for even *Magnum* tonight.

Pulling up to my apartment, I took the first available parking spot along the curb and jumped out. The night air floated across my skin, and memories of Jake popped into my mind. It was dark, and the only light was from a streetlight across the street. The feeling of being watched fell over me. I hurried my steps, but when I'd made it halfway up the sidewalk, I glanced over my shoulder.

There were several palm trees across the street, and a man stood behind one of those trees. I guess he thought he was covered by the dark of night. But the streetlight in the distance was breaking his cover. I was sure that he didn't think I'd noticed him as he hid behind the tree and watched me. I wasn't as dumb as he thought, though. I hurried my steps, but when I glanced back, he had moved. I was pretty sure he was making his way toward me. If I took off at a run, then he might try to catch up to me. I didn't want this to escalate into something ugly. I could guarantee him that

I wouldn't go down without a fight. I'd use whatever means I had to in order to survive.

My heart thumped as I rushed around the corner. They really needed to add more lights around this place. I had my gun concealed at my waist. Was this a killer? Had Kristin's killer tracked me down? After all, my name had been in the paper. Maybe he'd found out that I was investigating the case. In spite of the fact that the man was trying to hide, I'd gotten a glimpse of his face.

I was almost sure that this man was the employee at the restaurant—the one I'd seen talking to the man on the boat. What did he want?

As I leaned against the building, I tried to steady my breathing and remain calm. I should turn around and ask this guy what the hell he was doing following me. He had some nerve. I glanced over my shoulder again but didn't see him. Was he hiding somewhere else now? The area was dark now, so there was no way for me to know. I could pull out the flashlight on my phone and hunt him down. I'd push him out into the light like the cockroach he was.

I inched around the building so that it would offer more cover for me. Pausing again, I looked around, waiting for this guy to pop out.

There was no movement, and after a while I figured he must have left. One thing was for sure—I intended on getting to the bottom of why he was following me.

Even though he was nowhere in sight, I couldn't get it out of my head that he had followed me. I wanted to know if this guy was still around. If I found him, I should definitely call the police, although that would probably ruin my investigation. I would no longer be able to find out anything about the murder because my cover would be blown.

This guy would soon find out who I was, though, if he was poking around. Not seeing him still, I headed back down the path toward my car. When I peered across the street, I saw that his car was still parked along the curb.

He had to still be around somewhere. For all I knew, he could be watching me at this very moment. I was out there in the open, with no cover. It was a vulnerable feeling with the streetlight shining nearby, highlighting my every move. Of course, I was curious about this guy and where he was at the moment. The allure of checking out his car was too great. I had to take a peek in the window. I would just take a quick look. If he came back—well, I'd be brave and confront him. I'd ask him why the heck he was following me.

With my adrenaline racing, I hurried across the street. A few cars passed by, but no one seemed to notice me. When I reached the passenger side of the vehicle, I peeked in. The door was locked, but when I saw that the driver's door was open, I figured it wouldn't hurt to take a little peek inside.

I glanced over my shoulder but didn't see the guy, so I immediately hurried to the other side of the car. With one last glance around, I opened the door. I cringed when it creaked loudly. My heart thumped in my chest. I sucked in a deep breath of night air and tried to calm my nerves.

I crawled into the car and peered around. It kind of smelled bad—like dirty socks and rotten food. I wasn't sure of what I was looking for now that I was inside. This was another one of those crazy things that I do that seems like a good idea beforehand, but when I'm in the midst of the action, I question my sanity.

Food wrappers littered the floor of the car. Other than that, it I didn't notice anything significant. I just hoped I didn't find a rodent hiding in this mess. Leaning over the backseat, I peered into the back. This guy liked fast food.

A black duffle bag was on the floor in the back. I peeked up again to see if the guy was coming back or if anyone was watching me. He had to return soon. Where could he have gone? Was he still looking for me? Maybe he was in my apartment waiting for me. That was a scary thought. I scooped up the bag by its handles and hoisted it over the seat. Placing it in the middle of the front seats, I grabbed the zipper and unzipped the bag in one swift motion. My heart rate increased. What if I found a severed body part in this bag?

When I opened the bag, I didn't find a head or arm, but there was a bunch of cash. All of the money was in one-hundred-dollar bills. I had no idea how much money was in there, but it had to be a lot. What was he doing with all of this money? If it was the guy from the restaurant and he had that kind of cash, then why was he working there? Did he always carry this much around in a bag? I peered over the seat again to make sure he wasn't coming. If he saw me with my hands on the bag, he'd think I was stealing it.

I zipped the bag up and tossed it back to the spot where I'd found it. When the sound of a phone ringing filled the car, I jumped and banged my arm on the steering wheel. Where was the phone? It wasn't my ring because I had the theme song for *Magnum, P.I.* as my ringtone. After checking the seats, I still hadn't found the source of the loud ring. It seemed to be coming from the front of the car, though. I flipped open the glove compartment, and not only did I find the source of the ringing, but there was even more ringing.

The glove compartment contained a bunch of phones. If I counted them correctly, there were ten phones in there and two of them were currently ringing. I didn't like the looks of this at all. What had I gotten myself into this time? Why would anyone need this many phones? There was only one reason, and it wasn't a good one.

I pulled out one of the phones and looked at the screen. I didn't recognize the number, but then again, I hadn't expected to anyway. I stuffed the phone back and picked up the other ringing phone. That number looked familiar, but I couldn't place it. There was no way that I knew anyone calling these phones, though, so I figured I was just I imagining that I'd seen the number before.

I stuffed that phone back in and slammed the glove compartment closed. It was time for me to get the heck out of there. I was kind of shocked that I hadn't been caught already. It would be surprising if I made it away from his car without the guy returning. For a moment, the thought of claiming that I'd innocently thought this was my car if he caught me came to mind, but I knew even the most gullible person wouldn't believe that story. No, if I were caught, I'd just have to admit the truth. But so far, I was good; now it was time to get out of there and see what happened next.

I backed out of the car and slammed the door shut. Again the hinges squeaked, echoing through the area. If he were anywhere near, he'd probably hear the sound and know someone was in his car.

What exactly did he want with me? Running across the street and back down the path, I rushed over to my door, ran inside, and quickly turned the lock. I leaned against the door and released a deep breath. It had been one heck of a day.

Chapter Eighteen

The next morning, I was at the office early. I hadn't stopped off for coffee, and I wondered if I'd missed Jake. Had he stopped for coffee too? Because I was sluggish and couldn't focus, I was regretting my decision to forgo the coffee. But I intended on finding an address for the guy who had followed me last night. I decided I would pay him a little visit. I didn't want to confront him at work, though, because I didn't want the others to know anything about the situation. Asking this guy what he was up to would definitely blow my cover.

"Are you ready for work?" I asked Dorothy.

"As ready as I'll ever be, I guess," Dorothy said as she packed up her knitting needles.

I leaned over and glanced at the project Dorothy was working on. "What are you knitting?"

"They're pastry covers." She beamed at me.

"You cover pastry with yarn?" I asked.

She waved her hand. "I thought it was odd too, at first, but I think they're actually to set your cupcakes and stuff on. Just to make them pretty."

A knitting book set on her desk, open to the page on which I assumed she'd gotten this pattern. "Did you find this in that book?"

She nodded and tapped the page. "Yes, right there."

I picked up the book. "Dorothy, this pattern is for pasties."

Her face turned red. "What? Why would I want to knit pasties?"

I laughed. "Maybe you'll need an extra pair."

She grabbed the book and slammed it shut. "Let's just go before we're late."

Dorothy draped her purse on her arm and marched toward the car. She ignored my chuckling.

The guy I'd talked to at work the night before was standing at the bar when we stepped inside. I headed toward him right away.

"Hey, how's it going?" he asked when he saw me.

"Remember the guy I asked you about last night?"

He looked over his shoulder. "Yeah, what about him?"

"What's his name?" I asked.

He stared for a beat and then said, "Spencer Johnson. Why are you so interested in this guy?"

Obviously, I couldn't tell him the truth. "I accidentally took one of his tips, and I need to give it back," I said as I walked away.

"Oh, that was really good. He'll never be suspicious of us now." Dorothy rolled her eyes.

"Okay, so I'm not good under pressure. So sue me," I said.

There were a few employees in the side dining area, prepping the tables for the customers who would soon be there for dinner. "I wonder if Megan is here yet?" I asked.

Dorothy looked around the room. "I don't see her. Unfortunately, we don't know what kind of car she drives, so looking in the parking lot won't help."

"Maybe she's in the back room," I said as I motioned for Dorothy to follow me.

Dorothy and I stepped across the room. No one seemed to notice us or care what we did. I walked into the break room and was surprised to see Megan sitting at the table. She was just sitting there, staring blankly at the wall. I exchanged a look with Dorothy.

"I think I'll get something to drink," Dorothy said and walked out of the room.

Oh great, she left *me* to talk with her. Megan was kind of weird, and she freaked me out every time I was around her. I stepped across the room. The whole time, I kept my eyes on her. Finally, I said, "Are you okay?"

She continued to stare at the wall in front of her.

"Do you mind if I sit down?" I asked and pointed at the chair across from her.

She shrugged, which other than giving me her name was the only reaction I'd gotten out of her. I sat in the chair and smiled when she glanced at me.

"Is everything okay?" I asked.

"I think she wanted him." Megan didn't make eye contact as she picked at the edge of her shirt.

I raised an eyebrow. "She wanted who?"

"Kristin wanted to have a relationship with Justin." Megan met my stare.

"Her business partner, Justin?" I asked.

She nodded. "Justin and I are dating, you know. He doesn't want me to tell anyone, but I figure what difference does it make if he really loves me like he says he does?"

I nodded. "That's true." Her admission was a shock to me because Justin and Megan had never given a clue that they were dating. I figured I would have seen a wink or a smile or some kind of flirtatious look. "How long have you been dating?" I asked.

Megan looked down at the table. "Six months. Anyway, I guess it doesn't matter now that Kristin is gone. Does that sound bad?"

I didn't know what to say, so I opted for a casual shrug. "I don't know."

"They just spent so much time together, and I saw the way that she looked at him."

This conversation was making me very uncomfortable. Megan stood from her chair and stared at me. "Forget that I said anything, okay?"

She didn't take her eyes off me. I had no choice but to agree, so I nodded. "No, I won't say a word. Heck, I don't know anyone around here to even tell," I said breezily.

She didn't return my smile. After a couple more seconds of her weird stare down, she walked over to the door and left the room without looking back. I didn't even know what my next move would be. I had to get Justin's side of the story. Of course, I'd told her that I wouldn't tell anyone what she'd said, so that made things more difficult. I'd have to get the information from him without telling him what I knew.

I tapped my fingers against the table and contemplated my dilemma. Could Megan have gotten rid of Kristin just because she thought she'd be in the way of her relationship with Justin? Maybe she'd had the guy on the boat get rid of Kristin for her. Anything was possible. Plus, Megan had acted a little strange and secretive. Maybe Justin and Megan were in on Kristin's death together. Just exactly who was Justin anyway? I needed as much info about him as I could find.

The door opened slightly, and Dorothy peeked her head through. "I overheard a little of what she said."

I nodded as Dorothy walked over and sat down. "She thinks Kristin was having an affair with her business partner," I said, leaning back against the chair.

"What do you think?" Dorothy asked.

I shrugged. "Since I don't know either one of them very well, I don't know what to say. I know one thing though: we have to find out more about both of them. Why aren't more people here discussing Kristin?" I asked.

"Maybe they didn't like her," Dorothy offered.

"I still think that they would be talking about how much they didn't like her."

"Well, we can't ask any questions because we're always working," Dorothy said.

"We'll just have to make time," I said.

"You know, your uncle never made me work this many hours." Dorothy glared.

I frowned. "You're the one who got me this job in the first place."

"Yes, and you'll thank me later when we solve this case because of it," she said with a wave of her finger.

I looked over my shoulder. "You know, if you were to be my lookout, I could snoop around in his office. Maybe I'd find something," I said.

Dorothy pointed her index finger at me. "Or maybe you'd get caught and get both of us killed."

"Think positive, Dorothy."

"That *is* positive. Positive that you'll get us killed," she said.

"Oh, nonsense," I said with a wave of my hand. I jumped up and over to the door. I peeked out to see if anyone was coming our way. "It looks like the coast is clear."

"It seems like you're hell-bent on getting us into trouble," Dorothy said as she pushed to her feet. "Hurry up before someone comes." She wrung her hands.

I rushed over to the office door. I was surprised that Justin had left it open. Every time I'd tried before, it had been locked. I thought back on what Megan had said. How would I ask Justin if he'd been doing his partner? I glanced over my shoulder one last time, and Dorothy motioned for me to hurry.

When I stepped into the office, I didn't know where to start. I hurried over to the desk and looked at the planner that was open. I flipped back to the date of Kristin's murder. There was a meeting for that day, but it didn't say with whom—just that there was a meeting. It could have been with the uniform salesman, for all I knew.

I opened the drawers and looked around, but nothing looked important for my case. There was a photo of Kristin, though. It had been turned upside down in the drawer. That was odd. I was surprised he hadn't just thrown it away since he didn't seem too heartbroken over her death. I continued to rifle through pages, hoping I'd find the smoking gun.

Dorothy's coughing caught my attention, and I knew that was my sign to get out of there. I shoved the drawer closed and rushed to the door. Just as I'd slipped out and halfway back to where Dorothy stood, the manager walked in. He looked at me as if I'd been caught stealing the salt and pepper shakers off the tables.

"Is everything okay back here?" he asked with a frown.

"Why, everything is just peachy," Dorothy said with a smile. "Maggie and I were just discussing how much we enjoy working here."

He looked from Dorothy to me as if I'd let it slip that Dorothy was really lying. "Yes, we love it," I said. I glanced over at a photo of the restaurant that was hanging on the wall. "How long has this restaurant been in business?" I asked with a smile.

He frowned. "A couple of years."

I nodded. "Really? So Kristin and Justin started the place?"

He looked as if he'd seen a ghost when I mentioned her name. I hadn't expected such a reaction from him.

His face was pale, but he finally said, "Kristin started the place first, and then Justin came into it to help."

I shook my head. "It's such a shame that she was in such a terrible accident."

He walked back to the door, letting me know that he thought the conversation was over. It might have been over for now, but I had a lot more questions to ask him, and I wouldn't stop until I got answers.

I followed him out the door, but he walked so quickly that I couldn't keep up. I threw my hands up in frustration.

"He doesn't like to talk much to the wait staff," Megan said.

I turned around and was surprised to see that she was talking to me again. "I can see that," I said after a moment.

Now that she was speaking again, I wanted to take advantage of that and ask more questions about what she'd just told me. "Listen, Megan, I feel bad that you were so upset. Do you want to talk about it more? You said that you thought the co-owner and Kristin were having an affair?"

"No, I never said that. I said that I thought she wanted him. He didn't want her. As a matter of fact he was mad at her," Megan said.

"Why is that?" I asked with a frown.

Dorothy was standing behind me. "Yeah, why is that?"

"She wanted him out of the business. Can you believe that? After all this time and how much effort he put into this place. He wanted to buy her half of the restaurant."

"That is terrible," I said, trying to make her think that I didn't suspect her of anything. This was great, but I wanted Justin's side of the story.

"Anyway, I guess he doesn't have to worry about that now, does he?" she said matter-of-factly.

I stared at her. I couldn't believe her careless comment. That would be a possible motive for murder. If Kristin had said no, all Justin would have had to do was kill her, and she'd be out of the picture. I had no idea how evil this man could be or if he was completely innocent, but I'd been hired to find the killer, and getting to the bottom of his motives would put me one step closer to that goal.

The main thing that remained was finding the man with the boat. If the owner of the restaurant was connected to the man with the boat, then that would definitely make me more suspicious. I didn't think that the man on the boat had acted alone. Maybe it was just a gut instinct, but I got the feeling they hadn't been alone out there on the water that day.

I needed to spend some time at the marina and find out more about the boat's owner. Someone around there would be willing to talk.

"What is going on in that mind of yours?" Dorothy asked as she stepped into the room.

I tapped my fingers against the table. "I need to spend more time at the marina. If that man has kept his boat there, then someone should be able to share a little bit of info with me."

Chapter Nineteen

That evening, after our shift, it was time for the big Bunco night. Dorothy insisted that she pick me up for the game. I wasn't sure I trusted her to drive after my past experiences, but I gave her another shot. The game was being held at her place, so at least I knew that I wouldn't run into Jake. It wasn't that I didn't want to see him. I was kind of torn, actually. If I saw him, I knew I would end up telling him everything that I'd discovered about the case, and I wasn't giving up what I knew without him divulging what he knew about the case. And he seemed stubborn enough that I doubted he would do that. So in other words, I was afraid that I'd end up telling him what I knew, and he wouldn't give me any info in return.

I'd never been in Dorothy's home before. I wasn't sure what to expect other than lots of knitted items. Dorothy's place was decorated with a multitude of shades of pink, from a mauve sofa to the pink mixer that sat on the kitchen counter.

"You like pink, huh?" I asked as I absorbed the view.

There was a ton of natural light in her condo that came from the patio doors that led to the small outside space. Dorothy had insisted that I come to her place early so I could help her set up refreshments. She'd mixed up margaritas for the evening, and I knew we were in for a real treat when these women got a little tipsy.

The first guests had just started to arrive, and Dorothy was busy chatting with the ladies when the doorbell rang again. "Maggie, can you get the door for me?" Dorothy asked.

I nodded and headed over to the door, fully prepared to see another of the Bunco Babes, as Dorothy called them. When I opened the door, I almost immediately shut it again. Jake was standing in front of me. For a second, I wondered if I was at the condo of one of the other Bunco Babes who lived in the same condo complex as Jake.

He looked handsome in his khaki pants and blue button-down shirt. A smile spread across his face. "You look beautiful," he said.

I looked down at my pale yellow sundress, then looked back at him. "So do you," I said softly. "What are you doing here?"

"Dorothy invited me." Jake winked at Dorothy, who I assumed was smiling behind my back.

I turned around and glared at her. She gave a little wave and wink. I stepped out of the way and let Jake into the room.

"Hi, Jake," the room of women called out to him in unison.

"Hello, ladies. You're looking lovely this evening." One flash of his smile and the whole room melted . . . including me.

"So she talked you into playing tonight too, huh?" I asked.

"What do you mean 'too'? I have a feeling you enjoy this game night as much as she does," he said with a teasing grin.

Of course, once again the ladies placed me next to Jake as often as possible throughout the evening. I had to admit he smelled delicious. And that sexy smile of his didn't hurt matters either.

We were sitting at the table, and everyone seemed to be having fun, although I could tell by some of the frowns and scowls that tension was beginning to mount between the Bunco Babes. Tonight's game was for high stakes, after all. There was a big gift bag full of items at stake. The winner got all the goodies, so the ladies were taking every roll of the dice seriously. The woman beside me tapped her fingers nervously against the table. I thought

I remembered her name as Betsy, but I wasn't one hundred percent positive. There were a lot of women here, and I hadn't memorized all the names.

The woman leaned over toward the other lady who sat across from me. Alaina had introduced herself to me, and I remembered the name because that was my mother's best friend's name too. Anyway, Alaina frowned at the other woman. Apparently Betsy was interested in the score pad.

"We need to stop the game," Betsy demanded.

The women stopped and stared at Betsy.

"What's wrong, Betsy?" Dorothy asked.

"Alaina is cheating," Betsy said indignantly.

Gasps rang out around the room. Alaina had just been accused of the ultimate Bunco crime. I wasn't sure what the penalty was, though.

The women at my table jumped up. Both placed their hands on their hips and stared at each other. I watched in amazement, wondering what would happen next.

"Dorothy, you have to do something," Betsy insisted.

Dorothy hurried over from her table. I was ready to get out of the room before things got ugly. I had no idea why Betsy thought Alaina was cheating, but I knew we were about to find out.

I exchanged a look with Jake. Of course, he had a smile on his face, and that caused me to have to bite my lip to keep from laughing.

Dorothy lifted her eyeglasses and peered at the scorecard. After a few seconds, she looked from Alaina to Betsy. You could have heard a pin drop, definitely one of Dorothy's knitting needles.

We were all in suspense, wondering what she would say.

Finally, Dorothy said, "Betsy, I don't see any sign that Alaina is cheating. What makes you say that?"

"She changed the numbers." Betsy glared at Alaina.

"She just can't count," Alaina retorted, narrowing her eyes.

I was waiting to see which one would take the first punch. They'd rip the eyeglass chains off each other's necks within seconds.

Dorothy shrugged and placed the pad back on the metal card table. "I can't see that she was cheating."

Betsy straightened. "I can't believe that you doubt me."

"Well, you did accuse Donna of cheating not more than six months ago."

The other women around the room nodded in agreement.

"This time is different," she said defensively.

"We should just go back to playing. I'm sure everything's fine," I said, trying to soothe the situation.

Alaina and Betsy looked at me as though they wanted me to stay out of it, but I was only trying to help.

Based on the scowls on their faces, it didn't look as if this discussion were going to end soon. There was even further trouble when I noticed Betsy glance over at the tray of cupcakes on the nearby table. The next thing I knew, Betsy had grabbed a cupcake, but Alaina rushed over and snatched up a pretty pink confection too. The women stood in front of each other with cupcakes in hand, ready to toss at the first cross word or glare. I looked at Jake, but he shrugged. Apparently, he wasn't getting involved.

With their arms pulled back, I knew the cupcakes would start flying through the air soon. When one lady tossed, the other one would fire, and for all I knew, the whole room would erupt into a food fight.

"Don't do it, ladies," Dorothy said. "I am not cleaning up a food mess again."

Again? Had this happened before? I knew they took the game seriously, but this was a little extreme. I'd seen a candle and a bag of dried prunes in the gift bag. The items were hardly worth all this trouble.

"I'm not afraid to use this," Betsy warned, wiggling the cupcake through the air.

Okay, this had gone on long enough. If no one else were going to put a stop to this, then I would have to. I stepped forward and stood between the women. They looked around me.

"Ladies, it's not worth fighting over. Now I know you all love each other, so why don't you put the cupcakes down and just play the game." I used my best soothing voice and offered the women a wide smile.

Apparently, it wasn't what they wanted to hear, because neither woman surrendered her sweet-laced missile.

I had to take matters into my own hands. Or in this case, cupcakes into my own hands. I reached forward to remove the cupcake from Betsy's hand. She wasn't going down without a fight, though, because she tossed the cupcake in my direction. That was when Jake stepped forward and eased the cupcake from Alaina's hand before she tossed it. Lucky for me, the cupcake missed and landed on the floor in a smashed mess.

Dorothy marched over. "Betsy! You apologize to Maggie right now."

She scowled and said, "I'm sorry, Maggie. I don't know what came over me."

I released a deep breath and said, "That's okay."

Dorothy patted my hand. "Sorry about that, Maggie. Betsy has always had a bit of a temper."

"I can see that," I said.

When Jake and I stepped to the side, he said, laughing, "That was one dangerous game of Bunco."

"Yes, it was touch and go there for a minute," I said.

The women sat down and immediately went back to the game. Not a word of the incident was spoken, but I had a feeling that in another few months a cheating scandal would pop up again. Maybe Dorothy needed to rethink providing the refreshments.

More importantly, I hadn't won the big prize tonight—I guessed that meant the women would allow me to come back again.

It was getting late, and with as many margaritas as the ladies had consumed here, was no way I was letting Dorothy get anywhere near a car to drive me home.

"Dorothy, I need to take your car, so I can go home. I can pick you up in the morning," I said.

"Oh no. Remember, no one drives my car," she said as she stumbled over to me.

"How am I supposed to get home?" I asked.

Dorothy looked at Jake standing beside me. "How about Jake taking you home?" she asked with a huge smile.

My heart sped up at just the mention of his name.

"I'd love to take you home," Jake said.

Dorothy gave a satisfied smile. I realized then that she probably hadn't had as many drinks as I'd thought. This was just all part of her plan to get me alone with Jake. Well played, Dorothy, well played. Either Jake gave me a ride home, or I would have to walk. My feet still hadn't recovered from waiting tables, so I didn't relish the thought of walking all the way home.

Finally, I nodded. "Okay, thanks."

Dorothy and the other ladies had smiles on their faces. "Have fun, kids."

I climbed into the passenger seat of Jake's car, and he headed toward my apartment.

"You played well tonight," he said as he steered the wheel.

"Sorry that I beat you," I said.

He chuckled. "We'll have to have a rematch." I tried to hide my smile. "We haven't had a chance to talk about the case," he said.

I didn't say anything for a moment; then I finally looked at him. "You talk first."

He laughed. "What does that mean?"

"I'm not telling you what I know until you tell me what you know." I flashed a satisfied grin.

He glanced over at me. "You know something?"

"Maybe. Do *you* know something?" I asked. He looked at the road and nodded. "You go first," I said.

"Okay, I'll go first. We do know that Kristin was on a boat the day she died."

"That is your news?" I asked. "I told you that before she was even found."

"I know—just calm down," he said.

I released a deep breath. "Sorry. I got a little excited."

He glanced at me again. "Yeah, well, you do that a lot, but that's one thing I like about you."

I bit back a smile. It was good to know that he thought one of my annoying habits was a cute quirk. Jake parked the car by my apartment. He sat there for a moment after turning off the engine. A soft breeze floated through the window. He looked like there was something he wanted to say, and my heart rate increased as I wondered what he was about to tell me. The faint sound of the palm fronds brushing against the tree trunks carried across the air.

Finally, he said, "Well, I guess I'd better walk you to your door."

His statement caught me off guard because I was sure that he'd wanted to say more. "That's okay. I can walk by myself," I said, opening the door.

He opened his car door. "No, I want to walk you."

Jake hurried around and opened the door for me. I met his gaze as he held the door open for me. "Thank you," I said softly.

Jake and I walked to my door in silence. It wasn't awkward; instead, it was oddly calming. I pulled the keys out of my purse and shoved them into the lock.

Another sound came from over our shoulder, and Jake whipped around. It could have been a cat, but then again, it could have been the murderer. I prayed it was just a cat. I was just thankful that I wasn't alone. It was nice having someone to have my back and not having to check out the noises all by myself. Not that I wouldn't; it was just good to have backup occasionally. I would never admit that to Jake, though. It was my little secret.

We peered out into the darkness. The sound could have come from any direction. When another noise sounded, Jake took off, sprinting. I wasn't sure what he'd seen.

"Stay there. I'll be right back," he called over his shoulder.

Considering I had no idea where he was running to, I didn't think he'd have to worry about me going anywhere. Although I hated just standing around … and I kind of wanted to know what he was doing. Had he seen someone? I doubted he would take off running like that for a cat, so my guess was that he'd seen someone. Was that person alone? I looked to my side but didn't see anything.

So even though Jake had asked me to stay there and wait for him, I decided to do the opposite. I took off in a run down the pathway. There was a sidewalk in the courtyard that went around all the apartments' doors. I scanned the area as I ran, but it was dark and hard to see. They needed to add more lighting to this area. The one light at the front of the building was just not enough. When I reached the end of the path, I stopped to catch my breath.

As I scanned the area, I didn't see Jake. I was beginning to get nervous. What was he doing? Had something serious happened?

"Jake?" I whispered.

Of course, he didn't answer. I guessed the only option I had at this point was to turn around and go back to my apartment. Maybe Jake was already there, waiting for me. I knew the first thing he'd ask would be why I hadn't waited for him. He would know the answer to that question, but it still wouldn't stop him from asking.

I turned around to walk back to my apartment but stopped in my tracks. A man had walked out in front of me. I'd been looking down at the time and saw his dark shoes first. I slowly looked up at him. I released a deep breath when I realized it was my neighbor. He was holding a black trash bag. I'd only seen him a few times before, but I was thankful to run into him this time. Maybe Jake had spotted my neighbor and thought it was the bad guy.

I smiled. "Oh, I'm sorry. I didn't see you."

"That's okay. Sorry if I startled you." He stared at me.

I looked down at his trash bag. "So are you on your way to the dumpster?"

That was a stupid question.

He nodded.

"Did you see someone else go past? A tall guy with dark hair? He may or may not have had a gun in his hand," I said.

My neighbor's eyes widened. "Is there a problem?"

I waved off his concern. "No, he's a police officer. We thought we heard a strange noise."

He stared at me blankly.

"Anyway, have you seen anything strange lately? Anyone you don't recognize hanging around?" I asked.

He shook his head. "No."

He was a man of few words.

"Well, thanks anyway. I'm headed back to my apartment," I said and motioned over his shoulder.

He nodded and stepped around me. I turned and watched him walk away. He was a bit odd, but I guessed he was just the quiet type. After watching him for a few seconds, I headed down the path back to my apartment. I hoped Jake was there, waiting for me. Stars twinkled like rhinestones in the night sky. With Jake missing, I felt very much alone under those stars.

I'd almost made it back to the door when I felt someone grasp my shoulder. I grabbed the person's arm, spun around, and in one swift movement, slammed my attacker onto the ground. I'd practiced that move many times, but I'd never known if I'd be able to do it when I was actually in a life-or-death situation. It was good to know that I could, in fact, pull off that move.

Unfortunately, I'd just slammed Jake to the ground. He climbed to his feet.

"Nice move," he said.

I rushed over to him. "I'm so sorry."

"No." He waved off my apology. "I know better than to startle someone like that."

"Well, you did grab my shoulder," I said.

"Actually, it was more of a tap on the shoulder," he countered.

I studied his face for a moment. Okay, I guessed he was right. It hadn't been a complete grab, and maybe I'd overreacted just a little.

"What happened?" I asked.

"I thought you were going to wait here for me," he said, scowling.

"Why would I do that?" I said. "What if you needed my help?"

"I *am* law enforcement. I'm kind of used to taking care of myself."

I nodded. "Yeah, I guess you have a point. So what did you see? Why did you take off?"

"I thought I saw a man… now I'm not so sure. It may have been another resident."

"You didn't grab my neighbor, did you?"

"Just a little bit." He ran his hand through his hair. "I think he was just taking his trash out."

I shook my head. That guy is never going to talk to me again.

Before I had a chance to turn the key, the door pushed open. Jake and I exchanged a look, and then he motioned for me to step back. The speed at which he drew his gun out of its holster was especially impressive. I knew that I'd locked my door, so that could mean only one thing: someone had broken into my apartment.

Jake motioned for me to stay back while he walked into my place. I didn't want him going in there alone, but he seemed intent on carrying out his law enforcement inclinations. So I stayed by the door. It wasn't like it was going to take him long to search the place. He stood in the middle of the room, with his gun in his hand. Night cast a shadow over the room, but I could make out his silhouette.

After a few seconds, Jake moved back toward the door and flipped the light switch. Nothing happened. The lights weren't working.

"Do you have a flashlight?" he asked.

"Only on my phone," I said, retrieving the phone from my pocket and clicking on the app.

The small light lit a path through my apartment. Jake moved over to the closet and stepped to the side. After a brief pause, he yanked the door open. Thank goodness, no one was there, so he moved over to the bed. He leaned down and looked underneath.

"No one is in here," he said when he stepped closer to me.

"I don't know how the door could have gotten open."

"Where's the circuit breaker?"

"It's right over here." I moved into the room and over to the far wall.

I held my phone up while he opened the box and flipped the switch. Light flooded the room. Jake looked around, and I was suddenly aware of just how small the room was. I picked up the shirt I'd left on the chair that morning and stuffed it in the desk drawer.

"Well, no one is here. Does anything seem out of place?" He looked around the room instead of looking at me.

I tucked a stray strand of hair behind my ear. "No, nothing seems to be missing."

"You must have left the door unlocked, and it somehow blew open," he said.

I nodded. "I guess so."

I knew that I'd locked the door, but I had no way to prove that, so I'd let it go. I wondered if I should tell him about seeing the guy from the restaurant watching me. No, I would handle it myself. I felt as if I were close to discovering something important on the case and didn't want to lose my momentum now.

"Thank you for checking everything out," I said.

Jake moved past me. His clean and masculine smell circled me in his wake. When Jake reached the door, he turned around to face me. "You'll make sure to lock your door when I leave?" he asked.

I stepped over to the door and nodded. "I'll talk to you soon."

He stared for a moment and then said, "Good night, Maggie."

Chapter Twenty

The next day found Dorothy and me back on the investigation. Within a few minutes we'd made our way to the dock. I counted down to the third boat, and sure enough, it was there. I didn't see the woman, though, so I stepped closer. I was standing by the ramp to the boat when the woman came up behind us.

"May I help you?" she asked.

I flashed my wallet, which had nothing official in it, but she wouldn't know that. "Maggie Thomas, P.I." I rushed the words, hoping that she wouldn't understand what I'd said. "We'd like to ask you some questions about Kristin Grant."

Dorothy leaned close. "You just showed her your Bath and Body Works gift card."

I stood a little straighter, hoping that would make up for my flub.

The woman's expression turned. "Yeah, what do you want to know?"

"You were friends with her?" I asked.

She nodded. "Yes, we've known each other for about a year now. I met her here at the restaurant, but she spent a lot of time here."

"With her boyfriend?" I asked.

Her eyes widened. "Yes. His boat is sometimes docked right next to mine."

"But he doesn't leave his boat here all the time?" I asked.

"No, just when the spot is empty," she said.

I pulled out the picture. "Do you happen to know the other people in this photo of you?" I pointed.

"I don't know the other woman," she said.

I found that hard to believe, but I pressed on with questioning. "What about him?"

"You mean the hairy arm behind us?"

"Yes," I said.

She looked at me with a lifted eyebrow. "That's her boyfriend, I guess."

"Do you know his name?" I asked.

She nodded. "His name was Sam."

That was the name I was hoping she would say. "Do you know anything else about him?" I continued.

"I know he was pressuring Kristin into doing something that she didn't want to do, but she wouldn't tell me what. She said she didn't want to get me involved."

"What do you think it was?" I asked.

"I really have no idea. Kristin was a private person. We talked about general things, but never anything too personal."

I paused and looked out at the water. It looked as if this conversation wasn't going to produce any new information.

"Thanks for the information," I said.

As Dorothy and I made it away from the boat, I felt eyes on me. I looked back at the woman, and she was focused on something else and didn't notice at me. But that sensation remained. I took a couple more steps and glanced to my right. That was when I noticed the middle-aged man watching Dorothy and me as we walked by. I looked away, hoping that he would stop staring, but I still felt his eyes on me. Taking another quick peek, once again I found the dark-haired man staring at us. Was he looking at someone else? I peered over to my left but didn't see anyone.

He was definitely scrutinizing us. I quickened my step.

"Come on, Dorothy; that strange man is watching us. He's making me nervous."

Dorothy looked over in the direction.

"Don't look at him," I said.

"Okay, but he's coming after us," she replied.

I hoped that I'd heard her wrong, but when I glanced over my shoulder and saw the man walking briskly toward us, I knew that she'd spoken the truth. It was time for us to get the heck out of there. What did he want with us? I'd done nothing wrong... not yet anyway.

We'd made it to the end of the dock when the man yelled at us.

"Excuse me." He waved his arms.

Okay, that didn't sound like a threatening comment, but I wasn't going to take a chance. He called out again, but I ignored him. Instead, I focused on getting to the parking lot. We'd just turned to our left when the man jumped out in front of us. With one swift kick, I knocked him down. That would serve him right for trying to attack two women. Who did he think he was anyway? What a creep. He'd think twice before attacking another woman.

The man clutched his side and looked up at me. "I need to talk with you about the woman on the boat," he said breathlessly.

I glanced over at Dorothy.

"Oops," she said.

"Are you okay?" I asked.

He nodded.

"I'm sorry. Why didn't you say something sooner?"

He sat up. "It was my fault."

Yeah, it kind of was his fault. Could he blame me for thinking that he was about to attack us? After another couple of seconds, he stood.

"What did you want to tell us?" I asked.

"I overheard your conversation with the woman on the boat."

I looked at him questioningly. "Oh, yeah?"

He nodded. "Yes, you were asking about the woman who was killed and her boyfriend."

"Yes, that's right," I replied.

He rubbed his side again. "I saw him here on the day that the young woman was killed. He was talking with that woman on the boat."

"Are you sure about that?" I asked.

"I'm positive. I have the boat slip right next to hers. I overheard them talking," he said.

It seemed that this man did a lot of listening.

"So what were they talking about?" I asked.

"Oh, well, he was asking her out, and they were flirting."

I looked at Dorothy. She had a huge frown on her face.

The man nodded. "Anyway, she was definitely talking to him on the day of the woman's death."

"So has he been back here since?" I asked.

He shrugged. "That I don't know. But he was around here a lot."

I supposed that didn't automatically mean he was guilty of something just because he had been here. It was suspicious, though. If she was having a romantic relationship with the boyfriend, she had certainly hidden it well from me.

"I don't normally listen to people's conversations, in case you were wondering," he added.

I waved off his comment. "Hey, it's none of my business."

"You say he came around here often?" Dorothy asked.

"Yes, everyone knew them here because they were loud."

"Did you see the woman who was murdered?" I asked.

His eyes widened. "She was murdered? I didn't hear that."

I didn't answer. Maybe I'd said too much already.

He continued, "Yes, I had seen her here before. Like I said, I'm right next to the boat where they were."

I nodded. "I really appreciate your help."

"No problem," he said. "I figured you were the police. I always thought that guy was trouble. Now that I know the police are asking about him, that just confirms that I was right."

I didn't bother correcting him.

"Uh-oh, the woman is headed this way," he said.

I looked back and saw that she was in fact headed our way. I couldn't tell if she was watching us, though. I didn't want to cause any problems for this man. She'd probably want to know why I was speaking with him.

"If we just step over here, then maybe she won't see us," he said, pointing toward a small building.

Dorothy and I moved over beside the building. The man peeked out. It was as if he was afraid of her. Had she said something to him in the past?

After a couple of seconds, he glanced at us. "She walked on by."

"Did she say something to you in the past?" I asked.

"Well, she had warned me not to listen to her conversations."

"Oh," I said with a nod. "Thanks again for the information."

He smiled. "It was my pleasure to help."

"I'm sorry about kicking you." I pointed at his stomach.

He patted it. "I'm tough."

Dorothy and I waved goodbye and headed toward the parking lot. Now he had me nervous and looking for her. I had to figure out if what he'd said was true. It wouldn't do any good for me to confront her. She would just tell me what I wanted to hear.

When Dorothy and I returned to the parking lot, a car alarm was going off. As I neared, I realized it was my car that was making the noise. I saw a man run away, but he was already so far away that I couldn't tell who he was. Of course, I had my suspicions. Why was this guy following me if not for the fact that he knew who I was? I didn't know for sure that he'd been by my car, but what other reason would he have for running? I hurried over, turning off the loud alarm, and looked around the car.

Dorothy stood beside me. Nothing seemed to be out of place. The windows weren't smashed, and all the tires still had the same amount of air in them as when I'd parked the car.

"What do you think that was about?" I asked Dorothy.

She adjusted the pocketbook on her arm. "Maybe someone was just breaking into cars, looking for something to steal."

I wished she was right, but it had happened twice now, so that made it a little less likely that it was a coincidence. It gave me the creeps to know that he had been messing around my car.

"It looks like we at least scared him away." I unlocked the car, and we climbed in.

I shoved the key into the ignition and turned it. Nothing happened. The car tried to start but despite my best efforts, turning the key and pumping the gas, nothing happened.

"I thought you replaced the battery," she said.

"I did." I turned the ignition again.

"It sounds like it was a bad one." She took out her needles.

I leaned my head back against the headrest. This was not going as I'd planned. What would Magnum have done?

"What are we going to do now?" I asked.

"Well, for one, you need to get a reliable car. I mean, a private eye can't go driving around in a rattletrap," Dorothy said.

"Duly noted, but what do we do in the meantime?" I asked.

"There's only one thing we can do."

"What's that?" I looked at her for an answer.

"We have to call Jake." She stared me right in the eyes.

I waved my hands. "Oh, no. No way."

"Have you kissed him yet?" she asked.

"What does *that* have to do with anything?"

"You need to get it over with if you haven't. Now pick up that sparkly thing you call a phone and call him to come and get us."

Doing as I was told, I pulled out my phone and punched in his number. Dorothy stared at me. "What?" I asked.

"You have his number memorized?" she asked.

"It's an easy number to remember," I said defensively.

She shrugged and went back to her knitting. About twenty minutes passed before I noticed Jake's car pull into the parking lot. Since there were shops at the marina, at least I could lie to him and say we'd just been shopping.

He stepped out of his car and strolled over to us. There was no mistaking the cocky grin on his face as he leaned down, placing his hands on my car door.

"Hello, ladies. Having car trouble?"

"Yes, I'm not sure what's wrong," I said.

I seriously needed to learn more about car repair. My mother's third husband had tried to show me a little, but it was hard to understand his instructions after he'd had a half dozen beers.

Jake tapped the side of my car. "Pop the hood."

I hopped out and joined him in front of the car. "Any idea what's wrong?"

Jake reached under the hood and reconnected the cable onto the battery. "Looks like the battery cable came off. You should be fine now. Try to start it and see what happens."

I jumped back in and turned the ignition. The car started right away. I glanced at Dorothy. "It was just the cable."

She nodded but didn't stop knitting.

Jake closed the hood, and I hopped out again.

"I'm sorry that I had to call you," I said.

"Think nothing of it. I'm glad you called."

Jake looked around, then gestured over his shoulder. "What are you all up to?"

"What makes you think we were up to something?" I asked.

He stared for a beat, then said, "Wild guess."

"We were shopping," I said, knowing that I didn't sound convincing.

"Are you going back to the Captain's Quarters?" he asked.

I nodded. "We're supposed to go back."

"Have you found anything interesting?" he asked.

"There are some weird people there. One of the female employees, Megan Cass, thought that Kristin wanted to have an affair with the co-owner, Justin Mack. Megan is apparently having a relationship with him. Anyway, there's another employee who I think may be involved with the man on the boat."

I hadn't told Jake about the picture with the two women and the man's arm. Or about the bracelet that I'd found. One thing was for sure: I needed to talk with this Sam who was supposedly Kristin's boyfriend. If that was his bracelet I'd found, then he was probably involved with the man on the boat, and I told this to Jake.

Jake's eyebrows arched. "Really? What makes you say that?"

"I saw the man from the boat talking with him," I said.

"Why didn't you call me when you saw him?" he asked.

"He was gone too fast. Why aren't you talking to the employees?" I asked.

"We're looking into things," he said.

"You just like being mysterious. That's kind of annoying, you know," I said.

"I think you secretly like it," he said.

"Well, you're wrong," I said, climbing back behind the steering wheel.

"What are you planning next?" he asked as he leaned down to my window again. It was hard to resist looking at his handsome face.

"How do you know I have something planned?" I asked.

"You always have something planned," he said with a smile.

I shrugged. "Just going to check some leads I have."

"Are you going to share that info with me?" he asked.

"I'll think about it." I smiled.

Jake stepped back and I pulled the car out. I glanced in the rearview mirror. He was watching me and I couldn't help but smile.

Chapter Twenty-One

"Now that Jake is gone, we can go over to the other marina near the restaurant and see if that boat is there. I need to track down the guy on the boat and find this other guy. The boyfriend named Sam." I shifted the car into reverse.

Dorothy shook her head. "I am not making my daily knitting quota."

I released a deep breath. "Okay, you're right. I should just go by myself."

I knew that Dorothy would never go for that. She wanted to be a part of this, no matter what she admitted right now.

"No, it's dangerous. You definitely need someone to go with you." She set her needles down and peered at me from over the top of her eyeglasses. "You should let me drive though."

"We did that before, and I still haven't recovered," I said.

"I'll have you know that I've never had an accident or gotten a speeding ticket," Dorothy retorted.

"Well, there's always a first for everything," I said.

After a few minutes, we'd pulled up to the other marina. Dorothy and I walked around to the deck. If I didn't get any answers here, I'd have to go to the restaurant and ask more questions. I was trying to avoid the restaurant right now. For one, I didn't want them to ask me to work tonight, and for two, I didn't want them to wonder why I was there on my day off.

There were quite a few people around their boats. I didn't know where to even begin this clue-seeking mission.

"Why don't you take this side, and I'll take the other side," I said, motioning for Dorothy to start on the right. "Ask around and try to find out if the man with the boat has been here."

Dorothy nodded. "Come and find me if you find out, and I'll do the same."

I nodded and moved over to the first boat. I'd made my way to the fifth boat and was beginning to become discouraged when I spotted a man moving around the bow of his boat. I'd just stepped closer when he noticed me.

"Hello," he said.

"I wondered if I could ask you a few questions," I said.

He nodded. "Sure. What can I do for you?"

"I know this is a long shot, but I'm looking for a boat. The name has 'Vida' in it, but that's about all I know," I said.

He looked over and pointed toward the water. "Is that the boat?"

I strained to see, but I soon realized he was pointing out the boat that I'd been looking for. This was my chance, but what would I do now?

"Thank you," I said, running away.

Dorothy spotted me as I ran toward her. "What's wrong?"

"The boat is out there. It's leaving," I said breathlessly.

"Well, you're in luck," Dorothy said, motioning for me to follow her.

I was almost afraid to find out what this idea was.

"It'll work. I promise," she said.

I hurried after her. "Okay, let me have it. What idea do you have now?"

"I know someone with a boat. He'll let us take it out and follow that boat. That's one way to find out who this man is," she said.

"I guess that makes sense, but it sounds like a risky move."

"Since when do you let something like a risky move stop you?"

"Well, never, I guess," I said.

Jake would definitely not go for this plan. But it wasn't his case, so it didn't matter. How could he be a cop and never take a risk? Well, other than the risk of possibly being shot every day he was at work.

I couldn't believe I was allowing her to talk me into this. It had disaster written all over it, but since I was low on options, I had to give it a try. Believe me, if I could have thought of a better idea, I would have definitely tried it. I'd never driven a boat, but how hard could it be? Turn it on and steer with the wheel, right? It would be just like driving a car, right? Maybe even better because I wouldn't have to stay in the lanes or wait for red lights. As long as we could see land we'd be okay.

Heck, maybe I'd like it so much I'd eventually get a boat of my own, although that would require solving a whole lot of cases in order to afford one. Maybe I could get one of those houseboats and live on it. Then I thought better of that idea when I realized I would be constantly floating. Always up and down. I wondered if I would have seasickness. It would be too late once I got out there and realized that was the case.

"Are you sure this person will let you use the boat?" I asked.

Dorothy waved her hand. "Of course. This guy owes me a favor. I got him out of a lot of trouble one night."

I wasn't even going to ask what that was all about. "What are we going to do when we catch up to the boat?" I asked.

"We'll make him stop and ask him questions."

She made it sound so easy. If only it could be that simple.

"By the way, do you know how to swim?" Dorothy asked.

"I can stay above water, I guess," I said. "What about you?"

"Same here," she said.

I hoped this boat had lifejackets, because it looked as if we both needed them. The only boat I'd ever been on was my mom's third husband's old fishing boat. That thing had been a rust bucket and I couldn't believe that we hadn't sunk the moment we'd gotten on the water. That had been one of the most boring summers of my life. I would probably never be able to go fishing again because of that experience. The lake had reeked of hot fish, and the mosquitoes had had a buffet on my skin.

We reached the boat. It was small, and I was thankful for that. It would be easier for me to handle a small boat. My stomach flipped just thinking about navigating the waters. I barely knew how to turn the thing on.

Dorothy rushed over to her friend, and I stayed back to watch. I didn't want any part of that conversation. The boat was still in view, but the longer we waited, the farther away he would get. The man frowned at Dorothy, and it didn't look as if things were going in our favor. But after another minute he smiled and nodded.

The next thing, I knew he'd handed Dorothy the keys.

She bounced back over to where I stood. "We need to hurry before the boat gets away. Are you ready to go?"

"Yeah, sure. Is he okay with us taking his boat?" I asked.

She waved the keys in the air. "I have the keys, don't I?"

I nodded. "Well, yes, you do."

"Okay, then. Let's do this." She motioned over her shoulder. Dorothy climbed onto the boat and sat behind the wheel.

"Whoa. What are you doing?" I asked.

She looked at me incredulously. "What does it look like I'm doing? I told you we are going to find the boat." Dorothy sat behind the wheel of the boat with both hands wrapped tightly around the steering wheel.

"Dorothy, something tells me you don't know what you're doing. Have you ever driven a boat before?" I asked.

"No, but how hard can it be?" she said, adjusting the throttle on the boat.

Chapter Twenty-Two

I stared at her, but Dorothy didn't look over at me. "Why don't you let me give it a try?" I said in a sweet voice as if I were trying to talk her off the ledge of a building right before she jumped.

I'd experienced Dorothy's driving skills on the highway. Her driving on the waterway was something I didn't know if I could handle. How would I convince her to let me navigate the boat?

"Dorothy, I'll buy you a bunch of knitting supplies if you let me drive," I said.

She scoffed. "You don't have any money. You couldn't afford to buy me a ball of yarn. Now we're wasting time."

Dorothy pulled on the starter cord, and I knew my time was running out. "What if after I solve this case, I get you a date with Mr. Grant?"

She looked at me, and for a moment and I thought that my offer had worked, but instead she shrugged and turned her attention back to the wheel.

Dorothy put the throttle in the starting position and then adjusted the choke. We took off at what I thought was Mach speed. The wind almost knocked me over, and I was rendered speechless for a moment. It was like being on a boat in the middle of a hurricane. I held onto my seat, trying to steady myself.

"Dorothy, for the love of all things knitting will you slow down," I yelled over the roar of the engine.

She whipped the steering wheel around, and we headed in the opposite direction.

"I think you're supposed to navigate that way, not go in circles, Dorothy. We're losing the boat. He's getting away," I said.

"I know that, Maggie," Dorothy yelled as she spun the wheel around.

It wouldn't take much of Dorothy's driving to give me seasickness. I looked around for a radio on this thing so that I could call the Coast Guard. Dorothy turned the boat in the other direction again and pushed the throttle. Finally, at least we were pointing in the right direction, but unfortunately, I couldn't see the man's boat anymore.

Dorothy spun us around again, so much so that I didn't know up from down. I was pretty sure that she didn't know up from down or left from right now either. I had to put a stop to this madness right now.

"Don't get too far away from the coast, Dorothy," I said as she turned the boat in the wrong direction again.

"This is the right direction," she said with her eyes wide and focused on the water in front of her.

"No, no, it's that way," I said, motioning over my shoulder.

She eased off the throttle for a moment while she pondered what I'd said; then she pushed the gas again. "I'm sure it's this way."

"Look over at the buildings. We're going away from the marina. It's in the opposite direction," I said.

Dorothy glanced over, and it finally clicked. "Oh, dear. I guess we are going the wrong way."

There was no telling where we would end up if she were behind the wheel for much longer. I was ready to plant my feet on the land again. My first true boating experience might just be my last.

Dorothy whipped the boat around again, and I thought at any moment we would go flying off like little rag dolls. Water splashed up on the side of the boat and soaked the skin on my arms. I looked around for a lifejacket. That was something I should have done before Dorothy had ever turned on the ignition.

Finally, I grabbed the jackets and tried to make my way over to Dorothy. I stumbled and grabbed onto the edge, trying to keep my balance. I was secretly hoping that we'd run out of gas, except that would mean we'd be stuck out there in the middle of the water.

I made it over to Dorothy because I was going to insist that she put the jacket on. "I'll hold the wheel while you put this on."

She finally relinquished control of the boat over to me while she hurriedly put the jacket on and then grabbed the wheel again.

"Now you put your jacket on," she said as she attempted to steer in the correct direction.

I nodded and slipped into the jacket. Just then the boat started to sputter.

"What's happening?" Dorothy asked as she glanced back at me.

I shook my head. "I don't know, but it doesn't sound good."

I looked over at the gas gauge to see if my secret wish had come true. But it indicated that the boat had gas.

"What did you do to the boat?" Dorothy asked with a frown.

"Me? I didn't do anything. How could I? You've been driving, not me," I said.

"Well, you held the wheel for a moment," she said.

"Yes, for a few seconds. I hardly think that would cause the boat to break," I said.

"What will I tell the owner?" she asked.

"I'll go to the back and look." I held on to the side of the boat, trying to make my way to the stern.

Heck, I had no idea what I was looking for, though. The engine, maybe? What would I do once I got back there? Make sure that the boat still had an engine? The way Dorothy had been driving, it wouldn't surprise me if it had fallen off. At least for the time being, Dorothy had stopped the boat, though.

My hair was plastered to my head from the spray of water that had splashed across the boat, and I felt as if I'd been on one hell of a ride at the amusement park. I looked over the edge of the boat. The engine was still back there, but I had no idea if it was still working.

"Well, we still have an engine," I said.

"Thank heavens for small favors."

"Are you sure we have gas? Maybe the gauge is broken," I said.

"Oh dear, I hope we didn't break it," Dorothy said.

"There should be no *we* in that sentence. I had nothing to do with it," I said.

"Is there a way to see if the boat has gas?" she asked.

"Other than using the throttle, I have no idea."

I leaned over a little again and the boat lurched forward. I fell forward, and the next thing I knew, I'd hit the water.

Chapter Twenty-Three

The splash startled me, and the water was colder than I'd expected. I was definitely underneath the water for a moment. For a second, I saw my life flash before my eyes. Okay, maybe it wasn't my life, but more of a montage of what could have been. This was it for me, and I was going to drown.

My head finally emerged from under the ocean, and I spat out the water in my mouth and gasped for air. Dorothy was standing at the edge of the boat, staring down at me with a look of panic in her eyes. My legs dangled in the deep water, and all I could think about was that damn movie *Jaws*.

The more I thought about it, the more I was convinced that there were sharks circling me. I'd heard the stories, and I knew there were a lot of sharks in the water right off the coast.

"Dorothy," I gasped. "Get me out of here. I'm sure there are sharks all around me."

"You're panicking," she said.

"Well, do you blame me for panicking?"

"There are no sharks. Now swim over here and grab my hand." Dorothy motioned for me to come closer.

"I told you, I can't swim well. The sharks are going to eat me alive, and it will be your fault. I think I'm sinking." My voice had reached an all-time high panic level.

She shook her head. "You're wearing a lifejacket. You can't sink."

"Something is touching my leg," I said breathlessly.

"Oh, for heaven's sake. Now get yourself together and swim back over here to the boat," Dorothy demanded.

She was right. I had to get hold of myself. I'd take a deep breath and just kick my legs and arms. After all, I could almost touch the boat from where I was now.

"Your phone is ringing," Dorothy said.

"Well, I'm a little busy right now. They'll have to leave a message. I'm trying to save myself from the sharks," I yelled.

Dorothy rolled her eyes. "I've never seen anyone freak out as much as you. You should be ashamed." She wiggled her finger.

Really? Dorothy was shaming me now? I was in the middle of the freaking Atlantic Ocean. Personally, I thought she should have already called the Coast Guard. How the heck was she going to help pull me up onto the boat?

With lots of kicking and struggle, I made my way over to the boat again.

"Aren't you going to give me a hand?" I asked breathlessly.

"Can't you just use the ladder over there?" Dorothy pointed.

"Yeah, I guess that would be the more practical way of getting back on the boat. Forget about calling the Coast Guard."

She snorted. "I wasn't going to call them anyway."

After what seemed like an eternity, I made it to the little ladder on the side of the boat. I was sure I felt a shark brush past my legs again. Dorothy ran over to me as I climbed up onto the boat. I hoisted one leg over the side and then the other.

"You really shouldn't have leaned over the side like that," she admonished me.

"Yeah, that's sage advice that I will make sure to file away for future reference."

My phone rang again, and Dorothy and I exchanged a look. It was a look that said we knew we were doing something that we never wanted to tell anyone about. It would be our little secret. No one had to know what had happened out there today.

Chapter Twenty-Four

I was shocked that my purse hadn't somehow tumbled over the side of the boat too. I reached in and grabbed the phone. When I saw the number on the screen, I almost tossed the phone over the side of the boat. Why was Jake Jackson calling me now? There was no way he knew what we were doing… or did he? I looked around for another boat. I refused to believe that he could have discovered our little plan.

"Who is it?" Dorothy leaned closer.

"It's Jake."

"Aren't you going to answer?" she asked.

"I'm afraid he'll know what we're doing," I said.

"He can't possibly know," she said.

I sucked in a deep breath and clicked on the phone.

"Are you okay?" he immediately asked.

I glanced around again as if I expected him to be standing behind me on the boat. "Yes," I said, my voice wavering. "Why do you ask?" I chuckled nervously.

"I got a call from another detective who happened to be at the marina. He was out on his boat and said he thought the boat you went out on was doing circles in the water. Is that possible, Maggie?" he asked.

Oh, heavens. Did Jake have spies all over town? There was no point in lying because I knew he'd find out the truth.

"Well, if you must know, then yes. Dorothy and I went out on a boat," I said with confidence in my voice.

He snorted.

"What is so funny about that?" I asked as I stood soaked from falling in the water.

"Who was driving the boat?" he asked.

"Dorothy."

Dorothy tugged on my shirt. "Who is it?"

"Oh . . . are you back on dry land?" he asked with a worried tone.

"Well, not exactly, but we're on our way," I said.

"Do you need help? Should I call the Coast Guard?" he asked.

"No, I don't think so; we'll be fine. I'll call you soon." I hung up before he had a chance to ask any more questions.

"I think this trip is definitely over," I said to Dorothy. "We have to abandon our mission. Besides, the boat we were following is long gone anyway."

I hurried over and jumped onto the seat behind the steering wheel before Dorothy had a chance to claim it again. I didn't know if I'd be any better at driving, but I wanted to give it a try.

"Well, if you think my driving is so bad, then we'll just see how you do. It's not as easy as it looks," Dorothy said with a flip of her hand.

"I never said it looked easy, because I think it looks hard. Why do you think I was worried from the beginning?" I asked.

Now that I was behind the wheel, I maneuvered the boat and after some struggle, it was headed in the right direction. When we neared the marina, I lined it up with the dock and had a straight shot in. All I had to do was coast forward. When I finally had it docked, I realized I'd been holding my breath. It was a wonder I hadn't passed out from lack of oxygen.

"I thought you said you knew how to drive a boat," the man said with a frown when I handed him the key.

"Dorothy told you she knew how. I never said anything like that," I said as I walked away from him.

When Dorothy and I reached the end of the dock, Jake was standing there, waiting for me.

"Oh, great, are you here to arrest me? I swear I had permission to use the boat. Well, Dorothy had permission—unless she made that up." I looked at Dorothy.

"Of course I didn't make it up. Would I ever do something like that?" she said with an innocent smile.

Jake stepped closer. "Are you okay?" He brushed the wet hair off my forehead.

"I'm fine," I said.

"You look like hell," he said.

I glared at him. "Thanks for confirming what I already suspected."

"Do you want to tell me what happened?" he asked.

I started walking toward the parking lot. I needed out of the wet clothes. "Dorothy isn't a very good driver—that's what happened," I said.

"Did you actually fall off the boat?" He looked me up and down.

I nodded. "Yes, I did. Right into the water."

He chuckled and I cut him a look. "Sorry. What were you doing out there?"

"We had a lead on the boat that I saw that night."

"Why didn't you call me? I could have checked it out for you. I thought we were going to share info now," he said.

"You were serious about that?"

He stared at me as if he was a little offended that I would even ask that question. "Of course I was serious. Did you find the boat?"

"No, after I fell off the boat, we abandoned the mission," I said.

"That's probably for the best," he said. "Give me the information you have, and I'll check it out, okay?"

I shrugged. "I guess I can do that, but you'd think you could find out some of this on your own."

I leaned against my car, and Jake stepped closer.

"I'm glad you're okay. You had me worried," he said.

I met his gaze. Jake leaned in and placed his lips on mine. The air was sucked from my lungs more so than when I was underwater. It was exhilarating and terrifying at the same time. I broke away when I heard the car door behind me.

When I glanced over my shoulder, Dorothy was already sitting in the car, taking her knitting needles out of her purse. She waved when she noticed us watching her. Jake laughed.

"I guess I should drive Dorothy home," I said, motioning toward her with a tilt of my head.

"No more boat rides tonight?" he asked.

I nodded. "No, I need to get out of these clothes."

Jake's gaze took in my appearance, and my heart sped up. After a minute, he touched my cheek, and I opened the car door.

"I'll call you," he said.

I nodded. "Talk to you soon."

"I didn't mean to interrupt," Dorothy said when I got into the car.

"That's quite all right," I said as I turned the ignition.

"It's about time you stopped avoiding your feelings for him," she said.

"I don't know what my feelings are, but I'm not ignoring them," I said.

"Well, you'd better figure them out soon before you lose him," she said.

I dropped Dorothy off at her home and made my way back over to my apartment. I tried to think about my next move. As much as I tried to think about the case, thoughts of Jake popped into my head. His kiss lingered on my lips.

Chapter Twenty-Five

The next day, Dorothy and I drove the short distance to the jewelry store to pay a visit to Mr. Grant. I hadn't spoken with him since the first day, although we'd exchanged voicemails. I really needed to speak with him in person.

Mr. Grant was the only person I had left to ask about the woman and man in the picture. We circled around the block a few times until I found a parking space nearby, and then we made our way down the sidewalk. Dorothy was walking just a little faster than usual.

"Why are you in such a hurry?" I asked her.

Dorothy didn't look at me. "I'm just curious to hear what he has to say."

"Yeah, sure, that's why you're in a hurry," I said.

She snorted but didn't refute my statement. The jewelry store was small, but the inventory was fairly jam-packed. There was a large selection. We stepped into the store and looked around for Mr. Grant. There were a handful of customers and a few employees assisting them.

"I'm not a fan of diamonds," Dorothy said as we looked around.

"Oh yeah, why?" I asked.

"Just seems like an overrated stone to me. I'd rather have a ruby," she said.

We made eye contact with one of the employees. He nodded, letting us know he'd be right over to help us. I didn't want to take him away from a paying customer, but I couldn't get Mr. Grant's attention.

Dorothy was most interested in what Mr. Grant was doing. She inched closer to the back of the room in order to get a better look at him.

"He does look handsome in his suit, doesn't he?" she asked.

I nodded. "He does look nice."

We went from display case to display case, and I began to think that maybe we should come back at a different time. Maybe I should have called first to let him know we were on our way. I just needed to ask him about the picture, and I'd get going. It was probably a wasted trip anyway, because what would he be able to tell me about this picture? It was very little to go on.

Nevertheless, I hoped that maybe he could provide more details about his granddaughter. Any little detail might be just the clue that I needed to crack this case.

Dorothy and I were still looking around the store when she poked me in the side. I glared at her.

"Do you see that man over there?" she asked?

I glanced over to her left. "The one with the spiky blonde hair, wearing a tie?"

She nodded. "Yeah, that's the one."

"What about him?" I asked.

Dorothy looked to her left and then to her right as if to see if anyone else were listening in on our conversation. When she was satisfied no one was, she leaned closer to me. "I think he is going to rob this place."

My eyes widened. "What on earth makes you think that?" I asked.

"Just look at the way he's looking at all the stuff and then keeps looking around at all the people." Dorothy said, pointing at him again.

"I think they could say the same thing about us," I said.

Dorothy stared at me for a moment, and then finally she waved her hand. "Don't be silly. I'm serious. You should keep your eye on him."

I had no idea why Dorothy was suspicious of this man. So what if he was looking around. He might be looking for help with the jewelry.

Dorothy motioned over her shoulder. "We should follow him around."

"I don't think we should follow him around. He'll call the police and tell them that a couple of women are stalking him. Maybe he'll think we're trying to rob him." I shook my head. "I don't want that to happen."

"What if we stop him from robbing this place and save the day? Morton will be so happy. Don't you want to make your customers happy?" she asked.

"Yes, of course he will be happy. And yes, I want to make my customers happy, but I really don't think the guy is about to rob the store," I said.

And I thought *I* had a vivid imagination, but Dorothy had me beat.

Dorothy stepped closer to the man, and then she motioned for me to come over to where she stood.

I reluctantly went over there. "What is it?"

"See that? He has a gun." She pointed with a tilt of her head.

I looked at the man and, sure enough, noticed the gun at his waistband. "I'm pretty sure he's probably a policeman," I said. The gun was poking out from under his shirt.

"I don't think so. Did you see his beady little eyes?" She narrowed her own eyes.

"No, I didn't," I said.

"Well, you should look a little closer."

Before I answered, Dorothy marched over to the man. I prayed that she wasn't going to confront him. When she tapped him on the shoulder, I figured we were in trouble. We'd get kicked out of the store before I had any of my questions answered. I rushed over to try to stop her before it got out of hand.

"What are you doing, Dorothy?" I asked through a fake smile.

"Oh, I'm just talking to this man," she said with a wave of her hand.

He stared at us. I couldn't read his expression. I didn't know if he was mad or just confused. What had she said to him?

"We should leave the man alone," I said.

"I'm just helping him pick out jewelry," she said with a smile.

I stared for a beat and then said, "Well, *I* really need your help."

"That's okay, I think I know which one I want. You can help her," he said.

I pulled on Dorothy's arm. "What did you say to him?" I asked when we stepped away.

"I asked him who he was buying jewelry for, and he didn't have an answer," she said.

"He doesn't have to answer you," I said. "Maybe he's just not that friendly. It happens."

Dorothy tapped the first employee she found on the shoulder. The man turned around and looked at her.

"May I help you?" he asked.

"I just wanted to alert you that that man over there has a gun. I think you need to contact the police right away."

The male employee smiled. Just then the other man started walking toward us. Suddenly, I just wanted to get out of the store. I needed an escape door or something. Unfortunately, I didn't have one, so I'd have to deal with this situation.

The man approached. "I'm sorry for upsetting you, ladies. I work security for the store."

I stared at Dorothy. "See? I told you he was fine."

She blushed. "Oh, I'm sorry. But you do have those beady eyes."

It was time to get Dorothy out of there. We needed to speak with Mr. Grant and then leave.

"Again I'm sorry if I frightened you, ladies," he said.

I waved my hand. "That's okay. We're just being vigilant. The employee had stepped away."

"We're just going to step over here and look around. Thanks again," I said with a wave of my hand.

He nodded. "I told you he wasn't robbing the place," I hissed at Dorothy.

"Well, you can never be too careful," Dorothy said.

We made our way all the way to the back of the store, and there was nowhere else for us to go unless to the back office. We had to wait patiently, which Dorothy was having a hard time with.

After another minute, we made eye contact with a woman. She smiled and hurried over.

"May I help you?" she asked in a squeaky voice.

Her hair was a bright blonde, and she wore a tight blue pantsuit. Her lips were painted a bright red. She was probably a little younger than Dorothy, but they were almost the same age.

"We're here to see Mr. Grant," I said.

"Oh, is he expecting you?" She looked from me to Dorothy.

"We don't have an appointment, but I know he'll want to see us," I said.

"Yes, he'll be happy to see us," Dorothy added, eyeing the woman up and down. Uh-oh. I knew that Dorothy didn't like this woman already.

"I'm sure he'll just be a few more minutes," the employee said.

"Thank you," I said.

"Have you known Mr. Grant long?" she asked.

I exchanged a look with Dorothy. "We have business with him," I said.

She stared at me for a moment and then said, "Oh, are you the private eye? He told me all about you last night when we went to dinner."

The expression on Dorothy's face changed instantly. No, Dorothy didn't like this woman one bit.

"So you know about his granddaughter?" I asked.

"Oh yes, of course, it's just terrible. I know he tried to help her, but some people just don't want help, you know? She seemed to be doing so well, though. I think she had her own demons, but then don't we all," she added.

I nodded. "I suppose."

"My name is Annie Merrick, by the way. I've been working here with Morty for a long time."

I glanced over at Dorothy. She was pretending to look in one of the display cases, but I knew she was all ears.

"So you're close friends with Mr. Grant?" I asked. Dorothy looked over when I asked that question.

"Oh yes, we're very close." Annie smiled coyly. I didn't want to be rude and ask if they were an item. It didn't look as if she was going to offer the information either.

"Morty is such a wonderful man," she said.

Apparently, she had a nickname for him. This didn't look like it was going in Dorothy's favor. Dorothy's face had turned a shade redder.

"I do hope you can help him. I hate to see him so upset," Annie added.

"Well, it's understandable considering he just lost his granddaughter," I said.

Annie nodded. "Yes, but I'm glad you're trying to help him." She smiled. "You know, I can help you. I always wanted to be a private eye."

I stared at her.

She nodded. "If you need anything, just let me know." Maybe I'd take her up on that offer. Since it seemed that she was so close to Mr. Grant, maybe she could offer information as well. It was worth a try, although I knew Dorothy wouldn't be happy with that. But it was always good to have inside information.

"Did you know Kristin at all? You must have met her, since you've worked at the store for so long."

"Well, like I said, she didn't want to be around family, so I only saw her once in the past five years," she said.

"When was the last time you saw her?" I asked.

"Oh, we went by her home about two years ago."

"We?" I asked, cutting a glance at Dorothy.

Annie nodded. "Yes, me and Morty."

Dorothy snorted. I knew the use of the nickname was not making her happy.

"Well, I'll just go see if he's about done with his appointment now. If you'll excuse me." Annie smiled.

I nodded. "Thank you."

When Annie walked away, Dorothy snorted again. "Well, she seems to be awfully cozy with Morty."

I choked back my laughter. "Oh, she seems nice." That statement garnered a glare. "Okay, she seems to be nice to Morty," I corrected.

"Oh, never mind about her," Dorothy said, looking around again. "This trip is probably just a waste of time anyway."

"What a way to keep a positive attitude."

"I would think that he would have shared everything that he knew with you earlier."

"Sometimes people forget things. Maybe this will jar his memory. It's worth a shot," I said.

"If you say so. I still say that the people Kristin worked around are being too secretive."

I nodded. "I agree, but there's nothing I can do to make them talk."

I walked around the store, gazing in the display cases while we waited. Dorothy followed along beside me.

"There has to be a way to find out more about Kristin. Something that I'm missing," I said. "She had to have friend other than the mysterious ones in the photo. I refuse to believe she had nothing going on other than work."

"That's all some people do—work." Dorothy shrugged.

"But if it makes them happy ..."

"That's all *you* do," Dorothy said.

"I have a new business. You have to put in a lot of hours at first," I said.

Just then Mr. Grant walked up to us. Dorothy stepped forward right away. Out of the corner of my eye, I saw her fluff her hair just a little. Mr. Grant looked at her and smiled appreciatively. Annie had walked over with Mr. Grant and was standing nearby.

"Nice to see you again, Ms. Raye," he said.

"Please call me Dorothy," she said coyly.

Mr. Grant turned his attention to me. "Are there any updates?"

I hated that I didn't have much information to give him, but sadly, that was the truth. "Nothing solid yet. I'm sorry. I just wanted to stop by and see if there was something maybe you'd left out or forgotten to share with me."

He frowned. "Is something wrong?"

"Oh no, I'm sorry; it's just that sometimes people forget things, and a couple days later they remember, even if it's a small detail. I just want to make sure I get as much info as possible," I said.

He nodded. "Of course. You said you went to her place. Did you find anything?"

"Well, there was a photo I found." I pulled it from my purse and handed it to him. "Do you recognize anyone in this photo?"

Annie was leaning closer, trying to view the photo but to pretend that she wasn't paying attention at the same time.

Mr. Grant studied the photo and then handed it back to me. "I'm sorry, but I don't know these women." I could tell that looking at the photo was difficult for him.

I took the photo back. "Thanks anyway, Mr. Grant. I'll be in touch soon. Please rest assured I am working hard on the case."

"I have faith in you." He waved at someone across the room. "If you'll excuse me. It's been very busy today."

"That's quite all right. I'm sorry that we stopped in at such a busy hour," I said.

Mr. Grant gave a halfhearted smile and hurried across the room. He flashed another look at Dorothy. I think Dorothy actually batted her eyelashes at him. I had to get her out of there. Annie crossed her arms in front of her chest and stared at Dorothy.

"Did he just wink at you?" I whispered after he'd walked away.

Dorothy blushed. "I don't know. I wasn't looking."

"I think he was flirting with you, Dorothy," I said.

She waved her hand. "He's just being nice. After all, he has Annie." She cut a look at Annie.

Coincidentally, Annie had been watching us too. I'd spotted her bright blonde hair out of the corner of my eye. I thought they had a rivalry thing going on. Mr. Grant seemed to be clueless that Annie was trying to get his attention. I wondered what their situation was. Were they dating? Dorothy had been a widow for many years now. She could use the companionship of Mr. Grant. Not that I wanted to play matchmaker, but they seemed perfect for each other.

Chapter Twenty-Six

Annie glared at us. Then, as if she'd realized what she was doing, she threw her hand up in a wave and smiled.

"What a phony," Dorothy said.

I had to admit that Annie's smile hadn't seemed sincere.

Annie sashayed over to us. "Did Morty answer all of your questions?" She smiled again, but I knew it was forced. Dorothy crossed her arms in front of her chest and stared right back at Annie. Maybe that was the reason Annie wasn't being all that friendly. Had she heard Dorothy's comments?

I sighed and looked around the store. "Yes, I think he answered all that he could."

Annie shook her head. "It looks like you're a little upset. Maybe there's something I can help you with," she said.

If she was offering to help me investigate the case again, then no way.

"That's doubtful," Dorothy said under her breath.

Before I had a chance to answer, Annie held up her index finger. "I'll be right back. A customer needs me. Don't go away, okay?"

"We should get out of here," Dorothy said. "She can't help us."

"Maybe I should show her the picture. She was looking over at it. It's worth a shot," I said.

Dorothy shrugged. "She's just so smug. Even if she knew something, she probably wouldn't help us."

"Maybe if you were a little nicer, then she'd help," I said.

Dorothy shook her head.

"I guess your answer is no. That's fine, but you let me do the talking if you're not going to be nice."

"Like they say, if you don't have anything nice to say," Dorothy said.

After helping the customer, Annie hurried back over. "Okay, now what were we talking about?"

"You said maybe you could help me," I said.

"Yes, that's right. Is there something I can help with?" she asked.

Dorothy didn't comment.

"Well, maybe. I doubt you would know, but I thought I'd ask," I said.

"Of course. Anything, dear." She smiled.

I pulled out the picture and handed it to her. She took the photo from me and studied it. "Do you know the women in the picture with Kristin?" I asked. I didn't bother to inquire about the arm because that would have just been weird.

She handed the photo back to me. "As a matter of fact, I do know one of them."

My eyes widened. I hadn't expected that answer. I hoped it wasn't the one I'd already talked to.

"Who is she?" I asked.

She pointed out the woman I hadn't already spoken with, and I released a sigh of relief.

"That was Kristin's friend. Her name is …" Annie tapped her brightly polished fingers against the counter. "Um, her name is Grace. Yeah, Grace Stanley. Wait here and I'll get her address."

This was almost too good to be true. Dorothy and I exchanged a look.

"I don't trust this woman," Dorothy said.

"Maybe not, but I want the address," I said.

"Why didn't she mention this earlier when Morty was looking at the photo?" Dorothy asked.

"I guess maybe we just thought she was looking at it when he was," I said.

After a few seconds, Annie returned. She handed me a piece of paper. There was an address written down. I recognized the street name.

"Thanks," I said, gesturing toward the paper.

"You're welcome, doll. I'd do anything to help Morty," she said.

I knew Dorothy wanted to say something but was biting her tongue.

"Please tell Mr. Grant again that I'll talk with him soon," I said.

"Sure will," she said with a little wave. "Let me know if I can do anything else."

"She can stop being so annoying," Dorothy said as we walked toward the door.

Dorothy and I hurried to the car. I was excited that I'd gotten an address for the other woman. Now maybe I could find out more information about Kristin's murder.

"That woman is a complete phony," Dorothy said.

"I think you already said that," I pointed out.

"Well, it bears repeating," she said.

"She's probably sweet if you get to know her," I added.

"Gutter slut," Dorothy mumbled under her breath.

"What did you call her? Did you just call her a gutter slut?" I asked.

Dorothy looked at me coyly. "I'm not usually for calling people names, but she provoked me."

"How did she provoke you?" I asked.

"You saw the way she was looking at me," Dorothy said.

"Yes, but I still don't see how that was provoking," I said. She smirked at me. "Okay, fine, she provoked you, but what is a gutter slut?"

"A slut who lives in the gutter, what else?"

"Of course," I said.

I climbed into the car and turned on the ignition. "We'll go check out the address right away."

"I hope this woman cooperates more than the other woman," Dorothy said.

"She'd have to be completely silent for her to be any worse," I said.

Dorothy still didn't look happy that we'd left Mr. Grant with Annie. "Do you think she is dating him?" Dorothy asked as she grabbed her needles out of her purse and began feverishly knitting.

"Well, if they are, I don't think it's serious. It looked like they were just friends," I said, steering the car onto the next street.

My phone rang, and I pulled over so that I could answer the call. When I looked at the screen, I saw that it was Mr. Grant's number.

"It's Mr. Grant," I whispered, as if he'd hear me.

Dorothy's eyes lit up.

"Sorry to call you so soon after you left," he said when I answered.

"That's okay. Is everything all right?" I asked.

"Well . . ." He paused. "There was one thing. It's your assistant."

I glanced over at Dorothy. She looked at me with her wide, innocent eyes. Uh-oh. What had she done?

"Yes, what about her?" I asked.

Dorothy's expression dropped.

"I wondered if she'd be interested in having coffee with me sometime." He rushed his words as if he hadn't uttered that phrase in a long time.

I smiled and looked at the unsuspecting Dorothy. "Well, why don't you ask her yourself?"

Dorothy's eyes were about to pop out of her head. "Do you think she'd mind?" he asked.

“No, not at all. Here, I’ll give her the phone,” I said, handing it over to Dorothy.

She had a huge smile on her face when she hung up. “He wants to have coffee,” she said.

“That’s what I heard. See? I told you he liked you.”

She waved off my comment. “Oh, he’s just being friendly.”

“Yes, my point exactly,” I said.

Chapter Twenty-Seven

I punched in the address that Annie had given us on the GPS and pointed the car in the right direction. Within a few minutes, we were pulling up to the ranch-style stucco home. There was a car parked in the driveway.

After turning off the engine, I paused and looked over at the house. I wanted to know what this Grace Stanley had to say, but I was worried that I wouldn't find any new information. Finding no information wouldn't bode well for my investigative abilities.

"Well, what are you waiting for? Let's go talk with her," Dorothy said as she climbed out of the car and motioned over her shoulder.

I forced myself to open the door and climbed out from behind the wheel. I wondered if Dorothy had one of those peppermints that she claimed calmed nerves—preferably one still in the wrapper.

Dorothy and I made our way up the sidewalk and to the front door. We stood side by side on the little front porch, and I rang the doorbell. I shifted from one foot to the other while we waited. I'd started to wonder if maybe she wasn't home after all when the door finally opened.

Grace Stanley, the woman from the picture, was standing in front of us.

"May I help you?" she asked.

By the way she held the door and her stiffened body stance, it looked as if she was ready to slam the door in our faces at any second.

A dog barked from inside her house. I wasn't sure about the size, but the dog sounded huge and like he wanted to use my arm as a chew toy. Not only was the dog barking, but he was scratching at the door too. I was beginning to think this wasn't such a good idea. Then again, a lot of things I did weren't good ideas, but that hadn't stopped me yet. The barking only grew louder, and now there was a pounding on the door. I thought the dog might be charging at the door or something.

I was about to open my mouth to speak when a loud crash rang out. In one big, white fluffy blur, the dog ran toward us. He wasn't huge after all. With his ears pinned back, he ran toward the door.

The woman yelled out, "No, Patches! Come back here."

Patches had broken free, and he wasn't listening to a word she said. He had kicked his speed into full gear and was making a beeline toward the front door. I doubted there was anything she could do to stop him. Surprisingly, he'd stopped barking.

The little white dog ran out the door. She reached out for him but came nowhere near catching him. He quickly hopped down the step, off the front porch, and into the yard. He never looked back as she yelled for him to stop. Luckily, he hadn't gone out of the yard. He was running in circles, probably trying to decide which way he wanted to go or which flower to water first. I glanced over at Dorothy, and she shrugged. The woman ran past us, practically shoving me out of her way.

"Don't just stand there. Help me catch the dog!" she yelled over her shoulder as she ran around the yard. "It's your fault that he got out."

How was it my fault that the dog had gotten out? I'd never even been in her house. I exchanged a look with Dorothy. She shook her head and said, "Well, come on. Let's go get Fluffy or whatever his name is."

Dorothy shuffled off the porch and onto the sidewalk. It looked as if I would have to catch the dog, because neither of them seemed to know what they were doing. Okay, I didn't know how to catch him either, but I had to give it a shot. Patches looked like he was enjoying the game, though.

Dorothy took off in one direction, and I went the opposite way. I couldn't see Patches at the moment, and I hoped he'd left the yard. He didn't look concerned about getting too far away. It seemed he was more interested in just having us chase him. I ran toward the edge of the lawn, then paused and looked around. Where was the dog? Dorothy had stopped and was peering around for him too. I didn't even see the woman. Maybe she'd already found him. I waved at Dorothy and headed her way.

As Dorothy approached, her eyes widened and she pointed over my shoulder. I whipped around, thinking that the dog was behind me. There *was* a dog behind me, but it wasn't Patches. This dog had his lips curled up in a snarl showing off his canines.

"Hi, doggie. Nice doggie. Please don't bite me," I said.

Where had this large black dog come from? I was frozen and didn't know what to do. Fortunately, this dog wasn't moving toward me either. Just then, out of the corner of my eye, I saw a white streak. The black dog took off after Patches.

The woman ran around the side of the house. "Did you see Patches come this way?" she asked.

I nodded. "He went that way. The black dog is chasing him."

"Oh, that's Patches's friend from next door. They play all the time."

Dorothy was up ahead, and I saw her lunge forward in an apparent attempt to catch Patches. If she wasn't careful, she would break a hip. Dorothy nearly missed capturing Patches. The other dog and Patches were now chasing each other in the neighbor's yard.

We sprinted over to the other yard. This had gone on long enough. Patches was just playing games with us.

"Does he do this often?" I asked as we ran alongside each other.

She nodded. "Every chance he gets."

Maybe she should secure the door. I guessed that was why she'd blamed me, because we'd come to her front door and she'd obviously had to put Patches in the other room. Now the three of us stood in her neighbor's yard. We had all edges of the yard covered, but something told me this dog would have no problem outsmarting us.

When Patches made a run for it, I lunged forward but landed on my face. As I was lying there with my face in the grass, I felt something licking my cheek. I looked over to see Patches's face an inch from mine. I laughed and reached out, then grabbed the dog in my arms. The woman ran over.

"Oh, thank goodness, you got him."

No matter that I'd almost broken an arm or leg in the process. Patches wiggled in my arms when she came near. She took the dog from me.

I pushed to my feet, and Dorothy hurried over.

"Are you okay, Maggie?" Dorothy brushed grass from my hair and shirt.

"I'm fine. I'm just glad we caught Patches before he was hurt." I glanced over and noticed that the other dog had returned to his home and was sitting innocently on the front porch. He looked at us as if we were the crazy ones. We headed back to the woman's front door as she placed the dog back inside. She closed the door so he couldn't get out, and stood on the front porch, glaring at us. Clearly, she was still blaming me for his escape.

"Grace? I hope we're not bothering you, but Annie from Grant Jewelers gave us your address. I was hoping I could ask you a few questions," I said, trying to sound casual after what had happened.

An odd expression spread across Grace's face. "First of all, you need to tell me who you are before I'll answer any questions." She looked from me to Dorothy.

"My name is Maggie Thomas, and this is my assistant, Dorothy Raye. I'm a private investigator."

I thought for a moment by the look on her face that she would definitely shut the door. If it hadn't been for Dorothy giving her that sweet grandmotherly look she probably would have. Looks could be deceiving, though. This woman would be wise to look out for the kindly smiles from Dorothy. Oh, well, she'd have to learn that for herself.

"What are your questions?" Grace asked hesitantly.

"Like I said, I'm a private investigator. I've been hired to look into the death of Kristin Grant," I said.

Her face paled, but she didn't say anything.

I continued, "Her grandfather hired me." I pulled out the picture and handed it to her. "You're in this picture with her."

Grace took the picture, then looked down and nodded. "Yes, that's me. That was a fun night," she said with a smile. "We were at a nightclub, and we danced all night."

"How long ago was the picture taken?" I asked.

"Oh, that was just about two months ago."

At least I was getting some information out of her. Finally, now I was getting somewhere.

"There was one other thing," I said. She looked up at me. I tapped the photo with my finger. "Do you know this man in the photo? I know it's just his arm, but I know he's with you all because he's sitting at the same table."

She was shaking her head before I'd even finished the question.

"This is really important. You do want to help your friend, right? I know you know who this is," I said with a pleading look.

"How did you get this photo?" Grace asked, changing the subject.

How had I lost control of the conversation? "Her grandfather gave the photo to me," I said. That wasn't exactly a lie, because he had given me access to the house. He would have given me the picture if he'd had it. Now I needed to steer the conversation back to the important subject. I had to convince her to share more information.

"So back to the picture … can you tell me who's in the photo? It's very important," I said.

Grace looked down and at her feet and sighed. Finally, she looked at me. "That was Kristin's boyfriend."

Now we were really getting somewhere. "What can you tell me about him?" I asked.

She shrugged. "There's not a lot to tell."

"Any info you can provide would be a huge help," Dorothy added with a smile.

Grace paused and then said, "His name is Henry Reynolds." She paused again and then continued, "I don't like the guy, and I don't know what she saw in him."

I glanced down at the photo. "What didn't you like about him?"

"Besides that he was a pompous ass?" Grace asked.

Dorothy snickered.

"Yes, well, besides that," I said.

"Henry wanted her to do everything in the relationship. She paid for every single date. She drove her car. They did everything he wanted. I mean, what happened to sharing?" she asked.

"That's a pompous ass, all right," Dorothy said.

"Can you tell me where I can find him?" I asked.

Grace hesitated again. Now was not the time for her to stop talking after I'd gotten this far. She looked around as if someone would overhear her. "Well, you didn't get this information from me, but I do have his address."

"That would be great if you could give it to me," I said.

This had been a totally worthwhile trip. We'd get this guy's address and go see him right away. Of course, I couldn't just come right out and ask if he'd killed his girlfriend, though. That was an entirely too dangerous question.

"I'll give you the address, but you don't want to go," she said with all seriousness.

I stared for a moment, but she didn't change her statement. "What makes you say that?" I asked. "Is it just because you think he's a jerk? Because trust me, I'm very accustomed to dealing with jerks. I've dealt with more than my share of them over the years."

Dorothy nodded. "Maggie is a jerk magnet ... well, except for Jake, but that's a story for another day."

I stared at Dorothy and then focused my attention on Grace again. "He's no match for us."

Grace shook her head. "No, it's not just because he's a jerk."

"Then what is it?" I asked. How long was she going to keep me in suspense? "Why shouldn't we go see him?"

"I think he's involved with a lot of bad people." She rushed her words.

My stomach dropped. This was the kind of info I'd been looking for. Someone like this could definitely be involved with Kristin's death. Why hadn't she mentioned this earlier?

"Who are these bad people?" I asked.

Grace looked around again. "I think they were involved with drugs ... a lot of big stuff. Like selling it."

"Her boyfriend did that?" I asked.

Grace nodded. "Yes, and he tried to get Kristin involved. I stopped talking to her about a month ago, so I'm not sure what was going on," she said.

"How did Kristin meet this guy?" I asked.

"He came in the restaurant a lot. I guess they got to talking and then started dating. I can see how she would fall for his charm at first," she said.

That was interesting. The guy with the boat had come into the restaurant too. Was there a connection? I hoped I could find out.

I wasn't sure how Kristin could have fallen for Henry's charm, because he didn't sound like a very nice guy. Some people could be deceiving, though, and he probably put on a good act. I wouldn't fall for it. I'd be able to see right through him.

"Hold on and I'll write down the address of where you can find him, but remember, I didn't tell you, and you never talked to me. I don't want to be involved in this." She waved her hands through the air. "And I should warn you again that you shouldn't get involved either."

"It's my job," I said.

I wanted to sound confident, but a little doubt had slipped into my mind. I couldn't lie and act like I wasn't a little frightened.

Grace grabbed paper and a pen from the table next to the door. She jotted down the address and handed me the paper. "Good luck," she said as she closed the door.

"Well, either she's being overly dramatic, or maybe we should be worried," I said as we made our way back to the car.

Dorothy nodded softly. The conversation had left even her speechless, and that never happened.

I started the car and pointed it in the direction of the address. I hoped this didn't end badly—like with either of us killed. Maybe I should have consulted with Jake before I set out on this trip, but that was the logical thing to do, and I wasn't known for doing anything logical. Where was the fun in that?

Chapter Twenty-Eight

"There's one thing that I forgot to ask her," I said as I navigated the car.

"What's that?" Dorothy asked as she fished around in her purse.

I had a feeling she was going to shove a peppermint in my mouth soon. Just because she was nervous didn't mean that I was too. "How did Annie know who this woman was?" I asked.

"That's a good question," Dorothy said.

"I mean, Mr. Grant said that Kristin didn't come around often, so how would Annie know this woman?"

"That's something we definitely need to find out," Dorothy said, shoving a peppermint at me.

We'd almost arrived at the address that Grace had given us, when I recognized the place. It was the same house that Dorothy and I had already visited once. We'd found the address at Kristin's place. I had to confess that I was apprehensive. How could I not be anxious with Grace's dire warnings? Now I knew that this man had been lying to me when I questioned him.

"This is the same house," Dorothy pointed out.

"I know. What should we do now?" I asked.

"We sure as heck shouldn't go up there," she said.

"I kind of have to," I said.

She shook her head. "You should call Jake."

I waved off her statement as I climbed out of the car. "Yeah, yeah. I'll call him later."

I'd only made it halfway up the driveway when the guy appeared from around the side of the house. His hand was on the gun at the side of his waist. I swallowed hard. This wasn't going as planned.

"What the hell do you want?" he asked.

I froze and for a moment was unable to speak. His expression said he wanted to shoot first and ask questions later.

Finally, I said, "Are you Sam?"

The scowl on his face deepened. "What the hell? Did Sam send you?"

It was time for me to abandon this mission. "No, I must have the wrong address."

I turned around and ran toward my car. The whole time I prayed he wouldn't shoot me in the back. I jumped in the car and cranked the engine.

"Well, that was a fine mess. I told you to call Jake."

I wasn't going to admit to her face that Dorothy was right, but she *was* right. I should have called Jake. This guy looked like he meant business.

The next day, Dorothy and I made our way to the restaurant. I really didn't want to go back in that place. The smell of seafood was making me sick. But I had no other choice. Dorothy and I hopped out of the car. I really hoped I would discover some kind of good clue today. I'd gladly give away all my tips for another kind of tip regarding the case.

First on my agenda was to find Spencer Johnson, the waiter from Captain's Quarters who'd been talking to the boat guy, since I was pretty sure he had been following me. Next, I needed to talk with Megan. I hadn't gotten the chance to speak with her again since the time in the break room. Not that it would do any good, because she hadn't been very forthcoming that time, and I doubted things had changed since.

When I spotted the waiter who'd given me information about Spencer, I hurried over to him. "Hey, is Spencer here today?" I asked.

He set his tray down on a table and looked around. "No, I think he quit."

Just then the manager called out to him. I got the weird impression that he didn't want anyone to talk with me.

"I have to go." He grabbed his tray and hurried away.

I stood there wondering what had happened. Had Spencer really quit? Since I had Spencer's name, I'd have to do a quick search to see if I could find his address. Unfortunately, it would have to wait until after work.

Dorothy was already at the bar, surrounded by a group of customers. They were hanging on to every word. She regaled them with fascinating stories, but when I walked up, everyone stopped talking, like I couldn't be included in their fun. I assumed the stories weren't about me, but with Dorothy I never knew. She seemed to be doing a good job with the drinks, though, and the customers loved her. I just hoped she kept it up and wouldn't blow our cover.

As I sat at the bar, watching Dorothy fulfill orders, she seemed to know what she was doing. She apparently knew every drink available . . . or so I thought.

The blonde woman beside me waved Dorothy over. "I'd like a Screaming Orgasm, please."

I did not want to know where this was going to end. But surprisingly, Dorothy took the order and immediately turned around to gather items. Dorothy was focused and completely serious about her work. She turned around and gathered bottles and glass, mixed the drink, and brought it back over.

Dorothy sat the fruity-looking drink on the bar in front of the woman.

When the woman looked up, Dorothy said, "Okay, now meet me in the back, and we'll take care of the screaming orgasm."

The crowd gathered around the bar laughed. The blonde blushed a little and joined in the laughter.

"Dorothy, I can't believe you said that," I said.

Dorothy pointed at the other female bartender. "She told me to say it."

The other bartender chuckled, then turned around and walked away.

"I don't think I'd do everything she tells you to do, Dorothy," I said.

After taking out orders for some of my customers, I went back over to the bar to see how Dorothy was doing. Apparently, I needed to keep a close eye on her. Nonetheless, she was still obviously doing a lot better at this job than I was.

A dark-haired man was sitting at the bar. Since I had a few minutes' break, I sat next to him and sipped on a glass of water. After the man placed an order of bourbon neat, Dorothy turned around and grabbed a glass and started to make his order. He glanced at me, and I smiled. He didn't return the smile but instead just looked back at Dorothy. Apparently he wasn't in a talking mood, which was fine with me because I was really just trying to be polite.

Dorothy turned and started wiping off the counter in front of the man. She cleaned up the space around him and made it look really nice. She placed a napkin down in front of him, all neat and orderly. He watched her as if she'd lost her mind. Finally, Dorothy placed the glass down and then wiped up the extra liquid that had dripped off the side of the glass. She looked at him, smiling.

He stared for a moment and then said, "What is this?" He looked at me as if I would be able to answer.

"The drink you wanted," she said, her smile becoming more fixed.

He stared at her as if she were speaking a foreign language. "I ordered a bourbon neat. This is not a bourbon neat."

"I made it as neat as possible for you," she said.

I touched Dorothy's arm. "Dorothy, that's not what he means."

"I thought he wanted it clean around the bar," she said.

"No, that just means bourbon and nothing else."

The man got up and tossed a couple of crumpled dollars onto the counter and then stormed off. He was probably going to talk to the manager.

"Dorothy, I thought you knew what you were doing over here!"

She waved her hand. "I've been faking it. No one has complained ... much."

"Maybe you should study up on the drinks before you blow our cover," I said.

She shook her head, grabbed a towel, and began wiping off the rest of the counter. "I've been doing a great job up until now. I'm not going to blow our cover."

"Just try not to do anything else to draw attention to us," I said.

"I think we're doing great. Before you know it, we'll find out everything we need to do, and then we can get out of here."

"It will be none too soon for me because I'm terrible at this job."

I was pretty sure I was going to be fired soon, before I even had a chance to quit.

Dorothy's eyes widened, and she got a funny look on her face. She motioned over my shoulder, and I turned around. Megan was standing nearby.

"Did she hear us talking about being undercover?" I whispered to Dorothy.

Dorothy shrugged. "I don't know, but I think she may have. Watch what you're saying from now on. You'll blow our cover for both of us."

This job wasn't going exactly how I planned it and definitely not the way things would have worked out for Charlie's Angels or Magnum, P.I.

Chapter Twenty-Nine

I was at the back of the restaurant and hadn't expected to see Jake. When I looked up and spotted his face, I couldn't help but smile. He walked back toward me. I was standing by the door that led to the little employees' lounge area. The office and dressing area with lockers were also back there.

When Jake approached, he didn't crack a smile. "Can I talk to you in private?"

I didn't like the sound of this, but I sucked it up and nodded. "Yeah, we can go in the back dressing area. There's a table and chair back there."

He followed me through the door. That was when he grabbed my hand and led me around to the back, behind the lockers.

"I don't think anyone can hear us back here," he said.

I had to admit the touch of his hand caused a thrill to run through my body.

"What do you want to talk about?" I asked, dreading to hear what he might have to say.

Jake looked at me and then said, "I'm just worried about you here. I don't like the way things are going."

"Why do you say that? What makes you so worried? Do you know something that you're not telling me?

Before he answered, voices carried through the air. Apparently, we weren't alone in the room anymore. We stopped talking in order to listen. The sound of footsteps echoed as they moved across the room. Obviously, they didn't know we were in there. Just then they started talking. I recognized the voices. It was Megan and Spencer again.

Jake and I stood completely still, being as quiet as possible. Jake leaned forward as they spoke so that he could hear more of their conversation. "What are they saying?" I whispered.

"They're talking about getting the job done."

They must have stepped closer because that was when I was able to make out some of their conversation. Megan and Spencer were once again discussing what they were going to do with the money. Well, Megan was really the only one talking about what she was doing with the money, but I assumed Spencer was in on this too.

Unfortunately, I still didn't know what any of this meant. They were being secretive and not letting on to exactly what they were talking about. All I knew was that it couldn't be good.

Jake shook his head. "I don't know what they're talking about."

Yeah, that was what we had to find out. We stepped to the edge of the lockers, the only thing blocking us from view. But maybe we'd be able to hear more of the conversation, since some of it was still muffled.

In spite of us being extremely quiet, the couple stopped talking. I held my breath, wondering if they knew somehow that we were back there listening to them. How would they have known we were here unless they'd seen us come back here? Because they'd been talking already, I was sure they hadn't seen us. Sure, we'd spoken, but I doubted the sound would carry over to where they stood.

Just then the sound of footsteps clicked against the floor as if they were moving closer. I held my breath. Jake moved closer to me, then turned around so that his back was to me. He stood in front of me as if he were ready to attack whoever came back there.

The footsteps finally paused when they were just at the edge of the lockers. We waited, but no other sounds came from the other side of the lockers. Had they gone? It had been a long time since we'd heard anything.

I'd just released a deep breath, thinking we were safe, when the footsteps sounded again, and I knew they were coming closer. They hadn't left the room after all. Maybe they were just playing games with us.

Jake grabbed my hand and rushed over to the broom closet. He thrust open the door and shoved me in. Jake jumped in the tiny space with me, then eased the door shut behind us. His body was pressed against mine. Yeah, needless to say, there wasn't a ton of space. Not to mention, I couldn't even see my hand in front of my face. I knew Jake's face was extremely close to mine because I couldn't almost feel it.

"What the hell are you doing?" I whispered.

He covered my mouth with his hand and said, "Don't talk now."

I felt Jake's sweet breath against my lips as he spoke.

In spite of us being extremely quiet, footsteps drew closer to us. I knew that soon someone would yank open the door, and we'd be caught. What would my excuse be for hiding in a closet with a very handsome man? The footsteps had stopped, and I wondered if Megan and Spencer were listening to us. They probably heard the sound of my breathing because I heard it loud and clear in the tiny space.

The door yanked open, and light flooded the little space. At that moment Jake stopped. His lips had just brushed against mine. The tingle hadn't even left my limbs yet. "What the hell are you all doing in there like a couple of teenagers?" Dorothy stood in front of the door, with her hands on her hips. "Get out here."

I knew she wouldn't believe me when I told her the true reason we'd been hiding in the closet. Jake moved out of the closet first. I pushed a broom out of my way and stepped out from the tiny space. Dorothy looked us up and down, then shook her head. A huge, satisfied smile spread across her face.

"We were just hiding from Spencer and Megan." I looked around at the empty space.

"It was probably not the best idea," Jake added.

Dorothy crossed her arms in front of her chest, her bangle jewelry jingling with the movement.

Jake gestured over his shoulder. "I'll be going now, Maggie. Just be careful, okay?"

Dorothy continued looking at us.

I nodded. "It's okay. I promise we'll be careful."

I shrugged as I followed him out the door. I knew Dorothy was staring at our backs with that smug smile on her face. So I'd almost kissed Jake. Big deal.

Chapter Thirty

I only had a couple small tables and was managing quite nicely when a large group of people entered the restaurant. It was a struggle just getting their drink order, and I figured I'd already lost the tip by the looks of disdain on their faces.

"You are a terrible waitress," one of the men said.

Dorothy was standing behind me at this point. "She's trying her best, and if that's not good enough for you, then maybe you should go somewhere else to eat."

Unfortunately, the manager was standing beside us when Dorothy uttered these words. The next thing I knew, Dorothy and I were headed to my car. We'd been relieved of our duties. Permanently.

"To be honest, I'm shocked that we lasted this long," Dorothy said as she climbed into the car.

"Yeah, me too," I said with a chuckle. "I really like the way you stood up to that guy for me."

"Well, someone needed to tell him," she said. And Dorothy was just that person. "Now what do we do?" she asked.

"I have to find Spencer's address, and then we'll pay him a little visit," I said.

No sooner had I spoken the words than I saw Spencer. Dorothy had decided that we should move closer to him and listen in on his conversation with another man. I figured it was a good idea, so I agreed.

Spencer approached a blue sedan, and the other man jumped out of the car. Dorothy and I walked across the lot. My car was backed into a spot near the men at the rear of the lot, so we casually stood by the car. I opened the trunk so that it would look like we were busy.

"Do you live in your car? Why do you have this clothing?" Dorothy picked up a hat.

"I don't have a lot of room in my apartment," I said.

"We should have disguises," Dorothy said, slipping on a pair of sunglasses from her purse. She picked out one of the hats from my trunk and placed it on her head.

I grabbed a hat from the trunk and sunglasses from my purse. When I looked over at Dorothy, she was wearing a Miami Heat cap and huge black sunglasses with rhinestones on the sides.

"Don't look at me that way," she said. "You look just as ridiculous as me."

I knew she was right when I glanced in the mirror and saw my appearance. I had on a blue-and-white plaid newsboy cap and aviator sunglasses. This was our attempt at disguises.

"We need to be closer," I said.

Dorothy adjusted her sunglasses. "Let's do this."

So with our hats and shades in place, Dorothy and I took off across the parking lot to see what we could discover about Spencer. He was up next to the car, and the other man had stepped in front of him at this point. They were talking to each other, but unless I got closer, I wasn't going to find out what they were saying. Dorothy and I wove around the cars, slinking down, trying not to be noticed. I didn't know if we were any good at hiding, but we were sure giving it a shot.

Dorothy and I were crouched down behind a red sports car. We had a good spot for listening now.

Spencer said, "I told you to bring me the money. Where's the money?"

The young guy replied, "I just couldn't get it. If you can give me a few more days, I promise I'll have it."

"That's not good enough," Spencer yelled.

"I promise I'll get it," the man pleaded.

"I told you to bring it now."

A loud thump sounded, and I didn't know what had happened. I peeked up over the side of the car.

"What's going on?" Dorothy whispered, pulling on my arm.

I glanced back, crouching down again. "They're arguing and now Spencer is beating the guy up."

Dorothy covered her mouth and then said, "This isn't good."

Another loud noise sounded from next to the car again. I eased up and saw Spencer pull his arm back and swing. He hit the guy again. The guy was trying to defend himself by throwing punches too. Groans and grunts sounded across the air. I had to do something. I couldn't just let this guy get beat up.

I was ready to call the police, so I fumbled around and finally found my phone in my pocket. I pulled it out, but when I punched in the numbers, it beeped and immediately lost a signal.

"Dorothy, do you have your phone with you?" I asked.

"I left it in the car." She gestured in that direction.

I knew I'd have to go back for it, so I crouched down and inched over to the edge of the car. I'd have to weave my way around the cars again.

Before I took off for my car, I glanced over and saw the men still fighting, but the young man finally managed to break loose from Spencer. He ran for his car and jumped in, backing out and squealing the tires as he took off out of the parking lot. Spencer immediately jumped in his car. How the heck would Dorothy and I get back to my car in time? I wouldn't be able to catch up to find out where they were going.

"Dorothy, they're leaving. We have to try to catch up to them," I said.

Dorothy and I ran across the parking lot. When we finally made it to the car, Spencer was pulling out of the parking lot. He was so occupied with catching up with the guy that I knew there was no way he'd seen us, probably not because of our disguises, though. Dorothy and I jumped in the car as quickly as possible, and I cranked the engine and took off out of the parking lot. Spencer seemed to do everything fast—drive, walk, talk. What was his hurry?

After just a short distance, I'd amazingly caught up with Spencer. Surprisingly, we'd turned a complete circle, and Spencer had turned into the restaurant's parking lot again, but I didn't see the man he'd beaten up. But there was another man waiting for him.

Chapter Thirty-One

I wasn't sure, but I suspected Spencer was talking to the man from the boat. His back was to me, so I couldn't be sure.

These men were on my radar, however, so now that I'd spotted him out there in the parking lot talking, I had to know what they were saying.

"Come on, Dorothy; let's go listen." I pointed at the men.

"How are we going to do that?" she asked.

"We'll just have to hide," I said.

We'd officially ditched our disguises.

Dorothy pointed toward some shrubbery. "What about those bushes? We can hide in there. It's close, but they won't see us."

"I'm not sure that's a great idea," I said.

"Yeah? Do you see any other place to hide?" she asked.

"Well, no, but . . ."

"Okay, well, how about we don't hide it all?" she suggested in a sarcastic voice, her hands on her hips.

"That's not what private investigators are supposed to do. Remember, we have to listen and find out details of what's going on. How else will we ever solve a case if I don't spy on people?" I said.

"That's my point. We have no options other than the bushes."

We made our way over to the bushes and got down on the ground. Dorothy and I crawled between the branches. I was doing my best to keep the twigs out of her hair. I pulled one out and tossed it on the ground.

"Here," Dorothy said, handing me her pocketbook.

"What am I supposed to do with this?" I asked.

"It's just in case one of them comes over here. You'll need something to hit them with. I think you're a much better aim than I am." She gestured for me to take the purse.

How could I argue with that? I took the big brown leather purse and then peeked out of the bushes.

Dorothy and I watched the men and listened closely, but I just couldn't make out what they were saying. As they spoke, they moved their arms and were having an animated conversation. It didn't look like they were fighting, but just really intent on what they were talking about. If I could just move closer to them... I looked for more shrubs to hide behind, but there was nothing. I could possibly sneak around some of the cars, but I thought it was just a little bit too risky. We would just have to stay put. Obviously, we weren't going to find out what they were saying anyway.

"We're just like Charlie's Angels," Dorothy whispered.

I snorted. "Yeah, just like the Angels. Which one are you?"

"Definitely Farrah, don't you think?" She smiled.

Just as I was about to give up on them, they quit talking for a second. Spencer reached in the car and grabbed something out. He handed it to the man, and then the man gave him something in return. I couldn't make out what exactly was in their hands. It was just too dark to see. I had to know what it was that they were doing, though. I didn't know how to find out without getting caught.

A tickle formed in my throat, and I knew I was about to cough. I had to keep it in. If I made any noise, the men would figure out we were behind the bushes. Who knew what they would do if they found us spying on them? My gun was in the car, so I didn't have any protection other than Dorothy's purse. I didn't know how much good that would be if the men actually came after us. I tried to suppress my cough again, but all of a sudden I let out a big cough.

Dorothy slapped her hand over my mouth. "You can't cough out here," she hissed. "See? I knew you should have taken that peppermint candy from me."

I kept my composure and moved her hand from my mouth. When I peeked out, the men had stopped talking and were looking around the parking lot. They were trying to figure out where the noise had come.

The man stepped closer to us. Since the sun had set, I still couldn't make out which man was talking to Spencer. As they moved even closer to the bushes, my heart pounded in my chest, and I was pretty they would hear my heavy breathing. Dorothy grabbed my hand and squeezed, but didn't say a word. The most important thing was that I hoped I didn't have to cough again. One little noise and they would find us in the bushes. I didn't know what they would say when that happened.

Finally the man stopped looking and marched back over to their cars. I let out a sigh of relief.

"That was a close one," Dorothy whispered.

I nodded my head, saying, "It was too close."

The men shook hands and then got into each car and took off out of the parking lot. We slumped down. I didn't want them to shine the car headlights on us. We'd be like a couple of cats in the night.

"What exactly is going on here?" Jake's voice sounded from behind me.

I didn't want to turn around, but I knew I had to eventually. I stood quickly and saw his handsome face staring at us. The corners of his mouth twisted and his brow rose in amusement.

"Did you lose something?" he asked, trying to get an answer out of me.

Dorothy grabbed her purse from me. "Thanks for finding my purse, Maggie. I don't know how it got in the bushes."

She stepped away from the bushes and over to the car, leaving me alone with Jake to explain myself.

"Listen, I'm sorry about earlier," he said.

I shook my head. "It's okay."

"No, it wasn't very professional of me."

I was beginning to rub off on him. Professional wasn't always the way to go with this job.

"So what exactly were you doing in the bushes?"

"Just research. What are you doing back here? I thought you left," I said.

He shrugged. "Thought I might find something I missed."

Okay, if he was going to keep things from me, then I didn't feel so bad about not telling him everything.

"Well, I'd better get Dorothy home," I said, gesturing over my shoulder.

He nodded. "Call me if you need anything."

"You know I will," I said with a smile.

Chapter Thirty-Two

It was early the next morning when I made it back to my office. I'd spent so little time there lately, and now I really missed the cramped place. After running in to do a quick search, I'd found out that Spencer lived not far from the restaurant. I'd also found out that he'd been arrested a couple of times in the past few years—once for disorderly conduct, and another time for drugs. It looked like he wasn't such a nice guy, but I had suspected as much.

I jotted down the address and headed back outside, where Dorothy was waiting in the car for me. Before I could visit Spencer, I had to drop Dorothy off at Mr. Grant's house, so they could go on their coffee date.

Dorothy was busy putting on a bright red lipstick instead of messing around with her knitting needles and crossword puzzle book.

I hid my smile. "That shade looks nice on you."

She smacked her lips together. "Thank you. I appreciate your driving me here. You can never be too safe. I didn't want to go to a strange man's house without an escort."

"I completely understand," I said.

When we pulled up in front of Mr. Grant's house, Dorothy said, "Now you wait out here until I make sure he's home. Don't leave until we're safely in his car and pulling away from the house."

"Yes, ma'am," I said.

Dorothy released a deep breath and then climbed out of the car, clutching her big brown purse.

"Don't do anything I wouldn't do," I warned.

"That leaves me a lot of options," Dorothy said with a smirk.

Mr. Grant lived in a beautiful two-story brick home with a landscaped yard and gorgeous glass front door. I watched as Dorothy walked up the front path, with her pocketbook draped across her arm. She'd worn her best gold shoes and bright red pants, with a white silky blouse. I knew she'd taken extra time to fix her hair this morning.

I tapped my fingers against the steering wheel and stared up at the cloudless blue sky. My thoughts were lost in the case, and occasionally visions of Jake popped into my head. I flipped on the radio for distraction and began scanning the channels. I finally settled on oldies from the eighties. The songs reminded me of simpler times when I was at home with my mother.

I leaned my head back against the seat and tried to relax. I hoped that Dorothy wouldn't be too long. But if she started chatting with Mr. Grant, they might let the time slip away from them.

Somehow, I sensed Dorothy's presence and looked up to see her hurrying down the path toward me. She had a look of distress on her face. I knew something was wrong right away.

"What's wrong?" I asked as she opened the car door.

"I think you should come inside right away," she said breathlessly.

"Is there something wrong with Mr. Grant?" I asked in a panic.

She shook her head. "I don't know. He's not there."

"What do you mean he's not there?" I asked.

"Exactly what I said. The door is open, but he doesn't appear to be home." Dorothy glanced back at the house.

I stepped out of the car and moved around to the front path.

"Is his car here?" I asked.

She shook her head. "I don't know. The front door was open a little, so I just stepped in the house and called out for him. But he didn't answer."

"Okay, we'll just remain calm. I'm sure he just stepped out for a moment, and he'll be right back."

I hoped that he didn't stand Dorothy up, because then I'd really have to let him have it. Dorothy and I made our way up the sidewalk to the front door. I paused when I reached the threshold. She motioned for me to go on in.

"Mr. Grant, it's Maggie Thomas and Dorothy Raye," I called out. "Are you home?"

"He didn't answer before, so I doubt that he'll answer now," she said.

I stepped into the house and looked around. I wasn't quite sure at first, but once I saw some of the furniture turned over, I knew we had a serious problem. I didn't want to alarm Dorothy any more than she already was. There was no need to panic just yet. Visions of when I had discovered my last client murdered in his home flashed through my mind, and I hoped that I wouldn't find Mr. Grant in that same situation.

We stepped further into the room, and I noticed a chair turned over. I had hoped I could keep it from Dorothy, but when she let out a gasp I knew that it was too late.

"It doesn't mean anything bad happened to him," I said, trying to reassure her. "Just in case though, don't touch anything," I said as if I were a pro at crime scenes. I'd learned the hard way last time after I'd touched a bunch of stuff at the scene of a murder.

"Why don't we want to touch anything? Do you really think something happened to him?" she asked.

"No, I don't," I said, knowing it was a lie.

"We'll just look around the rest of the house," Dorothy said.

She took off across the room, headed for the kitchen.

"What are you doing?" I called after her.

She was surprisingly fast for her age. I honestly always had a hard time keeping up with her. By the time I caught up with her, she was already standing in the kitchen, looking around with her hands on her hips.

"What are you doing in here?" I asked.

She shrugged. "I just wanted to have a little look. Nothing wrong with that, right?"

"No, I guess not," I said, peeking around the space.

The room was mostly white with stainless steel appliances. There was a small window over the sink and a door that led out to the backyard. I stepped over to the door and peered out the window. There was a fenced-in area and a neighbor's home nearby. As a matter of fact, that neighbor was standing in his backyard and just so happened to glance up at that moment. He noticed me watching him and threw his hand up in a small wave. I wondered if Mr. Grant knew his neighbors well. Would they know where he'd gone?

When I turned back around, I found Dorothy looking through Mr. Grant's cabinets.

"What on earth are you doing? I really don't think you'll find him in the cabinets. He's a small man, but not that small."

She waved off my comment. "I thought I'd check to see if he needed groceries."

"Do you plan to shop for him?" I asked.

"No." She smirked. "But maybe he went to pick up a few things."

I didn't believe her excuse. I think she just wanted to be snoopy. I didn't blame her, though. I was curious and wanted to know where he was and why his living room looked disturbed.

Dorothy closed the cabinet door and picked up a nearby dishcloth. She started wiping down the counter.

"Dorothy, we didn't come here to clean his house. We're here to find him—remember?"

"I remember, but I need to keep busy when I'm nervous." She stepped over to the sink. "Maybe we should wash his dishes." She reached for the dish-washing detergent, and I grabbed her arm.

"No way. I have to stop you right there."

Someone had to put an end to this madness.

Dorothy frowned. "I really think you should let me have my way."

Holding Dorothy's arm, I pulled her toward the kitchen's entrance.

"It's not bad in here, for a bachelor," she said.

I was surprised she hadn't grabbed onto something and tried to stop me from taking her out of the room. Dorothy and I hadn't known each other long, but I was already starting to recognize that look in her eyes. And right now that look said she wanted to clean the house to release her nervous energy. I'd just have to find another way for her to do that.

"Yes, he's a good housekeeper. Let's get out of here."

I'd almost gotten Dorothy out of the room when she stopped in her tracks. She made a beeline for the refrigerator. I spotted what she was going for and knew there was no way I would be able to stop her now. A big greeting card was stuck to the front of the refrigerator with a magnet. It was a cartoon card with a drawing of a couple of cute dogs. From what I saw, there were little red hearts on the card too. Dorothy couldn't take the card down fast enough, to read it. I could tell her not to go through personal things, but maybe this would be a clue that would lead us to Mr. Grant.

Dorothy and I exchanged a glance as she clutched the card in her hands.

"What does it say?" I asked, leaning over her shoulder for a closer look.

"It's a card from Annie to Morton. It's for the best boss in the world." Dorothy's eyes narrowed.

I snorted. "The nerve of that woman."

Dorothy waved the card at me. "Don't you mock me. Annie is a phony, and I don't trust her. Look, she even wrote smooches on it. That's not very professional. You wouldn't write smooches on a card to me." She scowled.

"I most certainly would not. Hugs, maybe, if you caught me on a good day."

Dorothy frowned.

"Okay, so she sent him a card that doesn't mean anything. Just put it back, and let's go."

Dorothy didn't budge as she continued to look at the card as if that would make it say something different or make it go away. Finally, I took the card from her hands and placed it back on the refrigerator.

Dorothy mumbled as we stepped out of the kitchen. "The worst part is, she actually kissed the card. It had her lip print on it," Dorothy fumed.

Okay, I could see how that would be hard for Dorothy to handle.

When we made it back into the foyer, I lost track of Dorothy again. She was headed up the stairs.

"Where are you going now?" I asked.

"I thought we should check the bedrooms." She pointed up the stairway.

"Oh, no way." That was the last thing I needed. "There's nothing else we can find up there. Let's just leave. I'm sure he'll be back soon."

Dorothy persisted. "But what if he's up there? What if he's hurt and can't call out to us?"

I frowned. Okay, she had another point, but I didn't want her to go up there. It had been bad enough when she'd gone into the kitchen.

"You wait down here, and I'll go up there and check the rooms."

She frowned but ultimately caved and nodded.

I hurried up the stairs and went to my right. There was one bedroom on that side that I figured was the master bedroom. I didn't like going through Mr. Grant's house. After opening the door, I stuck my head in. When I didn't see him, I backed out in a rush. I checked the other bedrooms on the other side of the stairs. Mr. Grant wasn't in either room, so I made my way back downstairs.

I found Dorothy straightening up the living room.

"He wasn't up there," I said.

Just then the sound of a car came from the front of the house.

"See? I bet he's here now. Nothing to worry about," I said.

Dorothy and I went to the front door. She rushed in front of me and peeked out. "The man coming up the driveway isn't Mr. Grant, and he doesn't look as if he's a nice guy either. He has a gun in his hand," Dorothy said in a panic.

"I don't know who it is, but I think we'd better hide," I said, pointing to the closet.

Unfortunately, I didn't have my gun with me, and I'd be no match for his bullets. Dorothy and I slipped into the closet and waited as we listened to the man move around the house. A flashback of being in the closet with Jake came to me. This was no time to think of Jake Jackson.

Finally, the sound of the footsteps faded, and after a moment Dorothy and I peeked out from the closet.

"I don't see anyone," I said, motioning for her to come out.

I stepped back over to the door and looked out. Apparently, the car and man Dorothy had seen were gone.

"We need to call the police right away," I said, pulling my phone out of my pocket.

I dialed Jake's number, but it went straight to his voicemail. When he didn't answer, I had no choice but to dial 911. Dorothy and I waited in the car until the police came. When I looked in my rearview mirror, I saw that Jake was with the other officers. How did he know I was the one who'd made the call? I wasn't looking forward to explaining this one.

Jake stepped over to the window but didn't say anything.

Finally, I said, "I guess you're wondering what's going on, huh?"

"I kind of wondered, yes," he said.

I quickly explained about Mr. Grant not being in the house and how we'd hidden from a man with a gun.

"Hey, at least I wasn't shot at this time," I said.

"Why does trouble always seem to find you?" he asked.

"Do you have any idea what happened to him?" I asked Jake.

Dorothy had a worried look on her face.

Jake ran his hand through his hair. "At this point, I just don't know. But we'll do a thorough investigation here." He motioned with a tilt of his head toward Mr. Grant's home.

"Did you see the way all the furniture was knocked over?" Dorothy asked. "That can't be good. I just know something bad has happened."

We watched as police moved in and out of Mr. Grant's home. I knew all the action was making Dorothy even more nervous.

"We have to assume he left on his own," Jake said when one of the police walked by.

"What do you mean?" Dorothy asked in a loud voice. "There is no way he left on his own. Why would the furniture be turned over like that?" she asked.

"Just because his house is a mess doesn't mean anything." Jake tried to reassure her.

"What about the fact that a strange man was in his house?" I asked.

"Maybe he was a stranger to you, but for all we know, Mr. Grant knew the man," Jake said.

Dorothy rolled her eyes. She wasn't buying it.

Jake looked at me and gave a half smile. "I'd better get back to work. Please, ladies, try to stay out of trouble."

Now was my turn to roll my eyes, but I refrained out of professionalism.

"If something really happened to him, then I can guarantee that we'll do everything we can to find him," Jake said.

He touched my chin and then walked away.

I watched him for a moment and then turned to Dorothy.

"You know we have to find him, right?" she asked.

I nodded while looking at Jake again. "Yes, I know."

Jake must have felt eyes on him, because he looked over and smiled at me.

Dorothy was right. I had to find Mr. Grant. Now I'd lost another client. This wasn't looking good for my business referrals.

Dorothy and I drove away. I hated leaving Mr. Grant's house. It was somehow like I was letting him down by driving away. But I wouldn't let this go. I had to find him. Of course, I should have known that the police wouldn't take a missing person's report for Mr. Grant because there was no proof that there was any foul play involved.

Dorothy knitted as we drove back to my office. She was going on and on about how we needed to do something to help Mr. Grant.

"That man probably came back because he forgot something," Dorothy said.

I looked at her. "You know, you've got a good point. We'll go back to his house when we can, but how will we get inside? The police will probably secure the door."

Dorothy waved her hand. "Oh, you'll think of something."

Chapter Thirty-Three

We'd only been back at the office for a short time when a loud knock sounded against the door. I exchanged a look with Dorothy.

"Did you schedule an appointment?" I asked.

She shook her head. "No, you haven't got a single thing going on."

I frowned. "Thanks for reminding me."

I eased over to the door. I couldn't see exactly who was standing in front of the tempered glass, but by the size and height I figured it was a woman. I opened the door and was surprised to see Annie standing in front of me.

"Annie, what are you doing here?" I asked.

Dorothy closed the distance between us in record time. "Yes, Annie, what are you doing here?" Her tone was icy.

"I just heard the news." She clutched her chest as if she would faint if she didn't. "The police won't tell us anything. They came by asking questions and said that Morty might be missing."

Now why hadn't I thought to go by the jewelry store and ask questions? I'd have to do better than that if I wanted to stay in business.

"I really don't know anything that the police don't know. Dorothy was going for coffee with him, and he wasn't home when I dropped her off at his house," I said.

Annie gave Dorothy a dirty look. Dorothy returned it with a smirk.

"Why don't you come in and sit down?" I suggested.

Annie waved off my offer. "No, I can't stay. I just wanted to know what happened. The store is closed without Morty there."

Dorothy snorted.

"I can help you find him," Annie said.

I cut a glance at Dorothy. "I'm sure that won't be necessary. He'll show up in no time."

Annie nodded. "You'll call me if you need anything?" She handed me a business card with her number.

"Did you notice anything unusual about Mr. Grant?" I asked.

Annie shook her head. "Not that I can think of." She looked irritated at me that I would even ask, but I was just doing my job. After all, we all wanted to find Mr. Grant.

"I have a question for you, Annie," Dorothy said as she stepped closer.

This wasn't going to end well. The last thing I needed was for these women to start hitting each other with their purses. Peppermint candies would be everywhere once Dorothy started swinging that thing around.

"How did you meet Mr. Grant?" Dorothy asked, staring at Annie for an answer.

Annie looked at me as if I would answer for her.

When I didn't speak, she said, "We met when I applied for a job at the jewelry store."

Annie furrowed her brow. She was obviously perplexed as to why Dorothy was questioning her.

Dorothy paced her hands on her hips. "Well, how long have you been working there?"

She stared at Annie; there was no way she was going to let her get out of answering. Annie shifted from one foot to the next. "I don't remember."

"You don't remember how long you've been working there?" Dorothy asked accusingly. "You have to have some idea."

"It's been a few years, I guess." Annie stumbled over her words.

She didn't seem all that confident in her answer. That didn't matter to Dorothy, though. I knew she would keep up the questions as long as I didn't put a stop to it.

Dorothy wouldn't stop with just two questions. I figured she had at least twenty. That meant eighteen more to go.

"Do you have hobbies?" Dorothy crossed her arms in front of her chest.

"Why are you asking me that question?" Annie asked with a frown.

Dorothy offered a fake smile. "I'm just trying to be friendly, dear."

"Oh," Annie said. "Well, I guess I like to go boating and fishing, and I like to read."

Dorothy quirked a brow and looked over at me. Annie still looked totally confused, as if she knew she's said the wrong thing but was unaware of what that was.

Dorothy moved even closer by stepping up to the window. She looked out as she asked, "Do you know where he may be?"

"Do I know where Morty is? If I knew, wouldn't I tell police?"

Dorothy faced Annie. "What I meant was, are there places he likes to go? Maybe a place he likes to go to get away from it all for a while?" Dorothy pressed her.

Annie twisted her hands. "Oh, not that I know of. You know, I already talked with the police."

I actually think Annie had started to sweat. Who knew that Dorothy was this good at interrogating people?

Dorothy stepped back over to her desk. "What does he like to do in his spare time?"

Annie shrugged. "I don't know."

"Well, I thought you knew him so well. At least that's the way you acted," Dorothy said.

"I don't think I can answer any more questions. I really need to go now." Annie moved toward the door.

"You'll have to excuse Dorothy," I said. "She gets a little into the job sometimes."

Dorothy frowned.

"I guess I didn't know she was a private eye too," Annie said.

Dorothy folded her arms in front of her chest but didn't answer.

"What about the store? Who will take care of it? Will it be closed until he comes back?" I asked.

Annie waved her hand. "The manager is handling everything until Morty comes back. I'm sure it will be soon." She frowned. "At least I hope it will be soon. I'll make sure that everything is taken care of at his store. I'd never let anything happen to Morty."

"Yeah, that's why you give him cards with kisses on it," Dorothy said under her breath.

"What did she say?" Annie asked, looking at me.

"Oh, never mind her," I said with a wave of my hand. "Dorothy, I think you've asked enough questions. We should let Annie go. I know she's really upset over what's happened to her boss."

Dorothy's scowl deepened when I said "boss." That was a painful reminder of what she'd found. I stepped over toward Annie, hoping to put some distance between the women. It would have turned out like the Bunco party if I'd had cupcakes.

Annie glared at Dorothy. They'd now become enemies. At least we'd gotten some questions answered, though. Maybe I should have let Dorothy continue. Although I sensed that Annie wasn't going to answer any more of Dorothy's or my questions. She had to know that Dorothy was interested in Mr. Grant. Anyone could see that.

"I'll definitely call you if I hear from him or find out anything. I hope you'll do the same," I said.

She nodded. "Oh, by the way, did you speak with Grace?"

"Yes, as a matter of fact, we did. I meant to ask you how you know her."

Annie paused, and a terrified look flickered in her eyes. "Oh, she came by one day with Kristin. So you'll be spending all your time working on that case, right? How will you possibly have time to find Mr. Grant?"

"I'm sure I'll manage," I said.

Annie stared for a moment and then offered a small grin. "Okay, well, good luck."

Dorothy and I watched in silence as she turned around and walked out to the parking lot. She climbed into her black Toyota and drove away. She never looked back at us, but she had to feel our stares. She was a little strange.

Dorothy shook her head. "No way do we need her help."

"Well, we may need her help since she knows him better than we do," I said.

"There's just something about her that I don't like," Dorothy said with a frown.

"Maybe it's because she has a little nickname for Mr. Grant," I said.

Dorothy shook her head, "No, that's not it at all. Why did she assume something had happened to him?" Dorothy asked.

"Well, the police were asking questions. And you assumed the same thing," I said.

"Yeah, but they didn't tell her that anything was wrong." Dorothy went back to her desk. "I still think something is suspicious."

We were quiet as I went back to my desk. I tapped my pen against my desk as I replayed the day's events in my mind. "Dorothy, I've had time to think about it, and I think you may be right about Annie. She was acting strange. And she said Kristin never came in the store, yet just now she said she'd met Grace when she came in the store with Kristin. Something doesn't add up."

Dorothy set her crossword puzzle book down. She stared at me for a moment and then said, "Well, I'm glad that you finally came to your senses. You should listen to me more often."

"I don't know about that," I said.

"What do you think she's hiding?" she asked.

I tapped my pen against the desk again, then shrugged. "I don't know, but I started thinking about how anxious she seemed. It was almost as if she wanted to feel us out to see what we knew."

Dorothy pointed her finger at me. "Exactly. Yes, that's what it was. I couldn't quite describe it, but you hit it right. What do you think she's up to?"

"I don't know, but I'll try to find out more about her. More important is whether Mr. Grant's disappearance is connected to his daughter's death," I said. "I'd say Annie knows something about it. It would be creepy to find out she was working with him the whole time and knew something about Kristin."

"We have to find out who that man was at Mr. Grant's house," Dorothy said.

"That's not as easy as it seems. We have nothing to go on," I said.

"We can start by asking around."

I nodded. "Yeah, I guess that's a start."

"There has to be something else we can do."

"I think if we continue to look for Kristin's killer, then that will lead us right to Mr. Grant," I said.

Dorothy nodded. "I think that sounds like a good plan, but I hope he's okay."

It was a good thing because that was the only plan I had. I felt a little helpless.

"Did you get a good look at the man at Mr. Grant's house?" I asked.

She looked at me from over the top of her eyeglasses. "Unfortunately, I wasn't wearing my glasses. You know I wanted to look nice for Morton."

"It would have been nice if I could get one of those police artists to sketch the gunman," I said.

"Why don't they?" Dorothy asked.

"Because they don't consider him a missing person yet. Maybe if he's gone longer," I said.

"Let's hope it doesn't come to that," Dorothy said with a sigh.

I nodded. I had a bad vibe about the whole thing, though.

"Was there anything that stood out about him?" I asked.

"He was big. Like not overweight, but just a solid, thick guy. Oh, and he had a lot of hair on his arms . . . and a gold bracelet on his right wrist," Dorothy said.

I looked at her. "I thought you said you couldn't see him. That's a lot of detail."

"Well, I couldn't see any facial features. What are you thinking?" she asked.

"That the jewelry could be connected. It would make sense, right?" I asked.

"A lot of people in Miami have jewelry," she reminded me.

"That's true, but I found that other piece of jewelry at the dock. I think it's connected to the case," I said.

Chapter Thirty-Four

After stepping outside to get fresh air, I came back inside the office and caught Dorothy at my laptop. She looked up at me like I'd just caught her stealing someone's yarn stash.

"What are you doing, Dorothy?" I asked.

She flashed a sheepish grin. "I was just searching the Internet."

"Wow. I didn't know you could Google."

"Well, I'm not that old. I can learn new things," she said.

I stepped closer to her and peered over her shoulder. "So what did you find? Are you on one of those matchmaker services? Oh no, you didn't sign me up for an account, did you?"

She wagged her finger at me. "No, but that's not a bad idea."

Oh, great. Now I'd put ideas into her head. I leaned closer and saw the name Annie on the screen. "Oh, my goodness. You're searching for her," I said. "What did you find out?"

Dorothy looked at me with a smirk. "I found out that she isn't all that she seems. I knew she was up to something."

I waved my hand. "Oh, I'm sure she's okay. You're just being suspicious because you like Mr. Grant."

"Why do you keep saying that? It's not true." She frowned.

Dorothy pulled out a giant yellow legal pad. Notes that she'd taken were written at the top of the page.

There were only a couple of lines of notes. The first one had nothing more than Annie's address listed, and the next line had the name of a souvenir shop here in town.

"What's that for?" I asked.

Dorothy looked up at me. "Annie said she had worked at Grant Jewelers for a long time. Well, unless she had a second job that's not true because until recently, like maybe about two months ago, she worked at this souvenir shop too," she said with a satisfied smile.

"Let me see that." I scrolled down the screen and saw the information Dorothy had been talking about. It seemed to be legitimate.

So of course, Dorothy and I piled in my car and headed out for this shop where Annie had supposedly worked. With any luck, we would find someone who could give us information on whether she really had worked there and for how long—maybe even why she had quit. Within a few minutes, Dorothy and I had arrived at the Sunset Souvenir Shop. It was a small place down by the marina.

When we stepped into the shop, we looked around for a few seconds. There were the usual souvenir-type items: T-shirts, magnets, key chains, glasses, and mugs—that kind of stuff. Only a few customers were at the back of the store, looking at T-shirts, and a couple of employees were busy behind the counter.

"Let's go ask the woman behind the counter," I said, pointing her out.

"I hope we get details about Annie," Dorothy said as she marched toward the counter.

"Excuse me," I said to the woman behind the counter.

She was probably a few years older than me. Her brown hair reached to her shoulders.

She smiled cheerfully. "Yes, ma'am, may I help you?

"I'm looking for someone who works here or possibly worked here a short time ago. Her name is Annie."

The woman's smile instantly turned into a frown. "She's not here anymore. May I help you with something?"

I knew that she probably wouldn't give me information about Annie, so I would have to make up a story.

"Annie told me that I could come here to apply for a job. She was the manager here—is that right?" I asked.

"Yes, she was, but she's not a manager now. That lady over there is the manager." She gestured toward the other woman. "I can give you an application if you'd like."

I glanced over at the woman who was busy with customers. "Oh no, that won't be necessary."

"If you're sure," she said.

"I'll come back. Thank you; you've been very helpful." I smiled.

Dorothy and I turned to leave. I didn't look back, but I felt the woman staring at my back. Somehow, I knew she was suspicious of my story, but it didn't matter because I would probably never see her again. She would never know the real reason that I was in the shop.

We'd made it halfway through the store when I paused for reasons I didn't quite know. When I glanced to my side, I spotted Megan at the back of the store. She was helping customers and wearing the same uniform polo shirt as the other woman behind the counter.

I pulled on Dorothy's arm. "Look who's also working in the store."

"Very interesting," Dorothy said.

Now that we'd seen Megan, there was no way we could leave. Dorothy and I turned around and moved farther into the shop.

"When she's finished with the customers, we'll talk to her. We'll act like it was a complete coincidence that we stopped here," I said.

"Of course." Dorothy nodded. "That sounds like a good plan."

Dorothy and I moved over to the T-shirts with “Miami Beach” written across the front and started sorting through the rack.

We can’t just hang around here waiting for her to stop talking to the customers. They’ll get suspicious. We have to do something to make us look like customers,” Dorothy said.

Dorothy was right.

“Why don’t you try on something?” she said.

I shook my head. “Why don’t *you* try on something?”

Dorothy rolled her eyes. “I am not wearing shorts that have ‘Beach Bum’ written across my rear end.”

“Well, we have to do something while we wait. I’ll try on something if you try on something,” I said with a smile.

Dorothy stared at me for a moment and then finally nodded. “Okay, it’s a deal.”

She’d better keep her end of the bargain, I thought.

Dorothy wandered around, trying to find something to take into the dressing room. I kept my eye on Megan while I looked around too. It didn’t really matter what we tried on because I didn’t plan on making a purchase anyway, although I would if I had to. If it meant getting info that I needed. Dorothy would search for hours if I didn’t stop her, so I grabbed two T-shirts and took her by the arm.

“I got us a couple of T-shirts,” I said.

“Did you get the right size? I like my shirts to fit big. I can’t stand fabric binding up around me.”

“I think they are one size fits all.” I handed her the T-shirt.

“Oh, great. This should look wonderful,” Dorothy said drily.

Dorothy and I picked dressing rooms, went in, and closed the curtains. I had planned on just slipping the T-shirt over my shirt. Like I said, we were just wasting time and pretending to be customers anyway. I’d just gotten the shirt over my head when I heard the curtain pulled back. I struggled to get the thing over my head so I could see who had entered my room.

“Who is it?” I asked in a panic.

"Quit thrashing around like a fish out of water," Dorothy ordered. "It's just me."

She pulled the shirt down over my head, and I blew my hair out of my eyes. "What are you doing in here?"

She waved her hand. "We can't talk if I'm in the other room."

I stared at her. "Do we need to talk right now?"

She shrugged. "Well, we need to discuss what is going on here. What better place than in here? It's private, and no one will hear us."

"I don't know about that." I tapped on the flimsy wall. "This thing isn't very thick. Why don't you try on your T-shirt?" I asked.

Dorothy held the shirt up and frowned. "Do you seriously think I am going to wear this thing? Was this some kind of joke?"

I bit my lip to keep from laughing. "I wasn't trying to be funny, honest. I just picked up the first shirt that I found."

Dorothy looked skeptical. "Yeah, sure." Dorothy held up the shirt with the image of a woman's body in a bikini printed on the front. "And look at the back." She flipped the shirt over.

I bit my lip again. The back of the shirt had the rear view of the woman's body, of course—wearing a thong.

"Well, forget me trying this shirt on." She crossed her arms in front of her chest.

I chuckled. "You don't have to wear it."

A voice from the next dressing room caught our attention. We stopped talking so we could listen in. The voice sounded familiar—it was a lot like Megan's. I peeked out the curtain but didn't see her. I stepped closer to the dressing room wall in the hope that I could overhear the conversation. I strained, but it was almost impossible to make out what was being said.

"I'll be there as soon as I get off work. If you'd given me some cash, now I wouldn't have to work these jobs," the woman said.

I looked at Dorothy and said, "I think she called the person she's talking to 'Annie.'"

Dorothy's eyes widened.

Could it be the same Annie? The one who had worked here? It was probably just a coincidence. After all, there were a lot of people with that name.

Finally, the voice stopped. I had to know if it was Megan that we'd heard. I rushed over to the curtain and peeked out. I didn't see anyone. Was she still in the dressing room? Did she know that we had been listening? I glanced down and noticed that the wall didn't go all the way to the floor. My heart rate increased. She could have easily looked down and noticed that we were standing next to the wall. Having two women standing next to the dressing room wall like that wasn't normal. I had no explanation for why we'd been standing there if she asked.

I tugged at the T-shirt and got it over my head.

"Do you think it was her?" Dorothy asked.

"I think it was," I whispered. "But I also think she may have seen us eavesdropping."

"Well, she shouldn't expect a private conversation in the dressing room," Dorothy said.

"Actually, you suggested that it would be private to talk in here."

Dorothy frowned. "Oh, don't be sassy."

I rolled my eyes. Then quickly I realized that would be considered sassy too. I grabbed my purse and motioned for Dorothy to follow my lead. I pulled the curtain back and peeked out.

When I poked my head out from the curtain, I noticed Megan leaving her area, but I had no way of knowing if she'd been in that dressing room. She could have been with a customer for all I knew.

Dorothy and I stepped out from the dressing room. A woman standing next to the rack of clothing beside us frowned.

"My sister can never make up her mind about clothing," Dorothy said, gesturing toward me.

The woman smiled and nodded.

"So I'm your sister now?" I asked under my breath.

"It's better than me being your grandmother, don't you think?"

"So did you want to buy that T-shirt, Dorothy?" I asked.

"Very funny," she said, placing it back on the rack.

Megan was with another customer again, so we were back in the same predicament as when we started.

A few seconds passed and Megan noticed us. She must have felt eyes on her because Dorothy and I couldn't stop looking her way. Finally, she flashed a fake smile and waved. I hoped the customers she was helping would leave soon.

After another minute, Megan bounced over like she was headed to a pep rally. I had never seen her like that in the restaurant. I wondered if maybe this was her twin or if I had the right person.

When she stepped over to us, she said, "I'm so glad to see you all."

A strange expression was probably on my face. There was no way I could control my reaction. "Do you work here?" I asked.

"Yeah, it's just a second job. You know, I have to pay the bills. It's a lot of fun here, though."

This was probably the first time I'd seen her smile.

"What are you all doing here?" she asked.

"Um, I was looking for a shirt." I grabbed the first one I saw.

She raised her eyebrows. "Can I help you find one?"

I stuffed the shirt back on the rack. "Actually, I don't think you have the one I was looking for. There is one question I have for you, though."

Megan glanced from me to Dorothy. "Yes?"

"Do you know Annie?" I searched her gaze for a reaction.

Without pausing, she said, "Annie who? No, I don't know an Annie. Why do you ask?"

"She's a friend of mine, and we lost touch," Dorothy said before I had a chance to respond. "She used to work here."

Megan might be able to verify whether this story was true or not, so our cover could be in jeopardy. But it was too late now.

Megan smiled. “Sorry I couldn’t help you.”

I nodded. “Thanks anyway.”

As we walked out the door, Dorothy said, “Sorry about that. I got a little anxious. That’s not what Magnum would have done, huh?”

Chapter Thirty-Five

"Since we don't have to work anymore, I guess we have plenty of time to go to Spencer's address. And if he's not at work, maybe there's a good chance he'll be at home," I said as I slipped back into the car.

"He's probably still sleeping," Dorothy said.

I pointed the car in the direction of his place, hoping that I'd find out why he'd been watching me. The drive from my office to his address wasn't a long one. If it hadn't been for the heavy traffic, we would have been there within minutes. It was a beautiful day in Miami, and the sun had just started to set.

Jake called my cell phone, but by the time I answered, he'd hung up. I punched in his number again, but he didn't pick up. I hoped he had good news for me.

We pulled up in front of Spencer's place. There were quite a few cars parked on the street, so I had to drive by several times before I found a place to park.

"So what do we do now?" Dorothy asked.

"One of your favorite things," I said. "We sit and wait."

"So we're just going to sit out in front of his house too? I'm not so sure that worked out well for us the last time." Dorothy and I had spent way too much time on stakeouts with the last case.

"What are you talking about? We got a lot of info from doing that before. It's what Magnum would do," I said.

She rolled her eyes. I watched Spencer's house as Dorothy clacked her knitting needles.

I glanced over at her. "What are you knitting anyway? That's got to be the longest scarf in the history of scarves."

I hadn't mentioned the pasties debacle again.

"I thought I'd knit you a full-body suit," she said snarkily.

I focused my attention on the building again.

Silence filled the car for a moment until Dorothy finally said, "Maggie, do you ever wonder why they drive on a parkway but park in a driveway?"

I shook my head. "No, Dorothy, I can honestly say that the thought never crossed my mind."

Finally, I spotted movement. "He's coming out the front door," I said excitedly.

"Thank goodness. My butt is starting to fall asleep," Dorothy said, putting her needles in her purse.

I watched as Spencer walked along the sidewalk and stopped at a car. He looked around, and I lowered my head.

"Is he looking this way?" Dorothy asked. "Follow him."

"Not yet, but he was looking around. I think he senses us," I said.

"He's not a dog. I doubt he'll sniff us out," she said.

"No, but he can probably feel four beady eyes on him," I said.

Spencer finally climbed behind the wheel and pulled away from the curb. I waited a few seconds, then cranked the engine and pulled out a few car lengths behind him.

"I have to admit you're getting good at this following cars business," Dorothy said.

"Why thank you, Dorothy. That's very sweet of you." I smiled.

"That doesn't mean that your driving skills are any better than mine, though," she warned with a wave of her finger.

"Of course not," I said.

I followed Spencer through the streets, and for a while I wondered if he knew where the heck he was going.

"This had better not be a wasted trip," I said as I turned right and followed him down the next street.

We neared the park, and finally his car slowed down. Spencer pulled into the parking lot that was for park access. It was dark, but there was a light on in the street nearby, and I could make out most of what was going on.

I stayed back and waited. Another car pulled up a few minutes later, and a man got out of his car. He walked up to Spencer, and they talked for a moment. I was pretty sure this man was the one from the boat, but I needed a closer view to know positively.

This meant that, just as I'd expected, that there had to be a connection to Spencer and Kristin's murder. But what about Mr. Grant's disappearance? How would I get a closer look? Was I brave enough to walk through the park? There weren't a lot of areas that would conceal me. Even though it was dark, the men would probably see me if I got that close.

But from my vantage point, I couldn't even see them at all now, so I had no idea what they were doing or where they'd gone. After a couple minutes, the men came into view again. Both of them climbed into Spencer's car this time. The headlights came on, and Spencer put the car in reverse. It looked like I was going to have to follow him again.

As they were pulling out, I dialed Jake's number.

"Is he answering?" Dorothy asked.

"Jake," I said breathlessly when he answered the phone. "I'm following the guy from my work. The one who was messing around with my car."

"A guy was messing around with your car? Why are you following him?" Jake asked.

"Because I wanted to see what he was up to—why else?" I asked. "Listen, they're going somewhere."

"Well, I figure if they're in a car driving, then they are going somewhere. By the way, who are these men?"

"One of the men works with me at the restaurant. Well, until we were fired I worked with him. His name is Spencer. And I think the other one is the guy from the boat."

"Where are you?" Jake asked with tension in his voice. His tone had definitely changed. "Tell me the name of the street. I'm coming there right now."

"Why, what's going on?" I asked.

"Just tell me where you are," he said.

"I'm on Second Street, turning on to Biscayne."

"I'll call you right back, okay?" he asked.

"Yeah, okay."

I was glad he hadn't told me to stop following the men because his request would have fallen on deaf ears. As I drove, I concentrated on following Spencer's car so that I wouldn't lose it. There was no way I would let him get away from me.

"You'd better punch it," Dorothy said.

"I think they're headed to the beach," I said.

"Good observation," Dorothy said.

I drove behind them for a little longer, and sure enough, they were going to the beach. Spencer pulled up in the parking lot for beach access and parked. There was only one other car there. Were they meeting the person who had driven that car? There was only one way to find out.

The men got out of the car and headed toward the beach.

"I have to follow them," I said.

"I don't think that's a good idea. You should wait for Jake to call you back. He's probably on his way. You'll tell him exactly where we are, and he'll be here in no time," Dorothy said.

"I don't think I have time to wait for him to show up," I said.

"At least call and see if he's on his way," she said.

"Fine." I dialed Jake's number while I kept my eye on the men.

They walked over to the beach access and disappeared from my view. Jake's line rang repeatedly.

"He's not answering."

Dorothy released a sigh. "I guess we'll have to take care of this then," she said, climbing out of the car.

Chapter Thirty-Six

I jumped out and joined her. We crossed the road and headed in the same direction the men had taken. Dorothy and I walked across the parking lot. I stepped close to the car and peered in but didn't see anything. We stepped over to the other car, but there was nothing unusual about it either. Food wrappers and a bunch of junk littered the back seat. I was just glad not to see a dead body in the car. But heck, maybe that was in the trunk.

I swallowed hard and then said, "I guess we should look on the beach now."

Dorothy nodded. "Yes, I guess we'd better."

Dorothy and I walked across the access and made our way to the sand. A slight breeze glided by. I looked up and down the shore but didn't spot the men.

"Do you see them?" Dorothy asked.

I shook my head. "No, I don't see them."

"Maybe we should walk over there?" Dorothy pointed toward a little covered area with a few picnic benches.

I wanted to find out what the men were doing, but I was afraid to find them at the same time. What would they say if they knew I'd followed them?

The men were still nowhere in sight as Dorothy and I made our way across the sand toward the covered picnic area. The waves lapped against the sand, causing an eerie roar. Other than that, silence filled the air… definitely spooky.

Once we reached the covered area, Dorothy and I stopped and scanned it.

"Well, they're obviously not here." I released a deep breath.

Dorothy placed her hands on her hips. "Well, do you think they drowned?"

I looked out at the water. "I guess I hadn't thought of that, but no, that's not possible."

Dorothy shrugged. "Anything is possible."

"It's certainly strange that they would walk out here and disappear. They haven't been gone long enough to walk that far down the beach to where we wouldn't see them." I stepped out onto the sand and looked to my left and then to my right. I'd expected to see someone, but it was just us.

I glanced down at my phone, expecting to get a call back from Jake, but it didn't ring. It looked as if my service was out. Had he tried to call and my phone wasn't working? Maybe I should go back to the car and see if I could get it to work.

But before I did that, I wanted to go out by the water.

"Let's step over to the water," I said. Dorothy adjusted her purse on her arm and nodded. "Maybe we can see farther down the beach if we go out there."

"Okay, but we can't stay long. I want you to try to call Jake again," Dorothy said.

We walked across the beach, away from the covered picnic area, and my feet sank into the soft, wet sand. I slid out of my shoes and let the water rush over my feet and beat against my ankles.

Dorothy slipped off her shoes and stuck her feet in the water too.

"It's cold," I said.

I looked from left to right again but still didn't see anything. It was obvious that the men weren't there. We needed to just go back to the car and give up. I wasn't even sure that they'd done anything wrong, so it probably was for the best that I hadn't found them anyway.

"Are you ready to go?" I asked.

I was surprised that I could even get near the water after what had just happened to me. I'd come narrowly close to being eaten by a shark.

Dorothy nodded. "I'm ready to go."

Just then my phone rang. I reached in my pocket and pulled it out. It was Jake's number.

"Are you looking for us?" I said when I answered the phone.

There was no noise and no Jake. I glanced down at the phone. The call had been dropped.

"My phone service is terrible out here," I said, holding the phone up, trying to get a better signal.

The little bars at the top of the screen increased, so I punched in Jake's number again. It took a few seconds, but it finally began to ring.

"It's ringing," I said, answering Dorothy's silent question.

It rang several times, but then it was silent. I looked down at the screen again.

"It stopped working again. It's pointless out here," I said.

"We should go back to the car," Dorothy said.

"I'm sure he's trying to find us," I said.

I reached down, grabbed my shoes, and slipped them back on. Of course, now I had sand on my feet, but I didn't want to accidentally step on one of those crabs as I walked back to the car. As I waited for Dorothy to put her shoes back on, I looked down at my phone again. The service was still not available.

My focus was on Dorothy when someone knocked the phone out of my hand. I let out a gasp and looked up. It was the man who had been on the boat. He was tall and looked even bigger than I remembered. He glared at me with his dark eyes.

"Why the hell are you following us?" he asked.

He studied my face, and I knew that he was trying to recognize where he'd seen me. His eyes narrowed, and I knew that he'd just remembered that I'd been on his boat with Jake.

"You're a cop," the man said.

I shook my head. "No, I'm not."

"She worked with me at the restaurant. I knew she was a narc. I told you," Spencer said.

My eyes widened. "A narc? No," I said again.

"Is that why you were following me?"

A terrified look was splashed across Dorothy's face. I felt so bad that I'd brought her into this dangerous situation, although she had insisted on coming. I should have insisted that she stay out of it.

"Answer my question," the man said.

"I'm not following you," I said.

"We were just going for a walk on the beach," Dorothy answered.

"I saw you on my boat, and then we saw you follow us tonight. That's not a coincidence," he said with a growl in his voice.

The next thing I knew, he had grabbed me by the arms. I wasn't prepared for his strength as his hands tightened on my arms.

"Let go of me!" I demanded.

When I looked over, I saw that Spencer had grabbed Dorothy. My stomach turned at the sight.

"Let her go," I said.

I jerked my arms to try to get away from his grip, but it was no use. I couldn't break free. I had to think quickly because I didn't know what they would do next. If he had killed Kristin, then he wouldn't think twice about doing the same thing to us. If I could get this guy in just the right position, I might be able to break free from his grip. What would I do if I got away, though? I couldn't run and leave Dorothy there. I didn't want to use the gun, but it looked as though that might be my only option. Maybe just pointing it at the guy would be enough to get him to stop. Then I could race back up to the road to see if my phone would work.

I turned my body to the side and jerked. Thank goodness, the motion had put me in the correct spot. I jerked to my right and jabbed the guy in the stomach. He groaned and released his hold on me. I immediately ran toward water. Dorothy was still trying to get away from Spencer, but mostly he was just holding her arms. Why, I didn't know. What was the most she could do? Hit him with her pocketbook? Though she did have those knitting needles. Would she think to use them?

Chapter Thirty-Seven

I jumped in the water. For the second time in less than twenty-four hours, I was in the ocean. I'd made it to waist-deep when the man ran in the water after me. I had nowhere else to go. I couldn't go farther out into the water. He had me trapped.

Within seconds, he reached me, and I fell down. Water splashed over me, covering me completely. Visions of Kristin's lifeless body flashed through my mind. He would drown me in this water too. He wrapped his arms around me, and I struggled to break free from his hold once again.

Water splashed around us as the man and I struggled in the water. I knew he was trying to get me down so that he could hold me underwater. I had my gun, but I couldn't get to it at the moment. I didn't want to allow him the chance to get hold of my weapon either. Now that water was in the barrel, it could be dangerous to fire it. He might not know that, though. There was little hope that I would get away from him this time. He was bigger and much stronger than me.

I wondered what was happening with Dorothy. The noise from the waves was drowning out any sound that she might be making. She could call out for help, and I wouldn't know—not that I could help her anyway. I felt powerless. I would have to pull off some pretty impressive moves to get this guy off me.

Hitting in the lower portion of my attacker's body wasn't possible. I would have to go for the head area. I managed to get one hand free. I had only seconds to make a move. With the palm of my hand I jabbed upward on my attacker's nose. He let out a wail that sounded more like a bear's.

He stumbled backward, and I looked over at Dorothy. At that moment Dorothy had lifted her leg and jabbed Spencer right in the groin with her knee. The guy fell to his knees and then to the side so that his entire body was in the sand. Dorothy reached down and picked up her purse that had fallen to the ground.

She draped the big brown bag on her arm as if she did this kind of thing all the time, dusting off the sand from her purse and hands. Nobody messed with Dorothy and her pocketbook. Dorothy and I made eye contact. It was as if at that moment she realized what had happened. I knew she was just as shocked by what she'd done as I was. I guess I shouldn't have been too surprised, though; Dorothy could be tough when she needed to take care of business.

My attacker was still on the ground, and it looked like he wasn't going anywhere for a few moments. I glanced down at the man and a wave of water flowed over him. There was blood on his face. It served him right for attacking me. He was lucky that I hadn't done more bodily harm.

The man looked over and saw what Dorothy had done. He groaned again, but he didn't attempt to get up. Just then a wave slammed into my legs and knocked me backward. I landed in the water again on my butt.

When I looked over, I saw that he was climbing up. I should have run away when I'd had the chance. Now I would have to fight him off again. Where was a jellyfish to sting him when I needed it? I prayed that one didn't get me.

I pushed and struggled up before another wave crashed into me again. The man had gotten to his feet at this point, and we stared at each other, each trying to gauge what move the other would make next. He glared at me but didn't speak a word. I'd almost expected to see Dorothy run up and smack him in the head with her purse, but I was glad she hadn't tried that. Who would make the first move? That was when I remembered I had one advantage over him.

I reached down quickly and grabbed my gun that was still at my waist. He looked down, and at that moment he knew what I was going to do. He knew that I had something over him. I didn't want to use the gun, but he didn't know that. I had to plaster the toughest look on my face that I could muster.

I pointed the gun at him. "Don't make another move."

My hands were surprisingly steady, and he held his hands up. I glanced over and saw that Spencer was now sitting up, but he clearly still wasn't ready to stand. It didn't look like he would cause any problems for a while. I had to get Dorothy to show me that move sometime. It was practically lethal. Where had she learned to be so tough?

"Dorothy, did you call the police yet?" I asked.

This guy didn't know that our phones wouldn't work out here.

She nodded. "They're on the way."

I looked at my attacker again with a satisfied grin. They thought they would take us down because we were smaller than they were, but smaller didn't always mean weaker. They'd learned that lesson the hard way.

The guy stared at me. I knew he was trying to think of ways to get the gun away from me, but it was no use. There was no way he could get it out of my hands.

In one way, it seemed like forever before Jake showed up with the other police, but in another way, it seemed like he was there instantly. The lights from the police cars flooded the area, and I spotted Jake running my way.

"We got it from here, Maggie," he called out.

Apparently, Dorothy's phone had worked after all. The moment I lowered my gun was when my hands finally started shaking. It must have been the adrenaline that I was now noticing running through my veins.

I moved over to Dorothy. "Are you okay?" I asked.

She had a death grip on her pocketbook. "I'm fine now. That will teach him to grab me," she said, shooting another nasty look Spencer's way.

"I'm sorry that I put you in that danger," I said.

She waved off my comment. "You're just lucky that you have me."

I smiled. "Yes, I am lucky."

Jake stepped into the water and grabbed the man by his shirt. He dragged him onto the sand, like he was hauling in a fish. I watched as he handcuffed the guy and released him to another officer.

Spencer was finally able to climb to his feet. His hands were cuffed as well, and he was escorted away. It was only now that I began to notice my surroundings again. I'd been so consumed in my struggle with the man that I'd forgotten we were at the edge of the water. The stars twinkled in the sky, and the water rushed at the sand.

"At least you were able to keep your purse safe," I said.

Dorothy patted the bag. "No one was getting at this baby. This is my lifeline." She reached in her purse and fumbled around, finally dragging out a mint. She pushed it at me. "Here, take this. It will calm your nerves."

I waved it away. "I don't want it, thanks."

"It will help you. Take it," she insisted.

"But I don't want it. I'm not stressed now," I said.

"Oh, hogwash. Of course you are. That man almost killed you. Now take the mint." She shoved it at me again.

I sighed and took the mint, then reluctantly popped it in my mouth. This one didn't have a wrapper either.

Jake walked over to us.

"Looks like you found me after all," I said.

He shook his head. "It wasn't easy. Why didn't you wait for me?" he asked.

"I didn't have time. I almost lost them. Now aren't you glad I didn't wait?"

"Not really. You all could have been killed," he said.

"But I wasn't, so now everything is fine." I smiled.

"We had just learned more about this guy. I was moving in on him," Jake said.

"But I figured it out first." I stood a little straighter.

He smiled. "Maybe we should have you on the police force."

I shrugged. "Maybe you should."

Chapter Thirty-Eight

"Apparently, Kristin had been blackmailed to run the drugs for her boyfriend. She didn't know what she was involved in. Spencer was working for her at the Captain's Quarters and told his dealer. They realized she was working for the competition. They told Kristin's boyfriend they would kill her if he didn't get out of the area. He didn't believe them, so he sent her to do his dirty work again, and they really killed her," Jake explained.

I shook my head. "That is terrible."

"Thank goodness, we figured it out before it was too late," Dorothy said. Her expression turned bleak. "Did you find out what happened to Mr. Grant?"

I looked at Jake and was afraid to hear his answer. "Did they say where he was?" I asked.

Jake stared for a moment and then said, "They said they have nothing to do with his disappearance. They didn't know who he was."

I frowned. "That isn't possible. Where else would he be?"

"We still don't know if he left on his own," he said.

"Oh, don't be ridiculous. Of course he didn't leave on his own," Dorothy said.

I ran my hand through my hair. "This doesn't make sense. He wouldn't just leave his business."

Jake shook his head. "I know, and we'll try to find him."

"Well, at least you are on the same page as me with this," I said with relief.

He smiled. "Are you okay?"

I nodded. "I'm feeling great."

We walked away from the water. I thought I'd seen enough of water and the beach for the day. Once again I had to go home and get out of wet clothing.

Jake walked me to my car. Dorothy had already gotten in, but she didn't bother reaching for the knitting needles this time.

"This is the second time you've seen me all wet," I said.

He looked me up and down. "It's not a bad look on you."

I couldn't hold back a smile. "Thank you for getting here so quickly."

"It's my job," he said.

I stared at him. "Is that the only reason why you got here so quickly? Because it's your job?"

Jake touched my chin with his fingers, then leaned down and placed his lips against mine. My pulse skittered alarmingly. For the second time tonight, adrenaline raced through my body, but this was for an entirely different reason. His lips were soft against mine and felt oh so good. He didn't just kiss me, but caressed my mouth with his lips.

Jake leaned back and looked me in the eyes. "I'd planned on asking you if you wanted to go for a walk along the beach tonight, but this isn't what I had in mind."

I chuckled. "I would hope not."

"Listen, I need to wrap things up here. Can I call you later?" he asked.

I nodded. "Yeah, I'd like that."

For once I could drive home and not have to worry about who might be following me. It had been nonstop craziness since I'd arrived in Miami. What happened to the simple lost love or deadbeat parent cases? I really needed one of those right now.

After dropping Dorothy off, I headed home, showered, and collapsed into bed. Jake's kiss still lingered on my lips.

Chapter Thirty-Nine

Although Kristin's killer had been found, we still had to find Mr. Grant. Dorothy and I had returned to the restaurant. I still hadn't figured out what Megan had been talking about when we'd overheard her in the break room. Dorothy and I had decided to follow that lead. It was the only thing we had.

Megan walked out of the restaurant and jumped in her car. Dorothy and I exchanged a look.

"Are you ready?" I asked.

Dorothy nodded. "I'm as ready as I'll ever be."

I had no idea if following Megan would do any good, but it couldn't hurt. Maybe if I was lucky I'd find out something... something that she didn't want to tell me.

Megan backed her car out of the spot, and I waited a few minutes before pulling out behind her. I didn't want to her to see me. It was hard to stay far enough behind a car and not lose it in the process. But I was becoming an old pro at this by now.

Dorothy and I followed her through the streets of downtown Miami, and for a minute I was sure she had noticed me.

"I think our cover is blown," I said.

Dorothy had been knitting and totally not paying attention. She was still on edge about Mr. Grant, and so was I.

"What makes you say that?" she asked, looking at me over the top of her glasses.

"Megan sped up," I said.

Dorothy went back to knitting. "She's probably just driving the speed limit. You should try it sometime."

"Just because I don't want to drive at warp speed doesn't mean there is anything wrong with my driving," I said.

Megan turned onto a street and finally came to a stop in front of a house.

Dorothy looked up. "Where are we?"

"You should have been paying attention. What if I need your help to get out of here?"

"You were driving. Why would you need my help getting out of here?"

"Never mind," I said.

Dorothy and I watched as Megan got out of the car and walked up to the nice house. She rang the doorbell, and I was anxious to see who would answer the door. After a few seconds, the door finally opened, and I was surprised to see Justin, the owner of the restaurant.

Apparently, Megan hadn't lied when she said she'd been having a relationship with him.

"I hope she isn't in there long," Dorothy said.

"We should plan on her being in here for a while because I think something is going on between the two. Romantically, you know."

"Please, I don't want the details." Dorothy rummaged through her purse. "It's a good thing I brought snacks. Do you want some trail mix?" She shoved a handful toward me.

I looked over at her and scowled. After a second, I said, "Yeah, I'll take some of the trail mix."

Dorothy gave me a smug, satisfied smile. So she'd been right to bring snacks. It had been a long morning, and I hadn't eaten much. I grabbed a handful of trail mix and continued to watch the house.

"There's no telling how long we could be out here waiting for them to come out," Dorothy said as she munched on the mix.

"This is part of the job," I said.

When she finished chewing, she said, "I think we should go up there and look in the windows."

I shook my head. "I don't think that's a good idea. What if they see us? How would I explain that we were peeking in the windows?" I asked.

"Oh, we won't get caught. We can just go up there and listen. We don't have to actually look in the window."

I paused. "Well, okay, I guess I am tired of sitting here."

Dorothy and I got out of the car and hurried up to the house. I hid behind a small scrub while Dorothy hid behind an even smaller one. I doubted either of us was concealed from view, but it felt good to have some kind of shield.

"We need to go closer if we want to hear anything," I said, motioning for Dorothy to follow.

"Maybe we should find the bedroom and listen outside the window," Dorothy said.

"Ugh, no way. I don't want to solve the case that badly," I said.

Okay, I did want to solve the case badly, and I'd probably do what I had to, but I hoped to find an easier way.

Dorothy and I maneuvered over to one of the windows, like a couple of cat burglars. Well, I hurried, but Dorothy had more of a shuffle thing going on, although she got there pretty darn quickly all the same. I leaned up close to the window and listened.

"I don't hear anything," I said.

Even if I had wanted to look in the windows, I wouldn't have been able to because the blinds were closed, and there was no way to see in.

"I don't hear anything either," Dorothy said. "What do we do now?"

As I was thinking of a fix for our dilemma, sound came from the side of the house. A neighbor was in his backyard.

"Let's get out of here before we're caught or they call the police," I said.

We jumped into the car just in time, because Megan was coming out of the front door. I'd fastened my seat belt and was ready to drive off, thinking she'd be in there all night. Megan got in her car, never glancing over and noticing my car. I'd give her just a little bit of time and then I'd take off behind her, although there probably was no point because I'd already followed her here. There was probably no other reason to follow her. I'd have to give up.

Within another few seconds, Justin stepped out the front door and got behind the wheel of his car. Now I had no choice but to follow him. I'd abandon my mission of spying on Megan and trail after him instead. I wouldn't have followed him if I hadn't noticed the Grant Jewelers bag in his hand. It was probably nothing, but I was curious just the same.

"Did you see his bag?" Dorothy asked as she sat up straighter in her seat.

I nodded. "Yeah, I saw it."

It seemed as though following people around was all I was doing, and it wasn't really giving me any answers. Maybe I should give up on this private-eye tactic. There had to be a better way to find the info. I just hadn't found it yet.

Dorothy and I watched as Justin sat in his car for a moment. Megan had already driven down the street, so it was too late to change my mind and follow her instead. I guess he wasn't waiting to follow her, because she'd already left him behind. Finally he backed his car down the driveway.

I pulled out slowly and followed him out of the subdivision and through downtown. When he stopped at a bank ATM, I pulled up to the curb and waited. Luckily, he still hadn't noticed me. Justin pulled out again, driving even faster than Dorothy. Maybe I should have let her drive so that we could have kept up.

"You're going to have to speed it up if you don't want to lose him," she said.

I nodded. "Yeah, I know. Everyone is driving too fast."

She shook her head and went back to the knitting. I was about to abandon this mission because I couldn't keep up, but I pushed through, managing to get closer to him again. I wasn't a quitter.

Chapter Forty

He turned onto another street, and I had a suspicion about where he was headed. When he turned into the marina parking lot, I knew that I'd been right. Why was he going there? I hoped that I was about to find out. Maybe it was a coincidence; after all, a lot of people had boats and a lot of people knew people with boats. Not to mention, he could be doing something else at the marina because there were other shops here. I parked my car, not taking my eyes off the spot where he parked, and jumped out as soon as he did.

After following Justin, I realized that this trip was truly getting me nowhere. He was sitting on a bench near the marina. It looked as if he were waiting for someone, but after ten minutes I was no longer patient enough to find out exactly whom he was meeting.

"That was a waste of time. Come on. Let's go back to Mr. Grant's house," I said.

Dorothy draped her giant pocketbook over her arm and marched across the parking lot.

"What are we going to do when we get there?" she asked.

"We'll just look for a clue. Maybe he had an appointment with someone. He probably has a schedule or a cell phone. If he left that behind, then we know something happened."

"Don't you think the police looked for that?"

I scowled. "Are you serious? I doubt they looked for anything. They think he just took off," I said.

Dorothy nodded. "But Jake doesn't believe that."

"That still doesn't mean anything," I said.

Dorothy and I made the quick drive back to Mr. Grant's house. I hadn't expected to see the police car in the driveway. It wasn't Jake's car, but it was a police car, nonetheless. There were no other cars—well, not that I saw anyway.

"What do you think that means?" Dorothy pointed at the police car.

"I guess Jake really did take me seriously," I said.

"I think they know more than they're telling us," Dorothy said.

"Well, if that's true, then I'd better find out from Jake."

Okay, he didn't owe me anything, but I hoped that he would share something this important with me. Since the police were there, we couldn't get in.

Dorothy and I pulled out of the driveway.

"Now what do we do?" Dorothy asked with frustration in her voice.

I tapped the steering wheel with my fingers. "I don't know. Let me think about this one."

I had to think of something soon because I didn't want to drive around in circles.

"How about we go back to the marina and see if Justin is still there? He can't sit on that bench all day," I said.

Dorothy nodded. "If he's still there, we should just confront him and ask if he knew Mr. Grant."

"That's exactly what I was thinking," I said.

I pointed the car in the direction of the marina, and within a short time I was circling the parking lot, looking for a space. I squeezed the car in between a delivery truck and an SUV.

"I don't think I can get out. The car is too close for the door to open. I'm not that skinny," Dorothy said with a frown.

I shoved the key back in the ignition and pulled out. "I'll drive back around and get a better shot at pulling in."

I circled the lot again and made my way back to the spot, but just as I was about to pull in, a black Porsche whizzed across the lot and zipped into the spot as if I hadn't even been sitting there. For a moment I wondered if I were suddenly invisible.

"What a jerk," Dorothy said.

She shook her fist at him. I expected her to pull out her knitting needles and threaten to poke him in the butt with them. He glared at us as we sat there.

"Hey, that's the guy from Mr. Grant's house." Dorothy yelled at him as he walked away. "Get back here, you dirtbag!"

"How sure are you?" I asked.

"I'm positive. Hurry up," she said. "He's going to get away."

"I don't know what to do. I can't find a spot to park the car."

"Let me out and I'll follow him while you find a place to park this jalopy."

"That's too dangerous," I said.

"We don't have any other options." She'd already opened the car door.

"Okay, but turn that giant old-lady phone of yours on, so I can find you."

She nodded and hopped out of the car. I didn't have a good feeling about this, but I didn't have any other options. After circling around another time, I finally found a spot and whipped my car in.

I hurried across the parking lot and finally caught up with Dorothy. She'd done a good job of keeping up with him, but he was steadily putting distance between us. It was hard trying to keep up with the pace of this guy. He was a fast walker, and our shorter legs were having a hard time keeping up.

"I wish he would slow down. Where's the fire?" Dorothy said.

We rounded the corner and spotted him walking down the sidewalk.

"Are you okay?" I asked.

She nodded. "Oh yeah, I'm as fit as a twenty-year-old. Let's see where he's headed," she said, motioning for us to continue with a tilt of her head.

We hurried around a couple people and kept him in sight. He turned down the sidewalk and walked onto the dock. So Dorothy and I continued down to the dock too. We paused when we got to the edge. He was talking with a man beside a boat. Of course, Dorothy and I tried to act casual so that they wouldn't look over and notice us watching him. I knew he would recognize us right away, but he'd probably think we'd followed him because of the parking space. The men talked, and I wondered what their conversation was about. After a couple seconds they started walking, so we followed them. To my surprise they stepped up to the bench where Justin was sitting. He was still there and apparently had been waiting for the men. Megan was there too now. Dorothy and I stepped over to a bench, hoping that they didn't spot us.

"Whose idea was it to kidnap the guy anyway?" the man who we'd followed asked Justin.

Justin looked at Megan, but I couldn't hear what he said.

"What are the odds that his granddaughter would be murdered at the very time we'd planned to kidnap him?" the guy with the boat said.

So the kidnapping hadn't been related to Kristin's death at all.

"Do you think someone will pay ransom?" the guy we'd followed asked Justin.

Justin shook his head, and my stomach turned. So they'd kidnapped him, and now they had no one to pay the ransom. What would happen to Mr. Grant? Justin handed the men the Grant Jewelers bag, and then they walked away. When Megan and Justin stood up from the bench, Dorothy and I were hot on their trail.

"We have to follow them," Dorothy whispered.

"I plan on doing just that," I said.

Chapter Forty-One

Justin and Megan picked up Annie. I had to admit I hadn't seen that one coming. We followed them back to the marina, where they met up with the man in the black Porsche. Justin and Megan had dropped her off beside what I assumed was Annie's car. Once Annie finished talking to the man, we followed her down the sidewalk.

"What do you think she's up to?" Dorothy asked.

"I don't know how involved she is with this, but the fact that she's talking to the man who was in Mr. Grant's house doesn't look good for her. We'll follow her, if possible," I said as we walked across the parking lot.

Annie paused once and looked back. Dorothy and I rushed over and crouched behind a car to block her view.

"Do you think she saw us?" Dorothy asked.

"I don't think so," I whispered, as if Annie could hear me.

Finally, Annie turned around and continued toward her car. We'd have to be more careful, so we didn't get caught.

"If she knew we were following her, she would freak out," I said.

"She probably would freak out over a lot of things," Dorothy said.

We followed Annie out of the parking lot and across town. I was getting better at following people, because this time I had no problem keeping up with her.

"Where is she going?" Dorothy asked as Annie turned into a parking lot.

There was a small building that looked like it had several separate offices inside. Annie parked in front of the doors, so I pulled into a space at the back of the parking lot. I had a great view of her, though. I'd be able to watch every move she made. Annie sat in the car and talked on her phone for a minute, and I began to wonder if she knew Dorothy and I were watching her. Maybe that was why she wasn't getting out of the car.

Finally, she climbed out from behind the wheel. She flung her purse strap over her shoulder and marched up to one of the doors. Annie took a key out and shoved it into the lock. She looked back, then stepped through the open door.

"This is our chance. Let's go see what she's doing," Dorothy said.

We made our way across the parking lot, weaving through the parked cars. I kept glancing over my shoulder because, at this point, I didn't know what to expect. We reached the building and noticed there was a window next to the door. I knew it was in the office that Annie had gone in. Would we see anything when we looked in? I knew Dorothy was anxious to find Mr. Grant, and I hoped that we found him soon.

Dorothy and I stepped over to the window. I leaned close and peered in. A gasp escaped my lips when I saw Mr. Grant inside the room. He looked as if his hands were tied behind his back.

"What is it?" Dorothy asked as she leaned close. I knew she wouldn't be happy when she saw him. "Oh, my heavens. What has she done to him?" Dorothy clutched her chest.

"I think she's holding him against his will."

Dorothy had been right all along: Annie was a bad person. Now I had to figure out how I was going to get Mr. Grant out of there. I couldn't just break in. There was no telling what Annie would do to him. She was obviously crazy.

I pulled out my cell phone.

"What are you doing?" Dorothy asked.

"I'm going to call Jake. He needs to get over here right away and arrest her."

Dorothy nodded. "Yeah, I hope he gives her the business."

When Jake answered, I told him where we were and what was going on. Of course, he didn't believe me at first. But seriously, would I make up something like a kidnapping? I knew it was crazy, but after the events of late he shouldn't have been too surprised.

I clicked off the phone and said, "He'll be here soon."

"What do we do in the meantime?" Dorothy asked.

That was an excellent question. Unfortunately, I didn't have an answer. I'd better think of something quick. What if Annie did something to Mr. Grant before Jake got there?

Finally, I decided that I would call Annie's phone. She wouldn't know that I was standing right outside her door. I punched in her number.

Dorothy was staring at me with wide eyes. "I hope this works."

"Me too." I nodded.

"Maggie, what a surprise to hear from you," she said with a sweet voice, as if nothing were wrong.

"I followed you, Annie. I need to speak with you. I'm right outside, and I can't believe you didn't see me trying to get your attention," I said sweetly.

I hoped she wouldn't think anything was wrong.

"Oh," she said and then there was a huge pause. "I'm sorry I didn't see you. You said you followed me?"

"Yes, I'm beside your car. Can you come outside?"

At this point, I thought she was a little suspicious. But I knew she was also curious.

"Sure, I'll be right out," Annie said sweetly.

"What do we do now? What will we say to her when she comes outside? *If* she comes outside," Dorothy said.

I hadn't thought that far in advance. I'd just have to wing it. I hoped that something good came to mind.

"I'll figure out something," I said, trying to make Dorothy feel better.

Finally, the door opened, and Annie appeared. She looked at me, expressionless. I smiled, trying to act as if nothing were wrong. I just had to keep her busy until the police arrived.

Chapter Forty-Two

"Hi, Annie," I said.

When I glanced over, I noticed Dorothy wasn't standing beside me. Where had she gone? That's when I spotted her going into the office. Oh no. I had to keep Annie from turning around and seeing Dorothy. Apparently, Dorothy was going to save Mr. Grant.

"What do you want to ask me?" Annie asked.

I stared at her for a moment, trying to think of something good to say. "Do you know if Mr. Grant had any friends that he may have left with?"

She scowled as if she couldn't believe that was what I had bothered her for. She shook her head and ran her hand through her hair. "No, I just can't think of anyone that he would have left with, but maybe he decided he needed a vacation," she said causally.

I stared for a moment. "Yeah, that's possible."

Annie knew that wasn't the case, and the way she was staring at me let me know that she knew that I knew too.

She looked over her shoulder, and I worried that she would catch Dorothy with Mr. Grant. What was going on inside that room anyway? Annie looked at me again. "I don't know exactly why you're here," she said.

I knew she was growing extremely frustrated with me. "I told you why. I wanted to talk with you."

Annie scowled, and I knew that the charade was over. I looked at the door, and she followed my gaze. She knew at that point that I knew who was inside that office. Just as she was about to turn around and run back into the office, Jake pulled up.

He jumped out with his gun pointed at her. "Don't move," he ordered.

Annie lifted her hands into the air but didn't say a word.

Jake rushed over and handcuffed Annie. "Where's Dorothy?" he asked.

I stepped around Annie and moved toward the door. "She's in the office with Mr. Grant, but I want to make sure she's okay. I don't know if anyone else was in that building when she went in."

Jake motioned for me to stay back. Another police officer stood with Annie.

When we stepped close to the door, Dorothy and Mr. Grant emerged from the room.

"Dorothy, are you okay?" I asked.

She smiled. "Everything is just fine. I had a hard time getting the rope off Mr. Grant."

"Thank you again, Dorothy." He smiled gratefully. Mr. Grant looked tired but was otherwise in good condition. Dorothy had actually saved Mr. Grant.

Just when I thought things had finally settled down, the man who had been at Mr. Grant's home showed up. He was the one who had cut us off and had stolen our parking spot, and now he was here.

He casually climbed out of his car and locked its doors. I guessed he was afraid someone would steal it, because he obviously hadn't seen the police standing there. He walked up to Annie's car. That was when he glanced up and noticed us looking at him. I don't know how he'd missed the police cars.

The man stared at us in his panicked state. He looked like an animal ready to run. I knew he was going to take off soon. He froze on the spot; then in one swift motion, he turned around and ran off. He sprinted across the parking lot, with the police chasing closely behind him. It wasn't long until they'd tackled him. He was down on the ground and in handcuffs within seconds. The officers pulled him up from the concrete and then dragged him back over to where we stood.

Mr. Grant and Dorothy stood next to each other. They were whispering and looking into each other's eyes. He grinned, and I knew he was so grateful that Dorothy had saved him. By the smile on Dorothy's face, I knew it made her feel equally good that she had been there for him. I didn't know what would become of their relationship, but I thought they made a great couple. I hoped they would soon be an item.

"Please put her in the back of the cruiser." Jake gestured toward Annie.

Annie had been the mastermind behind this failed kidnapping attempt. She'd wanted to get a ransom for Mr. Grant. Apparently, the police had been close to discovering her scheme, but not quickly enough. They had to move a lot faster if they wanted to keep up with Dorothy and Maggie.

Maggie Thomas, P.I. was on the case and the police would just have to catch up to me. I didn't think Jake wanted to hear that, though.

I prayed that when I went to the office today the craziness would be over. Dorothy was already there when I stepped in the door. She even had a coffee and pastry waiting for me.

"You look awfully bright and cheery this morning after what happened last night," I said.

Dorothy smiled and waved her hand through the air. "It's a beautiful day to be alive."

I was surprised. That was definitely not like her. Something was going on and I knew she was up to something.

"What's going on, Dorothy? What do you want?"

She smiled. "Oh, nothing. By the way, Mr. Grant called this morning, and he wants to stop by and thank you."

I smiled. "Now I know why you're smiling."

She blushed. "Don't be silly. That has nothing to do with it."

"Whatever you say, but you have the hots for Mr. Grant. I bet I'm not the reason why he wants to come by here today."

She couldn't hold back the smile. "He is a very nice man."

"And not bad-looking either, huh?" I asked.

She beamed again. "So what about Jake? That was one hot kiss he laid on you."

I shrugged, trying to act nonchalant. "Oh, that reminds me." I glanced at my watch. "I'm supposed to meet him. We're going for a quick walk along the beach. You don't mind, do you? I'm sure you can keep Mr. Grant company until I get back." I winked.

Dorothy waved her hand and pushed to her feet. "I don't mind at all, dear, not at all. As a matter of fact, I got you something." Dorothy walked over to me and pulled something out of her pocket. She opened the top on the lip gloss and then proceeded to smear it on my lips. She reached up and fluffed my hair out. "Now, go and have a good time." She winked.

I stared at her for a second, then shook my head and walked out the door.

I definitely had a spring in my step. The sun shone down, and a warm breeze drifted from the nearby water. With my coffee in hand, I was headed to meet up with Jake. His kiss had been on my mind a lot. When I reached the beach access where Jake and I were supposed to meet, I stopped in my tracks. Police tape was draped across the area. What was happening?

I stepped closer for a better look and spotted an officer. "Excuse me, what happened? Can I get to the beach from here?"

Before he answered, someone grabbed my arm and I spun around.

Jake stood behind me. "Maggie, I need to talk with you."

"What happened? Why is there police tape around the beach access?" I asked.

He stared for a beat, and then said, "There was another murder. I hate to ask this, but where were you last night around eleven?"

Acknowledgments

To my son, who brings me joy every single day. To my mother, who introduced me to the love of books. To my husband, who encourages me and always has faith in me. A huge thank-you to Anh Schluep for loving Maggie and Dorothy as much as I do. And to the readers who make writing fun.

3755

About the Author

Rose Pressey is a *USA Today*, Amazon, and Barnes & Noble Top 100 bestselling author. She enjoys writing quirky and fun novels with a paranormal twist. The paranormal has always captured her interest. The thought of finding answers to the unexplained fascinates her.

When she's not writing about werewolves, vampires, and every other supernatural creature, she loves eating cupcakes with sprinkles, reading, spending time with family, and listening to oldies from the fifties.

Rose suffers from psoriatic arthritis and has knee replacements. She might just set the world record for joint replacements. She's soon having her hips replaced.

Rose lives in the beautiful commonwealth of Kentucky with her husband, son, and three sassy Chihuahuas.

Visit her online at:
http: //www.rosepressey.com
http: //www.facebook.com/rosepressey
http: //www.twitter.com/rosepressey

Rose loves to hear from readers. You can email her at rose@rosepressey.com.

If you're interested in receiving information when a new Rose Pressey book is released, you can sign up for her newsletter at www.rosepressey.com. Join her on Facebook for lots of fun and prizes.

FROM THE PAGES OF *PETER PAN*

All children, except one, grow up. (page 7)

"You see, children know such a lot now, they soon don't believe in fairies, and every time a child says, 'I don't believe in fairies,' there is a fairy somewhere that falls down dead." (page 29)

"Wake up," she cried, "Peter Pan has come and he is to teach us to fly." (page 32)

In the midst of them, the blackest and largest jewel in that dark setting, reclined James Hook, or as he wrote himself, Jas. Hook, of whom it is said he was the only man that the Sea-Cook feared. He lay at his ease in a rough chariot drawn and propelled by his men, and instead of a right hand he had the iron hook with which ever and anon he encouraged them to increase their pace. (page 52)

"I want their captain, Peter Pan. 'Twas he cut off my arm." He brandished the hook threateningly. "I've waited long to shake his hand with this. Oh, I'll tear him!" (page 56)

Then all went on their knees, and holding out their arms cried, "O Wendy lady, be our mother." (page 68)

"If you believe," he shouted to them, "clap your hands; don't let Tink die." (page 118)

Then he sought to close and give the quietus with his iron hook, which all this time had been pawing the air; but Peter doubled under it and, lunging fiercely, pierced him in the ribs. At sight of his own blood, whose peculiar colour, you remember, was offensive to him, the sword fell from Hook's hand, and he was at Peter's mercy. (page 135)

"The last thing he ever said to me was, 'Just always be waiting for me, and then some night you will hear me crowing.'" (page 154)

PETER FLEW IN

PETER PAN

J. M. BARRIE

With an Introduction and Notes
by Amy Billone

Illustrated by F. D. Bedford

GEORGE STADE
CONSULTING EDITORIAL DIRECTOR

BARNES & NOBLE CLASSICS
NEW YORK

BARNES & NOBLE CLASSICS
NEW YORK

Published by Barnes & Noble Books
122 Fifth Avenue
New York, NY 10011

www.barnesandnoble.com/classics

Peter Pan was first published as *Peter and Wendy* in 1911.

Published in 2005 by Barnes & Noble Classics with new Introduction, Notes, Biography, Chronology, Inspired By, Comments & Questions, and For Further Reading.

Peter Pan
ISBN 978-1-59308-213-0
LC Control Number 2005923984

Produced and published in conjunction with:
Fine Creative Media, Inc.
322 Eighth Avenue
New York, NY 10001

Michael J. Fine, President & Publisher

Printed in the United States of America

QM

15 17 19 20 18 16 14

J. M. BARRIE

James Matthew Barrie was born on May 9, 1860, in Kirriemuir, Scotland, the ninth child and third and youngest son of David Barrie, a handloom weaver, and Margaret Ogilvy, who, following Scottish tradition, kept her maiden name among friends and family. In January 1867, when Barrie was six years old, his older brother David died in a skating accident on the eve of his fourteenth birthday, an event that haunted Barrie for the rest of his life.

Barrie's love of the theater bloomed at Dumfries Academy, which he attended for five years, beginning at age thirteen. He earned his master of arts degree in English literature from Edinburgh University in 1882. The next year he became leader-writer and sub-editor for the *Nottingham Journal*. In 1885 he moved to London, where he worked as a free-lance journalist; he self-published his first novel, *Better Dead*, two years later. With his second book, a collection of sketches titled *Auld Licht Idylls* (1888), he achieved recognition as a writer, and his reputation increased with the publication the same year of the novel *When a Man's Single*. In 1889 his *A Window in Thrums* appeared, and in 1891 he published the popular novel *The Little Minister*.

Barrie had his first commercial theatrical success with *Walker, London* (1892). Two years later he married Mary Ansell, an actress who had performed one of the play's leading roles. In 1896 two of Barrie's works were published: the novel *Sentimental Tommy* (its sequel, *Tommy and Grizel*, appeared in 1900), and *Margaret Ogilvy*, a memoir of his mother. Barrie first met George and Sylvia Llewelyn Davies and their sons George and Jack in 1897. The author's play-acting with the boys was the principal source of material for his play *Peter Pan; or, The Boy Who Would Not Grow Up*.

Barrie's 1902 novel *The Little White Bird* contains an early version of *Peter Pan* and describes Peter's life as a baby. Over the course of the next nine years, Barrie refined *Peter Pan* in various stage productions and publications. The play version of the story opened at the Duke of York's Theatre on December 27, 1904. Two years later, Barrie extracted six chapters from *The Little White Bird* that he published as *Peter Pan in Kensington Gardens*, and in 1911 he published the novel *Peter and Wendy*; longer than *Peter Pan in Kensington Gardens*, this book is now known simply as *Peter Pan*.

Barrie and his wife divorced in 1909. He never remarried, but the next year he acquired a family when Sylvia, the mother of the Llewelyn Davies boys, died (her husband had died in 1907) and Barrie adopted her sons (there were now five boys). In 1915 George, the oldest boy, was killed in World War I during an advance on the Germans. The same year Charles Frohman, Barrie's producer, went down on the passenger ship the *Lusitania* when a German torpedo hit it. Nevertheless, the next six years were fairly productive for Barrie as a writer and happy for him as a father, until Michael, the fourth of the brothers, drowned while swimming in a millpond with a friend. Barrie never recovered from Michael's death, which effectively brought his creative output to a halt.

In addition to the play *Peter Pan*, Barrie had a string of hits in the theater: the theatrical version of *The Little Minister* (1897), *Quality Street* and *The Admirable Crichton* (both 1902), and *What Every Woman Knows* (1908). *A Kiss for Cinderella* opened in 1916 and was often revived in London around Christmastime. Two fantasy plays followed: In *Dear Brutus* (1917), a group of people encounter their alternate destinies when they enter a magic forest, and in *Mary Rose* (1920), a woman dies young and returns to her family years later as a ghost, unable to recognize her now aged son. Barrie's last play, *The Boy David*, opened in 1936 and was not successful. On June 19, 1937, J. M. Barrie died. He was buried with his family in Kirriemuir cemetery.

TABLE OF CONTENTS

THE WORLD OF J. M. BARRIE AND *PETER PAN*

1860 James Matthew Barrie is born on May 9 in Kirriemuir, Scotland. The third son of seven surviving children, James shares two rooms with his entire family. The cottage also houses the handlooming tools with which his father, David, earns a living. The countryside surrounding Kirriemuir features breathtaking glens and stark mountains, and lush vegetation, lochs, and castles abound; the setting will influence Barrie's later writings.

1865 Lewis Carroll's *Alice's Adventures in Wonderland* is published.

1867 Barrie's brother David is killed in a skating accident. Margaret Ogilvy, Barrie's mother, never recovers from the loss of her second son, and the death will haunt James for the rest of his life.

1868 James leaves home to live with his brother Alexander and attend Glasgow Academy, where Alexander teaches classics.

1871 When Alexander leaves Glasgow, James moves with the rest of the family to the town of Forfar, where he enrolls in Forfar Academy. Lewis Carroll's *Through the Looking Glass and What Alice Found There* is published.

1872 George Eliot's *Middlemarch* is published.

1873 James again moves in with his brother to attend Dumfries Academy in Dumfries, in southwestern Scotland; Alexander is the inspector of schools for the district. James will study at the academy for five years. Jules Verne's *Around the World in Eighty Days* is published.

1878 Barrie enters Edinburgh University, supported financially by Alexander, who lectures there. While a student he becomes a part-time professional journalist, reviewing literature for the *Edinburgh Courant* and music for the *Dumfries Herald*.

1879 Henrik Ibsen's *A Doll's House* premieres.

1882 Barrie receives his master of arts degree.

1883 He is selected as leader-writer and sub-editor for the *Nottingham Journal*. Every week he writes five leaders (opinion columns on political and other public affairs that average 1,200 words), signing them "Hippomenes" and "A Modern Peripatetic." Soon he is contributing book reviews, literary columns, stories, and even a one-act farce; he will stay with the paper for two years. Robert Louis Stevenson's *Treasure Island* is published.

1885 Back in Kirriemuir after losing his *Journal* job, Barrie writes and submits articles to London newspapers. When several are accepted, he moves to London to further his writing career.

1886 Robert Louis Stevenson publishes *The Strange Case of Dr. Jekyll and Mr. Hyde.*

1887 Barrie self-publishes his first novel, *Better Dead. A Study in Scarlet*, Arthur Conan Doyle's debut Sherlock Holmes story, is published.

1888 Barrie publishes *Auld Licht Idylls*, a collection of sketches that had appeared in London newspapers beginning in 1885. With this book he is recognized as a writer, and his reputation grows with the publication of the novel *When a Man's Single* at the end of the year. Jack the Ripper terrorizes London's East End.

1889 With the publication of the novel *A Window in Thrums*, Barrie's fame as a writer is firmly established.

1891 His play *Richard Savage*, written with H. B. Marriott Watson, is presented in a special charity matinee at the Criterion Theatre in London. Barrie also publishes the successful novel *The Little Minister*. On May 30 his one-act play *Ibsen's Ghost* (a humorous sequel to *Hedda Gabler*) opens and runs for twenty-seven performances. Barrie begins keeping extensive notebooks of his ideas for stories. Oscar Wilde's *The Picture of Dorian Gray* and Thomas Hardy's *Tess of the d'Urbervilles* are published.

1892 On February 25 Barrie's play *Walker, London* opens at Toole's

Theatre in London; it is Barrie's first commercial success in the theater. The cast includes Mary Ansell, his future wife.

1894 On June 25 Barrie's play *The Professor's Love Story* opens at the Comedy Theatre in London; it also opens in New York, the first of his plays to be produced there. On July 9 he marries Mary Ansell, but the marriage is unhappy from the start; Barrie proves to be an indifferent, perhaps impotent, husband. "Boys can't love" is his explanation. Rudyard Kipling's *The Jungle Book* is published.

1895 Barrie's unmarried sister, Jane Ann, dies on September 1; three days later his mother dies. H. G. Wells publishes *The Time Machine*.

1896 Barrie's doting memoir of his mother, *Margaret Ogilvy*, is published, revealing the intensity of his attachment to her and providing a record of her major, complex influence on his private and creative life. *Sentimental Tommy*, his semi-autobiographical novel about a child who role-plays to the point of losing his identity, is published. While visiting the United States, Barrie first meets Charles Frohman, who will later produce several of his theatrical ventures, including *Peter Pan; or, The Boy Who Would Not Grow Up*.

1897 Barrie meets the Llewelyn Davies family. The five sons of George and Sylvia Llewelyn Davies will be the inspiration for *Peter Pan*. The theatrical version of Barrie's novel *The Little Minister* premieres in New York on September 27 and opens in London shortly after. A much-needed hit for Barrie, it is revived several times and tours widely. Bram Stoker's *Dracula* is published.

1900 Barrie publishes his novel *Tommy and Grizel* (a sequel to *Sentimental Tommy*), in which his hero attempts to embrace reality but fails to return the love of Grizel, whose life he destroys—a direct reflection of Barrie's marital unhappiness. Barrie's play *The Wedding Guest* premieres at the Garrick Theatre in London on September 27. Sigmund Freud's *The Interpretation of Dreams* is published.

1901 Queen Victoria dies.

1902 Barrie publishes his novel *The Little White Bird*, which contains an early version of *Peter Pan*. His play *Quality Street* opens at the Vaudeville Theatre in London on September 17, after premiering in New York. *The Admirable Crichton*, a play that probes the validity of the British class structure, is performed at the Duke of York's Theatre in London on November 4. A. E. W. Mason's *The Four Feathers* and Joseph Conrad's *Heart of Darkness* are published.

1903 Barrie's play *Little Mary* is performed at the Wyndham's Theatre in London on September 24.

1904 *Peter Pan* debuts at the Duke of York's Theatre on December 27; its enormous success brings Barrie considerable wealth and fame.

1905 *Alice Sit-By-the-Fire* opens at the Duke of York's Theatre. Written as a fallback for producer Frohman in case *Peter Pan* had flopped, it is not nearly as popular. George Bernard Shaw's *Major Barbara* debuts.

1906 Barrie publishes *Peter Pan in Kensington Gardens*—six self-contained chapters about Peter Pan as a baby, reproduced from his 1902 novel *The Little White Bird*. To prevent children from thinking they need only wish and jump out the window in order to fly, Barrie adds fairy dust to the *Peter Pan* story as the necessary ingredient for becoming airborne.

1907 Arthur Llewelyn Davies dies of cancer of the jaw after a year of debilitating illness. Barrie begins supporting Arthur's widow, Sylvia, and her children.

1908 Barrie's play *What Every Woman Knows*, based on the idea that women are intellectually superior to men, opens at the Duke of York's Theatre on December 19. An epilogue to *Peter Pan*, called "When Wendy Grew Up: An Afterthought," is added to the final show of the season, though it will not be performed again in Barrie's lifetime; now recognized as an integral part of the *Peter Pan* story, it provokes such applause that Barrie takes a rare curtain call. Barrie campaigns against theatrical censorship. Friendships with such writers as George Bernard Shaw and John Galsworthy fill his social calendar. He becomes a founding member of the Dramatist's Club in London. Kenneth Grahame's *The Wind in the Willows* is published.

1909 Mary divorces Barrie to be with her lover, writer Gilbert

Cannan. Barrie will never remarry. Edinburgh University awards him an honorary degree. On April 6 Robert E. Peary reaches the North Pole.

1910 Sylvia Llewelyn Davies dies of cancer. Barrie adopts her children—the youngest, Nico, is seven years old and the oldest, George, is seventeen. E. M. Forster's *Howards End* is published.

1911 Barrie publishes the novel *Peter and Wendy*, which elaborates the story about the baby Peter Pan in *Peter Pan in Kensington Gardens*; the novel is now known as *Peter Pan*.

1912 The Titanic hits an iceberg and sinks on its maiden voyage, killing 1,500 people.

1913 Barrie is made a baronet. His plays *The Adored One* and *The Will* open as a double bill on September 4 at the Duke of York's Theatre.

1914 World War I begins. Barrie travels to the United States. James Joyce's *Dubliners* is published. Shaw's *Pygmalion* premieres in London.

1915 George Llewelyn Davies, the family's oldest son, is killed in battle on the Western Front in Flanders. Charles Frohman, Barrie's patron and producer, is one of 1,201 deaths on the *Lusitania*, the British passenger liner torpedoed by a German submarine. Ford Madox Ford's *The Good Soldier* is published.

1916 Barrie's play *A Kiss for Cinderella* opens on March 16 at the Wyndham's Theatre. The film *The Real Thing at Last*, his parody of American movies using *Macbeth* as a vehicle, opens. The English translation of C. G. Jung's *Psychology of the Unconscious* (which appeared in German in 1912) is published.

1917 *Dear Brutus*, Barrie's play about a group of characters who enter a magic wood and are given the chance to turn back time and reshape their lives, debuts on October 17 at the Wyndham's Theatre. After one of the greatest adventures of all time, Ernest Shackleton's expedition to Antarctica is rescued. T. S. Eliot's *Prufrock and Other Observations* is published.

1919 Barrie becomes rector of St. Andrews University.

1920 His play *Mary Rose* is first performed on April 22 at the

Haymarket Theatre in London. The play, which deals with aging, youth, death, and memory, enjoys enormous popularity among an audience of theatergoers who are mourning a generation largely wiped out by World War I.

1921 Barrie's favorite adopted son, Michael, drowns in a millpond at Oxford; his death may be a suicide. *Shall We Join the Ladies?* opens on May 27 in celebration of the opening of the Royal Academy of Dramatic Art.

1922 Barrie is awarded the Order of Merit. Eliot's *The Waste Land* and Joyce's *Ulysses* are published.

1924 A silent film of *Peter Pan* appears; Barrie has written a scenario for a film, but his version is not used.

1927 Virginia Woolf's *To the Lighthouse* is published. Charles Lindbergh flies across the Atlantic Ocean alone.

1928 *Peter Pan* is published as a single volume and in *The Plays of J. M. Barrie*; it carries Barrie's dedication to the five Davies boys. Evelyn Waugh's *Decline and Fall* is published.

1929 Barrie gives all rights to and royalties from *Peter Pan* to the Great Ormond Street Hospital for Sick Children. Robert Graves's *Goodbye to All That* is published.

1930 Barrie receives an honorary degree from Cambridge University and is appointed chancellor of Edinburgh University. W. H. Auden's *Poems* is published.

1936 *The Boy David*, Barrie's last dramatic work and his only play to premiere in his native Scotland, opens at the King's Theatre in Edinburgh on November 21 and in London three weeks later. The piece reflects aspects of his own life, including the untimely death of his brother David; it is not a success.

1937 On June 19 J. M. Barrie dies. He is buried beside his family in Kirriemuir cemetery.

INTRODUCTION

At six years old, James Matthew Barrie believed he was his mother's last hope. Inconsolable after the sudden death of her son David, who had fractured his skull in a skating accident, Barrie's mother fell ill with grief. In his memoir about his mother, *Margaret Ogilvy*, Barrie recalls how his sister Jane Ann came to him "with a very anxious face and wringing her hands" and told him to go quickly to his mother "and say to her that she still had another boy" (Barrie, *Margaret Ogilvy*, see p. 12; see "For Further Reading"). Barrie went that day and for many days afterward to his mother's bed, where, through jokes and antics, he strove to make her laugh. He even kept a record of her laughs on a piece of paper. The first time he slipped the laugh chart into her doctor's hand, it showed that his mother had laughed five times. When the doctor saw the chart, he laughed so hard that the young Barrie exclaimed, "I wish that was one of hers!" (p. 14). The doctor took sympathy on him and suggested he show the chart to his mother, at which point she would laugh again and the five laughs would increase to six. Barrie writes, "I did as he bade me, and not only did she laugh then but again when I put the laugh down, so that though it was really one laugh with a tear in the middle I counted it as two" (p. 15).

Barrie's sister said that in addition to making his mother laugh he needed to encourage her to talk about her dead son. While Barrie couldn't see how this would make her "the merry mother she used to be" (p. 15), he was advised that if he could not do it, "nobody could," which made him "eager to begin." At first, he often was jealous of his mother's "fond memories" and would interrupt them with the cry "Do you mind nothing about me?" But this resentment did not last. Instead, Barrie countered his jealousy by trying to become so like his dead brother that his mother would not see the difference. He asked Margaret many artful questions about David, and he practiced imitating him in secret. For example, his mother told him that David had "such a cheery way of whistling . . . with his legs apart and his hands in the pockets of his knickerbockers" (p. 16) and that it always brightened her workday. One day, after Barrie had learned his brother's whistle (which took much practice), he disguised himself in a suit of David's dark gray clothes and slipped into his mother's room. With his legs stretched wide apart, and his hands plunged deep into his knickerbockers, he began to whistle.

No matter what Barrie's successes were in coaxing his mother to laugh, he could not make her "forget the bit of her that was dead" (p. 19). Often she fell asleep speaking to David. Even while she slept, her lips moved and she smiled as if the dead boy had come back to her. Sometimes when she woke, he vanished so suddenly that she would rise bewildered, saying slowly, "My David's dead!" Or perhaps David "remained long enough to whisper why he must leave her now, and then she lay silent with filmy eyes." Just as his mother was perpetually haunted by her dead son, Barrie himself became preoccupied by a ghost child who kept returning to him from the other side of the grave. Most famously, this ghost appears in the shape of Peter Pan—a boy who materializes from the world of children's dreams.

The combination of laughter and tears, or the effort to make his audience laugh in the face of tragedy, distinguishes all of J. M. Barrie's writing. We encounter the most flawless example of this mixture of humor and heartbreak in *Peter Pan*—the story of a never-aging boy who takes other children on fantastic adventures and is eventually abandoned by them. "All Barrie's life," wrote Roger Lancelyn Green, "led up to the creation of Peter Pan, and everything that he had written so far contained hints or foreshadowings of what was to come" (*J. M. Barrie*, p. 34).

The idea behind *Peter Pan* first appeared in *Tommy and Grizel*, a novel that Barrie published in 1900 as a sequel to *Sentimental Tommy*, which had come out in 1896. In *Tommy and Grizel*, the main character, Tommy, contemplates writing a story about a boy who hates the idea of growing up. Like the character in his story, Tommy cannot make the passage from childhood to adulthood; he is doomed to love his wife, Grizel, in exactly the same way that he loves his sister Elspeth. Peter Pan first appears by name in a strange novel, *The Little White Bird*, that Barrie published in 1902. Written for adults, the book is narrated by Captain W——, a middle-aged bachelor and member of the Junior Old Fogies' Club. Like Barrie, he has a St. Bernard dog named Porthos. As the narrative develops, Captain W—— invents and then kills off a son in order to become close to a little boy named David. Six chapters of the book consist of a story that the Captain and David create together: the tale of Peter Pan's birth and his escapades with the birds and fairies in Kensington Gardens. Peter is much younger in this novel than in later stories—in spirit, he is only one week old. In 1906 Barrie extracted the six chapters about Peter, and they were published, accompanied by Arthur Rackham's illustrations, under the title *Peter Pan in Kensington Gardens*.

Appearing the same year as *The Little White Bird*, Barrie's play *The Admirable Crichton* opened in 1902. Drama scholar Harry Geduld calls *The Admirable Crichton* Barrie's "comedic masterpiece" (*Sir James Barrie*, p. 120). In it, a wealthy family and its servants are stranded on a "wrecked island," where the rules of power reverse, only to restore themselves completely when the group is rescued at the end. *The Admirable Crichton* resembles *Peter Pan* in that it begins realistically, converts into a fantasy with the shipwreck, and returns to normalcy in the concluding scenes. On the island the butler (Crichton) becomes the group's leader, and Lady Mary, the aristocratic daughter of his employer, falls passionately in love with him. Two years later, she is about to marry him—and then the marooned group is discovered. In act 4, Lady Mary loses all interest in Crichton when the power relations reverse a second time. While the play is a comedy, it is also poignant, for the natural and truthful love that the characters feel on the island proves impossible to sustain in real life.

Written just before *Peter Pan*, Barrie's play *Little Mary* was first performed in 1903. *Little Mary* is the story of a girl named Moira (Wendy's full name in *Peter Pan* is Wendy Moira Angela Darling) who is able to cure illnesses with the aid of an invisible medium called Little Mary. Moira becomes known throughout society as the Stormy Petrel, the name of a species of seabird that is used for someone who appears at the onset of trouble. The play is quite entertaining until Moira's strategy is at last revealed at the end of the final act—she has simply changed her patients' diets, for her grandfather had proved that we are what we eat. (Such a twist was fitting in that "Little Mary" was Moira's pet name for "stomach.") Because of the play's unfortunate climax, *Little Mary* was mocked by reviewers and satirized in comic strips, although it ran for 207 performances. It may have done better if, like *Peter Pan*, it had permitted the existence of a certain degree of magic. It was not until the following year that Barrie more than made up for *Little Mary* with *Peter Pan; or, The Boy Who Would Not Grow Up*, which was first performed at the Duke of York's Theatre in 1904.

The story of Peter Pan developed in the company of the five sons of Arthur and Sylvia Llewelyn Davies: George, Jack, Peter, Michael, and Nicholas (Nico). Barrie first met this family in 1897. At the time, he was married to Mary Ansell, an actress who had played one of the girls in his 1892 play *Walker, London*. Their marriage of three years was an unhappy one, troubled by Barrie's likely impotence and his consequent lack of interest in sex. Although both adored children, the marriage remained childless. One day while walking his dog, Barrie met four-year-old George Llewelyn Davies and George's younger brother Jack. George and Jack took an interest in Barrie's dog, and Barrie began meeting the children every day in Kensington Gardens.

Barrie's involvement with the family grew intimate—he began to visit the Davies home for tea and for dinner. After he met their baby brother, Peter, Barrie began to weave Peter's name into the stories he made up and performed for George and Jack. In one of these stories, all babies are birds before they turn into human beings; Peter was a child who had not completely stopped being a bird and therefore could still fly. Peter Llewelyn Davies's failure to demonstrate his flying ability compelled Barrie to invent a fictional version of him—Peter Pan.

As the Davies boys grew older, Barrie converted his early tales about Peter, in which Peter was only one week old and played with the birds and fairies in Kensington Gardens, into stories about pirates and fantasy islands. Michael Llewelyn Davies was born in 1900—the first child in the family whom Barrie knew from birth.

In 1901 the Davies family summered in Surrey a short distance away from the house on the Black Lake that the Barries had purchased the previous year. Barrie played with the boys all that summer, and their fantasy games supplied material for a book called *The Boy Castaways of Black Lake Island* (another early version of *Peter Pan*). The book—supposedly written by four-year-old Peter Llewelyn Davies (even though it was purportedly "published" by J. M. Barrie)—consisted of a preface and thirty-six captioned photographs. Barrie put together two copies of the manuscript, one of which he gave to Arthur Llewelyn Davies, who promptly lost it. At Christmas that same year, a visit to the theater with the Davies boys to see *Bluebell in Fairyland* gave Barrie the idea that he might write his own play for children.

On November 23, 1903, the day before the birth of Nicholas Llewelyn Davies, Barrie began to work seriously on the play that would later become *Peter Pan*. At first, it was simply called "Anon. A Play." Barrie finished the first draft of the Peter Pan play on March 1, 1904, but he was worried that his American producer, Charles Frohman, would not like it. *Peter Pan* was an incredibly expensive show to put on, requiring massive sets and a cast of more than fifty, including a dog, a fairy, a crocodile, an eagle, wolves, pirates, and redskins, and at least four cast members would be required to fly. It was also unclear what sort of audience Barrie had in mind for the play—it seemed to be oriented to children, but the dialogue was quite sophisticated. The first version of the play combined harlequins and columbines (from the old pantomime tradition) with pirates and redskins, and it curiously blended outrageous farce with grave sentimentality. Barrie first showed his play to Beerbohm Tree, one of the most famous actors and directors of the period. Tree's intricate and luxurious productions at His Majesty's Theatre had won him a substantial reputation for excessiveness, and Barrie thought he might be willing to put on *Peter Pan* if Frohman rejected it. However, Tree did not at all approve of the play; he wrote the following assessment and sent it to Frohman:

> Barrie has gone out of his mind. . . . I am sorry to say it, but you ought to know it. He's just read me a play. He is going to read it to you, so I am warning you. I know I have not gone woozy in my mind,

because I have tested myself since hearing the play; but Barrie must be mad (quoted in *Maude Adams: An Intimate Portrait*, p. 90).

Tree's reaction intimidated Barrie, who prepared another, much more realistic drama, *Alice Sit-by-the-Fire*, hoping it would give him negotiating power. When he met with Frohman in April 1904, Barrie gave him two works—*Peter Pan*, which he had retitled *The Great White Father*, and *Alice Sit-by-the-Fire*. He told Frohman he was sure the former would not be a commercial success, but it was a dream-child of his, and he was so eager to see it on stage that he would provide a second play to make up for the losses the first would incur. While Frohman thought *Alice Sit-by-the-Fire* was rather entertaining, he loved everything about *The Great White Father* (except for the title). Barrie had assumed Peter Pan would be played by a boy. But Frohman suggested that Peter should be played by American actress Maude Adams, who at the time was thirty-three years old. After all, Peter Pan was the star role. If Peter were to be played by a boy, the ages of the Lost Boys would have to be scaled down, and in England actors under fourteen years old could not perform after 9 P.M. Even though Maude Adams was not available until the following summer, Frohman was so anxious to see the play produced that he directed his London manager, William Lestocq, to go ahead at once with a West End production that would open in time for Christmas.

Once rehearsals for *Peter Pan* began at the Duke of York's in late October 1904, an aura of secrecy began to surround the play. Few cast members knew the play's title or story—most were given only those pages pertinent to their parts. Frohman's decision to have Maude Adams play Peter in America meant that a woman should also fill the role in the London production. Thirty-seven-year-old Nina Boucicault seemed a suitable choice—she had just played Moira in *Little Mary*, and her brother Dion was directing *Peter Pan*. For the part of Wendy, Barrie chose Hilda Trevelyan (who had replaced Nina Boucicault as Moira in a touring production of *Little Mary*). And he hired George Kirby's Flying Ballet Company to devise the flying apparatus. Kirby invented a revolutionary new harness to allow for difficult flight movements, requiring extraordinary skill on the part of the actors, who had to endure an exhausting two weeks of training. The coat of Barrie's Newfoundland dog Luath (a replacement for his Saint Bernard, Porthos) was reproduced for the actor playing Nana, and the Davies boys' clothes were duplicated for those of the Darling children and the Lost Boys.

The night before the play was to open, an automatic lift broke down, ruining much of the scenery. Consequently, the opening had to be postponed from December 22 to December 27. Because of other problems, Barrie had to cut the final twenty-two pages of the script; he rewrote what was at that point the fifth modified conclusion. By opening night, everyone expected a minor catastrophe. When Peter endeavors to save Tinker Bell's life, he shouts to the audience, "Do you believe in fairies? If you believe, wave your handkerchiefs and clap your hands!" Because Barrie was convinced that the play would be a disaster and that this line would be greeted with silence from the stylish adult audience, he had arranged with the musical director to have the orchestra put down their instruments and clap. As it turned out, when Nina Boucicault asked if anyone believed in fairies, the audience applauded so enthusiastically that she burst into tears. The first night ended with many curtain calls and rave reviews. Even Beerbohm Tree's half-brother, Max Beerbohm, complimented Barrie in the *Saturday Review*: "Mr. Barrie is not that rare creature, a man of genius. He is something even more rare—a child who, by some divine grace, can express through an artistic medium the childishness that is in him" (quoted in Birkin, *J. M. Barrie and the Lost Boys*, pp. 117–118).

In its stage history, *Peter Pan* displays a good deal of gender fluidity. Theatrical cross-dressing originates in the traditions of pantomime, where gender swapping is essential—actresses typically portray the leading young male heroes in these shows, and men often play the parts of women. Traditionally, in *Peter Pan* the same actor would play both Mr. Darling and Captain Hook, although originally Barrie asked that Hook be played by a woman—the same woman, in fact, who played Mrs. Darling. And, of course, the show has a long history of casting women in the role of Peter. As described above, Nina Boucicault created the title role in London, and Maude Adams was Peter in New York. With rare exceptions, women would continue to act the part of Peter for almost fifty years. In the 1954 musical production of the play (which was later filmed for television and broadcast seven times between 1955 and 1973), Mary Martin played Peter. Two major Broadway revivals starred Sandy Duncan, in the late 1970s, and gymnast Cathy Rigby, in the 1990s.

In 1938 an American production cast a male, Leslie C. Gorall, as Peter Pan, and in 1952 a German production put a male in the role. The English did not break their cross-dressing tradition until 1982 when Trevor Nunn and John Caird produced their version of *Peter Pan* at the Barbican Theatre in London.

Although elements of Peter Pan's story appeared in Barrie's *Tommy and Grizel* and *The Little White Bird*, Barrie did not officially write his novel about Peter Pan until 1911, when he published *Peter and Wendy*. (The original copyright expired in 1987, and the novel is now known by the title *Peter Pan*.) In terms of plot, it closely resembles the play. One exception is an epilogue to the play, which Barrie called "An Afterthought," where we are given a glimpse into the future, when Wendy is married and the mother of a little girl. This postscript was performed only once in Barrie's lifetime (on February 22, 1908)—he insisted that it remain a one-night-only addition. However, he included the scene about the future in the novel, where it appears as chapter XVII, "When Wendy Grew Up." "An Afterthought" in its original form was first published as part of the play in 1957, twenty years after Barrie's death.

Unlike characters in most other children's literature, Peter Pan has achieved mythological status. Even though many people have not read Barrie's novel or play, Peter Pan is now as well known as Cinderella or Sleeping Beauty. Why is *Peter Pan* such a memorable drama? The story may be so compelling partly because of its attentiveness to reversibility. Childhood and adulthood, birth and death, boys and girls, dreams and waking life all persistently change places in the story. But they change places in such a way that they reinforce rather than dismantle the oppositions that confuse and distress us. Children do become adults; birth leads to death; boys and girls cannot effortlessly change roles; dreams remain distinct from waking life. Time moves ferociously forward. Even though *Peter Pan* is the story of a boy who never grows older, the narrative proves that everyone else must age. The first sentence of the novel tells us so:

"All children, except one, grow up" (p. 7). While the legend tempts us with achingly desirable unions, it is about the difficulty (if not the impossibility) of fusing disparate worlds: life and death, dreams and reality, masculinity and femininity, childhood and adulthood. Through lively comedy, *Peter Pan* brilliantly masks the underlying sadness that threatens to pull the story apart.

The heartbreaking undercurrents in *Peter Pan* become evident when we consider the mirroring between fantasy and reality that took place in J. M. Barrie's life. Like Peter Pan, Barrie remained a ghostly outsider. He wanted children of his own but instead found himself staring in at the Llewelyn Davies family, with whom he shared no blood relationship. Peter Pan convinces the Darling children to fly away with him in an attempt to take them from their parents and make them his; Barrie inadvertently achieved the same result with the Davies boys. In 1907 Arthur Llewelyn Davies, their father, died of cancer of the jaw. In 1909 James and Mary Barrie were divorced because of her affair with Gilbert Cannan. And in 1910 Sylvia Llewelyn Davies died of cancer. Barrie was left with five boys—age seven to seventeen—all of whom were now orphans left to his care.

What was J. M. Barrie's relationship with the Davies brothers? There are certainly passages in some of Barrie's novels that read, a century after their publication, as suspiciously attentive to the attractiveness of little boys. Barrie's involvement with the Davies boys was unusually close—more intense, perhaps, than typical relationships between parents and their natural offspring. However, Nicholas Llewelyn Davies swore to Barrie's biographer Andrew Birkin that Barrie never showed one hint of homosexuality or pedophilia toward him or his brothers. Critics have for the most part concluded that Barrie was entirely sexless. Nevertheless, he loved the Davies brothers obsessively. We might even go so far as to say that he was in love with at least two of them, George and Michael. As Barrie himself wrote in *Margaret Ogilvy*, "The fierce joy of loving too much, it is a terrible thing" (p. 206). Years later, Barrie wrote to George Llewelyn Davies, then twenty-one years old and fighting in World War I:

> I do seem to be sadder today than ever, and more and more wishing you were a girl of 21 instead of a boy, so that I could say the things to you that are now always in my heart. For four years I have been waiting for you to become 21 & a little more, so that we could get closer & closer to each other, without any words needed (quoted in Birkin, p. 228).

Shortly after receiving Barrie's letter, George was killed in Flanders. This event was probably the most traumatic experience Barrie had endured since his brother's death. But the worst was still to come. On May 19, 1921, Michael Llewelyn Davies, the fourth of the boys, was drowned while swimming in Oxford with his best friend, Rupert Buxton, who also drowned. Like George, Michael died when he was twenty-one. Rumors circulated that the deaths of Michael and his friend Rupert were intentional, the result of a mutual suicide pact.

Barrie never recovered from Michael's death. His secretary, Lady Cynthia Asquith, wrote that he looked like a man in a nightmare. He became suicidal and grew quite ill with grief. "All the world is different to me now. Michael was pretty much my world" (letter to Elizabeth Lucas, December 1921; quoted in Birkin, p. 295). He explained in his notebook that he dreamed Michael came back to him, not knowing he had drowned, and that Barrie kept this knowledge from him. The two lived together for another year quite ordinarily though strangely close to each other. Little by little Michael realized what was going to happen to him. Even though Barrie tried to prevent him from swimming, both knew what was sure to happen. Barrie accompanied Michael to the dangerous pool, holding his hand, and when they reached the deadly place, Michael said "good-bye" to Barrie and went into the water and sank. Barrie interrupts his account of the dream with new insight into the import of *Peter Pan*: "It is as if, long after writing P. Pan, its true meaning came back to me, desperate attempt to grow up but can't." Although Barrie lived for another sixteen years, he was never able to write successfully after Michael died. The author passed away before the final scene of this tragedy, for Peter Llewelyn Davies, too, eventually took his own life; in 1960 he jumped beneath an underground train in London.

As much as Barrie associated Peter Pan with doomed children who die before they fully mature (such as his brother David, George, and Michael), he also identified with all that made Peter Pan a tragic boy. Barrie wanted to develop into a man—to have a reciprocal relationship with a woman and have children of his own. But as a boy in a man's body, he was possibly unable to consummate his marriage and would never experience these joys. Instead, he was driven to turn to a family of strangers and to adopt five boys who were not his own. Barrie's closeness with the Davies children was all-consuming and heartrending. Likewise, Peter Pan's happiness cloaks a fundamental sorrow. His rebellion against time might be seen as a form of make-believe; if he *could*, he would gladly grow up. In the play *Peter Pan*, Mrs. Darling tries to convince Peter to let her adopt him, and he asks if this means he will have to grow up. When she responds in the affirmative, he says passionately, "I don't want to go to school and learn solemn things. No one is going to catch me, lady, and make me a man. I want always to be a little boy and to have fun." But Barrie wisely adds this parenthetical remark: ("So perhaps he thinks, but it is only his greatest pretend"). With this aside, Barrie gives us an important clue as to what makes Peter Pan a tragic boy.

People who read the novel version of *Peter Pan* for the first time may be surprised by Peter's fits of sadness, considering that by nature he seems to be such a happy boy. In the chapter "Do You Believe in Fairies?" Barrie explains Peter's trouble with dreams: "Sometimes, though not often, he had dreams, and they were more painful than the dreams of other boys. For hours he could not be separated from these dreams, though he wailed piteously in them. They had to do, I think, with the riddle of his existence" (p. 115). Even on the night when Peter kills Captain Hook he has "one of his dreams" and he cries in his sleep "for a long time," while Wendy holds him tight (p. 138). Barrie drew these details about Peter Pan's dreams from notes he made about Michael Llewelyn Davies. As a child Michael had horrible nightmares or waking dreams, and he used to like for Barrie to sit by his bed at night doing something ordinary, like reading the newspaper. Some of Barrie's notes about Michael may have been for a sequel to *Peter Pan* about Peter's brother, "Michael Pan." However, this piece never got much further than the title, perhaps because Barrie interwove his notes about Michael into descriptions of Peter in the novel *Peter and Wendy*. Michael and Peter Pan merged in other ways as well. When *Peter and Wendy* was first published in 1911, ten years before Michael's death, Barrie gave the sculptor Sir George Frampton a picture of Michael to use as a model for a statue of Peter Pan. Barrie then had the statue placed in Kensington Gardens one night after Lock-out Time so it would seem the next day to have been put there by magic. The statue still stands in London's Kensington Gardens.

Although Barrie wrote some fine plays after he lost George, such as *Dear Brutus* in 1917 and *Mary Rose* in 1920, he was so wounded by Michael's death that he could not repeat his past glories. However, he did continue to be recognized in other capacities. In 1922 he received the Order of Merit; in 1929 he gave all rights and royalties from *Peter Pan* to the Great Ormond Street Hospital for Sick Children; in 1930 he received an honorary degree from Cambridge, and he was installed as chancellor of Edinburgh University. During his later years, Barrie developed a reputation as a public speaker. Nevertheless, his brightest days as a writer were over. He had been writing the play *Shall We Join the Ladies?*, which appeared in 1921, for Michael and with Michael's guidance. Barrie did not complete the play after Michael's death but let it stand as it was. In 1936 his last play, *The Boy David*, was performed. Based on the Bible, it is about the relationship that develops between Saul and David (who is still a child). Although Saul grows to love David, he feels he must murder him when he realizes that David will replace him as king. Like *Peter Pan*, *The Boy David* deals with attraction, terror, and obsession. Barrie had high hopes for the play but was disappointed by its lack of success. The production came to an end after only fifty-five performances, to Barrie's acute distress. He died shortly afterward, on June 19, 1937, at the age of seventy-seven and, at his request, was buried beside his family in the cemetery at Kirriemuir, his childhood home.

The best piece of Barrie's writing composed after his series of losses may be his 1928 dedication to the play *Peter Pan*. The same themes that run through all of Barrie's important work—the tension between childhood and adulthood, ferocious love and loss, memory and forgetfulness, realism and fantasy—take center stage in Barrie's dedication. He addresses all five Llewelyn Davies boys as if they are still alive, even though two of them were most likely already dead when he wrote it (George died in 1915 and Michael in 1921). Barrie begins the dedication by confessing that he has no recollection of ever having written *Peter Pan*. Speculating that he may have written the story, he still gives the boys all the credit: "As for myself, I suppose I always knew that I made Peter by rubbing the five of you violently together, as savages with two sticks produce a flame. That is all he is, the spark I got from you" (*Peter Pan and Other Plays*, p. 75). Barrie devotes much of the dedication to an exploration of the unsettling passage of time. He maintains that while some say that we are different people at different periods of our lives, he does not believe this. Rather, he supposes we remain the same from start to finish of our lives, "merely passing, as it were, in these lapses of time from one room to another, but all in the same house" (p. 78). Reminiscing about his own childhood, he remembers how he read feverishly about desert islands, which he called "wrecked islands." He pursues himself like a shadow, watching as he becomes an undergraduate who craves to be a real explorer. Still, he goes "from room to room," until he is a man, real exploration abandoned, though only because no one would have him. Soon he begins to write plays, many of which contain the wrecked islands that fascinated him so much in his youth. And he notes, "with the years the islands grow more sinister."

Barrie struggles to sustain the belief that we do not change as we grow older, but at last he concedes he may be wrong: "Of course this is over-charged. Perhaps we do change; except a little something in us which is no larger than a mote in the eye, and that, like it, dances in front of us beguiling us all our days. I cannot cut the hair by which it hangs" (p. 79). He concludes with what he considers to be his "grandest triumph," the best scene by far in *Peter Pan*, though the scene is not in *Peter Pan* at all (p. 85). This was the time long after Michael had ceased to believe in magic, the time when Barrie brought him back to the faith, even if only for a few minutes. Michael, Nico and Barrie were on their way in a boat to fish the Outer Hebrides. Even though Michael was excited to begin, he suffered from one pain: the absence of Johnny Mackay—a friend he had made the summer before who could not be with them, as he was in a distant country. As their boat drew nearer to the Kyle of Localsh pier, Barrie told Michael and Nico how this was such a famous wishing pier that all they had to do was to ask for something for their wish to be granted. Nico believed at once, but Michael refused to participate in the game. Barrie asked Michael whom he most wanted to see. When Michael answered "Johnny Mackay," Barrie told him that it couldn't do any harm to wish. At last Michael wished (quite contemptuously), and suddenly as the ropes were thrown on the pier, he saw Johnny waiting for him. Thus Barrie ends the dedication:

> I know no one less like a fairy than Johnny Mackay, but for two minutes No. 4 [Michael] was quivering in another world than ours. When he came to he gave me a smile which meant that we understood each other, and thereafter neglected me for a month, being always with Johnny. As I have said, this episode is not in the play; so though I dedicate *Peter Pan* to you I keep the smile, with the few other broken fragments of immortality that have come my way (p. 86).

The broken fragments of immortality come our way, too. Of children's adventures with Peter Pan, Barrie says in the last sentence of his novel, "and so it will go on, so long as children are gay and innocent and heartless" (p. 159). Miraculously, so it does—for all of us. We follow Barrie from room to room. The window is open. Expectantly, the stars wink and shout. A boy floats, beckoning us from the dream-like night sky. Laughing, but with tears in our eyes, we fly out.

Amy Billone teaches at the University of Tennessee, Knoxville. She received her Ph.D. in Comparative Literature at Princeton University. She has published articles on both children's literature and poetry in numerous places, including: *Children's Literature*, *Mosaic: A Journal for the Interdisciplinary Study of Literature*, *Browning Society Notes*, *Silence, Sublimity and Suppression in the Romantic Period*, *Victorian Poetry*, and *Nineteenth-Century French Studies*. In 2003 she was awarded the Sidonie Clauss Memorial Prize from Princeton University.

PETER PAN

CONTENTS

ILLUSTRATIONS

From Drawings by F. D. Bedford

CHAPTER I

Peter Breaks Through

ALL CHILDREN, EXCEPT ONE, grow up. They soon know that they will grow up, and the way Wendy knew was this. One day when she was two years old she was playing in a garden, and she plucked another flower and ran with it to her mother. I suppose she must have looked rather delightful, for Mrs. Darling put her hand to her heart and cried, "Oh, why can't you remain like this for ever!" This was all that passed between them on the subject, but henceforth Wendy knew that she must grow up. You always know after you are two. Two is the beginning of the end.

Of course they lived at 14, and until Wendy came her mother was the chief one. She was a lovely lady, with a romantic mind and such a sweet mocking mouth. Her romantic mind was like the tiny boxes, one within the other, that come from the puzzling East, however many you discover there is always one more; and her sweet mocking mouth had one kiss on it that Wendy could never get, though there it was, perfectly conspicuous in the right-hand corner.

The way Mr. Darling won her was this: the many gentlemen who had been boys when she was a girl discovered simultaneously that they loved her, and they all ran to her house to propose to her except Mr. Darling, who took a cab and nipped in first, and so he got her. He got all of her, except the innermost box and the kiss. He never knew about the box, and in time he gave up trying for the kiss. Wendy thought Napoleon[1] could have got it, but I can picture him trying, and then going off in a passion, slamming the door.

Mr. Darling used to boast to Wendy that her mother not only loved him but respected him. He was one of those deep ones who know about stocks and shares. Of course no one really knows, but he quite seemed to know, and he often said stocks were up and shares were down in a way that would have made any woman respect him.

Mrs. Darling was married in white, and at first she kept the books perfectly, almost gleefully, as if it were a game, not so much as a Brussels sprout was missing; but by and by whole cauliflowers dropped out, and instead of them there were pictures of babies without faces. She drew them when she should have been totting up.* They were Mrs. Darling's guesses.

Wendy came first, then John, then Michael.

For a week or two after Wendy came it was doubtful whether they would be able to keep her, as she was another mouth to feed. Mr. Darling was frightfully proud of her, but he was very honourable, and he sat on the edge of Mrs. Darling's bed, holding her hand and calculating expenses, while she looked at him imploringly. She wanted to risk it, come what might, but that was not his way; his way was with a pencil and a piece of paper, and if she confused him with suggestions he had to begin at the beginning again.

"Now don't interrupt," he would beg of her.

"I have one pound seventeen here,[2] and two and six at the office; I can cut off my coffee at the office, say ten shillings, making two nine and six, with your eighteen and three makes three nine seven, with five naught naught in my cheque-book makes eight nine seven,—who is that moving?—eight nine seven, dot and carry seven—don't speak, my own—and the pound you lent to that man who came to the door—quiet, child—dot and carry child—there, you've done it!—did I say nine nine seven? yes, I said nine nine seven; the question is, can we try it for a year on nine nine seven?"

"Of course we can, George,"[3] she cried. But she was prejudiced in Wendy's favour, and he was really the grander character of the two.

"Remember mumps,"† he warned her almost threateningly, and off he went again. "Mumps one pound, that is what I have put down, but I daresay it will be more like thirty shillings—don't

---

*Totaling up the bills.

†Contagious disease characterized by fever, sore throat, and puffy cheeks; it mainly affects children.

speak—measles[*] one five, German measles[†] half a guinea,[‡] makes two fifteen six—don't waggle your finger—whooping-cough,[§] say fifteen shillings"—and so on it went, and it added up differently each time, but at last Wendy just got through, with mumps reduced to twelve six, and the two kinds of measles treated as one.

There was the same excitement over John, and Michael had even a narrower squeak; but both were kept, and soon, you might have seen the three of them going in a row to Miss Fulsom's Kindergarten school, accompanied by their nurse.

Mrs. Darling loved to have everything just so, and Mr. Darling had a passion for being exactly like his neighbours; so, of course, they had a nurse. As they were poor, owing to the amount of milk the children drank, this nurse was a prim Newfoundland dog, called Nana,[4] who had belonged to no one in particular until the Darlings engaged her. She had always thought children important, however, and the Darlings had become acquainted with her in Kensington Gardens, where she spent most of her spare time peeping into perambulators,[||] and was much hated by careless nursemaids, whom she followed to their homes and complained of to their mistresses. She proved to be quite a treasure of a nurse. How thorough she was at bath-time, and up at any moment of the night if one of her charges made the slightest cry. Of course her kennel was in the nursery. She had a genius for knowing when a cough is a thing to have no patience with and when it needs stocking round your throat. She believed to her last day in old-fashioned remedies like rhubarb[#] leaf, and made sounds of contempt over all this new-fangled talk about germs, and so on. It was a lesson in propriety to see her escorting the

---

*Contagious disease usually affecting children; characterized by eruption of red spots on the skin, fever, and inflammation of the air passages of the head and throat.

†Also known as rubella. Starts with a mild fever and swollen lymph nodes; a day or two later, a rash appears on the face and spreads downward.

‡A guinea was one pound and one shilling, so "half a guinea" was ten shillings and sixpence.

§Symptoms include runny nose, fever, and a cough that ends in a "whooping" sound; exhausting coughing spells make it most lethal to babies.

||Strollers or baby carriages.

#Any of several plants of the genus *Rheum* that have large leaves with thick, succulent stalks. Victorians used the powdered root as a laxative.

children to school, walking sedately by their side when they were well behaved, and butting them back into line if they strayed. On John's footer days she never once forgot his sweater,[5] and she usually carried an umbrella in her mouth in case of rain. There is a room in the basement of Miss Fulsom's school where the nurses wait. They sat on forms,* while Nana lay on the floor, but that was the only difference. They affected to ignore her as of an inferior social status to themselves, and she despised their light talk. She resented visits to the nursery from Mrs. Darling's friends, but if they did come she first whipped off Michael's pinafore† and put him into the one with blue braiding, and smoothed out Wendy and made a dash at John's hair.

No nursery could possibly have been conducted more correctly, and Mr. Darling knew it, yet he sometimes wondered uneasily whether the neighbours talked.

He had his position in the city to consider.

Nana also troubled him in another way. He had sometimes a feeling that she did not admire him. "I know she admires you tremendously, George," Mrs. Darling would assure him, and then she would sign to the children to be specially nice to father. Lovely dances followed, in which the only other servant, Liza, was sometimes allowed to join. Such a midget she looked in her long skirt and maid's cap, though she had sworn, when engaged, that she would never see ten again.‡ The gaiety of those romps! And gayest of all was Mrs. Darling, who would pirouette so wildly that all you could see of her was the kiss, and then if you had dashed at her you might have got it. There never was a simpler, happier family until the coming of Peter Pan.

Mrs. Darling first heard of Peter when she was tidying up her children's minds. It is the nightly custom of every good mother after her children are asleep to rummage in their minds and put things straight for next morning, repacking into their proper places the many articles that have wandered during the day. If you could keep

---

*Long seats or benches (chiefly British).

†Sleeveless garment, worn over other clothing as an apron or a dress.

‡Liza looks like a young child, even though she swore when she was hired that she was would never see ten [years old] again.

awake (but of course you can't) you would see your own mother doing this, and you would find it very interesting to watch her. It is quite like tidying up drawers. You would see her on her knees, I expect, lingering humorously over some of your contents, wondering where on earth you had picked this thing up, making discoveries sweet and not so sweet, pressing this to her cheek as if it were as nice as a kitten, and hurriedly stowing that out of sight. When you wake in the morning, the naughtinesses and evil passions with which you went to bed have been folded up small and placed at the bottom of your mind, and on the top, beautifully aired, are spread out your prettier thoughts, ready for you to put on.

I don't know whether you have ever seen a map of a person's mind. Doctors sometimes draw maps of other parts of you, and your own map can become intensely interesting, but catch them trying to draw a map of a child's mind, which is not only confused, but keeps going round all the time. There are zigzag lines on it, just like your temperature on a card, and these are probably roads in the island, for the Neverland is always more or less an island, with astonishing splashes of colour here and there, and coral reefs and rakish-looking craft[*] in the offing,[†] and savages and lonely lairs, and gnomes[‡] who are mostly tailors, and caves through which a river runs, and princes with six elder brothers, and a hut fast going to decay, and one very small old lady with a hooked nose. It would be an easy map if that were all, but there is also first day at school, religion, fathers, the round pond,[6] needle-work, murders, hangings, verbs that take the dative, chocolate pudding day, getting into braces,[§] say ninety-nine,[||] three-pence for pulling out your tooth yourself, and so on, and either these are part of the island or they are another map showing through, and it is all rather confusing, especially as nothing will stand still.

Of course the Neverlands vary a good deal. John's, for instance, had a lagoon with flamingoes flying over it at which John was

---

*Boats with a trim, streamlined appearance, signifying speed.

†The area of deep sea that can be seen from the shore.

‡Dwarf-like, ageless creatures who live underground and guard treasure.

§Putting on suspenders.

||Technique doctors used to get patients to open their mouths wide.

shooting, while Michael, who was very small, had a flamingo with lagoons flying over it. John lived in a boat turned upside down on the sands, Michael in a wigwam,* Wendy in a house of leaves deftly sewn together. John had no friends, Michael had friends at night, Wendy had a pet wolf forsaken by its parents, but on the whole the Neverlands have a family resemblance, and if they stood still in a row you could say of them that they have each other's nose, and so forth. On these magic shores children at play are for ever beaching their coracles.† We too have been there; we can still hear the sound of the surf, though we shall land no more.

Of all delectable islands the Neverland is the snuggest and most compact, not large and sprawly, you know, with tedious distances between one adventure and another, but nicely crammed. When you play at it by day with the chairs and table-cloth, it is not in the least alarming, but in the two minutes before you go to sleep it becomes very nearly real. That is why there are night-lights.

Occasionally in her travels through her children's minds Mrs. Darling found things she could not understand, and of these quite the most perplexing was the word Peter. She knew of no Peter, and yet he was here and there in John and Michael's minds, while Wendy's began to be scrawled all over with him. The name stood out in bolder letters than any of the other words, and as Mrs. Darling gazed she felt that it had an oddly cocky appearance.

"Yes, he is rather cocky," Wendy admitted with regret. Her mother had been questioning her.

"But who is he, my pet?"

"He is Peter Pan, you know, mother."

At first Mrs. Darling did not know, but after thinking back into her childhood she just remembered a Peter Pan who was said to live with the fairies. There were odd stories about him, as that when children died he went part of the way with them, so that they should not be frightened. She had believed in him at the time, but now that

---

*Native American dwelling place, made with an arched framework of poles covered with bark, hides, or rush mats.

†Used in Britain for millennia, coracles are small boats consisting of a wicker frame covered with a hide or tarp.

she was married and full of sense she quite doubted whether there was any such person.

"Besides," she said to Wendy, "he would be grown up by this time."

"Oh no, he isn't grown up," Wendy assured her confidently, "and he is just my size." She meant that he was her size in both mind and body; she didn't know how she knew it, she just knew it.

Mrs. Darling consulted Mr. Darling, but he smiled pooh-pooh. "Mark my words," he said, "it is some nonsense Nana has been putting into their heads; just the sort of idea a dog would have. Leave it alone, and it will blow over."

But it would not blow over, and soon the troublesome boy gave Mrs. Darling quite a shock.

Children have the strangest adventures without being troubled by them. For instance, they may remember to mention, a week after the event happened, that when they were in the wood they met their dead father and had a game with him. It was in this casual way that Wendy one morning made a disquieting revelation. Some leaves of a tree had been found on the nursery floor, which certainly were not there when the children went to bed, and Mrs. Darling was puzzling over them when Wendy said with a tolerant smile:[7]

"I do believe it is that Peter again!"

"Whatever do you mean, Wendy?"

"It is so naughty of him not to wipe," Wendy said, sighing. She was a tidy child.

She explained in quite a matter-of-fact way that she thought Peter sometimes came to the nursery in the night and sat on the foot of her bed and played on his pipes to her. Unfortunately she never woke, so she didn't know how she knew, she just knew.

"What nonsense you talk, precious! No one can get into the house without knocking."

"I think he comes in by the window," she said.

"My love, it is three floors up."

"Weren't the leaves at the foot of the window, mother?"

It was quite true; the leaves had been found very near the window.

Mrs. Darling did not know what to think, for it all seemed so natural to Wendy that you could not dismiss it by saying she had been dreaming.

"My child," the mother cried, "why did you not tell me of this before?"

"I forgot," said Wendy lightly. She was in a hurry to get her breakfast.

Oh, surely she must have been dreaming.

But, on the other hand, there were the leaves. Mrs. Darling examined them carefully; they were skeleton leaves, but she was sure they did not come from any tree that grew in England.[8] She crawled about the floor, peering at it with a candle for marks of a strange foot. She rattled the poker up the chimney and tapped the walls. She let down a tape from the window to the pavement, and it was a sheer drop of thirty feet, without so much as a spout to climb up by.

Certainly Wendy had been dreaming.

But Wendy had not been dreaming, as the very next night showed, the night on which the extraordinary adventures of these children may be said to have begun.

On the night we speak of all the children were once more in bed. It happened to be Nana's evening off, and Mrs. Darling had bathed them and sung to them till one by one they had let go her hand and slid away into the land of sleep.

All were looking so safe and cosy that she smiled at her fears now and sat down tranquilly by the fire to sew.

It was something for Michael, who on his birthday was getting into shirts. The fire was warm, however, and the nursery dimly lit by three night-lights, and presently the sewing lay on Mrs. Darling's lap. Then her head nodded, oh, so gracefully. She was asleep. Look at the four of them, Wendy and Michael over there, John here, and Mrs. Darling by the fire. There should have been a fourth night-light.

While she slept she had a dream. She dreamt that the Neverland had come too near and that a strange boy had broken through from it. He did not alarm her, for she thought she had seen him before in the faces of many women who have no children. Perhaps he is to be found in the faces of some mothers also. But in her dream he had rent the film that obscures the Neverland,[9] and she saw Wendy and John and Michael peeping through the gap.

The dream by itself would have been a trifle, but while she was dreaming the window of the nursery blew open, and a boy did drop on the floor. He was accompanied by a strange light, no bigger than your fist, which darted about the room like a living thing, and I think it must have been this light that wakened Mrs. Darling.

She started up with a cry, and saw the boy, and somehow she knew at once that he was Peter Pan. If you or I or Wendy had been there we should have seen that he was very like Mrs. Darling's kiss. He was a lovely boy, clad in skeleton leaves and the juices that ooze out of trees, but the most entrancing thing about him was that he had all his first teeth. When he saw she was a grown-up, he gnashed the little pearls* at her.

---

*Peter's baby teeth—small, white, and evenly shaped, like pearls.

CHAPTER II

The Shadow

MRS. DARLING SCREAMED, AND, as if in answer to a bell, the door opened, and Nana entered, returned from her evening out. She growled and sprang at the boy, who leapt lightly through the window. Again Mrs. Darling screamed, this time in distress for him, for she thought he was killed, and she ran down into the street to look for his little body, but it was not there; and she looked up, and in the black night she could see nothing but what she thought was a shooting star.

She returned to the nursery, and found Nana with something in her mouth, which proved to be the boy's shadow. As he leapt at the window Nana had closed it quickly, too late to catch him, but his shadow had not had time to get out; slam went the window and snapped it off.

You may be sure Mrs. Darling examined the shadow carefully, but it was quite the ordinary kind.

Nana had no doubt of what was the best thing to do with this shadow. She hung it out at the window, meaning "He is sure to come back for it; let us put it where he can get it easily without disturbing the children."

But unfortunately Mrs. Darling could not leave it hanging out at the window, it looked so like the washing and lowered the whole tone of the house. She thought of showing it to Mr. Darling, but he was totting up winter great-coats* for John and Michael, with a wet towel round his head to keep his brain clear, and it seemed a shame to trouble him; besides, she knew exactly what he would say: "It all comes of having a dog for a nurse."

---

*Totaling the price of heavy winter overcoats needed for John and Michael.

She decided to roll the shadow up and put it away carefully in a drawer, until a fitting opportunity came for telling her husband. Ah me!

The opportunity came a week later, on that never-to-be-forgotten Friday. Of course it was a Friday.

"I ought to have been specially careful on a Friday," she used to say afterwards to her husband, while perhaps Nana was on the other side of her, holding her hand.

"No, no," Mr. Darling always said, "I am responsible for it all. I, George Darling, did it. *Mea culpa, mea culpa.*"* He had had a classical education.

They sat thus night after night recalling that fatal Friday, till every detail of it was stamped on their brains and came through on the other side like the faces on a bad coinage.†

"If only I had not accepted that invitation to dine at 27," Mrs. Darling said.

"If only I had not poured my medicine into Nana's bowl," said Mr. Darling.

"If only I had pretended to like the medicine," was what Nana's wet eyes said.

"My liking for parties, George."

"My fatal gift of humour, dearest."

"My touchiness about trifles, dear master and mistress."

Then one or more of them would break down altogether; Nana at the thought, "It's true, it's true, they ought not to have had a dog for a nurse. Many a time it was Mr. Darling who put the handkerchief to Nana's eyes.

"That fiend!" Mr. Darling would cry, and Nana's bark was the echo of it, but Mrs. Darling never upbraided Peter; there was something in the right-hand corner of her mouth that wanted her not to call Peter names.

They would sit there in the empty nursery, recalling fondly every smallest detail of that dreadful evening. It had begun so uneventfully, so precisely like a hundred other evenings, with Nana putting on the water for Michael's bath and carrying him to it on her back.

---

*My fault, my fault (Latin).

†Coins made of thin or poor-quality metals; the punch that creates the design on one side leaves marks visible from the other.

"I won't go to bed," he had shouted, like one who still believed that he had the last word on the subject, "I won't, I won't. Nana, it isn't six o'clock yet. Oh dear, oh dear, I shan't love you any more, Nana. I tell you I won't be bathed, I won't, I won't!"

Then Mrs. Darling had come in, wearing her white evening-gown. She had dressed early because Wendy so loved to see her in her evening-gown, with the necklace George had given her. She was wearing Wendy's bracelet on her arm; she had asked for the loan of it. Wendy so loved to lend her bracelet to her mother.

She had found her two older children playing at being herself and father on the occasion of Wendy's birth, and John was saying:

"I am happy to inform you, Mrs. Darling, that you are now a mother," in just such a tone as Mr. Darling himself may have used on the real occasion.

Wendy had danced with joy, just as the real Mrs. Darling must have done.

Then John was born, with the extra pomp that he conceived due to the birth of a male, and Michael came from his bath to ask to be born also, but John said brutally that they did not want any more.

Michael had nearly cried. "Nobody wants me," he said, and of course the lady in evening-dress could not stand that.

"I do," she said, "I so want a third child."

"Boy or girl?" asked Michael, not too hopefully.

"Boy."

Then he had leapt into her arms. Such a little thing for Mr. and Mrs. Darling and Nana to recall now, but not so little if that was to be Michael's last night in the nursery.

They go on with their recollections.

"It was then that I rushed in like a tornado, wasn't it?" Mr. Darling would say, scorning himself; and indeed he had been like a tornado.

Perhaps there was some excuse for him. He, too, had been dressing for the party, and all had gone well with him until he came to his tie. It is an astounding thing to have to tell, but this man, though he knew about stocks and shares, had no real mastery of his tie. Sometimes the thing yielded to him without a contest, but there were occasions when it would have been better for the house if he had swallowed his pride and used a made-up tie.

This was such an occasion. He came rushing into the nursery with the crumpled little brute of a tie in his hand.

"Why, what is the matter, father dear?"

"Matter!" he yelled; he really yelled. "This tie, it will not tie." He became dangerously sarcastic. "Not round my neck! Round the bed-post! Oh yes, twenty times have I made it up round the bed-post, but round my neck, no! Oh dear no! begs to be excused!"

He thought Mrs. Darling was not sufficiently impressed, and he went on sternly, "I warn you of this, mother, that unless this tie is round my neck we don't go out to dinner to-night, and if I don't go out to dinner to-night, I never go to the office again, and if I don't go to the office again, you and I starve, and our children will be flung into the streets."

Even then Mrs. Darling was placid. "Let me try, dear," she said, and indeed that was what he had come to ask her to do, and with her nice cool hands she tied his tie for him, while the children stood around to see their fate decided. Some men would have resented her being able to do it so easily, but Mr. Darling was far too fine a nature for that; he thanked her carelessly, at once forgot his rage, and in another moment was dancing round the room with Michael on his back.

"How wildly we romped!" says Mrs. Darling now, recalling it.

"Our last romp!" Mr. Darling groaned.

"O George, do you remember Michael suddenly said to me, 'How did you get to know me, mother?' "

"I remember!"

"They were rather sweet, don't you think, George?"

"And they were ours, ours! and now they are gone."

The romp had ended with the appearance of Nana, and most unluckily Mr. Darling collided against her, covering his trousers with hairs. They were not only new trousers, but they were the first he had ever had with braid on them, and he had to bite his lip to prevent the tears coming. Of course Mrs. Darling brushed him, but he began to talk again about its being a mistake to have a dog for a nurse.

"George, Nana is a treasure."

"No doubt, but I have an uneasy feeling at times that she looks upon the children as puppies."

"Oh no, dear one, I feel sure she knows they have souls."

"I wonder," Mr. Darling said thoughtfully, "I wonder." It was an opportunity, his wife felt, for telling him about the boy. At first he pooh-poohed the story, but he became thoughtful when she showed him the shadow.

"It is nobody I know," he said, examining it carefully, "but he does look a scoundrel."

"We were still discussing it, you remember," said Mr. Darling, "when Nana came in with Michael's medicine. You will never carry the bottle in your mouth again, Nana, and it is all my fault."

Strong man though he was, there is no doubt that he had behaved rather foolishly over the medicine. If he had a weakness, it was for thinking that all his life he had taken medicine boldly, and so now, when Michael dodged the spoon in Nana's mouth, he had said reprovingly, "Be a man, Michael."

"Won't; won't!" Michael cried naughtily. Mrs. Darling left the room to get a chocolate for him, and Mr. Darling thought this showed want of firmness.

"Mother, don't pamper him," he called after her. "Michael, when I was your age I took medicine without a murmur. I said 'Thank you, kind parents, for giving me bottles to make me well.'"

He really thought this was true, and Wendy, who was now in her night-gown, believed it also, and she said, to encourage Michael, "That medicine you sometimes take, father, is much nastier, isn't it?"

"Ever so much nastier," Mr. Darling said bravely, "and I would take it now as an example to you, Michael, if I hadn't lost the bottle."

He had not exactly lost it; he had climbed in the dead of night to the top of the wardrobe and hidden it there. What he did not know was that the faithful Liza had found it, and put it back on his wash-stand.

"I know where it is, father," Wendy cried, always glad to be of service. "I'll bring it," and she was off before he could stop her. Immediately his spirits sank in the strangest way.

"John," he said, shuddering, "it's most beastly stuff. It's that nasty, sticky, sweet kind."

"It will soon be over, father," John said cheerily, and then in rushed Wendy with the medicine in a glass.

"I have been as quick as I could," she panted.

"You have been wonderfully quick," her father retorted, with a vindictive politeness that was quite thrown away upon her. "Michael first," he said doggedly.

"Father first," said Michael, who was of a suspicious nature.

"I shall be sick, you know," Mr. Darling said threateningly.

"Come on, father," said John.

"Hold your tongue, John," his father rapped out.

Wendy was quite puzzled. "I thought you took it quite easily, father."

"That is not the point," he retorted. "The point is, that there is more in my glass than in Michael's spoon." His proud heart was nearly bursting. "And it isn't fair; I would say it though it were with my last breath; it isn't fair."

"Father, I am waiting," said Michael coldly.

"It's all very well to say you are waiting; so am I waiting."

"Father's a cowardy custard."*

"So are you a cowardy custard."

"I'm not frightened."

"Neither am I frightened."

"Well, then, take it."

"Well, then, you take it."

Wendy had a splendid idea. "Why not both take it at the same time?"

"Certainly," said Mr. Darling. "Are you ready, Michael?"

Wendy gave the words, one, two, three, and Michael took his medicine, but Mr. Darling slipped his behind his back.

There was a yell of rage from Michael, and "O father!" Wendy exclaimed.

"What do you mean by 'O father'?" Mr. Darling demanded. "Stop that row, Michael. I meant to take mine, but I—I missed it."

It was dreadful the way all the three were looking at him, just as if they did not admire him. "Look here, all of you," he said entreatingly, as soon as Nana had gone into the bathroom, "I have just thought of a splendid joke. I shall pour my medicine into Nana's bowl, and she will drink it, thinking it is milk!"

It was the colour of milk; but the children did not have their father's sense of humour, and they looked at him reproachfully as he poured the medicine into Nana's bowl. "What fun!" he said doubtfully, and they did not dare expose him when Mrs. Darling and Nana returned.

---

*British expression for "coward."

"Nana, good dog," he said, patting her, "I have put a little milk into your bowl, Nana."

Nana wagged her tail, ran to the medicine, and began lapping it. Then she gave Mr. Darling such a look, not an angry look: she showed him the great red tear that makes us so sorry for noble dogs, and crept into her kennel.

Mr. Darling was frightfully ashamed of himself, but he would not give in. In a horrid silence Mrs. Darling smelt the bowl. "O George," she said, "it's your medicine!"

"It was only a joke," he roared, while she comforted her boys, and Wendy hugged Nana. "Much good," he said bitterly, "my wearing myself to the bone trying to be funny in this house."

And still Wendy hugged Nana. "That's right," he shouted. "Coddle her! Nobody coddles me. Oh dear no! I am only the breadwinner, why should I be coddled—why, why, why!"

"George," Mrs. Darling entreated him, "not so loud; the servants will hear you." Somehow they had got into the way of calling Liza the servants.

"Let them!" he answered recklessly. "Bring in the whole world. But I refuse to allow that dog to lord it in my nursery for an hour longer."

The children wept, and Nana ran to him beseechingly, but he waved her back. He felt he was a strong man again. "In vain, in vain," he cried; "the proper place for you is the yard, and there you go to be tied up this instant."

"George, George," Mrs. Darling whispered, "remember what I told you about that boy."

Alas, he would not listen. He was determined to show who was master in that house, and when commands would not draw Nana from the kennel, he lured her out of it with honeyed words, and seizing her roughly, dragged her from the nursery. He was ashamed of himself, and yet he did it. It was all owing to his too affectionate nature, which craved for admiration. When he had tied her up in the back-yard, the wretched father went and sat in the passage, with his knuckles to his eyes.

In the meantime Mrs. Darling had put the children to bed in unwonted silence and lit their night-lights. They could hear Nana barking, and John whimpered, "It is because he is chaining her up in the yard," but Wendy was wiser.

"That is not Nana's unhappy bark," she said, little guessing what was about to happen; "that is her bark when she smells danger."

Danger!

"Are you sure, Wendy?"

"Oh yes."

Mrs. Darling quivered and went to the window. It was securely fastened. She looked out, and the night was peppered with stars. They were crowding round the house, as if curious to see what was to take place there, but she did not notice this, nor that one or two of the smaller ones winked at her. Yet a nameless fear clutched at her heart and made her cry, "Oh, how I wish that I wasn't going to a party to-night!"

Even Michael, already half asleep, knew that she was perturbed, and he asked, "Can anything harm us, mother, after the night-lights are lit?"

"Nothing, precious," she said; "they are the eyes a mother leaves behind her to guard her children."

She went from bed to bed singing enchantments over them,[1] and little Michael flung his arms round her. "Mother," he cried, "I'm glad of you." They were the last words she was to hear from him for a long time.

No. 27 was only a few yards distant, but there had been a slight fall of snow, and Father and Mother Darling picked their way over it deftly not to soil their shoes. They were already the only persons in the street, and all the stars were watching them. Stars are beautiful, but they may not take an active part in anything, they must just look on for ever. It is a punishment put on them for something they did so long ago that no star now knows what it was. So the older ones have become glassy-eyed and seldom speak (winking is the star language), but the little ones still wonder. They are not really friendly to Peter, who has a mischievous way of stealing up behind them and trying to blow them out; but they are so fond of fun that they were on his side to-night, and anxious to get the grown-ups out of the way. So as soon as the door of 27 closed on Mr. and Mrs. Darling there was a commotion in the firmament,* and the smallest of all the stars in the Milky Way screamed out:

"Now, Peter!"

---

*Disturbance in the sky.

CHAPTER III

Come Away, Come Away!

For a moment after Mr. and Mrs. Darling left the house the night-lights by the beds of the three children continued to burn clearly. They were awfully nice little night-lights, and one cannot help wishing that they could have kept awake to see Peter; but Wendy's light blinked and gave such a yawn that the other two yawned also, and before they could close their mouths all the three went out.

There was another light in the room now, a thousand times brighter than the night-lights, and in the time we have taken to say this, it has been in all the drawers in the nursery, looking for Peter's shadow, rummaged the wardrobe and turned every pocket inside out. It was not really a light; it made this light by flashing about so quickly, but when it came to rest for a second you saw it was a fairy, no longer than your hand, but still growing. It was a girl called Tinker Bell exquisitely gowned in a skeleton leaf, cut low and square, through which her figure could be seen to the best advantage. She was slightly inclined to *embonpoint.**

A moment after the fairy's entrance the window was blown open by the breathing of the little stars, and Peter dropped in. He had carried Tinker Bell part of the way, and his hand was still messy with the fairy dust.

"Tinker Bell," he called softly, after making sure that the children were asleep, "Tink, where are you?" She was in a jug for the moment, and liking it extremely; she had never been in a jug before.

---

*Having a plump or well-rounded figure.

"Oh, do come out of that jug, and tell me, do you know where they put my shadow?"

The loveliest tinkle as of golden bells answered him. It is the fairy language. You ordinary children can never hear it, but if you were to hear it you would know that you had heard it once before.

Tink said that the shadow was in the big box. She meant the chest of drawers, and Peter jumped at the drawers, scattering their contents to the floor with both hands, as kings toss ha'pence* to the crowd. In a moment he had recovered his shadow, and in his delight he forgot that he had shut Tinker Bell up in the drawer.

If he thought at all, but I don't believe he ever thought, it was that he and his shadow, when brought near each other, would join like drops of water, and when they did not he was appalled. He tried to stick it on with soap from the bathroom, but that also failed. A shudder passed through Peter, and he sat on the floor and cried.

His sobs woke Wendy, and she sat up in bed. She was not alarmed to see a stranger crying on the nursery floor; she was only pleasantly interested.

"Boy," she said courteously, "why are you crying?"

Peter could be exceedingly polite also, having learned the grand manner at fairy ceremonies, and he rose and bowed to her beautifully. She was much pleased, and bowed beautifully to him from the bed.

"What's your name?" he asked.

"Wendy Moira Angela Darling,"[1] she replied with some satisfaction. "What is your name?"

"Peter Pan."

She was already sure that he must be Peter, but it did seem a comparatively short name.

"Is that all?"

"Yes," he said rather sharply. He felt for the first time that it was a shortish name.

"I'm so sorry," said Wendy Moira Angela.

"It doesn't matter," Peter gulped.

She asked where he lived.

---

*Halfpennies, according to the pre-decimal system.

"Second to the right," said Peter, "and then straight on till morning."

"What a funny address!"

Peter had a sinking. For the first time he felt that perhaps it was a funny address.

"No, it isn't," he said.

"I mean," Wendy said nicely, remembering that she was hostess, "is that what they put on the letters?"

He wished she had not mentioned letters.

"Don't get any letters," he said contemptuously.

"But your mother gets letters?"

"Don't have a mother," he said. Not only had he no mother, but he had not the slightest desire to have one. He thought them very over-rated persons. Wendy, however, felt at once that she was in the presence of a tragedy.

"O Peter, no wonder you were crying," she said, and got out of bed and ran to him.

"I wasn't crying about mothers," he said rather indignantly. "I was crying because I can't get my shadow to stick on. Besides, I wasn't crying."

"It has come off?"

"Yes."

Then Wendy saw the shadow on the floor, looking so draggled,* and she was frightfully sorry for Peter. "How awful!" she said, but she could not help smiling when she saw that he had been trying to stick it on with soap. How exactly like a boy!

Fortunately she knew at once what to do. "It must be sewn on," she said, just a little patronisingly.

"What's sewn?" he asked.

"You're dreadfully ignorant."

"No, I'm not."

But she was exulting in his ignorance. "I shall sew it on for you, my little man," she said, though he was as tall as herself, and she got out her housewife,† and sewed the shadow on to Peter's foot.

"I daresay it will hurt a little," she warned him.

---

*Limp and soiled as if it has been dragged through wet mud.

†Small container for needles, thread, and other sewing equipment.

"Oh, I shan't cry," said Peter, who was already of opinion that he had never cried in his life. And he clenched his teeth and did not cry, and soon his shadow was behaving properly, though still a little creased.

"Perhaps I should have ironed it," Wendy said thoughtfully, but Peter, boylike, was indifferent to appearances and he was now jumping about in the wildest glee. Alas, he had already forgotten that he owed his bliss to Wendy. He thought he had attached the shadow himself. "How clever I am!" he crowed rapturously, "oh, the cleverness of me!"

It is humiliating to have to confess that this conceit of Peter was one of his most fascinating qualities. To put it with brutal frankness, there never was a cockier boy.

But for the moment Wendy was shocked. "You conceit," she exclaimed, with frightful sarcasm; "of course I did nothing!"

"You did a little," Peter said carelessly, and continued to dance.

"A little!" she replied with hauteur. "If I am no use I can at least withdraw," and she sprang in the most dignified way into bed and covered her face with the blankets.

To induce her to look up he pretended to be going away, and when this failed he sat on the end of the bed and tapped her gently with his foot. "Wendy," he said, "don't withdraw. I can't help crowing, Wendy, when I'm pleased with myself." Still she would not look up, though she was listening eagerly. "Wendy," he continued, in a voice that no woman has ever yet been able to resist, "Wendy, one girl is more use than twenty boys."

Now Wendy was every inch a woman, though there were not very many inches, and she peeped out of the bed-clothes.

"Do you really think so, Peter?"

"Yes, I do."

"I think it's perfectly sweet of you," she declared, "and I'll get up again," and she sat with him on the side of the bed. She also said she would give him a kiss if he liked, but Peter did not know what she meant, and he held out his hand expectantly.

"Surely you know what a kiss is?" she asked, aghast.

"I shall know when you give it to me," he replied stiffly, and not to hurt his feelings she gave him a thimble.

"Now," said he, "shall I give you a kiss?" and she replied with a slight primness, "If you please." She made herself rather cheap by inclining her face toward him, but he merely dropped an acorn button into her hand, so she slowly returned her face to where it had been before, and said nicely that she would wear his kiss on the chain round her neck. It was lucky that she did put it on that chain, for it was afterwards to save her life.

When people in our set are introduced, it is customary for them to ask each other's age, and so Wendy, who always liked to do the correct thing, asked Peter how old he was. It was not really a happy question to ask him; it was like an examination paper that asks grammar, when what you want to be asked is Kings of England.

"I don't know," he replied uneasily, "but I am quite young." He really knew nothing about it, he had merely suspicions, but he said at a venture, "Wendy, I ran away the day I was born."

Wendy was quite surprised, but interested; and she indicated in the charming drawing-room manner, by a touch on her night-gown, that he could sit nearer her.

"It was because I heard father and mother," he explained in a low voice, "talking about what I was to be when I became a man." He was extraordinarily agitated now. "I don't want ever to be a man," he said with passion. "I want always to be a little boy and to have fun. So I ran away to Kensington Gardens and lived a long long time among the fairies."

She gave him a look of the most intense admiration, and he thought it was because he had run away, but it was really because he knew fairies. Wendy had lived such a home life that to know fairies struck her as quite delightful. She poured out questions about them, to his surprise, for they were rather a nuisance to him, getting in his way and so on, and indeed he sometimes had to give them a hiding.* Still, he liked them on the whole, and he told her about the beginning of fairies.

"You see, Wendy, when the first baby laughed for the first time, its laugh broke into a thousand pieces, and they all went skipping about, and that was the beginning of fairies."

Tedious talk this, but being a stay-at-home she liked it.

"And so," he went on good-naturedly, "there ought to be one fairy for every boy and girl."

"Ought to be? Isn't there?"

---

*Spanking.

"No. You see children know such a lot now, they soon don't believe in fairies, and every time a child says, 'I don't believe in fairies,' there is a fairy somewhere that falls down dead."

Really, he thought they had now talked enough about fairies, and it struck him that Tinker Bell was keeping very quiet. "I can't think where she has gone to," he said, rising, and he called Tink by name. Wendy's heart went flutter with a sudden thrill.

"Peter," she cried, clutching him, "you don't mean to tell me that there is a fairy in this room!"

"She was here just now," he said a little impatiently. "You don't hear her, do you?" and they both listened.

"The only sound I hear," said Wendy, "is like a tinkle of bells."

"Well, that's Tink, that's the fairy language. I think I hear her too."

The sound came from the chest of drawers, and Peter made a merry face. No one could ever look quite so merry as Peter, and the loveliest of gurgles was his laugh. He had his first laugh still.

"Wendy," he whispered gleefully, "I do believe I shut her up in the drawer!"

He let poor Tink out of the drawer, and she flew about the nursery screaming with fury. "You shouldn't say such things," Peter retorted. "Of course I'm very sorry, but how could I know you were in the drawer?"

Wendy was not listening to him. "O Peter," she cried, "if she would only stand still and let me see her!"

"They hardly ever stand still," he said, but for one moment Wendy saw the romantic figure come to rest on the cuckoo clock. "O the lovely!" she cried, though Tink's face was still distorted with passion.

"Tink," said Peter amiably, "this lady says she wishes you were her fairy."

Tinker Bell answered insolently.

"What does she say, Peter?"

He had to translate. "She is not very polite. She says you are a great ugly girl, and that she is my fairy."

He tried to argue with Tink. "You know you can't be my fairy, Tink, because I am a gentleman and you are a lady."

To this Tink replied in these words, "You silly ass," and disappeared into the bathroom. "She is quite a common fairy," Peter explained apologetically, "she is called Tinker Bell because she mends the pots and kettles."[2]

They were together in the armchair by this time, and Wendy plied him with more questions.

"If you don't live in Kensington Gardens now——"

"Sometimes I do still."

"But where do you live mostly now?"

"With the lost boys."

"Who are they?"

"They are the children who fall out of their perambulators when the nurse is looking the other way. If they are not claimed in seven days they are sent far away to the Neverland to defray expenses.* I'm captain."

"What fun it must be!"

"Yes," said cunning Peter, "but we are rather lonely. You see we have no female companionship."

"Are none of the others girls?"

"Oh no; girls, you know, are much too clever to fall out of their prams."

This flattered Wendy immensely. "I think," she said, "it is perfectly lovely the way you talk about girls; John there just despises us."

For reply Peter rose and kicked John out of bed, blankets and all; one kick. This seemed to Wendy rather forward for a first meeting, and she told him with spirit that he was not captain in her house. However, John continued to sleep so placidly on the floor that she allowed him to remain there. "And I know you meant to be kind," she said, relenting, "so you may give me a kiss."

For the moment she had forgotten his ignorance about kisses. "I thought you would want it back," he said a little bitterly, and offered to return her the thimble.

"Oh dear," said the nice Wendy, "I don't mean a kiss, I mean a thimble."

"What's that?"

"It's like this." She kissed him.

"Funny!" said Peter gravely. "Now shall I give you a thimble?"

"If you wish to," said Wendy, keeping her head erect this time.

---

*Save money.

Peter thimbled her, and almost immediately she screeched. "What is it, Wendy?"

"It was exactly as if some one were pulling my hair."

"That must have been Tink. I never knew her so naughty before."

And indeed Tink was darting about again, using offensive language.

"She says she will do that to you, Wendy, every time I give you a thimble."

"But why?"

"Why, Tink?"

Again Tink replied, "You silly ass." Peter could not understand why, but Wendy understood, and she was just slightly disappointed when he admitted that he came to the nursery window not to see her but to listen to stories.

"You see I don't know any stories. None of the lost boys know any stories."

"How perfectly awful," Wendy said.

"Do you know," Peter asked, "why swallows build in the eaves of houses? It is to listen to the stories. O Wendy, your mother was telling you such a lovely story."

"Which story was it?"

"About the prince who couldn't find the lady who wore the glass slipper."

"Peter," said Wendy excitedly, "that was Cinderella, and he found her, and they lived happy ever after."

Peter was so glad that he rose from the floor, where they had been sitting, and hurried to the window. "Where are you going?" she cried with misgiving.

"To tell the other boys."

"Don't go, Peter," she entreated, "I know such lots of stories."

Those were her precise words, so there can be no denying that it was she who first tempted him.

He came back, and there was a greedy look in his eyes now which ought to have alarmed her, but did not.

"Oh, the stories I could tell to the boys!" she cried, and then Peter gripped her and began to draw her toward the window.

"Let me go!" she ordered him.

"Wendy, do come with me and tell the other boys."

Of course she was very pleased to be asked, but she said, "Oh dear, I can't. Think of mummy! Besides, I can't fly."

"I'll teach you."

"Oh, how lovely to fly."

"I'll teach you how to jump on the wind's back, and then away we go."

"Oo!" she exclaimed rapturously.

"Wendy, Wendy, when you are sleeping in your silly bed you might be flying about with me saying funny things to the stars."

"Oo!"

"And, Wendy, there are mermaids."

"Mermaids! With tails?"

"Such long tails."

"Oh," cried Wendy, "to see a mermaid!"

He had become frightfully cunning. "Wendy," he said, "how we should all respect you."

She was wriggling her body in distress. It was quite as if she were trying to remain on the nursery floor.

But he had no pity for her.

"Wendy," he said, the sly one, "you could tuck us in at night."

"Oo!"

"None of us has ever been tucked in at night."

"Oo," and her arms went out to him.

"And you could darn our clothes, and make pockets for us. None of us has any pockets."

How could she resist. "Of course it's awfully fascinating!" she cried. "Peter, would you teach John and Michael to fly too?"

"If you like," he said indifferently, and she ran to John and Michael and shook them. "Wake up," she cried, "Peter Pan has come and he is to teach us to fly."

John rubbed his eyes. "Then I shall get up," he said. Of course he was on the floor already. "Hallo," he said, "I am up!"

Michael was up by this time also, looking as sharp as a knife with six blades and a saw,* but Peter suddenly signed silence. Their faces assumed the awful craftiness of children listening for sounds from the

---

*Looking as alert and prepared for any kind of action as a large Swiss army knife.

grown-up world. All was as still as salt.[3] Then everything was right. No, stop! Everything was wrong. Nana, who had been barking distressfully all the evening, was quiet now. It was her silence they had heard!

"Out with the light! Hide! Quick!" cried John, taking command for the only time throughout the whole adventure. And thus when Liza entered, holding Nana, the nursery seemed quite its old self, very dark, and you could have sworn you heard its three wicked inmates breathing angelically as they slept. They were really doing it artfully from behind the window curtains.

Liza was in a bad temper, for she was mixing the Christmas puddings in the kitchen, and had been drawn away from them, with a raisin still on her cheek, by Nana's absurd suspicions. She thought the best way of getting a little quiet was to take Nana to the nursery for a moment, but in custody of course.

"There, you suspicious brute," she said, not sorry that Nana was in disgrace. "They are perfectly safe, aren't they? Every one of the little angels sound asleep in bed. Listen to their gentle breathing."

Here Michael, encouraged by his success, breathed so loudly that they were nearly detected. Nana knew that kind of breathing, and she tried to drag herself out of Liza's clutches.

But Liza was dense. "No more of it, Nana," she said sternly, pulling her out of the room. "I warn you if you bark again I shall go straight for master and missus and bring them home from the party, and then, oh, won't master whip you, just."

She tied the unhappy dog up again, but do you think Nana ceased to bark? Bring master and missus home from the party! Why, that was just what she wanted. Do you think she cared whether she was whipped so long as her charges were safe? Unfortunately Liza returned to her puddings, and Nana, seeing that no help would come from her, strained and strained at the chain until at last she broke it. In another moment she had burst into the dining-room of 27 and flung up her paws to heaven, her most expressive way of making a communication. Mr. and Mrs. Darling knew at once that something terrible was happening in their nursery, and without a good-bye to their hostess they rushed into the street.

But it was now ten minutes since three scoundrels had been breathing behind the curtains, and Peter Pan can do a great deal in ten minutes.

We now return to the nursery.

"It's all right," John announced, emerging from his hiding-place. "I say, Peter, can you really fly?"

Instead of troubling to answer him Peter flew round the room, taking the mantelpiece on the way.

"How topping!"* said John and Michael.

"How sweet!" cried Wendy.

"Yes, I'm sweet, oh, I am sweet!" said Peter, forgetting his manners again.

It looked delightfully easy, and they tried it first from the floor and then from the beds, but they always went down instead of up.

"I say, how do you do it?" asked John, rubbing his knee. He was quite a practical boy.

"You just think lovely wonderful thoughts," Peter explained, "and they lift you up in the air."

He showed them again.

"You're so nippy at it,"† John said, "couldn't you do it very slowly once?"

Peter did it both slowly and quickly. "I've got it now, Wendy!" cried John, but soon he found he had not. Not one of them could fly an inch, though even Michael was in words of two syllables, and Peter did not know A from Z.

Of course Peter had been trifling with them, for no one can fly unless the fairy dust has been blown on him. Fortunately, as we have mentioned, one of his hands was messy with it, and he blew some on each of them, with the most superb results.

"Now just wriggle your shoulders this way," he said, "and let go."

They were all on their beds, and gallant Michael let go first. He did not quite mean to let go, but he did it, and immediately he was borne across the room.

"I flewed!" he screamed while still in mid-air.

John let go and met Wendy near the bathroom.

"Oh, lovely!"

"Oh, ripping!"

---

*First-rate or excellent.

†Meaning "You're quick at it." From "nip," which means to move quickly or dart (chiefly British).

"Look at me!"

"Look at me!"

"Look at me!"

They were not nearly so elegant as Peter, they could not help kicking a little, but their heads were bobbing against the ceiling, and there is almost nothing so delicious as that. Peter gave Wendy a hand at first, but had to desist, Tink was so indignant.

Up and down they went, and round and round. Heavenly was Wendy's word.

"I say," cried John, "why shouldn't we all go out!"

Of course it was to this that Peter had been luring them.

Michael was ready: he wanted to see how long it took him to do a billion miles. But Wendy hesitated.

"Mermaids!" said Peter again.

"Oo!"

"And there are pirates."

"Pirates," cried John, seizing his Sunday hat, "let us go at once!"

It was just at this moment that Mr. and Mrs. Darling hurried with Nana out of 27. They ran into the middle of the street to look up at the nursery window; and, yes, it was still shut, but the room was ablaze with light, and most heart-gripping sight of all, they could see in shadow on the curtain three little figures in night attire circling round and round, not on the floor but in the air.

Not three figures, four!

In a tremble they opened the street door. Mr. Darling would have rushed upstairs, but Mrs. Darling signed to him to go softly. She even tried to make her heart go softly.

Will they reach the nursery in time? If so, how delightful for them, and we shall all breathe a sigh of relief, but there will be no story. On the other hand, if they are not in time, I solemnly promise that it will all come right in the end.

They would have reached the nursery in time had it not been that the little stars were watching them. Once again the stars blew the window open, and that smallest star of all called out:

"Cave,* Peter!"

---

*Beware (Latin).

THE BIRDS WERE FLOWN

Peter knew that there was not a moment to lose. "Come," he cried imperiously, and soared out at once into the night, followed by John and Michael and Wendy.

Mr. and Mrs. Darling and Nana rushed into the nursery too late. The birds were flown.[4]

CHAPTER IV

The Flight

SECOND TO THE RIGHT, and straight on till morning."

That, Peter had told Wendy, was the way to the Neverland; but even birds, carrying maps and consulting them at windy corners, could not have sighted it with these instructions. Peter, you see, just said anything that came into his head.

At first his companions trusted him implicitly, and so great were the delights of flying that they wasted time circling round church spires or any other tall objects on the way that took their fancy.

John and Michael raced, Michael getting a start.

They recalled with contempt that not so long ago they had thought themselves fine fellows for being able to fly round a room.

Not so long ago. But how long ago? They were flying over the sea before this thought began to disturb Wendy seriously. John thought it was their second sea and their third night.

Sometimes it was dark and sometimes light, and now they were very cold and again too warm. Did they really feel hungry at times, or were they merely pretending, because Peter had such a jolly new way of feeding them? His way was to pursue birds who had food in their mouths suitable for humans and snatch it from them; then the birds would follow and snatch it back; and they would all go chasing each other gaily for miles, parting at last with mutual expressions of good-will. But Wendy noticed with gentle concern that Peter did not seem to know that this was rather an odd way of getting your bread and butter, nor even that there are other ways.

Certainly they did not pretend to be sleepy, they were sleepy; and that was a danger, for the moment they popped off,* down they fell. The awful thing was that Peter thought this funny.

"There he goes again!" he would cry gleefully, as Michael suddenly dropped like a stone.

"Save him, save him!" cried Wendy, looking with horror at the cruel sea far below. Eventually Peter would dive through the air, and catch Michael just before he could strike the sea, and it was lovely the way he did it; but he always waited till the last moment, and you felt it was his cleverness that interested him and not the saving of human life. Also he was fond of variety, and the sport that engrossed him one moment would suddenly cease to engage him, so there was always the possibility that the next time you fell he would let you go.

He could sleep in the air without falling, by merely lying on his back and floating, but this was, partly at least, because he was so light that if you got behind him and blew he went faster.

"Do be more polite to him," Wendy whispered to John, when they were playing "Follow my Leader."

"Then tell him to stop showing off," said John.

When playing Follow my Leader, Peter would fly close to the water and touch each shark's tail in passing, just as in the street you may run your finger along an iron railing. They could not follow him in this with much success, so perhaps it was rather like showing off, especially as he kept looking behind to see how many tails they missed.

"You must be nice to him," Wendy impressed on her brothers. "What could we do if he were to leave us!"

"We could go back," Michael said.

"How could we ever find our way back without him?"

"Well, then, we could go on," said John.

"That is the awful thing, John. We should have to go on, for we don't know how to stop."

This was true, Peter had forgotten to show them how to stop.

John said that if the worst came to the worst, all they had to do was to go straight on, for the world was round, and so in time they must come back to their own window.

"And who is to get food for us, John?"

---

*Fell asleep.

"I nipped a bit out of that eagle's mouth pretty neatly, Wendy."

"After the twentieth try," Wendy reminded him. "And even though we became good at picking up food, see how we bump against clouds and things if he is not near to give us a hand."

Indeed they were constantly bumping. They could now fly strongly, though they still kicked far too much; but if they saw a cloud in front of them, the more they tried to avoid it, the more certainly did they bump into it. If Nana had been with them, she would have had a bandage round Michael's forehead by this time.

Peter was not with them for the moment, and they felt rather lonely up there by themselves. He could go so much faster than they that he would suddenly shoot out of sight, to have some adventure in which they had no share. He would come down laughing over something fearfully funny he had been saying to a star, but he had already forgotten what it was, or he would come up with mermaid scales still sticking to him, and yet not be able to say for certain what had been happening. It was really rather irritating to children who had never seen a mermaid.

"And if he forgets them so quickly," Wendy argued, "how can we expect that he will go on remembering us?"

Indeed, sometimes when he returned he did not remember them, at least not well. Wendy was sure of it. She saw recognition come into his eyes as he was about to pass them the time of day and go on; once even she had to call him by name.

"I'm Wendy," she said agitatedly.

He was very sorry. "I say, Wendy," he whispered to her, "always if you see me forgetting you, just keep on saying 'I'm Wendy,' and then I'll remember."

Of course this was rather unsatisfactory. However, to make amends he showed them how to lie out flat on a strong wind that was going their way, and this was such a pleasant change that they tried it several times and found they could sleep thus with security. Indeed they would have slept longer, but Peter tired quickly of sleeping, and soon he would cry in his captain voice, "We get off here." So with occasional tiffs, but on the whole rollicking,* they drew near the Neverland; for after many moons they did reach it,

---

*Carefree and high-spirited.

"LET HIM KEEP WHO CAN"

and, what is more, they had been going pretty straight all the time, not perhaps so much owing to the guidance of Peter or Tink as because the island was out looking for them. It is only thus that any one may sight those magic shores.

"There it is," said Peter calmly.

"Where, where?"

"Where all the arrows are pointing."

Indeed a million golden arrows were pointing it out to the children, all directed by their friend the sun, who wanted them to be sure of their way before leaving them for the night.

Wendy and John and Michael stood on tip-toe in the air to get their first sight of the island. Strange to say, they all recognised it at once, and until fear fell upon them they hailed it, not as something long dreamt of and seen at last, but as a familiar friend to whom they were returning home for the holidays.

"John, there's the lagoon!"

"Wendy, look at the turtles burying their eggs in the sand."

"I say, John, I see your flamingo with the broken leg!"

"Look, Michael, there's your cave!"

"John, what's that in the brushwood?"

"It's a wolf with her whelps.* Wendy, I do believe that's your little whelp!"

"There's my boat, John, with her sides stove in!"†

"No, it isn't! Why, we burned your boat."

"That's her, at any rate. I say, John, I see the smoke of the redskin camp!"

"Where? Show me, and I'll tell you by the way the smoke curls whether they are on the war-path."

"There, just across the Mysterious River."

"I see now. Yes, they are on the war-path right enough."

Peter was a little annoyed with them for knowing so much, but if he wanted to lord it over them his triumph was at hand, for have I not told you that anon‡ fear fell upon them?

It came as the arrows went, leaving the island in gloom.

---

*Young offspring of various carnivorous animals, especially dogs or wolves.
†Nautical term describing a boat rendered useless by holes broken in the hull.
‡Straightaway; at once; without hesitation.

THE NEVER NEVER LAND

In the old days at home the Neverland had always begun to look a little dark and threatening by bedtime. Then unexplored patches arose in it and spread, black shadows moved about in them, the roar of the beasts of prey was quite different now, and above all, you lost the certainty that you would win. You were quite glad that the night-lights were in. You even liked Nana to say that this was just the mantelpiece over here, and that the Neverland was all make-believe.

Of course the Neverland had been make-believe in those days, but it was real now, and there were no night-lights, and it was getting darker every moment, and where was Nana?

They had been flying apart, but they huddled close to Peter now. His careless manner had gone at last, his eyes were sparkling, and a tingle went through them every time they touched his body. They were now over the fearsome island, flying so low that sometimes a tree grazed their feet. Nothing horrid was visible in the air, yet their progress had become slow and laboured, exactly as if they were pushing their way through hostile forces. Sometimes they hung in the air until Peter had beaten on it with his fists.

"They don't want us to land," he explained.

"Who are they?" Wendy whispered, shuddering.

But he could not or would not say. Tinker Bell had been asleep on his shoulder, but now he wakened her and sent her on in front.

Sometimes he poised himself in the air, listening intently, with his hand to his ear, and again he would stare down with eyes so bright that they seemed to bore two holes to earth. Having done these things, he went on again.

His courage was almost appalling. "Would you like an adventure now," he said casually to John, "or would you like to have your tea first?"

Wendy said "tea first" quickly, and Michael pressed her hand in gratitude but the braver John hesitated.

"What kind of adventure?" he asked cautiously.

"There's a pirate asleep in the pampas* just beneath us," Peter told him. "If you like, we'll go down and kill him."

"I don't see him," John said after a long pause.

---

*Vast grass-covered plains located mostly in central Argentina.

"I do."

"Suppose," John said, a little huskily, "he were to wake up."

Peter spoke indignantly. "You don't think I would kill him while he was sleeping! I would wake him first, and then kill him. That's the way I always do."

"I say! Do you kill many?"

"Tons."

John said "how ripping," but decided to have tea first. He asked if there were many pirates on the island just now, and Peter said he had never known so many.

"Who is captain now?"

"Hook," answered Peter, and his face became very stern as he said that hated word.

"Jas. Hook?"[1]

"Ay."

Then indeed Michael began to cry, and even John could speak in gulps only, for they knew Hook's reputation.

"He was Blackbeard's bo'sun,"* John whispered huskily. "He is the worst of them all. He is the only man of whom Barbecue was afraid."†

"That's him," said Peter.

"What is he like? Is he big?"

"He is not so big as he was."

"How do you mean?"

"I cut off a bit of him."

"You!"

"Yes, me," said Peter sharply.

"I wasn't meaning to be disrespectful."

"Oh, all right."

"But, I say, what bit?"

"His right hand."

"Then he can't fight now?"

"Oh, can't he just!"

"Left-hander?"

---

*Variant of "boatswain," an officer in charge of a ship's rigging, anchors, cables, and deck crew.

†"Barbecue" was the crew's name for Long John Silver, the head pirate in Robert Lewis Stevenson's novel *Treasure Island* (1883).

"He has an iron hook instead of a right hand, and he claws with it."

"Claws!"

"I say, John," said Peter.

"Yes."

"Say, 'Ay, ay, sir.'"

"Ay, ay, sir."

"There is one thing," Peter continued, "that every boy who serves under me has to promise, and so must you."

John paled.

"It is this, if we meet Hook in open fight, you must leave him to me."

"I promise," John said loyally.

For the moment they were feeling less eerie, because Tink was flying with them, and in her light they could distinguish each other. Unfortunately she could not fly so slowly as they, and so she had to go round and round them in a circle in which they moved as in a halo. Wendy quite liked it, until Peter pointed out the drawback.

"She tells me," he said, "that the pirates sighted us before the darkness came, and got Long Tom* out."

"The big gun?"

"Yes. And of course they must see her light, and if they guess we are near it they are sure to let fly."

"Wendy!"

"John!"

"Michael!"

"Tell her to go away at once, Peter," the three cried simultaneously, but he refused.

"She thinks we have lost the way," he replied stiffly, "and she is rather frightened. You don't think I would send her away all by herself when she is frightened!"

For a moment the circle of light was broken, and something gave Peter a loving little pinch.

"Then tell her," Wendy begged, "to put out her light."

"She can't put it out. That is about the only thing fairies can't do. It just goes out of itself when she falls asleep, same as the stars."

---

*A large, long-range cannon.

"Then tell her to sleep at once," John almost ordered.

"She can't sleep except when she's sleepy. It's the only other thing fairies can't do."

"Seems to me," growled John, "these are the only two things worth doing."

Here he got a pinch, but not a loving one.

"If only one of us had a pocket," Peter said, "we could carry her in it." However, they had set off in such a hurry that there was not a pocket between the four of them.

He had a happy idea. John's hat!

Tink agreed to travel by hat if it was carried in the hand. John carried it, though she had hoped to be carried by Peter. Presently Wendy took the hat, because John said it struck against his knee as he flew; and this, as we shall see, led to mischief, for Tinker Bell hated to be under an obligation to Wendy.

In the black topper* the light was completely hidden, and they flew on in silence. It was the stillest silence they had ever known, broken once by a distant lapping, which Peter explained was the wild beasts drinking at the ford,† and again by a rasping sound that might have been the branches of trees rubbing together, but he said it was the redskins sharpening their knives.

Even these noises ceased. To Michael the loneliness was dreadful. "If only something would make a sound!" he cried.

As if in answer to his request, the air was rent by the most tremendous crash he had ever heard. The pirates had fired Long Tom at them.

The roar of it echoed through the mountains, and the echoes seemed to cry savagely, "Where are they, where are they, where are they?"

Thus sharply did the terrified three learn the difference between an island of make-believe and the same island come true.

When at last the heavens were steady again, John and Michael found themselves alone in the darkness. John was treading the air mechanically, and Michael without knowing how to float was floating.

---

*John's black top hat; a topper was typically made of silk.

†Place in a body of water where it is shallow enough to wade.

"Are you shot?" John whispered tremulously.

"I haven't tried yet," Michael whispered back.

We know now that no one had been hit. Peter, however, had been carried by the wind of the shot far out to sea, while Wendy was blown upwards with no companion but Tinker Bell.

It would have been well for Wendy if at that moment she had dropped the hat.

I don't know whether the idea came suddenly to Tink, or whether she had planned it on the way, but she at once popped out of the hat and began to lure Wendy to her destruction.

Tink was not all bad: or, rather, she was all bad just now, but, on the other hand, sometimes she was all good. Fairies have to be one thing or the other, because being so small they unfortunately have room for one feeling only at a time. They are, however, allowed to change, only it must be a complete change. At present she was full of jealousy of Wendy. What she said in her lovely tinkle Wendy could not of course understand, and I believe some of it was bad words, but it sounded kind, and she flew back and forward, plainly meaning "Follow me, and all will be well."

What else could poor Wendy do? She called to Peter and John and Michael, and got only mocking echoes in reply. She did not yet know that Tink hated her with the fierce hatred of a very woman. And so, bewildered, and now staggering in her flight, she followed Tink to her doom.

CHAPTER V

The Island Come True

FEELING THAT PETER WAS on his way back, the Neverland had again woke into life. We ought to use the pluperfect and say wakened, but woke is better and was always used by Peter.

In his absence things are usually quiet on the island. The fairies take an hour longer in the morning, the beasts attend to their young, the redskins feed heavily for six days and nights, and when pirates and lost boys meet they merely bite their thumbs at each other. But with the coming of Peter, who hates lethargy, they are all under way again: if you put your ear to the ground now, you would hear the whole island seething with life.

On this evening the chief forces of the island were disposed as follows. The lost boys were out looking for Peter, the pirates were out looking for the lost boys, the redskins were out looking for the pirates, and the beasts were out looking for the redskins. They were going round and round the island, but they did not meet because all were going at the same rate.

All wanted blood except the boys, who liked it as a rule, but tonight were out to greet their captain. The boys on the island vary, of course, in numbers, according as they get killed and so on; and when they seem to be growing up, which is against the rules, Peter thins them out; but at this time there were six of them, counting the twins as two. Let us pretend to lie here among the sugar-cane and watch them as they steal by in single file, each with his hand on his dagger.

They are forbidden by Peter to look in the least like him, and they wear the skins of bears slain by themselves, in which they are so round and furry that when they fall they roll. They have therefore become very sure-footed.

The first to pass is Tootles, not the least brave but the most unfortunate of all that gallant band. He had been in fewer adventures than any of them, because the big things constantly happened just when he had stepped round the corner; all would be quiet, he would take the opportunity of going off to gather a few sticks for firewood, and then when he returned the others would be sweeping up the blood. This ill-luck had given a gentle melancholy to his countenance, but instead of souring his nature had sweetened it, so that he was quite the humblest of the boys. Poor kind Tootles, there is danger in the air for you to-night. Take care lest an adventure is now offered you, which, if accepted, will plunge you in deepest woe. Tootles, the fairy Tink who is bent on mischief this night is looking for a tool, and she thinks you the most easily tricked of the boys. 'Ware Tinker Bell.

Would that he could hear us, but we are not really on the island, and he passes by, biting his knuckles.

Next comes Nibs, the gay and debonair, followed by Slightly,[1] who cuts whistles out of the trees and dances ecstatically to his own tunes. Slightly is the most conceited of the boys. He thinks he remembers the days before he was lost, with their manners and customs, and this has given his nose an offensive tilt. Curly is fourth; he is a pickle,* and so often has he had to deliver up his person when Peter said sternly, "Stand forth the one who did this thing," that now at the command he stands forth automatically whether he has done it or no. Last come the Twins, who cannot be described because we should be sure to be describing the wrong one. Peter never quite knew what twins were, and his band were not allowed to know anything he did not know, so these two were always vague about themselves, and did their best to give satisfaction by keeping close together in an apologetic sort of way.

The boys vanish in the gloom, and after a pause, but not a long pause, for things go briskly on the island, come the pirates on their

---

*Boy who is always causing trouble; wild young fellow (British).

track. We hear them before they are seen, and it is always the same dreadful song:

"Avast belay, yo ho, heave to,[*]
A-pirating we go,
And if we're parted by a shot
We're sure to meet below!"

A more villainous-looking lot never hung in a row on Execution dock.[†] Here, a little in advance, ever and again with his head to the ground listening, his great arms bare, pieces of eight[‡] in his ears as ornaments, is the handsome Italian Cecco, who cut his name in letters of blood on the back of the governor of the prison at Gao. That gigantic black behind him has had many names since he dropped the one with which dusky mothers still terrify their children on the banks of the Guadjo-mo. Here is Bill Jukes, every inch of him tattooed, the same Bill Jukes who got six dozen on the *Walrus* from Flint[§] before he would drop the bag of moidores;[||] and Cookson, said to be Black Murphy's brother (but this was never proved), and Gentleman Starkey, once an usher in a public school and still dainty in his ways of killing; and Skylights (Morgan's Skylights);[#] and the Irish bo'sun Smee, an oddly genial man who stabbed, so to speak, without offence, and was the only Nonconformist[**] in Hook's crew; and Noodler, whose hands were fixed on backwards; and Robt. Mullins and Alf Mason and many another ruffian long known and feared on the Spanish Main.

---

*Nautical commands meaning "stop," "secure a line," "turn the ship's head into the wind or sea and hold steady."

†In London's East End; the place where those sentenced to death (especially pirates) were hanged.

‡Old Spanish silver coins.

§He was whipped six dozen times on the *Walrus*, described in chapter 11 of *Treasure Island* as being "Flint's old ship."

||Portuguese or Brazilian gold coins that circulated in England in the early eighteenth century.

#Both Murphy and Morgan were real pirates in history; an usher was an assistant schoolmaster.

**Member of a church that has separated from the Church of England—a term meant to suppress non-Protestants; also, one who refuses to conform to a particular practice or course of action.

In the midst of them, the blackest and largest jewel in that dark setting, reclined James Hook, or as he wrote himself, Jas. Hook, of whom it is said he was the only man that the Sea-Cook* feared. He lay at his ease in a rough chariot drawn and propelled by his men, and instead of a right hand he had the iron hook with which ever and anon† he encouraged them to increase their pace. As dogs this terrible man treated and addressed them, and as dogs they obeyed him. In person he was cadaverous and blackavized,‡ and his hair was dressed in long curls, which at a little distance looked like black candles, and gave a singularly threatening expression to his handsome countenance. His eyes were of the blue of the forget-me-not,§ and of a profound melancholy, save when he was plunging his hook into you, at which time two red spots appeared in them and lit them up horribly. In manner, something of the grand seigneur still clung to him, so that he even ripped you up with an air, and I have been told that he was a *raconteur* of repute.|| He was never more sinister than when he was most polite, which is probably the truest test of breeding; and the elegance of his diction, even when he was swearing, no less than the distinction of his demeanour, showed him one of a different caste from his crew. A man of indomitable courage, it was said of him that the only thing he shied at was the sight of his own blood, which was thick and of an unusual colour. In dress he somewhat aped the attire associated with the name of Charles II,[2] having heard it said in some earlier period of his career that he bore a strange resemblance to the ill-fated Stuarts;[3] and in his mouth he had a holder of his own contrivance which enabled him to smoke two cigars at once. But undoubtedly the grimmest part of him was his iron claw.

Let us now kill a pirate, to show Hook's method. Skylights will do. As they pass, Skylights lurches clumsily against him, ruffling his lace collar; the hook shoots forth, there is a tearing sound and one

---

*Another name for Long John Silver (see note on p. 45); *The Sea Cook* was the original title of Stevenson's *Treasure Island*.

†Now and then; occasionally.

‡Having a dark complexion.

§Herbaceous plant of the genus *Myosotis* with clusters of small blue flowers; also called "scorpion grass."

||Storyteller (French) with a reputation for skill and wit.

screech, then the body is kicked aside, and the pirates pass on. He has not even taken the cigars from his mouth.

Such is the terrible man against whom Peter Pan is pitted. Which will win?

On the trail of the pirates, stealing noiselessly down the war-path which is not visible to inexperienced eyes, come the redskins, every one of them with his eyes peeled. They carry tomahawks and knives, and their naked bodies gleam with paint and oil. Strung around them are scalps, of boys as well as of pirates, for these are the Piccaninny tribe, and not to be confused with the softer-hearted Delawares or the Hurons. In the van, on all fours, is Great Big Little Panther, a brave of so many scalps that in his present position they somewhat impede his progress. Bringing up the rear, the place of greatest danger, comes Tiger Lily, proudly erect, a princess in her own right. She is the most beautiful of dusky Dianas and the belle of the Piccaninnies, coquettish, cold and amorous by turns; there is not a brave who would not have the wayward thing to wife, but she staves off the altar with a hatchet.* Observe how they pass over fallen twigs without making the slightest noise. The only sound to be heard is their somewhat heavy breathing. The fact is that they are all a little fat just now after the heavy gorging, but in time they will work this off. For the moment, however, it constitutes their chief danger.

The redskins disappear as they have come like shadows, and soon their place is taken by the beasts, a great and motley procession: lions, tigers, bears, and the innumerable smaller savage things that flee from them, for every kind of beast, and, more particularly, all the man-eaters, live cheek by jowl on the favoured island. Their tongues are hanging out, they are hungry to-night.

When they have passed, comes the last figure of all, a gigantic crocodile. We shall see for whom she is looking presently.

The crocodile passes, but soon the boys appear again, for the procession must continue indefinitely until one of the parties stops or changes its pace. Then quickly they will be on top of each other.

---

*She holds off or repels marriage with a fighting ax.

All are keeping a sharp look-out in front, but none suspects that the danger may be creeping up from behind. This shows how real the island was.

The first to fall out of the moving circle was the boys. They flung themselves down on the sward,* close to their underground home.

"I do wish Peter would come back," every one of them said nervously, though in height and still more in breadth they were all larger than their captain.

"I am the only one who is not afraid of the pirates," Slightly said, in the tone that prevented his being a general favourite, but perhaps some distant sound disturbed him, for he added hastily, "but I wish he would come back, and tell us whether he has heard anything more about Cinderella."

They talked of Cinderella, and Tootles was confident that his mother must have been very like her.

It was only in Peter's absence that they could speak of mothers, the subject being forbidden by him as silly.

"All I remember about my mother," Nibs told them, "is that she often said to father, 'Oh, how I wish I had a cheque-book of my own!' I don't know what a cheque-book is, but I should just love to give my mother one."

While they talked they heard a distant sound. You or I, not being wild things of the woods, would have heard nothing, but they heard it, and it was the grim song:

"Yo ho, yo ho, the pirate life,
The flag o' skull and bones,
A merry hour, a hempen rope,†
And hey for Davy Jones."

At once the lost boys—but where are they? They are no longer there. Rabbits could not have disappeared more quickly.

I will tell you where they are. With the exception of Nibs, who

---

*Land covered with grass.

†Rope made from the tough, woody fibers of the hemp plant; hempen ropes were used for hanging people.

has darted away to reconnoitre,* they are already in their home under the ground, a very delightful residence of which we shall see a good deal presently. But how have they reached it? for there is no entrance to be seen, not so much as a large stone, which if rolled away would disclose the mouth of a cave. Look closely, however, and you may note that there are here seven large trees, each with a hole in its hollow trunk as large as a boy. These are the seven entrances to the home under the ground, for which Hook has been searching in vain these many moons. Will he find it to-night?

As the pirates advanced, the quick eye of Starkey sighted Nibs disappearing through the wood, and at once his pistol flashed out. But an iron claw gripped his shoulder.

"Captain, let go!" he cried, writhing.

Now for the first time we hear the voice of Hook. It was a black voice. "Put back that pistol first," it said threateningly.

"It was one of those boys you hate. I could have shot him dead."

"Ay, and the sound would have brought Tiger Lily's redskins upon us. Do you want to lose your scalp?"

"Shall I after him, captain," asked pathetic Smee, "and tickle him with Johnny Corkscrew?" Smee had pleasant names for everything, and his cutlass† was Johnny Corkscrew, because he wriggled it in the wound. One could mention many lovable traits in Smee. For instance, after killing, it was his spectacles he wiped instead of his weapon.

"Johnny's a silent fellow," he reminded Hook.

"Not now, Smee," Hook said darkly. "He is only one, and I want to mischief all the seven. Scatter and look for them."

The pirates disappeared among the trees, and in a moment their captain and Smee were alone. Hook heaved a heavy sigh, and I know not why it was, perhaps it was because of the soft beauty of the evening, but there came over him a desire to confide to his faithful bo'sun the story of his life. He spoke long and earnestly, but what it was all about Smee, who was rather stupid, did not know in the least.

Anon he caught the word Peter.

---

*To examine or survey the scene in an attempt to find someone or something (French).

†Short, heavy sword with a curved, single-edged blade; once used by sailors on warships.

"Most of all," Hook was saying passionately, "I want their captain, Peter Pan. 'Twas he cut off my arm." He brandished the hook threateningly. "I've waited long to shake his hand with this. Oh, I'll tear him!"

"And yet," said Smee, "I have often heard you say that hook was worth a score of hands, for combing the hair and other homely uses."

"Ay," the captain answered, "if I was a mother I would pray to have my children born with this instead of that," and he cast a look of pride upon his iron hand and one of scorn upon the other. Then again he frowned.

"Peter flung my arm," he said, wincing, "to a crocodile that happened to be passing by."

"I have often," said Smee, "noticed your strange dread of crocodiles."

"Not of crocodiles," Hook corrected him, "but of that one crocodile." He lowered his voice. "It liked my arm so much, Smee, that it has followed me ever since, from sea to sea and from land to land, licking its lips for the rest of me."

"In a way," said Smee, "it's a sort of compliment."

"I want no such compliments," Hook barked petulantly. "I want Peter Pan, who first gave the brute its taste for me."

He sat down on a large mushroom, and now there was a quiver in his voice. "Smee," he said huskily, "that crocodile would have had me before this, but by a lucky chance it swallowed a clock which goes tick tick inside it, and so before it can reach me I hear the tick and bolt." He laughed, but in a hollow way.

"Some day," said Smee, "the clock will run down, and then he'll get you."

Hook wetted his dry lips. "Ay," he said, "that's the fear that haunts me."

Since sitting down he had felt curiously warm. "Smee," he said, "this seat is hot." He jumped up. "Odds bobs, hammer and tongs,[4] I'm burning."

They examined the mushroom, which was of a size and solidity unknown on the mainland; they tried to pull it up, and it came away at once in their hands, for it had no root. Stranger still, smoke began at once to ascend. The pirates looked at each other. "A chimney!" they both exclaimed.

They had indeed discovered the chimney of the home under the ground. It was the custom of the boys to stop it with a mushroom when enemies were in the neighbourhood.

Not only smoke came out of it. There came also children's voices, for so safe did the boys feel in their hiding-place that they were gaily chattering. The pirates listened grimly, and then replaced the mushroom. They looked around them and noted the holes in the seven trees.

"Did you hear them say Peter Pan's from home?" Smee whispered, fidgeting with Johnny Corkscrew.

Hook nodded. He stood for a long time lost in thought, and at last a curdling smile lit up his swarthy face. Smee had been waiting for it. "Unrip your plan, captain," he cried eagerly.

"To return to the ship," Hook replied slowly through his teeth, "and cook a large rich cake of a jolly thickness with green sugar on it. There can be but one room below, for there is but one chimney. The silly moles had not the sense to see that they did not need a door apiece. That shows they have no mother. We will leave the cake on the shore of the mermaids' lagoon. These boys are always swimming about there, playing with the mermaids. They will find the cake and they will gobble it up, because, having no mother, they don't know how dangerous 'tis to eat rich damp cake." He burst into laughter, not hollow laughter now, but honest laughter. "Aha, they will die!"

Smee had listened with growing admiration.

"It's the wickedest, prettiest policy ever I heard of!" he cried, and in their exultation they danced and sang:

"Avast, belay, when I appear,
  By fear they're overtook;
Nought's left upon your bones when you
  Have shaken claws with Hook."

They began the verse, but they never finished it, for another sound broke in and stilled them. It was at first such a tiny sound that a leaf might have fallen on it and smothered it, but as it came nearer it was more distinct.

Tick tick tick tick!

Hook stood shuddering, one foot in the air.

"The crocodile!" he gasped, and bounded away, followed by his bo'sun.

It was indeed the crocodile. It had passed the redskins, who were now on the trail of the other pirates. It oozed on after Hook.

Once more the boys emerged into the open; but the dangers of the night were not yet over, for presently Nibs rushed breathless into their midst, pursued by a pack of wolves. The tongues of the pursuers were hanging out; the baying of them was horrible.

"Save me, save me!" cried Nibs, falling on the ground.

"But what can we do, what can we do?"

It was a high compliment to Peter that at that dire moment their thoughts turned to him.

"What would Peter do?" they cried simultaneously.

Almost in the same breath they cried, "Peter would look at them through his legs."

And then, "Let us do what Peter would do."

It is quite the most successful way of defying wolves, and as one boy they bent and looked through their legs. The next moment is the long one, but victory came quickly, for as the boys advanced upon them in this terrible attitude, the wolves dropped their tails and fled.

Now Nibs rose from the ground, and the others thought that his staring eyes still saw the wolves. But it was not wolves he saw.

"I have seen a wonderfuller thing," he cried, as they gathered round him eagerly. "A great white bird. It is flying this way."

"What kind of a bird, do you think?"

"I don't know," Nibs said, awestruck, "but it looks so weary, and as it flies it moans, 'Poor Wendy.'"

"Poor Wendy?"

"I remember," said Slightly instantly, "there are birds called Wendies."

"See, it comes!" cried Curly, pointing to Wendy in the heavens.

Wendy was now almost overhead, and they could hear her plaintive cry. But more distinct came the shrill voice of Tinker Bell. The jealous fairy had now cast off all disguise of friendship, and was darting at her victim from every direction, pinching savagely each time she touched.

"Hullo, Tink," cried the wondering boys.

Tink's reply rang out: "Peter wants you to shoot the Wendy."

It was not in their nature to question when Peter ordered. "Let us do what Peter wishes," cried the simple boys. "Quick, bows and arrows."

All but Tootles popped down their trees. He had a bow and arrow with him, and Tink noted it, and rubbed her little hands.

"Quick, Tootles, quick," she screamed. "Peter will be so pleased."

Tootles excitedly fitted the arrow to his bow. "Out of the way, Tink," he shouted, and then he fired, and Wendy fluttered to the ground with an arrow in her breast.

CHAPTER VI

The Little House

FOOLISH TOOTLES WAS STANDING like a conqueror over Wendy's body when the other boys sprang, armed, from their trees.

"You are too late," he cried proudly, "I have shot the Wendy. Peter will be so pleased with me."

Overhead Tinker Bell shouted "Silly ass!" and darted into hiding. The others did not hear her. They had crowded round Wendy, and as they looked a terrible silence fell upon the wood. If Wendy's heart had been beating they would all have heard it.

Slightly was the first to speak. "This is no bird," he said in a scared voice. "I think it must be a lady."

"A lady?" said Tootles, and fell a-trembling.

"And we have killed her," Nibs said hoarsely.

They all whipped off their caps.

"Now I see," Curly said; "Peter was bringing her to us." He threw himself sorrowfully on the ground.

"A lady to take care of us at last," said one of the twins, "and you have killed her!"

They were sorry for him, but sorrier for themselves, and when he took a step nearer them they turned from him.

Tootles' face was very white, but there was a dignity about him now that had never been there before.

"I did it," he said, reflecting. "When ladies used to come to me in dreams, I said, 'Pretty mother, pretty mother.' But when at last she really came, I shot her."

He moved slowly away.

"Don't go," they called in pity.

"I must," he answered, shaking; "I am so afraid of Peter."

It was at this tragic moment that they heard a sound which made the heart of every one of them rise to his mouth. They heard Peter crow.

"Peter!" they cried, for it was always thus that he signalled his return.

"Hide her," they whispered, and gathered hastily around Wendy. But Tootles stood aloof.

Again came that ringing crow, and Peter dropped in front of them. "Greeting, boys," he cried, and mechanically they saluted, and then again was silence.

He frowned.

"I am back," he said hotly, "why do you not cheer?"

They opened their mouths, but the cheers would not come. He overlooked it in his haste to tell the glorious tidings.

"Great news, boys," he cried, "I have brought at last a mother for you all."

Still no sound, except a little thud from Tootles as he dropped on his knees.

"Have you not seen her?" asked Peter, becoming troubled. "She flew this way."

"Ah me!" one voice said, and another said, "Oh, mournful day."

Tootles rose. "Peter," he said quietly, "I will show her to you," and when the others would still have hidden her he said, "Back, twins, let Peter see."

So they all stood hack, and let him see, and after he had looked for a little time he did not know what to do next.

"She is dead," he said uncomfortably. "Perhaps she is frightened at being dead."

He thought of hopping off in a comic sort of way till he was out of sight of her, and then never going near the spot any more. They would all have been glad to follow if he had done this.

But there was the arrow. He took it from her heart and faced his band.

"Whose arrow?" he demanded sternly.

"Mine, Peter," said Tootles on his knees.

"Oh, dastard hand,"* Peter said, and he raised the arrow to use it as a dagger.

---

*Treacherous; betraying; underhanded.

Tootles did not flinch. He bared his breast. "Strike, Peter," he said firmly, "strike true."

Twice did Peter raise the arrow, and twice did his hand fall. "I cannot strike," he said with awe, "there is something stays* my hand."

All looked at him in wonder, save Nibs, who fortunately looked at Wendy.

"It is she," he cried, "the Wendy lady, see, her arm!"

Wonderful to relate, Wendy had raised her arm. Nibs bent over her and listened reverently. "I think she said 'Poor Tootles,'" he whispered.

"She lives," Peter said briefly.

Slightly cried instantly, "The Wendy lady lives."

Then Peter knelt beside her and found his button. You remember she had put it on a chain that she wore round her neck.

"See," he said, "the arrow struck against this. It is the kiss I gave her. It has saved her life."

"I remember kisses," Slightly interposed quickly, "let me see it. Ay, that's a kiss."

Peter did not hear him. He was begging Wendy to get better quickly, so that he could show her the mermaids. Of course she could not answer yet, being still in a frightful faint; but from overhead came a wailing note.

"Listen to Tink," said Curly, "she is crying because the Wendy lives."

Then they had to tell Peter of Tink's crime, and almost never had they seen him look so stern.

"Listen, Tinker Bell," he cried, "I am your friend no more. Begone from me for ever."

She flew on to his shoulder and pleaded, but he brushed her off. Not until Wendy again raised her arm did he relent sufficiently to say, "Well, not for ever, but for a whole week."

Do you think Tinker Bell was grateful to Wendy for raising her arm? Oh dear no, never wanted to pinch her so much. Fairies indeed are strange, and Peter, who understood them best, often cuffed† them.

But what to do with Wendy in her present delicate state of health?

"Let us carry her down into the house," Curly suggested.

---

*Holds back, restrains.

†Struck with an open hand.

"Ay," said Slightly, "that is what one does with ladies."

"No, no," Peter said, "you must not touch her. It would not be sufficiently respectful."

"That," said Slightly, "is what I was thinking."

"But if she lies there," Tootles said, "she will die."

"Ay, she will die," Slightly admitted, "but there is no way out."

"Yes, there is," cried Peter. "Let us build a little house round her."

They were all delighted. "Quick," he ordered them, "bring me each of you the best of what we have. Gut our house. Be sharp."

In a moment they were as busy as tailors the night before a wedding. They skurried this way and that, down for bedding, up for firewood, and while they were at it, who should appear but John and Michael. As they dragged along the ground they fell asleep standing, stopped, woke up, moved another step and slept again.

"John, John," Michael would cry, "wake up! Where is Nana, John, and mother?"

And then John would rub his eyes and mutter, "It is true, we did fly."

You may be sure they were very relieved to find Peter.

"Hullo, Peter," they said.

"Hullo," replied Peter amicably, though he had quite forgotten them. He was very busy at the moment measuring Wendy with his feet to see how large a house she would need. Of course he meant to leave room for chairs and a table. John and Michael watched him.

"Is Wendy asleep?" they asked.

"Yes."

"John," Michael proposed, "let us wake her and get her to make supper for us," and as he said it some of the other boys rushed on carrying branches for the building of the house. "Look at them!" he cried.

"Curly," said Peter in his most captainy voice, "see that these boys help in the building of the house."

"Ay, ay, sir."

"Build a house?" exclaimed John.

"For the Wendy," said Curly.

"For Wendy?" John said, aghast. "Why, she is only a girl!"

"That," explained Curly, "is why we are her servants."

"You? Wendy's servants!"

"Yes," said Peter, "and you also. Away with them."

The astounded brothers were dragged away to hack and hew and carry. "Chairs and a fender first," Peter ordered. "Then we shall build the house round them."

"Ay," said Slightly, "that is how a house is built; it all comes back to me."

Peter thought of everything. "Slightly," he cried, "fetch a doctor."

"Ay, ay," said Slightly at once, and disappeared, scratching his head. But he knew Peter must be obeyed, and he returned in a moment, wearing John's hat and looking solemn.

"Please, sir," said Peter, going to him, "are you a doctor?"

The difference between him and the other boys at such a time was that they knew it was make-believe, while to him make-believe and true were exactly the same thing. This sometimes troubled them, as when they had to make-believe that they had had their dinners.

If they broke down in their make-believe he rapped them on the knuckles.

"Yes, my little man," anxiously replied Slightly, who had chapped knuckles.

"Please, sir," Peter explained, "a lady lies very ill."

She was lying at their feet, but Slightly had the sense not to see her.

"Tut, tut, tut," he said, "where does she lie?"

"In yonder glade."*

"I will put a glass thing in her mouth," said Slightly, and he made-believe to do it, while Peter waited. It was an anxious moment when the glass thing was withdrawn.

"How is she?" inquired Peter.

"Tut, tut, tut," said Slightly, "this has cured her."

"I am glad!" Peter cried.

"I will call again in the evening," Slightly said; "give her beef tea out of a cup with a spout to it"; but after he had returned the hat to John he blew big breaths, which was his habit on escaping from a difficulty.

In the meantime the wood had been alive with the sound of axes; almost everything needed for a cosy dwelling already lay at Wendy's feet.

"If only we knew," said one, "the kind of house she likes best."

"Peter," shouted another, "she is moving in her sleep."

---

*Open space surrounded by trees, within sight.

"Her mouth opens," cried a third, looking respectfully into it. "Oh, lovely!"

"Perhaps she is going to sing in her sleep," said Peter. "Wendy, sing the kind of house you would like to have."

Immediately, without opening her eyes, Wendy began to sing:

> "I wish I had a pretty house,
> The littlest ever seen,
> With funny little red walls
> And roof of mossy green."

They gurgled with joy at this, for by the greatest good luck the branches they had brought were sticky with red sap, and all the ground was carpeted with moss. As they rattled up the little house they broke into song themselves:

> "We've built the little walls and roof
> And made a lovely door,
> So tell us, mother Wendy,
> What are you wanting more?"

To this she answered rather greedily:

> "Oh, really next I think I'll have
> Gay windows all about,
> With roses peeping in, you know,
> And babies peeping out."

With a blow of their fists they made windows, and large yellow leaves were the blinds. But roses——?

"Roses!" cried Peter sternly.

Quickly they made-believe to grow the loveliest roses up the walls.

Babies?

To prevent Peter ordering babies they hurried into song again:

> "We've made the roses peeping out,
> The babes are at the door,

We cannot make ourselves, you know,
'Cos we've been made before."

Peter, seeing this to be a good idea, at once pretended that it was his own. The house was quite beautiful, and no doubt Wendy was very cosy within, though, of course, they could no longer see her. Peter strode up and down, ordering finishing touches. Nothing escaped his eagle eye. Just when it seemed absolutely finished,

"There's no knocker on the door," he said.

They were very ashamed, but Tootles gave the sole of his shoe, and it made an excellent knocker.

Absolutely finished now, they thought.

Not a bit of it. "There's no chimney," Peter said; "we must have a chimney."

"It certainly does need a chimney," said John importantly. This gave Peter an idea. He snatched the hat off John's head, knocked out the bottom, and put the hat on the roof. The little house was so pleased to have such a capital chimney that, as if to say thank you, smoke immediately began to come out of the hat.

Now really and truly it was finished. Nothing remained to do but to knock.

"All look your best," Peter warned them; "first impressions are awfully important."

He was glad no one asked him what first impressions are; they were all too busy looking their best.

He knocked politely, and now the wood was as still as the children, not a sound to be heard except from Tinker Bell, who was watching from a branch and openly sneering.

What the boys were wondering was, would any one answer the knock? If a lady, what would she be like?

The door opened and a lady came out. It was Wendy. They all whipped off their hats.

She looked properly surprised, and this was just how they had hoped she would look.

"Where am I?" she said.

Of course Slightly was the first to get his word in. "Wendy lady," he said rapidly, "for you we built this house."

"Oh, say you're pleased," cried Nibs.

PETER ON GUARD

"Lovely, darling house," Wendy said, and they were the very words they had hoped she would say.

"And we are your children," cried the twins.

Then all went on their knees, and holding out their arms cried, "O Wendy lady, be our mother."

"Ought I?" Wendy said, all shining. "Of course it's frightfully fascinating, but you see I am only a little girl. I have no real experience."

"That doesn't matter," said Peter, as if he were the only person present who knew all about it, though he was really the one who knew least. "What we need is just a nice motherly person."

"Oh dear!" Wendy said, "you see I feel that is exactly what I am."

"It is, it is," they all cried; "we saw it at once."

"Very well," she said, "I will do my best. Come inside at once, you naughty children; I am sure your feet are damp. And before I put you to bed I have just time to finish the story of Cinderella."

In they went; I don't know how there was room for them, but you can squeeze very tight in the Neverland. And that was the first of the many joyous evenings they had with Wendy. By and by she tucked them up in the great bed in the home under the trees, but she herself slept that night in the little house, and Peter kept watch outside with drawn sword, for the pirates could be heard carousing far away and the wolves were on the prowl. The little house looked so cosy and safe in the darkness, with a bright light showing through its blinds, and the chimney smoking beautifully, and Peter standing on guard. After a time he fell asleep, and some unsteady fairies had to climb over him on their way home from an orgy. Any of the other boys obstructing the fairy path at night they would have mischiefed, but they just tweaked Peter's nose and passed on.

CHAPTER VII

The Home under the Ground

One of the first things Peter did next day was to measure Wendy and John and Michael for hollow trees. Hook, you remember, had sneered at the boys for thinking they needed a tree apiece, but this was ignorance, for unless your tree fitted you it was difficult to go up and down, and no two of the boys were quite the same size. Once you fitted, you drew in your breath at the top, and down you went at exactly the right speed, while to ascend you drew in and let out alternately, and so wriggled up. Of course, when you have mastered the action you are able to do these things without thinking of them, and then nothing can be more graceful.

But you simply must fit, and Peter measures you for your tree as carefully as for a suit of clothes: the only difference being that the clothes are made to fit you, while you have to be made to fit the tree. Usually it is done quite easily, as by your wearing too many garments or too few, but if you are bumpy in awkward places or the only available tree is an odd shape, Peter does some things to you, and after that you fit. Once you fit, great care must be taken to go on fitting, and this, as Wendy was to discover to her delight, keeps a whole family in perfect condition.

Wendy and Michael fitted their trees at the first try, but John had to be altered a little.

After a few days' practice they could go up and down as gaily as buckets in a well. And how ardently they grew to love their home under the ground; especially Wendy! It consisted of one large room, as all houses should do, with a floor in which you could dig if you wanted to go fishing, and in this floor grew stout mushrooms of a charming colour, which were used as stools. A Never tree tried hard to grow in the centre of the room, but every morning they sawed the trunk through, level with the floor. By tea-time it was always about two feet high, and then they put a door on top of it, the whole thus becoming a table; as soon as they cleared away, they sawed off the trunk again, and thus there was more room to play. There was an enormous fireplace which was in almost any part of the room where you cared to light it, and across this Wendy stretched strings, made of fibre, from which she suspended her washing. The bed was tilted against the wall by day, and let down at 6.30, when it filled nearly half the room; and all the boys slept in it, except Michael, lying like sardines in a tin. There was a strict rule against turning round until one gave the signal, when all turned at once. Michael should have used it also, but Wendy would have a baby, and he was the littlest, and you know what women are, and the short and the long of it is that he was hung up in a basket.

It was rough and simple, and not unlike what baby bears would have made of an underground house in the same circumstances. But there was one recess in the wall, no larger than a bird-cage, which was the private apartment of Tinker Bell. It could be shut off from the rest of the home by a tiny curtain, which Tink, who was most fastidious, always kept drawn when dressing or undressing. No woman, however large, could have had a more exquisite boudoir* and bed-chamber combined. The couch, as she always called it, was a genuine Queen Mab, with club legs; and she varied the bedspreads according to what fruit-blossom was in season. Her mirror was a Puss-in-boots, of which there are now only three, unchipped, known to the fairy dealers; the wash-stand was Pie-crust and reversible, the chest of drawers an authentic Charming the Sixth, and the carpet and rugs of the best (the early) period of Margery and Robin. There was a chandelier from Tiddlywinks for the look of the thing, but of course she lit the residence herself.[1] Tink was very contemptuous of the rest of the house, as indeed was perhaps inevitable, and her chamber, though beautiful, looked rather conceited, having the appearance of a nose permanently turned up.

I suppose it was all especially entrancing to Wendy, because those

---

*Woman's private dressing room (French).

rampagious boys of hers gave her so much to do. Really there were whole weeks when, except perhaps with a stocking in the evening, she was never above ground. The cooking, I can tell you, kept her nose to the pot, and even if there was nothing in it, even though there was no pot, she had to keep watching that it came aboil just the same. You never exactly knew whether there would be a real meal or just a make-believe, it all depended upon Peter's whim: he could eat, really eat, if it was part of a game, but he could not stodge* just to feel stodgy,† which is what most children like better than anything else; the next best thing being to talk about it. Make-believe was so real to him that during a meal of it you could see him getting rounder. Of course it was trying, but you simply had to follow his lead, and if you could prove to him that you were getting loose for your tree he let you stodge.

Wendy's favourite time for sewing and darning was after they had all gone to bed. Then, as she expressed it, she had a breathing time for herself; and she occupied it in making new things for them, and putting double pieces on the knees, for they were all most frightfully hard on their knees.

When she sat down to a basketful of their stockings, every heel with a hole in it, she would fling up her arms and exclaim, "Oh dear, I am sure I sometimes think spinsters are to be envied!"

Her face beamed when she exclaimed this.

You remember about her pet wolf. Well, it very soon discovered that she had come to the island and found her out, and they just ran into each other's arms. After that it followed her about everywhere.

As time wore on did she think much about the beloved parents she had left behind her? This is a difficult question, because it is quite impossible to say how time does wear on in the Neverland, where it is calculated by moons and suns, and there are ever so many more of them than on the mainland. But I am afraid that Wendy did not really worry about her father and mother; she was absolutely confident that they would always keep the window open for her to fly back by, and this gave her complete ease of mind. What did dis-

---

*Stuff himself full with food.

†Slow and plodding because of physical bulkiness.

turb her at times was that John remembered his parents vaguely only, as people he had once known, while Michael was quite willing to believe that she was really his mother. These things scared her a little, and nobly anxious to do her duty, she tried to fix the old life in their minds by setting them examination papers on it, as like as possible to the ones she used to do at school. The other boys thought this awfully interesting, and insisted on joining, and they made slates for themselves, and sat round the table, writing and thinking hard about the questions she had written on another slate and passed round. They were the most ordinary questions—"What was the colour of Mother's eyes? Which was taller, Father or Mother? Was Mother blonde or brunette? Answer all three questions if possible." "(A) Write an essay of not less than 40 words on How I spent my last Holidays, or The Carakters of Father and Mother compared. Only one of these to be attempted." Or "(1) Describe Mother's laugh; (2) Describe Father's laugh; (3) Describe Mother's Party Dress; (4) Describe the Kennel and its Inmate."

They were just everyday questions like these, and when you could not answer them you were told to make a cross; and it was really dreadful what a number of crosses even John made. Of course the only boy who replied to every question was Slightly, and no one could have been more hopeful of coming out first, but his answers were perfectly ridiculous, and he really came out last: a melancholy thing.

Peter did not compete. For one thing he despised all mothers except Wendy, and for another he was the only boy on the island who could neither write nor spell; not the smallest word. He was above all that sort of thing.

By the way, the questions were all written in the past tense. What was the colour of Mother's eyes, and so on. Wendy, you see, had been forgetting too.

Adventures, of course, as we shall see, were of daily occurrence; but about this time Peter invented, with Wendy's help, a new game that fascinated him enormously, until he suddenly had no more interest in it, which, as you have been told, was what always happened with his games. It consisted in pretending not to have adventures, in doing the sort of thing John and Michael had been doing all their lives, sitting on stools flinging balls in the air, pushing each other, going out for walks and coming back without having killed so much as a grizzly. To see Peter doing nothing on a stool was a great sight; he could not help looking solemn at such times, to sit still seemed to him such a comic thing to do. He boasted that he had gone a walk for the good of his health. For several suns these were the most novel of all adventures to him; and John and Michael had to pretend to be delighted also; otherwise he would have treated them severely.

He often went out alone, and when he came back you were never absolutely certain whether he had had an adventure or not. He might have forgotten it so completely that he said nothing about it; and then when you went out you found the body; and, on the other hand, he might say a great deal about it, and yet you could not find the body. Sometimes he came home with his head bandaged, and then Wendy cooed over him and bathed it in lukewarm water, while he told a dazzling tale. But she was never quite sure, you know. There were, however, many adventures which she knew to be true because she was in them herself, and there were still more that were at least partly true, for the other boys were in them and said they were wholly true. To describe them all would require a book as large as an English-Latin, Latin-English Dictionary, and the most we can do is to give one as a specimen of an average hour on the island. The difficulty is which one to choose. Should we take the brush with the redskins at Slightly Gulch? It was a sanguinary* affair, and especially interesting as showing one of Peter's peculiarities, which was that in the middle of a fight he would suddenly change sides. At the Gulch, when victory was still in the balance, sometimes leaning this way and sometimes that, he called out, "I'm redskin to-day; what are you, Tootles?" And Tootles answered, "Redskin; what are you, Nibs?" and Nibs said, "Redskin; what are you, Twin?" and so on; and they were all redskin; and of course this would have ended the fight had not the real redskins, fascinated by Peter's methods, agreed to be lost boys for that once, and so at it they all went again, more fiercely than ever.

The extraordinary upshot of this adventure was—but we have not decided yet that this is the adventure we are to narrate. Perhaps a better one would be the night attack by the redskins on the house under the ground, when several of them stuck in the hollow trees

---

*Bloodthirsty; murderous.

and had to be pulled out like corks. Or we might tell how Peter saved Tiger Lily's life in the Mermaids' Lagoon, and so made her his ally.

Or we could tell of that cake the pirates cooked so that the boys might eat it and perish; and how they placed it in one cunning spot after another; but always Wendy snatched it from the hands of her children, so that in time it lost its succulence, and became as hard as a stone, and was used as a missile, and Hook fell over it in the dark.

Or suppose we tell of the birds that were Peter's friends, particularly of the Never bird that built in a tree overhanging the lagoon, and how the nest fell into the water, and still the bird sat on her eggs, and Peter gave orders that she was not to be disturbed. That is a pretty story, and the end shows how grateful a bird can be; but if we tell it we must also tell the whole adventure of the lagoon, which would of course be telling two adventures rather than just one. A shorter adventure, and quite as exciting, was Tinker Bell's attempt, with the help of some street fairies, to have the sleeping Wendy conveyed on a great floating leaf to the mainland. Fortunately the leaf gave way and Wendy woke, thinking it was bath-time, and swam back. Or again, we might choose Peter's defiance of the lions, when he drew a circle round him on the ground with an arrow and dared them to cross it; and though he waited for hours, with the other boys and Wendy looking on breathlessly from trees, not one of them would accept his challenge.

Which of these adventures shall we choose? The best way will be to toss for it.

I have tossed, and the lagoon has won. This almost makes one wish that the gulch or the cake or Tink's leaf had won. Of course I could do it again, and make it best out of three; however, perhaps fairest to stick to the lagoon.

CHAPTER VIII

The Mermaids' Lagoon

IF YOU SHUT YOUR eyes and are a lucky one, you may see at times a shapeless pool of lovely pale colours suspended in the darkness; then if you squeeze your eyes tighter, the pool begins to take shape, and the colours become so vivid that with another squeeze they must go on fire. But just before they go on fire you see the lagoon. This is the nearest you ever get to it on the mainland, just one heavenly moment; if there could be two moments you might see the surf and hear the mermaids singing.

The children often spent long summer days on this lagoon, swimming or floating most of the time, playing the mermaid games in the water, and so forth. You must not think from this that the mermaids were on friendly terms with them: on the contrary, it was among Wendy's lasting regrets that all the time she was on the island she never had a civil word from one of them. When she stole softly to the edge of the lagoon she might see them by the score,* especially on Marooners' Rock, where they loved to bask, combing out their hair in a lazy way that quite irritated her; or she might even swim, on tiptoe as it were, to within a yard of them, but then they saw her and dived, probably splashing her with their tails, not by accident, but intentionally.

They treated all the boys in the same way, except of course Peter, who chatted with them on Marooners' Rock by the hour and sat on their tails when they got cheeky. He gave Wendy one of their combs.

The most haunting time at which to see them is at the turn of the moon, when they utter strange wailing cries; but the lagoon is

*In large groups; a score is twenty.

SUMMER DAYS ON THE LAGOON

dangerous for mortals then, and until the evening of which we have now to tell, Wendy had never seen the lagoon by moonlight, less from fear, for of course Peter would have accompanied her, than because she had strict rules about every one being in bed by seven. She was often at the lagoon, however, on sunny days after rain, when the mermaids come up in extraordinary numbers to play with their bubbles. The bubbles of many colours made in rainbow water they treat as balls, hitting them gaily from one to another with their tails, and trying to keep them in the rainbow till they burst. The goals are at each end of the rainbow, and the keepers* only are allowed to use their hands. Sometimes a dozen of these games will be going on in the lagoon at a time, and it is quite a pretty sight.

But the moment the children tried to join in they had to play by themselves, for the mermaids immediately disappeared. Nevertheless we have proof that they secretly watched the interlopers, and were not above taking an idea from them; for John introduced a new way of hitting the bubble, with the head instead of the hand, and the mermaids adopted it. This is the one mark that John has left on the Neverland.

It must also have been rather pretty to see the children resting on a rock for half an hour after their mid-day meal. Wendy insisted on their doing this, and it had to be a real rest even though the meal was make-believe. So they lay there in the sun, and their bodies glistened in it, while she sat beside them and looked important.

It was one such day, and they were all on Marooners' Rock. The rock was not much larger than their great bed, but of course they all knew how not to take up much room, and they were dozing or at least lying with their eyes shut, and pinching occasionally when they thought Wendy was not looking. She was very busy, stitching.

While she stitched a change came to the lagoon. Little shivers ran over it, and the sun went away and shadows stole across the water, turning it cold. Wendy could no longer see to thread her needle, and when she looked up, the lagoon that had always hitherto been such a laughing place seemed formidable and unfriendly.

It was not, she knew, that night had come, but something as dark as night had come. No, worse than that. It had not come, but it had sent that shiver through the sea to say that it was coming. What was it?

---

*Goalies or goal-keepers.

There crowded upon her all the stories she had been told of Marooners' Rock, so called because evil captains put sailors on it and leave them there to drown. They drown when the tide rises, for then it is submerged.

Of course she should have roused the children at once; not merely because of the unknown that was stalking toward them, but because it was no longer good for them to sleep on a rock grown chilly. But she was a young mother and she did not know this; she thought you simply must stick to your rule about half an hour after the mid-day meal. So, though fear was upon her, and she longed to hear male voices, she would not waken them. Even when she heard the sound of muffled oars, though her heart was in her mouth, she did not waken them. She stood over them to let them have their sleep out. Was it not brave of Wendy?

It was well for those boys then that there was one among them who could sniff danger even in his sleep. Peter sprang erect, as wide awake at once as a dog, and with one warning cry he roused the others.

He stood motionless, one hand to his ear.

"Pirates!" he cried. The others came closer to him. A strange smile was playing about his face, and Wendy saw it and shuddered. While that smile was on his face no one dared address him; all they could do was to stand ready to obey. The order came sharp and incisive.

"Dive!"

There was a gleam of legs, and instantly the lagoon seemed deserted. Marooners' Rock stood alone in the forbidding waters, as if it were itself marooned.

The boat drew nearer. It was the pirate dinghy,* with three figures in her, Smee and Starkey, and the third a captive, no other than Tiger Lily. Her hands and ankles were tied, and she knew what was to be her fate. She was to be left on the rock to perish, an end to one of her race more terrible than death by fire or torture, for is it not written in the book of the tribe that there is no path through water to the happy hunting-ground?† Yet her face was impassive; she was

---

*Small lifeboat carried on or towed behind a larger boat.
†Heaven, in Native American belief.

the daughter of a chief, she must die as a chief's daughter, it is enough.

They had caught her boarding the pirate ship with a knife in her mouth. No watch was kept on the ship, it being Hook's boast that the wind of his name guarded the ship for a mile around. Now her fate would help to guard it also. One more wail would go the round in that wind by night.

In the gloom that they brought with them the two pirates did not see the rock till they crashed into it.

"Luff,* you lubber,"† cried an Irish voice that was Smee's; "here's the rock. Now, then, what we have to do is to hoist the redskin on to it and leave her there to drown."

It was the work of one brutal moment to land the beautiful girl on the rock; she was too proud to offer a vain resistance.

Quite near the rock, but out of sight, two heads were bobbing up and down, Peter's and Wendy's. Wendy was crying, for it was the first tragedy she had seen. Peter had seen many tragedies, but he had forgotten them all. He was less sorry than Wendy for Tiger Lily: it was two against one that angered him, and he meant to save her. An easy way would have been to wait until the pirates had gone, but he was never one to choose the easy way.

There was almost nothing he could not do, and he now imitated the voice of Hook.

"Ahoy there, you lubbers!" he called. It was a marvellous imitation.

"The captain!" said the pirates, staring at each other in surprise.

"He must be swimming out to us," Starkey said, when they had looked for him in vain.

"We are putting the redskin on the rock," Smee called out.

"Set her free," came the astonishing answer.

"Free!"

"Yes, cut her bonds and let her go."

"But, captain——"

"At once, d' ye hear," cried Peter, "or I'll plunge my hook in you."

"This is queer!" Smee gasped.

"Better do what the captain orders," said Starkey nervously.

---

*Turn the head of the vessel toward the wind.

†Inexperienced sailor; variant of "landlubber."

"Ay, ay," Smee said, and he cut Tiger Lily's cords. At once like an eel she slid between Starkey's legs into the water.

Of course Wendy was very elated over Peter's cleverness; but she knew that he would be elated also and very likely crow and thus betray himself, so at once her hand went out to cover his mouth. But it was stayed even in the act, for "Boat ahoy!" rang over the lagoon in Hook's voice, but this time it was not Peter who had spoken.

Peter may have been about to crow, but his face puckered in a whistle of surprise instead.

"Boat ahoy!" again came the voice.

Now Wendy understood. The real Hook was also in the water.

He was swimming to the boat, and as his men showed a light to guide him he had soon reached them. In the light of the lantern Wendy saw his hook grip the boat's side; she saw his evil swarthy face as he rose dripping from the water, and, quaking, she would have liked to swim away, but Peter would not budge. He was tingling with life and also top-heavy with conceit. "Am I not a wonder, oh, I am a wonder!" he whispered to her, and though she thought so also, she was really glad for the sake of his reputation that no one heard him except herself.

He signed to her to listen.

The two pirates were very curious to know what had brought their captain to them, but he sat with his head on his hook in a position of profound melancholy.

"Captain, is all well?" they asked timidly, but he answered with a hollow moan.

"He sighs," said Smee.

"He sighs again," said Starkey.

"And yet a third time he sighs," said Smee.

"What's up, captain?"

Then at last he spoke passionately.

"The game's up," he cried, "those boys have found a mother."

Affrighted though she was, Wendy swelled with pride.

"O evil day!" cried Starkey.

"What's a mother?" asked the ignorant Smee.

Wendy was so shocked that she exclaimed, "He doesn't know!" and always after this she felt that if you could have a pet pirate Smee would be her one.

Peter pulled her beneath the water, for Hook had started up, crying, "What was that?"

"I heard nothing," said Starkey, raising the lantern over the waters, and as the pirates looked they saw a strange sight. It was the nest I have told you of, floating on the lagoon, and the Never bird was sitting on it.

"See," said Hook in answer to Smee's question, "that is a mother. What a lesson! The nest must have fallen into the water, but would the mother desert her eggs? No."

There was a break in his voice, as if for a moment he recalled innocent days when—but he brushed away this weakness with his hook.

Smee, much impressed, gazed at the bird as the nest was borne past, but the more suspicious Starkey said, "If she is a mother, perhaps she is hanging about here to help Peter."

Hook winced. "Ay," he said, "that is the fear that haunts me."

He was roused from this dejection by Smee's eager voice.

"Captain," said Smee, "could we not kidnap these boys' mother and make her our mother?"

"It is a princely scheme," cried Hook, and at once it took practical shape in his great brain. "We will seize the children and carry them to the boat: the boys we will make walk the plank, and Wendy shall be our mother."

Again Wendy forgot herself.

"Never!" she cried, and bobbed.

"What was that?"

But they could see nothing. They thought it must have been but a leaf in the wind. "Do you agree, my bullies?" asked Hook.

"There is my hand on it," they both said.

"And there is my hook. Swear."

They all swore. By this time they were on the rock, and suddenly Hook remembered Tiger Lily.

"Where is the redskin?" he demanded abruptly.

He had a playful humour at moments, and they thought this was one of the moments.

"That is all right, captain," Smee answered complacently; "we let her go."

"Let her go!" cried Hook.

"'Twas your own orders," the bo'sun faltered.

"You called over the water to us to let her go," said Starkey.

"Brimstone and gall,"* thundered Hook, "what cozening† is here!" His face had gone black with rage, but he saw that they believed their words, and he was startled. "Lads," he said, shaking a little, "I gave no such order."

"It is passing queer,"‡ Smee said, and they all fidgeted uncomfortably. Hook raised his voice, but there was a quiver in it.

"Spirit that haunts this dark lagoon to-night," he cried, "dost hear me?"

Of course Peter should have kept quiet, but of course he did not. He immediately answered in Hook's voice:

"Odds, bobs, hammer and tongs, I hear you."

In that supreme moment Hook did not blanch, even at the gills,[1] but Smee and Starkey clung to each other in terror.

"Who are you, stranger, speak?" Hook demanded.

"I am James Hook," replied the voice, "captain of the *Jolly Roger*."

"You are not; you are not," Hook cried hoarsely.

"Brimstone and gall," the voice retorted, "say that again, and I'll cast anchor in you."

Hook tried a more ingratiating manner. "If you are Hook," he said almost humbly, "come tell me, who am I?"

"A codfish," replied the voice, "only a codfish."

"A codfish!" Hook echoed blankly, and it was then, but not till then, that his proud spirit broke. He saw his men draw back from him.

"Have we been captained all this time by a codfish!" they muttered. "It is lowering to our pride."

They were his dogs snapping at him, but, tragic figure though he had become, he scarcely heeded them. Against such fearful evidence it was not their belief in him that he needed, it was his own. He felt his ego slipping from him. "Don't desert me, bully," he whispered hoarsely to it.

In his dark nature there was a touch of the feminine, as in all the greatest pirates, and it sometimes gave him intuitions. Suddenly he tried the guessing game.

---

*Strong language, similar to "Fire and brimstone!"

†Deceit by trickery or clever coaxing.

‡Rather strange.

"Hook," he called, "have you another voice?"

Now Peter could never resist a game, and he answered blithely in his own voice, "I have."

"And another name?"

"Ay, ay."

"Vegetable?" asked Hook.

"No."

"Mineral?"

"No."

"Animal?"

"Yes."

"Man?"

"No!" This answer rang out scornfully.

"Boy?"

"Yes."

"Ordinary boy?"

"No!"

"Wonderful boy?"

To Wendy's pain the answer that rang out this time was "Yes."

"Are you in England?"

"No."

"Are you here?"

"Yes."

Hook was completely puzzled. "You ask him some questions," he said to the others, wiping his damp brow.

Smee reflected. "I can't think of a thing," he said regretfully.

"Can't guess, can't guess!" crowed Peter. "Do you give it up?"

Of course in his pride he was carrying the game too far, and the miscreants saw their chance.

"Yes, yes," they answered eagerly.

"Well, then," he cried, "I am Peter Pan!"

Pan!

In a moment Hook was himself again, and Smee and Starkey were his faithful henchmen.

"Now we have him," Hook shouted. "Into the water, Smee. Starkey, mind the boat. Take him dead or alive!"

He leaped as he spoke, and simultaneously came the gay voice of Peter.

"Are you ready, boys?"

"Ay, ay," from various parts of the lagoon.

"Then lam into the pirates."

The fight was short and sharp. First to draw blood was John, who gallantly climbed into the boat and held Starkey. There was a fierce struggle, in which the cutlass was torn from the pirate's grasp. He wriggled overboard and John leapt after him. The dinghy drifted away.

Here and there a head bobbed up in the water, and there was a flash of steel followed by a cry or a whoop. In the confusion some struck at their own side. The corkscrew of Smee got Tootles in the fourth rib, but he was himself pinked in turn by Curly. Farther from the rock Starkey was pressing Slightly and the twins hard.

Where all this time was Peter? He was seeking bigger game.

The others were all brave boys, and they must not be blamed for backing from the pirate captain. His iron claw made a circle of dead water round him, from which they fled like affrighted fishes.

But there was one who did not fear him: there was one prepared to enter that circle.

Strangely, it was not in the water that they met. Hook rose to the rock to breathe, and at the same moment Peter scaled it on the opposite side. The rock was slippery as a ball, and they had to crawl rather than climb. Neither knew that the other was coming. Each feeling for a grip met the other's arm: in surprise they raised their heads; their faces were almost touching; so they met.

Some of the greatest heroes have confessed that just before they fell to they had a sinking. Had it been so with Peter at that moment I would admit it. After all, this was the only man that the Sea-Cook had feared. But Peter had no sinking, he had one feeling only, gladness; and he gnashed his pretty teeth with joy. Quick as thought he snatched a knife from Hook's belt and was about to drive it home, when he saw that he was higher up the rock than his foe. It would not have been fighting fair. He gave the pirate a hand to help him up.

It was then that Hook bit him.

Not the pain of this but its unfairness was what dazed Peter. It made him quite helpless. He could only stare, horrified. Every child is affected thus the first time he is treated unfairly. All he thinks he has a right to when he comes to you to be yours is fairness. After you have been unfair to him he will love you again, but he will never afterwards be quite the same boy. No one ever gets over the first unfairness; no one except Peter. He often met it, but he always forgot it. I suppose that was the real difference between him and all the rest.

So when he met it now it was like the first time; and he could just stare, helpless. Twice the iron hand clawed him.

A few minutes afterwards the other boys saw Hook in the water striking wildly for the ship; no elation on his pestilent* face now, only white fear, for the crocodile was in dogged pursuit of him. On ordinary occasions the boys would have swum alongside cheering; but now they were uneasy, for they had lost both Peter and Wendy, and were scouring the lagoon for them, calling them by name. They found the dinghy and went home in it, shouting "Peter, Wendy" as they went, but no answer came save mocking laughter from the mermaids. "They must be swimming back or flying," the boys concluded. They were not very anxious, they had such faith in Peter. They chuckled, boylike, because they would be late for bed; and it was all mother Wendy's fault!

When their voices died away there came cold silence over the lagoon, and then a feeble cry.

"Help, help!"

Two small figures were beating against the rock; the girl had fainted and lay on the boy's arm. With a last effort Peter pulled her up the rock and then lay down beside her. Even as he also fainted he saw that the water was rising. He knew that they would soon be drowned, but he could do no more.

As they lay side by side a mermaid caught Wendy by the feet, and began pulling her softly into the water. Peter, feeling her slip from him, woke with a start, and was just in time to draw her back. But he had to tell her the truth.

"We are on the rock, Wendy," he said, "but it is growing smaller. Soon the water will be over it."

She did not understand even now.

"We must go," she said, almost brightly.

"Yes," he answered faintly.

"Shall we swim or fly, Peter?"

He had to tell her.

---

*Morally, socially, or politically harmful; pernicious; deadly.

"TO DIE WILL BE AN AWFULLY BIG ADVENTURE"

"Do you think you could swim or fly as far as the island, Wendy, without my help?"

She had to admit that she was too tired.

He moaned.

"What is it?" she asked, anxious about him at once.

"I can't help you, Wendy. Hook wounded me. I can neither fly nor swim."

"Do you mean we shall both be drowned?"

"Look how the water is rising."

They put their hands over their eyes to shut out the sight. They thought they would soon be no more. As they sat thus something brushed against Peter as light as a kiss, and stayed there, as if saying timidly, "Can I be of any use?"

It was the tail of a kite, which Michael had made some days before. It had torn itself out of his hand and floated away.

"Michael's kite," Peter said without interest, but next moment he had seized the tail, and was pulling the kite toward him.

"It lifted Michael off the ground," he cried; "why should it not carry you?"

"Both of us!"

"It can't lift two; Michael and Curly tried."

"Let us draw lots," Wendy said bravely.

"And you a lady; never." Already he had tied the tail round her. She clung to him; she refused to go without him; but with a "Goodbye, Wendy," he pushed her from the rock; and in a few minutes she was borne out of his sight. Peter was alone on the lagoon.

The rock was very small now; soon it would be submerged. Pale rays of light tiptoed across the waters; and by and by there was to be heard a sound at once the most musical and the most melancholy in the world: the mermaids calling to the moon.

Peter was not quite like other boys; but he was afraid at last. A tremor ran through him, like a shudder passing over the sea; but on the sea one shudder follows another till there are hundreds of them, and Peter felt just the one. Next moment he was standing erect on the rock again, with that smile on his face and a drum beating within him. It was saying, "To die will be an awfully big adventure."

CHAPTER IX

The Never Bird

THE LAST SOUNDS PETER heard before he was quite alone were the mermaids retiring one by one to their bedchambers under the sea. He was too far away to hear their doors shut; but every door in the coral caves where they live rings a tiny bell when it opens or closes (as in all the nicest houses on the mainland), and he heard the bells.

Steadily the waters rose till they were nibbling at his feet; and to pass the time until they made their final gulp, he watched the only thing moving on the lagoon. He thought it was a piece of floating paper, perhaps part of the kite, and wondered idly how long it would take to drift ashore.

Presently he noticed as an odd thing that it was undoubtedly out upon the lagoon with some definite purpose, for it was fighting the tide, and sometimes winning; and when it won, Peter, always sympathetic to the weaker side, could not help clapping; it was such a gallant piece of paper.

It was not really a piece of paper; it was the Never bird, making desperate efforts to reach Peter on her nest. By working her wings, in a way she had learned since the nest fell into the water, she was able to some extent to guide her strange craft, but by the time Peter recognised her she was very exhausted. She had come to save him, to give him her nest, though there were eggs in it. I rather wonder at the bird, for though he had been nice to her, he had also sometimes tormented her. I can suppose only that, like Mrs. Darling and the rest of them, she was melted because he had all his first teeth.

She called out to him what she had come for, and he called out to her what was she doing there; but of course neither of them understood the other's language. In fanciful stories people can talk to the birds freely, and I wish for the moment I could pretend that this was such a story, and say that Peter replied intelligently to the Never bird; but truth is best, and I want to tell only what really happened. Well, not only could they not understand each other, but they forgot their manners.

"I—want—you—to—get—into—the—nest," the bird called, speaking as slowly and distinctly as possible, "and—then—you—can—drift—ashore, but—I—am—too—tired—to—bring—it—any—nearer—so—you—must—try—to—swim—to—it."

"What are you quacking about?" Peter answered. "Why don't you let the nest drift as usual?"

"I—want—you—" the bird said, and repeated it all over.

Then Peter tried slow and distinct.

"What—are—you—quacking—about?" and so on.

The Never bird became irritated; they have very short tempers.

"You dunderheaded little jay,"* she screamed, "why don't you do as I tell you?"

Peter felt that she was calling him names, and at a venture he retorted hotly:

"So are you!"

Then rather curiously they both snapped out the same remark.

"Shut up!"

"Shut up!"

Nevertheless the bird was determined to save him if she could, and by one last mighty effort she propelled the nest against the rock. Then up she flew; deserting her eggs, so as to make her meaning clear.

Then at last he understood, and clutched the nest and waved his thanks to the bird as she fluttered overhead. It was not to receive his thanks, however, that she hung there in the sky; it was not even to watch him get into the nest; it was to see what he did with her eggs.

There were two large white eggs, and Peter lifted them up and reflected. The bird covered her face with her wings, so as not to see the last of them; but she could not help peeping between the feathers.

I forget whether I have told you that there was a stave† on the rock,

---

*Overly talkative person, like a blue jay that won't stop twittering.
†Wooden staff.

driven into it by some buccaneers* of long ago to mark the site of buried treasure. The children had discovered the glittering hoard, and when in mischievous mood used to fling showers of moidores, diamonds, pearls and pieces of eight to the gulls, who pounced upon them for food, and then flew away, raging at the scurvy† trick that had been played upon them. The stave was still there, and on it Starkey had hung his hat, a deep tarpaulin,‡ watertight, with a broad brim. Peter put the eggs into this hat and set it on the lagoon. It floated beautifully.

The Never bird saw at once what he was up to, and screamed her admiration of him; and, alas, Peter crowed his agreement with her. Then he got into the nest, reared the stave in it as a mast, and hung up his shirt for a sail. At the same moment the bird fluttered down upon the hat and once more sat snugly on her eggs. She drifted in one direction, and he was borne off in another, both cheering.

Of course when Peter landed he beached his barque§ in a place where the bird would easily find it; but the hat was such a great success that she abandoned the nest. It drifted about till it went to pieces, and often Starkey came to the shore of the lagoon, and with many bitter feelings watched the bird sitting on his hat. As we shall not see her again, it may be worth mentioning here that all Never birds now build in that shape of nest, with a broad brim on which the youngsters take an airing.

Great were the rejoicings when Peter reached the home under the ground almost as soon as Wendy, who had been carried hither and thither by the kite. Every boy had adventures to tell; but perhaps the biggest adventure of all was that they were several hours late for bed. This so inflated them that they did various dodgy things to get staying up still longer, such as demanding bandages; but Wendy, though glorying in having them all home again safe and sound, was scandalised by the lateness of the hour, and cried, "To bed, to bed," in a voice that had to be obeyed. Next day, however, she was awfully tender, and gave out bandages to every one and they played till bed-time at limping about and carrying their arms in slings.

---

*People resembling the pirates who attacked or robbed Spanish settlements in the West Indies.

†Contemptible; mean.

‡Waxed, waterproof material used as a protection or covering.

§Variant of "bark," a small sailing vessel typically having three masts.

CHAPTER X

The Happy Home

ONE IMPORTANT RESULT OF the brush on the lagoon was that it made the redskins their friends. Peter had saved Tiger Lily from a dreadful fate, and now there was nothing she and her braves would not do for him. All night they sat above, keeping watch over the home under the ground and awaiting the big attack by the pirates which obviously could not be much longer delayed. Even by day they hung about, smoking the pipe of peace, and looking almost as if they wanted tit-bits to eat.

They called Peter the Great White Father,[1] prostrating themselves before him; and he liked this tremendously, so that it was not really good for him.

"The great white father," he would say to them in a very lordly manner, as they grovelled at his feet, "is glad to see the Piccaninny warriors protecting his wigwam from the pirates."

"Me Tiger Lily," that lovely creature would reply, "Peter Pan save me, me his velly nice friend. Me no let pirates hurt him."

She was far too pretty to cringe in this way, but Peter thought it his due, and he would answer condescendingly, "It is good. Peter Pan has spoken."

Always when he said, "Peter Pan has spoken," it meant that they must now shut up, and they accepted it humbly in that spirit; but they were by no means so respectful to the other boys, whom they looked upon as just ordinary braves. They said "How-do?" to them, and things like that; and what annoyed the boys was that Peter seemed to think this all right.

Secretly Wendy sympathised with them a little, but she was far too loyal a housewife to listen to any complaints against father. "Father knows best," she always said, whatever her private opinion must be. Her private opinion was that the redskins should not call her a squaw.*

We have now reached the evening that was to be known among them as the Night of Nights, because of its adventures and their upshot. The day, as if quietly gathering its forces, had been almost uneventful, and now the redskins in their blankets were at their posts above, while, below, the children were having their evening meal; all except Peter, who had gone out to get the time. The way you got the time on the island was to find the crocodile, and then stay near him till the clock struck.

This meal happened to be a make-believe tea, and they sat round the board, guzzling in their greed; and really, what with their chatter and recriminations, the noise, as Wendy said, was positively deafening. To be sure, she did not mind noise, but she simply would not have them grabbing things, and then excusing themselves by saying that Tootles had pushed their elbow. There was a fixed rule that they must never hit back at meals, but should refer the matter of dispute to Wendy by raising the right arm politely and saying, "I complain of so-and-so"; but what usually happened was that they forgot to do this or did it too much.

"Silence," cried Wendy when for the twentieth time she had told them that they were not all to speak at once. "Is your mug empty, Slightly darling?"

"Not quite empty, mummy," Slightly said, after looking into an imaginary mug.

"He hasn't even begun to drink his milk," Nibs interposed.

This was telling,† and Slightly seized his chance.

"I complain of Nibs," he cried promptly.

John, however, had held up his hand first.

"Well, John?"

"May I sit in Peter's chair, as he is not here?"

"Sit in father's chair, John!" Wendy was scandalised. "Certainly not."

---

*"Woman" or "wife" in some Native American languages.

†Acting the tattletale by informing on someone in order to bicker.

"He is not really our father," John answered. "He didn't even know how a father does till I showed him."

This was grumbling. "We complain of John," cried the twins.

Tootles held up his hand. He was so much the humblest of them, indeed he was the only humble one, that Wendy was specially gentle with him.

"I don't suppose," Tootles said diffidently, "that I could be father."

"No, Tootles."

Once Tootles began, which was not very often, he had a silly way of going on.

"As I can't be father," he said heavily, "I don't suppose, Michael, you would let me be baby?"

"No, I won't," Michael rapped out. He was already in his basket.

"As I can't be baby," Tootles said, getting heavier and heavier, "do you think I could be a twin?"

"No, indeed," replied the twins; "it's awfully difficult to be a twin."

"As I can't be anything important," said Tootles, "would any of you like to see me do a trick?"

"No," they all replied.

Then at last he stopped. "I hadn't really any hope," he said.

The hateful telling broke out again.

"Slightly is coughing on the table."

"The twins began with cheese-cakes."

"Curly is taking both butter and honey."

"Nibs is speaking with his mouth full."

"I complain of the twins."

"I complain of Curly."

"I complain of Nibs."

"Oh dear, oh dear," cried Wendy, "I'm sure I sometimes think that spinsters are to be envied."

She told them to clear away, and sat down to her work-basket, a heavy load of stockings and every knee with a hole in it as usual.

"Wendy," remonstrated Michael, "I'm too big for a cradle."

"I must have somebody in a cradle," she said almost tartly, "and you are the littlest. A cradle is such a nice homely thing to have about a house."

While she sewed they played around her; such a group of happy faces and dancing limbs lit up by that romantic fire. It had become a very familiar scene this in the home under the ground, but we are looking on it for the last time.

There was a step above, and Wendy, you may be sure, was the first to recognise it.

"Children, I hear your father's step. He likes you to meet him at the door."

Above, the redskins crouched before Peter.

"Watch well, braves. I have spoken."

And then, as so often before, the gay children dragged him from his tree. As so often before, but never again.

He had brought nuts for the boys as well as the correct time for Wendy.

"Peter, you just spoil them, you know," Wendy simpered.

"Ah, old lady," said Peter, hanging up his gun.

"It was me told him mothers are called old lady," Michael whispered to Curly.

"I complain of Michael," said Curly instantly.

The first twin came to Peter. "Father, we want to dance."

"Dance away, my little man," said Peter, who was in high good humour.

"But we want you to dance."

Peter was really the best dancer among them, but he pretended to be scandalised.

"Me! My old bones would rattle!"

"And mummy too."

"What!" cried Wendy, "the mother of such an armful, dance!"

"But on a Saturday night," Slightly insinuated.

It was not really Saturday night, at least it may have been, for they had long lost count of the days; but always if they wanted to do anything special they said this was Saturday night, and then they did it.

"Of course it is Saturday night, Peter," Wendy said, relenting.

"People of our figure, Wendy!"*

"But it is only among our own progeny."

"True, true."

---

*People of our stature or standing; Peter and Wendy are pretending to be parents, much older than they are.

So they were told they could dance, but they must put on their nighties first.

"Ah, old lady," Peter said aside to Wendy, warming himself by the fire and looking down at her as she sat turning a heel, "there is nothing more pleasant of an evening for you and me when the day's toil is over than to rest by the fire with the little ones near by."

"It is sweet, Peter, isn't it?" Wendy said, frightfully gratified. "Peter, I think Curly has your nose."

"Michael takes after you."

She went to him and put her hand on his shoulder.

"Dear Peter," she said, "with such a large family, of course, I have now passed my best, but you don't want to change me, do you?"

"No, Wendy."

Certainly he did not want a change, but he looked at her uncomfortably, blinking, you know, like one not sure whether he was awake or asleep.

"Peter, what is it?"

"I was just thinking," he said, a little scared. "It is only make-believe, isn't it, that I am their father?"

"Oh yes," Wendy said primly.

"You see," he continued apologetically, "it would make me seem so old to be their real father."

"But they are ours, Peter, yours and mine."

"But not really, Wendy?" he asked anxiously.

"Not if you don't wish it," she replied; and she distinctly heard his sigh of relief. "Peter," she asked, trying to speak firmly, "what are your exact feelings to me?"

"Those of a devoted son, Wendy."

"I thought so," she said, and went and sat by herself at the extreme end of the room.

"You are so queer," he said, frankly puzzled, "and Tiger Lily is just the same. There is something she wants to be to me, but she says it is not my mother."

"No, indeed, it is not," Wendy replied with frightful emphasis. Now we know why she was prejudiced against the redskins.

"Then what is it?"

"It isn't for a lady to tell."

"Oh, very well," Peter said, a little nettled. "Perhaps Tinker Bell will tell me."

"Oh yes, Tinker Bell will tell you," Wendy retorted scornfully. "She is an abandoned little creature."

Here Tink, who was in her bedroom, eavesdropping, squeaked out something impudent.

"She says she glories in being abandoned," Peter interpreted.

He had a sudden idea. "Perhaps Tink wants to be my mother?"

"You silly ass!" cried Tinker Bell in a passion.

She had said it so often that Wendy needed no translation.

"I almost agree with her," Wendy snapped. Fancy Wendy snapping! But she had been much tried, and she little knew what was to happen before the night was out. If she had known she would not have snapped.

None of them knew. Perhaps it was best not to know. Their ignorance gave them one more glad hour; and as it was to be their last hour on the island, let us rejoice that there were sixty glad minutes in it. They sang and danced in their night-gowns. Such a deliciously creepy song it was, in which they pretended to be frightened at their own shadows, little witting that so soon shadows would close in upon them, from whom they would shrink in real fear. So uproariously gay was the dance, and how they buffeted each other on the bed and out of it! It was a pillow fight rather than a dance, and when it was finished, the pillows insisted on one bout more, like partners who know that they may never meet again. The stories they told, before it was time for Wendy's good-night story! Even Slightly tried to tell a story that night, and the beginning was so fearfully dull that it appalled not only the others but himself, and he said happily:

"Yes, it is a dull beginning. I say, let us pretend that it is the end."

And then at last they all got into bed for Wendy's story, the story they loved best, the story Peter hated. Usually when she began to tell this story, he left the room or put his hands over his ears; and possibly if he had done either of those things this time they might all still be on the island. But to-night he remained on his stool; and we shall see what happened.

CHAPTER XI

Wendy's Story

LISTEN, THEN," SAID WENDY, settling down to her story, with Michael at her feet and seven boys in the bed. "There was once a gentleman——"

"I had rather he had been a lady," Curly said.

"I wish he had been a white rat," said Nibs.

"Quiet," their mother admonished them. "There was a lady also, and——"

"O mummy," cried the first twin, "you mean that there is a lady also, don't you? She is not dead, is she?"

"Oh no."

"I am awfully glad she isn't dead," said Tootles. "Are you glad, John?"

"Of course I am."

"Are you glad, Nibs?"

"Rather."

"Are you glad, Twins?"

"We are just glad."

"Oh dear," sighed Wendy.

"Little less noise there," Peter called out, determined that she should have fair play, however beastly a story it might be in his opinion.

"The gentleman's name," Wendy continued, "was Mr. Darling, and her name was Mrs. Darling."

"I knew them," John said, to annoy the others.

"I think I knew them," said Michael rather doubtfully.

"They were married, you know," explained Wendy, "and what do you think they had?"

WENDY'S STORY

"White rats!" cried Nibs, inspired.

"No."

"It's awfully puzzling," said Tootles, who knew the story by heart.

"Quiet, Tootles. They had three descendants."

"What is descendants?"

"Well, you are one, Twin."

"Do you hear that, John? I am a descendant."

"Descendants are only children," said John.

"Oh dear, oh dear," sighed Wendy. "Now these three children had a faithful nurse called Nana; but Mr. Darling was angry with her and chained her up in the yard, and so all the children flew away."

"It's an awfully good story," said Nibs.

"They flew away," Wendy continued, "to the Neverland, where the lost children are."

"I just thought they did," Curly broke in excitedly. "I don't know how it is, but I just thought they did!"

"O Wendy," cried Tootles, "was one of the lost children called Tootles?"

"Yes, he was."

"I am in a story. Hurrah, I am in a story, Nibs."

"Hush. Now I want you to consider the feelings of the unhappy parents with all their children flown away."

"Oo!" they all moaned, though they were not really considering the feelings of the unhappy parents one jot.

"Think of the empty beds!"

"Oo!"

"It's awfully sad," the first twin said cheerfully.

"I don't see how it can have a happy ending," said the second twin. "Do you, Nibs?"

"I'm frightfully anxious."

"If you knew how great is a mother's love," Wendy told them triumphantly, "you would have no fear." She had now come to the part that Peter hated.

"I do like a mother's love," said Tootles, hitting Nibs with a pillow. "Do you like a mother's love, Nibs?"

"I do just," said Nibs, hitting back.

"You see," Wendy said complacently, "our heroine knew that the mother would always leave the window open for her children to fly back by; so they stayed away for years and had a lovely time."

"Did they ever go back?"

"Let us now," said Wendy, bracing herself up for her finest effort, "take a peep into the future"; and they all gave themselves the twist that makes peeps into the future easier. "Years have rolled by, and who is this elegant lady of uncertain age alighting at London Station?"

"O Wendy, who is she?" cried Nibs, every bit as excited as if he didn't know.

"Can it be—yes—no—it is—the fair Wendy!"

"Oh!"

"And who are the two noble portly figures accompanying her, now grown to man's estate? Can they be John and Michael? They are!"

"Oh!"

"'See, dear brothers,' says Wendy, pointing upwards, "'there is the window still standing open. Ah, now we are rewarded for our sublime faith in a mother's love.' So up they flew to their mummy and daddy, and pen cannot describe the happy scene, over which we draw a veil."

That was the story, and they were as pleased with it as the fair narrator herself. Everything just as it should be, you see. Off we skip like the most heartless things in the world, which is what children are, but so attractive; and we have an entirely selfish time, and then when we have need of special attention we nobly return for it, confident that we shall be rewarded instead of smacked.

So great indeed was their faith in a mother's love that they felt they could afford to be callous for a bit longer.

But there was one there who knew better, and when Wendy finished he uttered a hollow groan.

"What is it, Peter?" she cried, running to him, thinking he was ill. She felt him solicitously, lower down than his chest. "Where is it, Peter?"

"It isn't that kind of pain," Peter replied darkly.

"Then what kind is it?"

"Wendy, you are wrong about mothers."

They all gathered round him in affright, so alarming was his agitation; and with a fine candour he told them what he had hitherto concealed.

"Long ago," he said, "I thought like you that my mother would always keep the window open for me, so I stayed away for moons and moons and moons, and then flew back; but the window was barred, for mother had forgotten all about me, and there was another little boy sleeping in my bed."

I am not sure that this was true, but Peter thought it was true; and it scared them.

"Are you sure mothers are like that?"

"Yes."

So this was the truth about mothers. The toads!

Still it is best to be careful; and no one knows so quickly as a child when he should give in. "Wendy, let us go home," cried John and Michael together.

"Yes," she said, clutching them.

"Not to-night?" asked the lost boys bewildered. They knew in what they called their hearts that one can get on quite well without a mother, and that it is only the mothers who think you can't.

"At once," Wendy replied resolutely, for the horrible thought had come to her: "Perhaps mother is in half mourning by this time."[1]

This dread made her forgetful of what must be Peter's feelings, and she said to him rather sharply, "Peter, will you make the necessary arrangements?"

"If you wish it," he replied, as coolly as if she had asked him to pass the nuts.

Not so much as a sorry-to-lose-you between them! If she did not mind the parting, he was going to show her, was Peter, that neither did he.

But of course he cared very much; and he was so full of wrath against grown-ups, who, as usual, were spoiling everything, that as soon as he got inside his tree he breathed intentionally quick short breaths at the rate of about five to a second. He did this because there is a saying in the Neverland that, every time you breathe, a grown-up dies; and Peter was killing them off vindictively as fast as possible.

Then having given the necessary instructions to the redskins he returned to the home, where an unworthy scene had been enacted in his absence. Panic-stricken at the thought of losing Wendy the lost boys had advanced upon her threateningly.

"It will be worse than before she came," they cried.

"We shan't let her go."

"Let's keep her prisoner."

"Ay, chain her up."

In her extremity* an instinct told her to which of them to turn.

"Tootles," she cried, "I appeal to you."

Was it not strange? she appealed to Tootles, quite the silliest one.

Grandly, however, did Tootles respond. For that one moment he dropped his silliness and spoke with dignity.

"I am just Tootles," he said, "and nobody minds me. But the first who does not behave to Wendy like an English gentleman I will blood him severely."

He drew his hanger;† and for that instant his sun was at noon. The others held back uneasily. Then Peter returned, and they saw at once that they would get no support from him. He would keep no girl in the Neverland against her will.

"Wendy," he said, striding up and down, "I have asked the redskins to guide you through the wood, as flying tires you so."

"Thank you, Peter."

"Then," he continued, in the short sharp voice of one accustomed to be obeyed, "Tinker Bell will take you across the sea. Wake her, Nibs."

Nibs had to knock twice before he got an answer, though Tink had really been sitting up in bed listening for some time.

"Who are you? How dare you? Go away," she cried.

"You are to get up, Tink," Nibs called, "and take Wendy on a journey."

Of course Tink had been delighted to hear that Wendy was going; but she was jolly well determined not to be her courier, and she said so in still more offensive language. Then she pretended to be asleep again.

"She says she won't!" Nibs exclaimed, aghast at such insubordination, whereupon Peter went sternly toward the young lady's chamber.

---

*Her condition of extreme urgency and desperation.

†Short, small sword once used by seamen.

"Tink," he rapped out, "if you don't get up and dress at once I will open the curtains, and then we shall all see you in your *negligée*."*

This made her leap to the floor. "Who said I wasn't getting up?" she cried.

In the meantime the boys were gazing very forlornly at Wendy, now equipped with John and Michael for the journey. By this time they were dejected, not merely because they were about to lose her, but also because they felt that she was going off to something nice to which they had not been invited. Novelty was beckoning to them as usual. Crediting them with a nobler feeling Wendy melted.

"Dear ones," she said, "if you will all come with me I feel almost sure I can get my father and mother to adopt you."

The invitation was meant specially for Peter, but each of the boys was thinking exclusively of himself, and at once they jumped with joy.

"But won't they think us rather a handful?" Nibs asked in the middle of his jump.

"Oh no," said Wendy, rapidly thinking it out, "it will only mean having a few beds in the drawing-room; they can be hidden behind screens on first Thursdays."

"Peter, can we go?" they all cried imploringly. They took it for granted that if they went he would go also, but really they scarcely cared. Thus children are ever ready, when novelty knocks, to desert their dearest ones.

"All right," Peter replied with a bitter smile, and immediately they rushed to get their things.

"And now, Peter," Wendy said, thinking she had put everything right, "I am going to give you your medicine before you go." She loved to give them medicine, and undoubtedly gave them too much. Of course it was only water, but it was out of a bottle, and she always shook the bottle and counted the drops, which gave it a certain medicinal quality. On this occasion, however, she did not give Peter his draught,† for just as she had prepared it, she saw a look on his face that made her heart sink.

---

*Woman's sheer, loose dressing gown, often of soft, delicate fabric (French).
†Dose of medicine poured out or mixed for drinking.

"Get your things, Peter," she cried, shaking.

"No," he answered, pretending indifference, "I am not going with you, Wendy."

"Yes, Peter."

"No."

To show that her departure would leave him unmoved, he skipped up and down the room, playing gaily on his heartless pipes. She had to run about after him, though it was rather undignified.

"To find your mother," she coaxed.

Now, if Peter had ever quite had a mother, he no longer missed her. He could do very well without one. He had thought them out, and remembered only their bad points.

"No, no," he told Wendy decisively; "perhaps she would say I was old, and I just want always to be a little boy and to have fun."

"But, Peter——"

"No."

And so the others had to be told.

"Peter isn't coming."

Peter not coming! They gazed blankly at him, their sticks over their backs, and on each stick a bundle. Their first thought was that if Peter was not going he had probably changed his mind about letting them go.

But he was far too proud for that. "If you find your mothers," he said darkly, "I hope you will like them."

The awful cynicism of this made an uncomfortable impression, and most of them began to look rather doubtful. After all, their faces said, were they not noodles to want to go?

"Now then," cried Peter, "no fuss, no blubbering; good-bye Wendy"; and he held out his hand cheerily, quite as if they must really go now, for he had something important to do.

She had to take his hand, as there was no indication that he would prefer a thimble.

"You will remember about changing your flannels, Peter?" she said, lingering over him. She was always so particular about their flannels.

"Yes."

"And you will take your medicine?"

"Yes."

That seemed to be everything, and an awkward pause followed. Peter, however, was not the kind that breaks down before people. "Are you ready, Tinker Bell?" he called out.

"Ay! ay!"

"Then lead the way."

Tink darted up the nearest tree; but no one followed her, for it was at this moment that the pirates made their dreadful attack upon the redskins. Above, where all had been so still, the air was rent with shrieks and the clash of steel. Below, there was dead silence. Mouths opened and remained open. Wendy fell on her knees, but her arms were extended toward Peter. All arms were extended to him, as if suddenly blown in his direction; they were beseeching him mutely not to desert them. As for Peter, he seized his sword, the same he thought he had slain Barbecue with, and the lust of battle was in his eye.

CHAPTER XII

The Children Are Carried Off

THE PIRATE ATTACK HAD been a complete surprise: a sure proof that the unscrupulous Hook had conducted it improperly, for to surprise redskins fairly is beyond the wit of the white man.

By all the unwritten laws of savage warfare it is always the redskin who attacks, and with the wiliness of his race he does it just before the dawn, at which time he knows the courage of the whites to be at its lowest ebb. The white men have in the meantime made a rude stockade on the summit of yonder undulating ground, at the foot of which a stream runs, for it is destruction to be too far from water. There they await the onslaught, the inexperienced ones clutching their revolvers and treading on twigs, but the old hands sleeping tranquilly until just before the dawn. Through the long black night the savage scouts wriggle, snake-like, among the grass without stirring a blade. The brushwood closes behind them as silently as sand into which a mole has dived. Not a sound is to be heard, save when they give vent to a wonderful imitation of the lonely call of the coyote. The cry is answered by other braves; and some of them do it even better than the coyotes, who are not very good at it. So the chill hours wear on, and the long suspense is horribly trying to the paleface* who has to live through it for the first time; but to the trained hand those ghastly calls and still ghastlier silences are but an intimation of how the night is marching.

That this was the usual procedure was so well-known to Hook that in disregarding it he cannot be excused on the plea of ignorance.

---

*White person.

The Piccaninnies, on their part, trusted implicitly to his honour, and their whole action of the night stands out in marked contrast to his. They left nothing undone that was consistent with the reputation of their tribe. With that alertness of the senses which is at once the marvel and despair of civilised peoples, they knew that the pirates were on the island from the moment one of them trod on a dry stick; and in an incredibly short space of time the coyote cries began. Every foot of ground between the spot where Hook had landed his forces and the home under the trees was stealthily examined by braves wearing their moccasins with the heels in front.* They found only one hillock† with a stream at its base, so that Hook had no choice; here he must establish himself and wait for just before the dawn. Everything being thus mapped out with almost diabolical cunning, the main body of the redskins folded their blankets around them, and in the phlegmatic‡ manner that is to them the pearl of manhood squatted above the children's home, awaiting the cold moment when they should deal pale death.§

Here dreaming, though wide-awake, of the exquisite tortures to which they were to put him at break of day, those confiding savages were found by the treacherous Hook. From the accounts afterwards supplied by such of the scouts as escaped the carnage, he does not seem even to have paused at the rising ground, though it is certain that in that grey light he must have seen it: no thought of waiting to be attacked appears from first to last to have visited his subtle mind; he would not even hold off till the night was nearly spent; on he pounded with no policy but to fall to.|| What could the bewildered scouts do, masters as they were of every war-like artifice save this one, but trot helplessly after him, exposing themselves fatally to view, the while they gave pathetic utterance to the coyote cry.

Around the brave Tiger Lily were a dozen of her stoutest warriors, and they suddenly saw the perfidious pirates bearing down upon them. Fell from their eyes then the film through which they

---

*Braves wear their moccasins backward to confuse pursuers about the direction of their footprints.

†Small hill.

‡Not easily excited to feeling or action; having a calm, self-possessed temperament.

§In other words, death to white people.

||To begin an activity energetically, often under command.

had looked at victory. No more would they torture at the stake. For them the happy hunting-grounds now. They knew it; but as their fathers' sons they acquitted themselves. Even then they had time to gather in a phalanx* that would have been hard to break had they risen quickly, but this they were forbidden to do by the traditions of their race. It is written that the noble savage must never express surprise in the presence of the white. Thus terrible as the sudden appearance of the pirates must have been to them, they remained stationary for a moment, not a muscle moving; as if the foe had come by invitation. Then, indeed, the tradition gallantly upheld, they seized their weapons, and the air was torn with the war-cry; but it was now too late.

It is no part of ours to describe what was a massacre rather than a fight. Thus perished many of the flower of the Piccaninny tribe. Not all unavenged did they die, for with Lean Wolf fell Alf Mason, to disturb the Spanish Main no more, and among others who bit the dust were Geo. Scourie, Chas. Turley, and the Alsatian Foggerty. Turley fell to the tomahawk of the terrible Panther, who ultimately cut a way through the pirates with Tiger Lily and a small remnant of the tribe.

To what extent Hook is to blame for his tactics on this occasion is for the historian to decide. Had he waited on the rising ground till the proper hour he and his men would probably have been butchered; and in judging him it is only fair to take this into account. What he should perhaps have done was to acquaint his opponents that he proposed to follow a new method. On the other hand this, as destroying the element of surprise, would have made his strategy of no avail, so that the whole question is beset with difficulties. One cannot at least withhold a reluctant admiration for the wit that had conceived so bold a scheme, and the fell† genius with which it was carried out.

What were his own feelings about himself at that triumphant moment? Fain‡ would his dogs have known, as breathing heavily and wiping their cutlasses, they gathered at a discreet distance from

---

*Body of armed troops in close formation.

†Malevolent.

‡Happily; willingly; with pleasure.

his hook, and squinted through their ferret eyes* at this extraordinary man. Elation must have been in his heart, but his face did not reflect it: ever a dark and solitary enigma, he stood aloof from his followers in spirit as in substance.

The night's work was not yet over, for it was not the redskins he had come out to destroy; they were but the bees to be smoked, so that he should get at the honey. It was Pan he wanted, Pan and Wendy and their band, but chiefly Pan.

Peter was such a small boy that one tends to wonder at the man's hatred of him. True he had flung Hook's arm to the crocodile, but even this and the increased insecurity of life to which it led, owing to the crocodile's pertinacity, hardly account for a vindictiveness so relentless and malignant. The truth is that there was a something about Peter which goaded the pirate captain to frenzy. It was not his courage, it was not his engaging appearance, it was not—. There is no beating about the bush, for we know quite well what it was, and have got to tell. It was Peter's cockiness.

This had got on Hook's nerves; it made his iron claw twitch, and at night it disturbed him like an insect. While Peter lived, the tortured man felt that he was a lion in a cage into which a sparrow had come.

The question now was how to get down the trees, or how to get his dogs down? He ran his greedy eyes over them, searching for the thinnest ones. They wriggled uncomfortably, for they knew he would not scruple to ram them down with poles.

In the meantime, what of the boys? We have seen them at the first clang of weapons, turned as it were into stone figures, open-mouthed, all appealing with outstretched arms to Peter; and we return to them as their mouths close, and their arms fall to their sides. The pandemonium above has ceased almost as suddenly as it arose, passed like a fierce gust of wind; but they know that in the passing it has determined their fate.

Which side had won?

The pirates, listening avidly at the mouths of the trees, heard the question put by every boy, and alas, they also heard Peter's answer.

---

*Eyes that endeavor to search out, discover, expose.

"If the redskins have won," he said, "they will beat the tom-tom; it is always their sign of victory."

Now Smee had found the tom-tom, and was at that moment sitting on it. "You will never hear the tom-tom again," he muttered, but inaudibly of course, for strict silence had been enjoined. To his amazement Hook signed to him to beat the tom-tom, and slowly there came to Smee an understanding of the dreadful wickedness of the order. Never, probably, had this simple man admired Hook so much.

Twice Smee beat upon the instrument, and then stopped to listen gleefully.

"The tom-tom," the miscreants heard Peter cry; "an Indian victory!"

The doomed children answered with a cheer that was music to the black hearts above, and almost immediately they repeated their good-byes to Peter. This puzzled the pirates, but all their other feelings were swallowed by a base delight that the enemy were about to come up the trees. They smirked at each other and rubbed their hands. Rapidly and silently Hook gave his orders: one man to each tree, and the others to arrange themselves in a line two yards apart.

CHAPTER XIII

Do You Believe in Fairies?

THE MORE QUICKLY THIS horror is disposed of the better. The first to emerge from his tree was Curly. He rose out of it into the arms of Cecco, who flung him to Smee, who flung him to Starkey, who flung him to Bill Jukes, who flung him to Noodler, and so he was tossed from one to another till he fell at the feet of the black pirate. All the boys were plucked from their trees in this ruthless manner; and several of them were in the air at a time, like bales of goods flung from hand to hand.

A different treatment was accorded to Wendy, who came last. With ironical politeness Hook raised his hat to her, and, offering her his arm, escorted her to the spot where the others were being gagged. He did it with such an air, he was so frightfully *distingué*,* that she was too fascinated to cry out. She was only a little girl.

Perhaps it is tell-tale to divulge that for a moment Hook entranced her, and we tell on her only because her slip led to strange results. Had she haughtily unhanded him (and we should have loved to write it of her), she would have been hurled through the air like the others, and then Hook would probably not have been present at the tying of the children; and had he not been at the tying he would not have discovered Slightly's secret, and without the secret he could not presently have made his foul attempt on Peter's life.

They were tied to prevent their flying away, doubled up with their knees close to their ears; and for this job the black pirate had

---

*Distinguished in appearance, manner, or bearing (French).

cut a rope into nine equal pieces. All went well with the trussing* until Slightly's turn came, when he was found to be like those irritating parcels that use up all the string in going round and leave no tags with which to tie a knot. The pirates kicked him in their rage, just as you kick the parcel (though in fairness you should kick the string); and strange to say it was Hook who told them to belay their violence. His lip was curled with malicious triumph. While his dogs were merely sweating because every time they tried to pack the unhappy lad tight in one part he bulged out in another, Hook's master mind had gone far beneath Slightly's surface, probing not for effects but for causes; and his exultation showed that he had found them. Slightly, white to the gills, knew that Hook had surprised his secret, which was this, that no boy so blown out could use a tree wherein an average man need stick.† Poor Slightly, most wretched of all the children now, for he was in a panic about Peter, bitterly regretted what he had done. Madly addicted to the drinking of water when he was hot, he had swelled in consequence to his present girth, and instead of reducing himself to fit his tree he had, unknown to the others, whittled his tree to make it fit him.

Sufficient of this Hook guessed to persuade him that Peter at last lay at his mercy, but no word of the dark design that now formed in the subterranean caverns of his mind crossed his lips; he merely signed that the captives were to be conveyed to the ship, and that he would be alone.

How to convey them? Hunched up in their ropes they might indeed be rolled down hill like barrels, but most of the way lay through a morass.‡ Again Hook's genius surmounted difficulties. He indicated that the little house must be used as a conveyance.§ The children were flung into it, four stout pirates raised it on their shoulders, the others fell in behind, and singing the hateful pirate chorus the strange procession set off through the wood. I don't know whether

---

*Tying up or tightly binding.

†No boy as bloated as Slightly could fit into a carved-out tree trunk that an average adult would get stuck in; carving the trunk bigger makes it large enough for a man to use and undermines a key defense of the Lost Boys' underground home.

‡Soft, wet area of low-lying ground that is difficult to cross.

§Something used for carrying things or people.

FLUNG LIKE BALES

any of the children were crying; if so, the singing drowned the sound; but as the little house disappeared in the forest, a brave though tiny jet of smoke issued from its chimney as if defying Hook.

Hook saw it, and it did Peter a bad service. It dried up any trickle of pity for him that may have remained in the pirate's infuriated breast.

The first thing he did on finding himself alone in the fast falling night was to tiptoe to Slightly's tree, and make sure that it provided him with a passage. Then for long he remained brooding; his hat of ill omen on the sward, so that a gentle breeze which had arisen might play refreshingly through his hair. Dark as were his thoughts his blue eyes were as soft as the periwinkle.* Intently he listened for any sound from the nether world,† but all was as silent below as above; the house under the ground seemed to be but one more empty tenement in the void. Was that boy asleep, or did he stand waiting at the foot of Slightly's tree, with his dagger in his hand?

There was no way of knowing, save by going down. Hook let his cloak slip softly to the ground, and then biting his lips till a lewd blood stood on them, he stepped into the tree. He was a brave man, but for a moment he had to stop there and wipe his brow, which was dripping like a candle. Then silently he let himself go into the unknown.

He arrived unmolested at the foot of the shaft, and stood still again, biting at his breath, which had almost left him. As his eyes became accustomed to the dim light various objects in the home under the trees took shape; but the only one on which his greedy gaze rested, long sought for and found at last, was the great bed. On the bed lay Peter fast asleep.

Unaware of the tragedy being enacted above, Peter had continued, for a little time after the children left, to play gaily on his pipes: no doubt rather a forlorn attempt to prove to himself that he did not care. Then he decided not to take his medicine, so as to grieve Wendy. Then he lay down on the bed outside the coverlet, to vex her still more; for she had always tucked them inside it, because you never know that you may not grow chilly at the turn of the night. Then he nearly cried; but it struck him how indignant she would be

---

*Trailing herb of the dogbane family, with blue flowers.
†Peter's home underground.

if he laughed instead; so he laughed a haughty laugh and fell asleep in the middle of it.

Sometimes, though not often, he had dreams, and they were more painful than the dreams of other boys. For hours he could not be separated from these dreams, though he wailed piteously in them. They had to do, I think, with the riddle of his existence. At such times it had been Wendy's custom to take him out of bed and sit with him on her lap, soothing him in dear ways of her own invention, and when he grew calmer to put him back to bed before he quite woke up, so that he should not know of the indignity to which she had subjected him. But on this occasion he had fallen at once into a dreamless sleep. One arm dropped over the edge of the bed, one leg was arched, and the unfinished part of his laugh was stranded on his mouth, which was open, showing the little pearls.

Thus defenceless Hook found him. He stood silent at the foot of the tree looking across the chamber at his enemy. Did no feeling of compassion stir his sombre breast? The man was not wholly evil; he loved flowers (I have been told) and sweet music (he was himself no mean performer on the harpsichord); and, let it be frankly admitted, the idyllic nature of the scene shook him profoundly. Mastered by his better self he would have returned reluctantly up the tree, but for one thing.

What stayed him was Peter's impertinent appearance as he slept. The open mouth, the drooping arm, the arched knee: they were such a personification of cockiness as, taken together, will never again one may hope be presented to eyes so sensitive to their offensiveness. They steeled Hook's heart. If his rage had broken him into a hundred pieces every one of them would have disregarded the incident, and leapt at the sleeper.

Though a light from the one lamp shone dimly on the bed Hook stood in darkness himself, and at the first stealthy step forward he discovered an obstacle, the door of Slightly's tree. It did not entirely fill the aperture, and he had been looking over it. Feeling for the catch, he found to his fury that it was low down, beyond his reach. To his disordered brain it seemed then that the irritating quality in Peter's face and figure visibly increased, and he rattled the door and flung himself against it. Was his enemy to escape him after all?

But what was that? The red in his eye had caught sight of Peter's medicine standing on a ledge within easy reach. He fathomed what it was straightway, and immediately he knew that the sleeper was in his power.

Lest he should be taken alive, Hook always carried about his person a dreadful drug, blended by himself of all the death-dealing rings that had come into his possession. These he had boiled down into a yellow liquid quite unknown to science, which was probably the most virulent poison in existence.

Five drops of this he now added to Peter's cup. His hand shook, but it was in exultation rather than in shame. As he did it he avoided glancing at the sleeper, but not lest pity should unnerve him; merely to avoid spilling. Then one long gloating look he cast upon his victim, and turning, wormed his way with difficulty up the tree. As he emerged at the top he looked the very spirit of evil breaking from its hole. Donning his hat at its most rakish angle, he wound his cloak around him, holding one end in front as if to conceal his person from the night, of which it was the blackest part, and muttering strangely to himself stole away through the trees.

Peter slept on. The light guttered* and went out, leaving the tenement in darkness; but still he slept. It must have been not less than ten o'clock by the crocodile, when he suddenly sat up in his bed, wakened by he knew not what. It was a soft cautious tapping on the door of his tree.

Soft and cautious, but in that stillness it was sinister. Peter felt for his dagger till his hand gripped it. Then he spoke.

"Who is that?"

For long there was no answer: then again the knock.

"Who are you?"

No answer.

He was thrilled, and he loved being thrilled. In two strides he reached his door. Unlike Slightly's door it filled the aperture, so that he could not see beyond it, nor could the one knocking see him.

"I won't open unless you speak," Peter cried.

Then at last the visitor spoke, in a lovely bell-like voice.

"Let me in, Peter."

---

*Burned low and unsteadily; flickered.

It was Tink, and quickly he unbarred to her. She flew in excitedly, her face flushed and her dress stained with mud.

"What is it?"

"Oh, you could never guess!" she cried, and offered him three guesses. "Out with it!" he shouted, and in one ungrammatical sentence, as long as the ribbons conjurers pull from their mouths, she told of the capture of Wendy and the boys.

Peter's heart bobbed up and down as he listened. Wendy bound, and on the pirate ship; she who loved everything to be just so!

"I'll rescue her!" he cried, leaping at his weapons. As he leapt he thought of something he could do to please her. He could take his medicine.

His hand closed on the fatal draught.

"No!" shrieked Tinker Bell, who had heard Hook muttering about his deed as he sped through the forest.

"Why not?"

"It is poisoned."

"Poisoned! Who could have poisoned it?"

"Hook."

"Don't be silly. How could Hook have got down here?"

Alas, Tinker Bell could not explain this, for even she did not know the dark secret of Slightly's tree. Nevertheless Hook's words had left no room for doubt. The cup was poisoned.

"Besides," said Peter, quite believing himself, "I never fell asleep."

He raised the cup. No time for words now; time for deeds, and with one of her lightning movements Tink got between his lips and the draught, and drained it to the dregs.

"Why, Tink, how dare you drink my medicine?"

But she did not answer. Already she was reeling in the air.

"What is the matter with you?" cried Peter, suddenly afraid.

"It was poisoned, Peter," she told him softly; "and now I am going to be dead."

"O Tink, did you drink it to save me?"

"Yes."

"But why, Tink?"

Her wings would scarcely carry her now, but in reply she alighted on his shoulder and gave his nose a loving bite. She whispered in his ear "you silly ass," and then, tottering to her chamber, lay down on the bed.

His head almost filled the fourth wall of her little room as he knelt near her in distress. Every moment her light was growing fainter; and he knew that if it went out she would be no more. She liked his tears so much that she put out her beautiful finger and let them run over it.

Her voice was so low that at first he could not make out what she said. Then he made it out. She was saying that she thought she could get well again if children believed in fairies.

Peter flung out his arms. There were no children there, and it was night time; but he addressed all who might be dreaming of the Neverland, and who were therefore nearer to him than you think: boys and girls in their nighties, and naked papooses* in their baskets hung from trees.

"Do you believe?" he cried.

Tink sat up in bed almost briskly to listen to her fate.

She fancied she heard answers in the affirmative, and then again she wasn't sure.

"What do you think?" she asked Peter.

"If you believe," he shouted to them, "clap your hands; don't let Tink die."

Many clapped.

Some didn't.

A few little beasts hissed.

The clapping stopped suddenly; as if countless mothers had rushed to their nurseries to see what on earth was happening; but already Tink was saved. First her voice grew strong, then she popped out of bed, then she was flashing through the room more merry and impudent than ever. She never thought of thanking those who believed, but she would have liked to get at the ones who had hissed.

"And now to rescue Wendy!"

The moon was riding in a cloudy heaven when Peter rose from his tree, begirt† with weapons and wearing little else, to set out upon

---

*Native American infants or very small children.

†Encircled with; Peter's gear is worn all around his body.

his perilous quest. It was not such a night as he would have chosen. He had hoped to fly, keeping not far from the ground so that nothing unwonted should escape his eyes; but in that fitful light to have flown low would have meant trailing his shadow through the trees, thus disturbing the birds and acquainting a watchful foe that he was astir.

He regretted now that he had given the birds of the island such strange names that they are very wild and difficult of approach.

There was no other course but to press forward in redskin fashion, at which happily he was an adept. But in what direction, for he could not be sure that the children had been taken to the ship? A slight fall of snow had obliterated all footmarks; and a deathly silence pervaded the island, as if for a space Nature stood still in horror of the recent carnage. He had taught the children something of the forest lore that he had himself learned from Tiger Lily and Tinker Bell, and knew that in their dire hour they were not likely to forget it. Slightly, if he had an opportunity, would blaze the trees, for instance, Curly would drop seeds, and Wendy would leave her handkerchief at some important place. But morning was needed to search for such guidance, and he could not wait. The upper world had called him, but would give no help.

The crocodile passed him, but not another living thing, not a sound, not a movement; and yet he knew well that sudden death might be at the next tree, or stalking him from behind.

He swore this terrible oath: "Hook or me this time."

Now he crawled forward like a snake; and again, erect, he darted across a space on which the moonlight played, one finger on his lip and his dagger at the ready. He was frightfully happy.

CHAPTER XIV

The Pirate Ship

ONE GREEN LIGHT SQUINTING over Kidd's Creek, which is near the mouth of the pirate river, marked where the brig,* the *Jolly Roger*, lay, low in the water; a rakish-looking craft foul to the hull, every beam in her detestable like ground strewn with mangled feathers. She was the cannibal of the seas, and scarce needed that watchful eye, for she floated immune in the horror of her name.

She was wrapped in the blanket of night, through which no sound from her could have reached the shore. There was little sound, and none agreeable save the whir of the ship's sewing machine at which Smee sat, ever industrious and obliging, the essence of the commonplace, pathetic Smee. I know not why he was so infinitely pathetic, unless it were because he was so pathetically unaware of it; but even strong men had to turn hastily from looking at him, and more than once on summer evenings he had touched the fount of Hook's tears and made it flow. Of this, as of almost everything else, Smee was quite unconscious.

A few of the pirates leant over the bulwarks† drinking in the miasma‡ of the night; others sprawled by barrels over games of dice and cards; and the exhausted four who had carried the little house lay prone on the deck, where even in their sleep they rolled skilfully to this side or that out of Hook's reach, lest he should claw them mechanically in passing.

Hook trod the deck in thought. O man unfathomable. It was his

---

*Two-masted sailing vessel.

†The parts of a ship's side that are above the upper deck.

‡Thick, vaporous atmosphere that corrupts or poisons.

hour of triumph. Peter had been removed for ever from his path, and all the other boys were on the brig, about to walk the plank. It was his grimmest deed since the days when he had brought Barbecue to heel; and knowing as we do how vain a tabernacle* is man, could we be surprised had he now paced the deck unsteadily, bellied out by the winds of his success?

But there was no elation in his gait, which kept pace with the action of his sombre mind. Hook was profoundly dejected.

He was often thus when communing with himself on board ship in the quietude of the night. It was because he was so terribly alone. This inscrutable man never felt more alone than when surrounded by his dogs. They were socially so inferior to him.

Hook was not his true name. To reveal who he really was would even at this date set the country in a blaze; but as those who read between the lines must already have guessed, he had been at a famous public school;† and its traditions still clung to him like garments, with which indeed they are largely concerned. Thus it was offensive to him even now to board a ship in the same dress in which he grappled her, and he still adhered in his walk to the school's distinguished slouch. But above all he retained the passion for good form.‡

Good form! However much he may have degenerated, he still knew that this is all that really matters.

From far within him he heard a creaking as of rusty portals, and through them came a stern tap-tap-tap, like hammering in the night when one cannot sleep. "Have you been good form to-day?" was their eternal question.

"Fame, fame, that glittering bauble, it is mine!" he cried.

"Is it quite good form to be distinguished at anything?" the tap-tap from his school replied.

"I am the only man whom Barbecue feared," he urged, "and Flint himself feared Barbecue."

"Barbecue, Flint—what house?"§ came the cutting retort.

---

*Pseudo-biblical phrase meaning the body is only a temporary and unworthy dwelling place for the soul.

†Hook was a student at Eton College, an exclusive English prep school.

‡Respectable manners; appropriate behavior meant to elicit respect and admiration.

§Eton College is divided into a number of houses, which compete with one another in academics and sports.

Most disquieting reflection of all, was it not bad form to think about good form?

His vitals* were tortured by this problem. It was a claw within him sharper than the iron one; and as it tore him, the perspiration dripped down his tallow† countenance and streaked his doublet.‡ Ofttimes he drew his sleeve across his face, but there was no damming that trickle.

Ah, envy not Hook.

There came to him a presentiment of his early dissolution. It was as if Peter's terrible oath had boarded the ship. Hook felt a gloomy desire to make his dying speech, lest presently there should be no time for it.

"Better for Hook," he cried, "if he had had less ambition!" It was in his darkest hours only that he referred to himself in the third person.

"No little children love me!"

Strange that he should think of this, which had never troubled him before; perhaps the sewing machine brought it to his mind. For long he muttered to himself, staring at Smee, who was hemming placidly, under the conviction that all children feared him.

Feared him! Feared Smee! There was not a child on board the brig that night who did not already love him. He had said horrid things to them and hit them with the palm of his hand, because he could not hit with his fist, but they had only clung to him the more. Michael had tried on his spectacles.

To tell poor Smee that they thought him lovable! Hooked itched to do it, but it seemed too brutal. Instead, he revolved this mystery in his mind: why do they find Smee lovable? He pursued the problem like the sleuth-hound that he was. If Smee was lovable, what was it that made him so? A terrible answer suddenly presented itself—"Good form?"

Had the bo'sun good form without knowing it, which is the best form of all?

---

*His body's vital organs.

†Pale, waxy.

‡Close-fitting garment worn by men.

He remembered that you have to prove you don't know you have it before you are eligible for Pop.*

With a cry of rage he raised his iron hand over Smee's head; but he did not tear. What arrested him was this reflection:

"To claw a man because he is good form, what would that be?"

"Bad form!"

The unhappy Hook was as impotent as he was damp, and he fell forward like a cut flower.

His dogs thinking him out of the way for a time, discipline instantly relaxed; and they broke into a bacchanalian† dance, which brought him to his feet at once, all traces of human weakness gone, as if a bucket of water had passed over him.

"Quiet, you scugs,"‡ he cried, "or I'll cast anchor in you"; and at once the din was hushed. "Are all the children chained, so that they cannot fly away?"

"Ay, ay."

"Then hoist them up."

The wretched prisoners were dragged from the hold, all except Wendy, and ranged in line in front of him. For a time he seemed unconscious of their presence. He lolled at his ease, humming, not unmelodiously, snatches of a rude song, and fingering a pack of cards. Ever and anon the light from his cigar gave a touch of colour to his face.

"Now then, bullies," he said briskly, "six of you walk the plank tonight, but I have room for two cabin boys. Which of you is it to be?"

"Don't irritate him unnecessarily," had been Wendy's instructions in the hold; so Tootles stepped forward politely. Tootles hated the idea of signing under such a man, but an instinct told him that it would be prudent to lay the responsibility on an absent person; and though a somewhat silly boy, he knew that mothers alone are always willing to be the buffer. All children know this about mothers, and despise them for it, but make constant use of it.

So Tootles explained prudently, "You see, sir, I don't think my

---

*Highly respected club at Eton, consisting of very few members, usually the top sportsmen in the school.

†Characterized by drunken revelry.

‡Lower boys in a school, or boys with untidy or ill-mannered habits.

mother would like me to be a pirate. Would your mother like you to be a pirate, Slightly?"

He winked at Slightly, who said mournfully, "I don't think so," as if he wished things had been otherwise. "Would your mother like you to be a pirate, Twin?"

"I don't think so," said the first twin, as clever as the others. "Nibs, would——"

"Stow this gab,"* roared Hook, and the spokesmen were dragged back. "You, boy," he said, addressing John, "you look as if you had a little pluck in you. Didst never want to be a pirate, my hearty?"

Now John had sometimes experienced this hankering at maths. prep.; and he was struck by Hook's picking him out.

"I once thought of calling myself Redhanded Jack," he said diffidently.

"And a good name too. We'll call you that here, bully, if you join."

"What do you think, Michael?" asked John.

"What would you call me if I join?" Michael demanded.

"Blackbeard Joe."

Michael was naturally impressed. "What do you think, John?" He wanted John to decide, and John wanted him to decide.

"Shall we still be respectful subjects of the King?" John inquired.

Through Hook's teeth came the answer: "You would have to swear, 'Down with the King.'"

Perhaps John had not behaved very well so far, but he shone out now.

"Then I refuse!" he cried, banging the barrel in front of Hook.

"And I refuse," cried Michael.

"Rule Britannia!" squeaked Curly.

The infuriated pirates buffeted them in the mouth; and Hook roared out, "That seals your doom. Bring up their mother. Get the plank ready."

They were only boys, and they went white as they saw Jukes and Cecco preparing the fatal plank. But they tried to look brave when Wendy was brought up.

No words of mine can tell you how Wendy despised those pi-

---

*Shut up.

rates. To the boys there was at least some glamour in the pirate calling; but all that she saw was that the ship had not been tidied for years. There was not a porthole, on the grimy glass of which you might not have written with your finger "Dirty pig"; and she had already written it on several. But as the boys gathered round her she had no thought, of course, save for them.

"So, my beauty," said Hook, as if he spoke in syrup, "you are to see your children walk the plank."

Fine gentleman though he was, the intensity of his communings had soiled his ruff,* and suddenly he knew that she was gazing at it. With a hasty gesture he tried to hide it, but he was too late.

"Are they to die?" asked Wendy, with a look of such frightful contempt that he nearly fainted.

"They are," he snarled. "Silence all," he called gloatingly, "for a mother's last words to her children."

At this moment Wendy was grand. "These are my last words, dear boys," she said firmly. "I feel that I have a message to you from your real mothers, and it is this: 'We hope our sons will die like English gentlemen.' "

Even the pirates were awed, and Tootles cried out hysterically, "I am going to do what my mother hopes. What are you to do, Nibs?"

"What my mother hopes. What are you to do, Twin?"

"What my mother hopes. John, what are——"

But Hook had found his voice again.

"Tie her up!" he shouted.

It was Smee who tied her to the mast. "See here, honey," he whispered, "I'll save you if you promise to be my mother."

But not even for Smee would she make such a promise. "I would almost rather have no children at all," she said disdainfully.

It is sad to know that not a boy was looking at her as Smee tied her to the mast; the eyes of all were on the plank: that last little walk they were about to take. They were no longer able to hope that they would walk it manfully, for the capacity to think had gone from them; they could stare and shiver only.

Hook smiled on them with his teeth closed, and took a step to-

---

*Stiffly starched, frilled, or pleated circular collar made of fine fabric.

ward Wendy. His intention was to turn her face so that she should see the boys walking the plank one by one. But he never reached her, he never heard the cry of anguish he hoped to wring from her. He heard something else instead.

It was the terrible tick-tick of the crocodile.

They all heard it—pirates, boys, Wendy—and immediately every head was blown in one direction; not to the water whence the sound proceeded, but toward Hook. All knew that what was about to happen concerned him alone, and that from being actors they were suddenly become spectators.

Very frightful was it to see the change that came over him. It was as if he had been clipped at every joint. He fell in a little heap.

The sound came steadily nearer; and in advance of it came this ghastly thought, "the crocodile is about to board the ship"!

Even the iron claw hung inactive; as if knowing that it was no intrinsic part of what the attacking force wanted. Left so fearfully alone, any other man would have lain with his eyes shut where he fell: but the gigantic brain of Hook was still working, and under its guidance he crawled on his knees along the deck as far from the sound as he could go. The pirates respectfully cleared a passage for him, and it was only when he brought up against the bulwarks that he spoke.

"Hide me!" he cried hoarsely.

They gathered round him, all eyes averted from the thing that was coming aboard. They had no thought of fighting it. It was Fate.

Only when Hook was hidden from them did curiosity loosen the limbs of the boys so that they could rush to the ship's side to see the crocodile climbing it. Then they got the strangest surprise of this Night of Nights; for it was no crocodile that was coming to their aid. It was Peter.

He signed to them not to give vent to any cry of admiration that might rouse suspicion. Then he went on ticking.

CHAPTER XV

"Hook or Me This Time"

ODD THINGS HAPPEN TO all of us on our way through life without our noticing for a time that they have happened. Thus, to take an instance, we suddenly discover that we have been deaf in one ear for we don't know how long, but, say, half an hour. Now such an experience had come that night to Peter. When last we saw him he was stealing across the island with one finger to his lips and his dagger at the ready. He had seen the crocodile pass by without noticing anything peculiar about it, but by and by he remembered that it had not been ticking. At first he thought this eerie, but soon he concluded rightly that the clock had run down.

Without giving a thought to what might be the feelings of a fellow-creature thus abruptly deprived of its closest companion, Peter began to consider how he could turn the catastrophe to his own use; and he decided to tick, so that wild beasts should believe he was the crocodile and let him pass unmolested. He ticked superbly, but with one unforeseen result. The crocodile was among those who heard the sound, and it followed him, though whether with the purpose of regaining what it had lost, or merely as a friend under the belief that it was again ticking itself, will never be certainly known, for, like all slaves to a fixed idea, it was a stupid beast.

Peter reached the shore without mishap, and went straight on, his legs encountering the water as if quite unaware that they had entered a new element. Thus many animals pass from land to water, but no other human of whom I know. As he swam he had but one thought: "Hook or me this time." He had ticked so long that he now went on ticking without knowing that he was doing it. Had he known he would have stopped, for to board the brig by the help of the tick, though an ingenious idea, had not occurred to him.

On the contrary, he thought he had scaled her side as noiseless as a mouse; and he was amazed to see the pirates cowering from him, with Hook in their midst as abject as if he had heard the crocodile.

The crocodile! No sooner did Peter remember it than he heard the ticking. At first he thought the sound did come from the crocodile, and he looked behind him swiftly. Then he realised that he was doing it himself, and in a flash he understood the situation. "How clever of me!" he thought at once, and signed to the boys not to burst into applause.

It was at this moment that Ed Teynte the quartermaster* emerged from the forecastle† and came along the deck. Now, reader, time what happened by your watch. Peter struck true and deep. John clapped his hands on the ill-fated pirate's mouth to stifle the dying groan. He fell forward. Four boys caught him to prevent the thud. Peter gave the signal, and the carrion was cast overboard. There was a splash, and then silence. How long has it taken?

"One!" (Slightly had begun to count.)

None too soon, Peter, every inch of him on tiptoe, vanished into the cabin; for more than one pirate was screwing up his courage to look round. They could hear each other's distressed breathing now, which showed them that the more terrible sound had passed.

"It's gone, captain," Smee said, wiping his spectacles. "All's still again."

Slowly Hook let his head emerge from his ruff, and listened so intently that he could have caught the echo of the tick. There was not a sound, and he drew himself up firmly to his full height.

"Then here's to Johnny Plank!" he cried brazenly, hating the boys more than ever because they had seen him unbend. He broke into the villainous ditty:

"Yo ho, yo ho, the frisky plank,
You walks along it so,

---

*Officer responsible for steering the ship.
†Section of the upper deck of a ship located at the bow forward of the foremast.

"HOOK OR ME THIS TIME"

Till it goes down and you goes down
To Davy Jones below!"

To terrorise the prisoners the more, though with a certain loss of dignity, he danced along an imaginary plank, grimacing at them as he sang; and when he finished he cried, "Do you want a touch of the cat* before you walk the plank?"

At that they fell on their knees. "No, no!" they cried so piteously that every pirate smiled.

"Fetch the cat, Jukes," said Hook, "it's in the cabin."

The cabin! Peter was in the cabin! The children gazed at each other.

"Ay, ay," said Jukes blithely, and he strode into the cabin. They followed him with their eyes; they scarce knew that Hook had resumed his song, his dogs joining in with him:

"Yo ho, yo ho, the scratching cat,
Its tails are nine, you know,
And when they're writ upon your back—"

What was the last line will never be known, for of a sudden the song was stayed by a dreadful screech from the cabin. It wailed through the ship, and died away. Then was heard a crowing sound which was well understood by the boys, but to the pirates was almost more eerie than the screech.

"What was that?" cried Hook.

"Two," said Slightly solemnly.

The Italian Cecco hesitated for a moment and then swung into the cabin. He tottered out, haggard.

"What's the matter with Bill Jukes, you dog?" hissed Hook, towering over him.

"The matter wi' him is he's dead, stabbed," replied Cecco in a hollow voice.

"Bill Jukes dead!" cried the startled pirates.

"The cabin's as black as a pit," Cecco said, almost gibbering, "but there is something terrible in there: the thing you heard crowing."

---

*Punishment using a cat-o'-nine tails, a whip, made with nine lines bound with a handle, that leaves marks like a cat's claws.

The exultation of the boys, the lowering* looks of the pirates, both were seen by Hook.

"Cecco," he said in his most steely voice, "go back and fetch me out that doodle-doo."†

Cecco, bravest of the brave, cowered before his captain, crying "No, no"; but Hook was purring to his claw.

"Did you say you would go, Cecco?" he said musingly.

Cecco went, first flinging up his arms despairingly. There was no more singing, all listened now: and again came a death-screech and again a crow.

No one spoke except Slightly. "Three," he said.

Hook rallied his dogs with a gesture. "S'death‡ and odds fish," he thundered, "who is to bring me that doodle-doo?"

"Wait till Cecco comes out," growled Starkey, and the others took up the cry.

"I think I heard you volunteer, Starkey," said Hook, purring again.

"No, by thunder!" Starkey cried.

"My hook thinks you did," said Hook, crossing to him. "I wonder if it would not be advisable, Starkey, to humour the hook?"

"I'll swing before I go in there," replied Starkey doggedly, and again he had the support of the crew.

"Is it mutiny?" asked Hook more pleasantly than ever. "Starkey's ringleader!"

"Captain, mercy!" Starkey whimpered, all of a tremble now.

"Shake hands, Starkey," said Hook, proffering his claw.

Starkey looked round for help, but all deserted him. As he backed Hook advanced, and now the red spark was in his eye. With a despairing scream the pirate leapt upon Long Tom and precipitated himself§ into the sea.

"Four," said Slightly.

"And now," Hook asked courteously, "did any other gentleman

---

*Angry, sullen, or threatening.

†Short for "cock-a-doodle-do"; a childish name for a rooster, from the sound it makes when crowing.

‡Short for "God's death."

§Flung himself down.

say mutiny?" Seizing a lantern and raising his claw with a menacing gesture, "I'll bring out that doodle-doo myself," he said, and sped into the cabin.

"Five." How Slightly longed to say it. He wetted his lips to be ready, but Hook came staggering out, without his lantern.

"Something blew out the light," he said a little unsteadily.

"Something!" echoed Mullins.

"What of Cecco?" demanded Noodler.

"He's as dead as Jukes," said Hook shortly.

His reluctance to return to the cabin impressed them all unfavourably, and the mutinous sounds again broke forth. All pirates are superstitious, and Cookson cried, "They do say the surest sign a ship's accurst is when there's one on board more than can be accounted for."

"I've heard," muttered Mullins, "he always boards the pirate craft at last. Had he a tail, captain?"

"They say," said another, looking viciously at Hook, "that when he comes it's in the likeness of the wickedest man aboard."

"Had he a hook, captain?" asked Cookson insolently; and one after another took up the cry, "The ship's doomed!" At this the children could not resist raising a cheer. Hook had well-nigh forgotten his prisoners, but as he swung round on them now his face lit up again.

"Lads," he cried to his crew, "here's a notion. Open the cabin door and drive them in. Let them fight the doodle-doo for their lives. If they kill him, we're so much the better; if he kills them, we're none the worse."

For the last time his dogs admired Hook, and devotedly they did his bidding. The boys, pretending to struggle, were pushed into the cabin and the door was closed on them.

"Now, listen!" cried Hook, and all listened. But not one dared to face the door. Yes, one, Wendy, who all this time had been bound to the mast. It was for neither a scream nor a crow that she was watching, it was for the reappearance of Peter.

She had not long to wait. In the cabin he had found the thing for which he had gone in search: the key that would free the children of their manacles,* and now they all stole forth, armed with such

---

*Handcuffs.

weapons as they could find. First signing to them to hide, Peter cut Wendy's bonds, and then nothing could have been easier than for them all to fly off together; but one thing barred the way, an oath, "Hook or me this time." So when he had freed Wendy, he whispered to her to conceal herself with the others, and himself took her place by the mast, her cloak around him so that he should pass for her. Then he took a great breath and crowed.

To the pirates it was a voice crying that all the boys lay slain in the cabin; and they were panic-stricken. Hook tried to hearten them, but like the dogs he had made them they showed him their fangs, and he knew that if he took his eyes off them now they would leap at him.

"Lads," he said, ready to cajole or strike as need be, but never quailing for an instant, "I've thought it out. There's a Jonah* aboard."

"Ay," they snarled, "a man wi' a hook."

"No, lads, no, it's the girl. Never was luck on a pirate ship wi' a woman on board. We'll right the ship when she's gone."

Some of them remembered that this had been a saying of Flint's. "It's worth trying," they said doubtfully.

"Fling the girl overboard," cried Hook; and they made a rush at the figure in the cloak.

"There's none can save you now, missy," Mullins hissed jeeringly.

"There's one," replied the figure.

"Who's that?"

"Peter Pan the avenger!" came the terrible answer; and as he spoke Peter flung off his cloak. Then they all knew who 'twas that had been undoing them in the cabin, and twice Hook essayed to speak and twice he failed. In that frightful moment I think his fierce heart broke.

At last he cried, "Cleave him to the brisket!"† but without conviction.

"Down, boys, and at them!" Peter's voice rang out; and in another moment the clash of arms was resounding through the ship. Had the pirates kept together it is certain that they would have won; but

---

*Person believed to bring bad luck to those around him; from the biblical tale of Jonah, who fled God's command onto a ship, only to be swallowed by a whale.

†Cut him to the breast!

the onset came when they were all unstrung, and they ran hither and thither, striking wildly, each thinking himself the last survivor of the crew. Man to man they were the stronger; but they fought on the defensive only, which enabled the boys to hunt in pairs and choose their quarry. Some of the miscreants leapt into the sea, others hid in dark recesses, where they were found by Slightly, who did not fight, but ran about with a lantern which he flashed in their faces, so that they were half blinded and fell an easy prey to the reeking* swords of the other boys. There was little sound to be heard but the clang of weapons, an occasional screech or splash, and Slightly monotonously counting—five—six—seven—eight—nine—ten—eleven.

I think all were gone when a group of savage boys surrounded Hook, who seemed to have a charmed life, as he kept them at bay in that circle of fire. They had done for his dogs, but this man alone seemed to be a match for them all. Again and again they closed upon him, and again and again he hewed a clear space. He had lifted up one boy with his hook, and was using him as a buckler,† when another, who had just passed his sword through Mullins, sprang into the fray.

"Put up your swords, boys," cried the newcomer, "this man is mine!"

Thus suddenly Hook found himself face to face with Peter. The others drew back and formed a ring round them.

For long the two enemies looked at one another, Hook shuddering slightly, and Peter with the strange smile upon his face.

"So, Pan," said Hook at last, "this is all your doing."

"Ay, James Hook," came the stern answer, "it is all my doing."

"Proud and insolent youth," said Hook, "prepare to meet thy doom."

"Dark and sinister man," Peter answered, "have at thee."

Without more words they fell to, and for a space there was no advantage to either blade. Peter was a superb swordsman, and parried with dazzling rapidity; ever and anon he followed up a feint with a lunge that got past his foe's defence, but his shorter reach stood him

---

*Wet with moisture, such as blood or sweat.

†Small, round shield or other armor carried by its handle at arm's length to intercept blows.

in ill stead, and he could not drive the steel home. Hook, scarcely his inferior in brilliancy, but not quite so nimble in wrist play, forced him back by the weight of his onset, hoping suddenly to end all with a favourite thrust, taught him long ago by Barbecue at Rio; but to his astonishment he found this thrust turned aside again and again. Then he sought to close and give the quietus* with his iron hook, which all this time had been pawing the air; but Peter doubled under it and, lunging fiercely, pierced him in the ribs. At sight of his own blood, whose peculiar colour, you remember, was offensive to him, the sword fell from Hook's hand, and he was at Peter's mercy.

"Now!" cried all the boys, but with a magnificent gesture Peter invited his opponent to pick up his sword. Hook did so instantly, but with a tragic feeling that Peter was showing good form.

Hitherto he had thought it was some fiend fighting him, but darker suspicions assailed him now.

"Pan, who and what art thou?" he cried huskily.

"I'm youth, I'm joy," Peter answered at a venture, "I'm a little bird that has broken out of the egg."

This, of course, was nonsense; but it was proof to the unhappy Hook that Peter did not know in the least who or what he was, which is the very pinnacle of good form.

"To't again," he cried despairingly.

He fought now like a human flail,† and every sweep of that terrible sword would have severed in twain‡ any man or boy who obstructed it; but Peter fluttered round him as if the very wind it made blew him out of the danger zone. And again and again he darted in and pricked.

Hook was fighting now without hope. That passionate breast no longer asked for life; but for one boon it craved: to see Peter bad form before it was cold for ever.

Abandoning the fight he rushed into the powder magazine§ and fired it.

---

*Death; final settlement. Hook means to stab Peter with a blow that will finish him off.

†Long wooden handle or staff with a shorter, free-swinging stick attached to its end.

‡Cut in two.

§Place where gunpowder is stored on board ship.

"THIS MAN IS MINE!"

"In two minutes," he cried, "the ship will be blown to pieces."

Now, now, he thought, true form will show.

But Peter issued from the powder magazine with the shell in his hands, and calmly flung it overboard.

What sort of form was Hook himself showing? Misguided man though he was, we may be glad, without sympathising with him, that in the end he was true to the traditions of his race. The other boys were flying around him now, flouting,* scornful; and as he staggered about the deck striking up at them impotently, his mind was no longer with them; it was slouching in the playing fields of long ago, or being sent up for good,† or watching the wall-game from a famous wall.‡ And his shoes were right, and his waistcoat was right, and his tie was right, and his socks were right.

James Hook, thou not wholly unheroic figure, farewell.

For we have come to his last moment.

Seeing Peter slowly advancing upon him through the air with dagger poised, he sprang upon the bulwarks to cast himself into the sea. He did not know that the crocodile was waiting for him; for we purposely stopped the clock that this knowledge might be spared him: a little mark of respect from us at the end.

He had one last triumph, which I think we need not grudge him. As he stood on the bulwark looking over his shoulder at Peter gliding through the air, he invited him with a gesture to use his foot. It made Peter kick instead of stab.

At last Hook had got the boon for which he craved.

"Bad form," he cried jeeringly, and went content to the crocodile.

Thus perished James Hook.

"Seventeen," Slightly sang out; but he was not quite correct in his figures. Fifteen paid the penalty for their crimes that night; but two reached the shore: Starkey to be captured by the redskins, who made him nurse for all their papooses, a melancholy come-down§ for a pi-

---

*Showing contempt and scorn for.

†Expression at Eton meaning "sent up for good work or effort"; a boy would show his work to the headmaster, who would give him a prize.

‡Unique to Eton, the wall-game is a modified soccer game on a field 5 meters wide; the best place to see it is from the top of a brick wall that runs along the field.

§Decline to lower status.

rate; and Smee, who henceforth wandered about the world in his spectacles, making a precarious living by saying he was the only man that Jas. Hook had feared.

Wendy, of course, had stood by taking no part in the fight, though watching Peter with glistening eyes; but now that all was over she became prominent again. She praised them equally, and shuddered delightfully when Michael showed her the place where he had killed one; and then she took them into Hook's cabin and pointed to his watch which was hanging on a nail. It said "half-past one"!

The lateness of the hour was almost the biggest thing of all. She got them to bed in the pirates' bunks pretty quickly, you may be sure; all but Peter, who strutted up and down on deck, until at last he fell asleep by the side of Long Tom. He had one of his dreams that night, and cried in his sleep for a long time, and Wendy held him tight.

CHAPTER XVI

The Return Home

BY THREE BELLS NEXT morning they were all stirring their stumps;* for there was a big sea running, and Tootles, the bo'sun, was among them, with a rope's end† in his hand and chewing tobacco. They all donned pirate clothes cut off at the knee, shaved smartly, and tumbled up, with the true nautical roll and hitching their trousers.

It need not be said who was the captain. Nibs and John were first and second mate. There was a woman aboard. The rest were tars before the mast,‡ and lived in the fo'c'sle.§ Peter had already lashed himself to the wheel; but he piped all hands and delivered a short address to them; said he hoped they would do their duty like gallant hearties,|| but that he knew they were the scum of Rio and the Gold Coast, and if they snapped at him he would tear them. His bluff strident words struck the note sailors understand, and they cheered him lustily. Then a few sharp orders were given, and they turned the ship round, and nosed her for the mainland.

Captain Pan calculated, after consulting the ship's chart, that if this weather lasted they should strike the Azores# about the 21st of June, after which it would save time to fly.

Some of them wanted it to be an honest ship and others were in

---

*By 3:00 the next morning they were all awake and moving their legs.

†The bo'sun (see note on p. 45) would beat negligent sailors with the end of a rope.

‡Ordinary sailors; "tar" is short for "tarpaulin" (sailor).

§Variant of "forecastle," the crew's quarters, typically located in the ship's bow.

||Good fellows; comrades; sailors.

#Group of volcanic islands in the northern Atlantic Ocean about 1,448 km (900 mi) west of mainland Portugal.

favour of keeping it a pirate; but the captain treated them as dogs, and they dared not express their wishes to him even in a round robin.* Instant obedience was the only safe thing. Slightly got a dozen† for looking perplexed when told to take soundings.‡ The general feeling was that Peter was honest just now to lull Wendy's suspicions, but that there might be a change when the new suit was ready, which, against her will, she was making for him out of some of Hook's wickedest garments. It was afterwards whispered among them that on the first night he wore this suit he sat long in the cabin with Hook's cigar-holder in his mouth and one hand clenched, all but the forefinger, which he bent and held threateningly aloft like a hook.

Instead of watching the ship, however, we must now return to that desolate home from which three of our characters had taken heartless flight so long ago. It seems a shame to have neglected No. 14 all this time; and yet we may be sure that Mrs. Darling does not blame us. If we had returned sooner to look with sorrowful sympathy at her, she would probably have cried, "Don't be silly, what do I matter? Do go back and keep an eye on the children." So long as mothers are like this their children will take advantage of them; and they may lay to that.

Even now we venture into that familiar nursery only because its lawful occupants are on their way home; we are merely hurrying on in advance of them to see that their beds are properly aired and that Mr. and Mrs. Darling do not go out for the evening. We are no more than servants. Why on earth should their beds be properly aired, seeing that they left them in such a thankless hurry? Would it not serve them jolly well right if they came back and found that their parents were spending the week-end in the country? It would be the moral lesson they have been in need of ever since we met them; but if we contrived things in this way Mrs. Darling would never forgive us.

One thing I should like to do immensely, and that is to tell her,

---

*Petition on which the signatures are arranged in a circle in order to conceal the order of signing.

†Got lashed with a whip twelve times (perhaps only in make-believe).

‡Take the depth measurement of the water.

in the way authors have, that the children are coming back, that indeed they will be here on Thursday week. This would spoil so completely the surprise to which Wendy and John and Michael are looking forward. They have been planning it out on the ship: mother's rapture, father's shout of joy, Nana's leap through the air to embrace them first, when what they ought to be preparing for is a good hiding. How delicious to spoil it all by breaking the news in advance; so that when they enter grandly Mrs. Darling may not even offer Wendy her mouth, and Mr. Darling may exclaim pettishly, "Dash it all, here are those boys again." However, we should get no thanks even for this. We are beginning to know Mrs. Darling by this time, and may be sure that she would upbraid us for depriving the children of their little pleasure.

"But, my dear madam, it is ten days till Thursday week; so that by telling you what's what, we can save you ten days of unhappiness."

"Yes, but at what a cost! By depriving the children of ten minutes of delight."

"Oh, if you look at it in that way!"

"What other way is there in which to look at it?"

You see, the woman had no proper spirit. I had meant to say extraordinarily nice things about her; but I despise her, and not one of them will I say now. She does not really need to be told to have things ready, for they are ready. All the beds are aired, and she never leaves the house, and observe, the window is open. For all the use we are to her, we might go back to the ship. However, as we are here we may as well stay and look on. That is all we are, lookers-on. Nobody really wants us. So let us watch and say jaggy* things, in the hope that some of them will hurt.

The only change to be seen in the night-nursery is that between nine and six the kennel is no longer there. When the children flew away, Mr. Darling felt in his bones that all the blame was his for having chained Nana up, and that from first to last she had been wiser than he. Of course, as we have seen, he was quite a simple man; indeed he might have passed for a boy again if he had been

---

*Prickly.

able to take his baldness off; but he had also a noble sense of justice and a lion courage to do what seemed right to him; and having thought the matter out with anxious care after the flight of the children, he went down on all fours and crawled into the kennel. To all Mrs. Darling's dear invitations to him to come out he replied sadly but firmly:

"No, my own one, this is the place for me."

In the bitterness of his remorse he swore that he would never leave the kennel until his children came back. Of course this was a pity; but whatever Mr. Darling did he had to do in excess, otherwise he soon gave up doing it. And there never was a more humble man than the once proud George Darling, as he sat in the kennel of an evening talking with his wife of their children and all their pretty ways.

Very touching was his deference to Nana. He would not let her come into the kennel, but on all other matters he followed her wishes implicitly.

Every morning the kennel was carried with Mr. Darling in it to a cab, which conveyed him to his office, and he returned home in the same way at six. Something of the strength of character of the man will be seen if we remember how sensitive he was to the opinion of neighbours: this man whose every movement now attracted surprised attention. Inwardly he must have suffered torture; but he preserved a calm exterior even when the young criticised his little home, and he always lifted his hat courteously to any lady who looked inside.

It may have been quixotic,* but it was magnificent. Soon the inward meaning of it leaked out, and the great heart of the public was touched. Crowds followed the cab, cheering it lustily; charming girls scaled it to get his autograph; interviews appeared in the better class of papers, and society invited him to dinner and added, "Do come in the kennel."

On that eventful Thursday week Mrs. Darling was in the night-nursery awaiting George's return home: a very sad-eyed woman. Now that we look at her closely and remember the gaiety of her in

---

*Unrealistic and idealistic; unconcerned with practicality. Taken from the name Don Quixote, the hero of a novel by Miguel de Cervantes.

the old days, all gone now just because she has lost her babes, I find I won't be able to say nasty things about her after all. If she was too fond of her rubbishy children she couldn't help it. Look at her in her chair, where she has fallen asleep. The corner of her mouth, where one looks first, is almost withered up. Her hand moves restlessly on her breast as if she had a pain there. Some like Peter best and some like Wendy best, but I like her best. Suppose, to make her happy, we whisper to her in her sleep that the brats are coming back. They are really within two miles of the window now, and flying strong, but all we need whisper is that they are on the way. Let's.

It is a pity we did it, for she has started up, calling their names; and there is no one in the room but Nana.

"O Nana, I dreamt my dear ones had come back."

Nana had filmy eyes, but all she could do was to put her paw gently on her mistress's lap, and they were sitting together thus when the kennel was brought back. As Mr. Darling puts his head out at it to kiss his wife, we see that his face is more worn than of yore, but has a softer expression.

He gave his hat to Liza, who took it scornfully; for she had no imagination, and was quite incapable of understanding the motives of such a man. Outside, the crowd who had accompanied the cab home were still cheering, and he was naturally not unmoved.

"Listen to them," he said; "it is very gratifying."

"Lot of little boys," sneered Liza.

"There were several adults to-day," he assured her with a faint flush; but when she tossed her head he had not a word of reproof for her. Social success had not spoilt him; it had made him sweeter. For some time he sat with his head out of the kennel, talking with Mrs. Darling of this success, and pressing her hand reassuringly when she said she hoped his head would not be turned by it.

"But if I had been a weak man," he said. "Good heavens, if I had been a weak man!"

"And, George," she said timidly, "you are as full of remorse as ever, aren't you?"

"Full of remorse as ever, dearest! See my punishment: living in a kennel."

"But it is punishment, isn't it, George? You are sure you are not enjoying it?"

"My love!"

You may be sure she begged his pardon; and then, feeling drowsy, he curled round in the kennel.

"Won't you play me to sleep," he asked, "on the nursery piano?" and as she was crossing to the day-nursery he added thoughtlessly, "And shut that window. I feel a draught."

"O, George, never ask me to do that. The window must always be left open for them, always, always."

Now it was his turn to beg her pardon; and she went into the day-nursery and played, and soon he was asleep; and while he slept, Wendy and John and Michael flew into the room.

Oh no. We have written it so, because that was the charming arrangement planned by them before we left the ship; but something must have happened since then, for it is not they who have flown in, it is Peter and Tinker Bell.

Peter's first words tell all.

"Quick, Tink," he whispered, "close the window; bar it! That's right. Now you and I must get away by the door; and when Wendy comes she will think her mother has barred her out, and she will have to go back with me."

Now I understand what had hitherto puzzled me, why when Peter had exterminated the pirates he did not return to the island and leave Tink to escort the children to the mainland. This trick had been in his head all the time.

Instead of feeling that he was behaving badly he danced with glee; then he peeped into the day-nursery to see who was playing. He whispered to Tink, "It's Wendy's mother! She is a pretty lady, but not so pretty as my mother. Her mouth is full of thimbles, but not so full as my mother's was."

Of course he knew nothing whatever about his mother; but he sometimes bragged about her.

He did not know the tune, which was "Home, Sweet Home," but he knew it was saying, "Come back, Wendy, Wendy, Wendy"; and he cried exultantly, "You will never see Wendy again, lady, for the window is barred!"

He peeped in again to see why the music had stopped, and now he saw that Mrs. Darling had laid her head on the box, and that two tears were sitting on her eyes.

"She wants me to unbar the window," thought Peter, "but I won't, not I!"

He peeped again, and the tears were still there, or another two had taken their place.

"She's awfully fond of Wendy," he said to himself. He was angry with her now for not seeing why she could not have Wendy.

The reason was so simple: "I'm fond of her too. We can't both have her, lady."

But the lady would not make the best of it, and he was unhappy. He ceased to look at her, but even then she would not let go of him. He skipped about and made funny faces, but when he stopped it was just as if she were inside him, knocking.

"Oh, all right," he said at last, and gulped. Then he unbarred the window. "Come on, Tink," he cried, with a frightful sneer at the laws of nature; "we don't want any silly mothers"; and he flew away.

Thus Wendy and John and Michael found the window open for them after all, which of course was more than they deserved. They alighted on the floor, quite unashamed of themselves, and the youngest one had already forgotten his home.

"John," he said, looking around him doubtfully, "I think I have been here before."

"Of course you have, you silly. There is your old bed."

"So it is," Michael said, but not with much conviction.

"I say," cried John, "the kennel!" and he dashed across to look into it.

"Perhaps Nana is inside it," Wendy said.

But John whistled. "Hullo," he said, "there's a man inside it."

"It's father!" exclaimed Wendy.

"Let me see father," Michael begged eagerly, and he took a good look. "He is not so big as the pirate I killed," he said with such frank disappointment that I am glad Mr. Darling was asleep; it would have been sad if those had been the first words he heard his little Michael say.

Wendy and John had been taken aback somewhat at finding their father in the kennel.

"Surely," said John, like one who had lost faith in his memory, "he used not to sleep in the kennel?"

"John," Wendy said falteringly, "perhaps we don't remember the old life as well as we thought we did."

A chill fell upon them; and serve them right.

"It is very careless of mother," said that young scoundrel John, "not to be here when we come back."

It was then that Mrs. Darling began playing again.

"It's mother!" cried Wendy, peeping.

"So it is!" said John.

"Then are you not really our mother, Wendy?" asked Michael, who was surely sleepy.

"Oh dear!" exclaimed Wendy, with her first real twinge of remorse, "it was quite time we came back."

"Let us creep in," John suggested, "and put our hands over her eyes."

But Wendy, who saw that they must break the joyous news more gently, had a better plan.

"Let us all slip into our beds, and be there when she comes in, just as if we had never been away."

And so when Mrs. Darling went back to the night-nursery to see if her husband was asleep, all the beds were occupied. The children waited for her cry of joy, but it did not come. She saw them, but she did not believe they were there. You see, she saw them in their beds so often in her dreams that she thought this was just the dream hanging around her still.

She sat down in the chair by the fire, where in the old days she had nursed them.

They could not understand this, and a cold fear fell upon all the three of them.

"Mother!" Wendy cried.

"That's Wendy," she said, but still she was sure it was the dream.

"Mother!"

"That's John," she said.

"Mother!" cried Michael. He knew her now.

"That's Michael," she said, and she stretched out her arms for the three little selfish children they would never envelop again. Yes, they did, they went round Wendy and John and Michael, who had slipped out of bed and run to her.

"George, George!" she cried when she could speak; and Mr. Darling woke to share her bliss, and Nana came rushing in. There could not have been a lovelier sight; but there was none to see it except a little boy who was staring in at the window. He had ecstasies innumerable that other children can never know; but he was looking through the window at the one joy from which he must be for ever barred.

CHAPTER XVII

When Wendy Grew Up

I HOPE YOU WANT to know what became of the other boys. They were waiting below to give Wendy time to explain about them, and when they had counted five hundred they went up. They went up by the stair, because they thought this would make a better impression. They stood in a row in front of Mrs. Darling, with their hats off, and wishing they were not wearing their pirate clothes. They said nothing, but their eyes asked her to have them. They ought to have looked at Mr. Darling also, but they forgot about him.

Of course Mrs. Darling said at once that she would have them; but Mr. Darling was curiously depressed, and they saw that he considered six a rather large number.

"I must say," he said to Wendy, "that you don't do things by halves," a grudging remark which the twins thought was pointed at them.

The first twin was the proud one, and he asked, flushing, "Do you think we should be too much of a handful, sir? Because if so we can go away."

"Father!" Wendy cried, shocked; but still the cloud was on him. He knew he was behaving unworthily, but he could not help it.

"We could lie doubled up," said Nibs.

"I always cut their hair myself," said Wendy.

"George?" Mrs. Darling exclaimed, pained to see her dear one showing himself in such an unfavourable light.

Then he burst into tears, and the truth came out. He was as glad to have them as she was, he said, but he thought they should have asked his consent as well as hers, instead of treating him as a cypher* in his own house.

"I don't think he is a cypher," Tootles cried instantly. "Do you think he is a cypher, Curly?"

"No, I don't. Do you think he is a cypher, Slightly?"

"Rather not. Twin, what do you think?"

It turned out that not one of them thought him a cypher; and he was absurdly gratified, and said he would find space for them all in the drawing-room if they fitted in.

"We'll fit in, sir," they assured him.

"Then follow the leader," he cried gaily. "Mind you, I am not sure that we have a drawing-room, but we pretend we have, and it's all the same. Hoop la!"

He went off dancing through the house, and they all cried "Hoop la!" and danced after him, searching for the drawing-room; and I forget whether they found it, but at any rate they found corners, and they all fitted in.

As for Peter, he saw Wendy once again before he flew away. He did not exactly come to the window, but he brushed against it in passing, so that she could open it if she liked and call to him. That was what she did.

"Hullo, Wendy, good-bye," he said.

"Oh dear, are you going away?"

"Yes."

"You don't feel, Peter," she said falteringly, "that you would like to say anything to my parents about a very sweet subject?"[1]

"No."

"About me, Peter?"

"No."

Mrs. Darling came to the window, for at present she was keeping a sharp eye on Wendy. She told Peter that she had adopted all the other boys, and would like to adopt him also.

"Would you send me to school?" he inquired craftily.

"Yes."

"And then to an office?"

---

*Person of no influence or importance.

"I suppose so."

"Soon I should be a man?"

"Very soon."

"I don't want to go to school and learn solemn things," he told her passionately. "I don't want to be a man. O Wendy's mother, if I was to wake up and feel there was a beard!"

"Peter," said Wendy the comforter, "I should love you in a beard;" and Mrs. Darling stretched out her arms to him, but he repulsed her.

"Keep back, lady, no one is going to catch me and make me a man."

"But where are you going to live?"

"With Tink in the house we built for Wendy. The fairies are to put it high up among the tree tops where they sleep at nights."

"How lovely," cried Wendy so longingly that Mrs. Darling tightened her grip.

"I thought all the fairies were dead," Mrs. Darling said.

"There are always a lot of young ones," explained Wendy, who was now quite an authority, "because you see when a new baby laughs for the first time a new fairy is born, and as there are always new babies there are always new fairies. They live in nests on the tops of trees; and the mauve ones are boys and the white ones are girls, and the blue ones are just little sillies who are not sure what they are."

"I shall have such fun," said Peter, with one eye on Wendy.

"It will be rather lonely in the evening," she said, "sitting by the fire."

"I shall have Tink."

"Tink can't go a twentieth part of the way round," she reminded him a little tartly.

"Sneaky tell-tale!" Tink called out from somewhere round the corner.

"It doesn't matter," Peter said.

"O Peter, you know it matters."

"Well, then, come with me to the little house."

"May I, mummy?"

"Certainly not. I have got you home again, and I mean to keep you."

"But he does so need a mother."

"So do you, my love."

"Oh, all right," Peter said, as if he had asked her from politeness merely; but Mrs. Darling saw his mouth twitch, and she made this handsome offer: to let Wendy go to him for a week every year and do his spring cleaning. Wendy would have preferred a more permanent arrangement, and it seemed to her that spring would be long in coming, but this promise sent Peter away quite gay again. He had no sense of time, and was so full of adventures that all I have told you about him is only a halfpenny worth of them. I suppose it was because Wendy knew this that her last words to him were these rather plaintive ones:

"You won't forget me, Peter, will you, before spring-cleaning time comes?"

Of course Peter promised, and then he flew away. He took Mrs. Darling's kiss with him. The kiss that had been for no one else Peter took quite easily. Funny. But she seemed satisfied.

Of course all the boys went to school; and most of them got into Class III., but Slightly was put first into Class IV. and then into Class V. Class I. is the top class. Before they had attended school a week they saw what goats they had been not to remain on the island; but it was too late now, and soon they settled down to being as ordinary as you or me or Jenkins minor. It is sad to have to say that the power to fly gradually left them. At first Nana tied their feet to the bed-posts so that they should not fly away in the night; and one of their diversions by day was to pretend to fall off buses; but by and by they ceased to tug at their bonds in bed, and found that they hurt themselves when they let go of the bus. In time they could not even fly after their hats. Want of practice, they called it; but what it really meant was that they no longer believed.

Michael believed longer than the other boys, though they jeered at him; so he was with Wendy when Peter came for her at the end of the first year. She flew away with Peter in the frock she had woven from leaves and berries in the Neverland, and her one fear was that he might notice how short it had become, but he never noticed, he had so much to say about himself.

She had looked forward to thrilling talks with him about old times, but new adventures had crowded the old ones from his mind.

"Who is Captain Hook?" he asked with interest when she spoke of the arch enemy.

"Don't you remember," she asked, amazed, "how you killed him and saved all our lives?"

"I forget them after I kill them," he replied carelessly.

When she expressed a doubtful hope that Tinker Bell would be glad to see her he said, "Who is Tinker Bell?"

"O Peter!" she said, shocked; but even when she explained he could not remember.

"There are such a lot of them," he said. "I expect she is no more."

I expect he was right, for fairies don't live long, but they are so little that a short time seems a good while to them.

Wendy was pained too to find that the past year was but as yesterday to Peter; it had seemed such a long year of waiting to her. But he was exactly as fascinating as ever, and they had a lovely spring cleaning in the little house on the tree tops.

Next year he did not come for her. She waited in a new frock because the old one simply would not meet, but he never came.

"Perhaps he is ill," Michael said.

"You know he is never ill."

Michael came close to her and whispered, with a shiver, "Perhaps there is no such person, Wendy!" and then Wendy would have cried if Michael had not been crying.

Peter came next spring cleaning; and the strange thing was that he never knew he had missed a year.

That was the last time the girl Wendy ever saw him. For a little longer she tried for his sake not to have growing pains; and she felt she was untrue to him when she got a prize for general knowledge. But the years came and went without bringing the careless boy; and when they met again Wendy was a married woman, and Peter was no more to her than a little dust in the box in which she had kept her toys. Wendy was grown up. You need not be sorry for her. She was one of the kind that likes to grow up. In the end she grew up of her own free will a day quicker than other girls.

All the boys were grown up and done for by this time; so it is scarcely worth while saying anything more about them. You may see the twins and Nibs and Curly any day going to an office, each carrying a little bag and an umbrella. Michael is an engine-driver. Slightly married a lady of title, and so he became a lord.[2] You see that judge in a wig coming out at the iron door? That used to be Tootles. The bearded man who doesn't know any story to tell his children was once John.

Wendy was married in white with a pink sash. It is strange to think that Peter did not alight in the church and forbid the banns.*

Years rolled on again, and Wendy had a daughter. This ought not to be written in ink but in a golden splash.

She was called Jane, and always had an odd inquiring look, as if from the moment she arrived on the mainland she wanted to ask questions. When she was old enough to ask them they were mostly about Peter Pan. She loved to hear of Peter, and Wendy told her all she could remember in the very nursery from which the famous flight had taken place. It was Jane's nursery now, for her father had bought it at the three per cents. from Wendy's father, who was no longer fond of stairs. Mrs. Darling was now dead and forgotten.

There were only two beds in the nursery now, Jane's and her nurse's; and there was no kennel, for Nana also had passed away. She died of old age, and at the end she had been rather difficult to get on with, being very firmly convinced that no one knew how to look after children except herself.

Once a week Jane's nurse had her evening off, and then it was Wendy's part to put Jane to bed. That was the time for stories. It was Jane's invention to raise the sheet over her mother's head and her own, thus making a tent, and in the awful darkness to whisper:—

"What do we see now?"

"I don't think I see anything to-night," says Wendy, with a feeling that if Nana were here she would object to further conversation.

"Yes, you do," says Jane, "you see when you were a little girl."

---

*Public announcement of a proposed marriage.

"That is a long time ago, sweetheart," says Wendy. "Ah me, how time flies!"

"Does it fly," asks the artful child, "the way you flew when you were a little girl?"

"The way I flew! Do you know, Jane, I sometimes wonder whether I ever did really fly."

"Yes, you did."

"The dear old days when I could fly!"

"Why can't you fly now, mother?"

"Because I am grown up, dearest. When people grow up they forget the way."

"Why do they forget the way?"

"Because they are no longer gay and innocent and heartless. It is only the gay and innocent and heartless who can fly."

"What is gay and innocent and heartless? I do wish I was gay and innocent and heartless."

Or perhaps Wendy admits she does see something. "I do believe," she says, "that it is this nursery!"

"I do believe it is!" says Jane. "Go on."

They are now embarked on the great adventure of the night when Peter flew in looking for his shadow.

"The foolish fellow," says Wendy, "tried to stick it on with soap, and when he could not he cried, and that woke me, and I sewed it on for him."

"You have missed a bit," interrupts Jane, who now knows the story better than her mother. "When you saw him sitting on the floor crying what did you say?"

"I sat up in bed and I said, 'Boy, why are you crying?'"

"Yes, that was it," says Jane, with a big breath.

"And then he flew us all away to the Neverland and the fairies and the pirates and the redskins and the mermaids' lagoon, and the home under the ground, and the little house."

"Yes! which did you like best of all?"

"I think I liked the home under the ground best of all."

"Yes, so do I. What was the last thing Peter ever said to you?"

"The last thing he ever said to me was, 'Just always be waiting for me, and then some night you will hear me crowing.'"

"Yes!"

"But, alas, he forgot all about me." Wendy said it with a smile. She was as grown up as that.

"What did his crow sound like?" Jane asked one evening.

"It was like this," Wendy said, trying to imitate Peter's crow.

"No, it wasn't," Jane said gravely, "it was like this"; and she did it ever so much better than her mother.

Wendy was a little startled. "My darling, how can you know?"

"I often hear it when I am sleeping," Jane said.

"Ah yes, many girls hear it when they are sleeping, but I was the only one who heard it awake."

"Lucky you!" said Jane.

And then one night came the tragedy. It was the spring of the year, and the story had been told for the night, and Jane was now asleep in her bed. Wendy was sitting on the floor, very close to the fire so as to see to darn, for there was no other light in the nursery; and while she sat darning she heard a crow. Then the window blew open as of old, and Peter dropped on the floor.

He was exactly the same as ever, and Wendy saw at once that he still had all his first teeth.

He was a little boy, and she was grown up. She huddled by the fire not daring to move, helpless and guilty, a big woman.

"Hullo, Wendy," he said, not noticing any difference, for he was thinking chiefly of himself; and in the dim light her white dress might have been the nightgown in which he had seen her first.

"Hullo, Peter," she replied faintly, squeezing herself as small as possible. Something inside her was crying "Woman, woman, let go of me."

"Hullo, where is John?" he asked, suddenly missing the third bed.

"John is not here now," she gasped.

"Is Michael asleep?" he asked, with a careless glance at Jane.

"Yes," she answered; and now she felt that she was untrue to Jane as well as to Peter.

"That is not Michael," she said quickly, lest a judgment should fall on her.

Peter looked. "Hullo, is it a new one?"

"Yes."

"Boy or girl?"

"Girl."

Now surely he would understand; but not a bit of it.

"Peter," she said, faltering, "are you expecting me to fly away with you?"

"Of course; that is why I have come." He added a little sternly, "Have you forgotten that this is spring-cleaning time?"

She knew it was useless to say that he had let many spring-cleaning times pass.

"I can't come," she said apologetically, "I have forgotten how to fly."

"I'll soon teach you again."

"O, Peter, don't waste the fairy dust on me."

She had risen, and now at last a fear assailed him. "What is it?" he cried, shrinking.

"I will turn up the light," she said, "and then you can see for yourself."

For almost the only time in his life that I know of, Peter was afraid. "Don't turn up the light," he cried.

She let her hands play in the hair of the tragic boy. She was not a little girl heart-broken about him; she was a grown woman smiling at it all, but they were wet smiles.

Then she turned up the light, and Peter saw. He gave a cry of pain; and when the tall beautiful creature stooped to lift him in her arms he drew back sharply.

"What is it?" he cried again.

She had to tell him.

"I am old, Peter. I am ever so much more than twenty. I grew up long ago."

"You promised not to!"

"I couldn't help it. I am a married woman, Peter."

"No, you're not."

"Yes, and the little girl in the bed is my baby."

"No, she's not."

But he supposed she was; and he took a step towards the sleeping child with his fist upraised. Of course he did not strike her. He sat down on the floor and sobbed, and Wendy did not know how to comfort him, though she could have done it so easily once. She

PETER AND JANE

was only a woman now, and she ran out of the room to try to think.

Peter continued to cry, and soon his sobs woke Jane. She sat up in bed, and was interested at once.

"Boy," she said, "why are you crying?"

Peter rose and bowed to her, and she bowed to him from the bed.

"Hullo," he said.

"Hullo," said Jane.

"My name is Peter Pan," he told her.

"Yes, I know."

"I came back for my mother," he explained, "to take her to the Neverland."

"Yes, I know," Jane said, "I have been waiting for you."

When Wendy returned diffidently she found Peter sitting on the bed-post crowing gloriously, while Jane in her nighty was flying round the room in solemn ecstasy.

"She is my mother," Peter explained; and Jane descended and stood by his side, with the look on her face that he liked to see on ladies when they gazed at him.

"He does so need a mother," Jane said.

"Yes, I know," Wendy admitted, rather forlornly; "no one knows it so well as I."

"Good-bye," said Peter to Wendy; and he rose in the air, and the shameless Jane rose with him; it was already her easiest way of moving about.

Wendy rushed to the window.

"No, no!" she cried.

"It is just for spring-cleaning time," Jane said; "he wants me always to do his spring cleaning."

"If only I could go with you!" Wendy sighed.

"You see you can't fly," said Jane.

Of course in the end Wendy let them fly away together. Our last glimpse of her shows her at the window, watching them receding into the sky until they were as small as stars.

As you look at Wendy you may see her hair becoming white, and her figure little again, for all this happened long ago. Jane is now a common grown-up, with a daughter called Margaret;[3] and every spring-cleaning time, except when he forgets, Peter comes for Margaret and takes her to the Neverland, where she tells him stories about himself, to which he listens eagerly. When Margaret grows up she will have a daughter, who is to be Peter's mother in turn; and so it will go on, so long as children are gay and innocent and heartless.

THE END

ENDNOTES

Chapter I: Peter Breaks Through

1. (p. 7) *Napoleon:* Napoleon Bonaparte (1769–1821) was a French general who, through his military genius and risk-taking, became emperor of the French twice. Napoleon was a short but powerful man (Barrie, too, was just over five feet tall); he appears in many of Barrie's writings.
2. (p. 8) *I have one pound seventeen here:* Mr. Darling performs his (at times inaccurate) calculations in pre-decimal British currency. "One pound seventeen" is one pound, seventeen shillings; "three nine seven" is three pounds, nine shillings, and seven pence.
3. (p. 8) *Of course we can, George:* Mr. Darling takes his first name from the oldest of the Davies boys, George Llewelyn Davies. The names of all but the youngest (Nico) of the boys appear in the novel: The second child after George was John (or Jack), the third was Peter, and the fourth was named Michael. Sir George Frampton modeled his statue of Peter Pan, which still stands in Kensington Gardens, after a photograph of Michael.
4. (p. 9) *This nurse was a prim Newfoundland dog, called Nana:* Barrie stressed how important it was that a man rather than a woman perform the part of Nana in the play *Peter Pan*. The portrait of Nana was drawn from two of Barrie's beloved dogs—his Saint Bernard, Porthos, and later a large Newfoundland named Luath. Barrie writes in his dedication to the play in 1928, "I must have sat at a table with that great dog waiting for me to stop, not complaining, for he knew it was thus we made our living, but giving me a look when he found he was to be in the play, with his sex changed. In after years when the actor who was Nana had to go to the wars he first taught his wife how to take his place as the dog till he came back, and I am glad that I see nothing funny in this; it seems to me to belong to the play. I offer this obtuseness on my part as my first proof that I am the author" (*Peter Pan and Other Plays*, p. 78; see "For Further Reading").
5. (p. 10) *On John's footer days she never once forgot his sweater:* Nana always remembers to bring along John's sweater on the days when he plays football (that is, soccer).
6. (p. 11) *It would be an easy map if that were all . . . but there is also . . . the round pond:* Barrie describes the Round Pond, which is still located in London's Kensington Gardens, in *The Little White Bird* (1902), the novel where Peter Pan first

appears by name: "It is round because it is in the very middle of the Gardens, and when you are come to it you never want to go any farther" (p. 149).

7. (p. 13) *Wendy said with a tolerant smile:* That is, with a forgiving, broad-minded smile. This passage recalls Barrie's memoir of his mother, *Margaret Ogilvy* (1896), in which he marvels at the effect his grandmother's death had on his mother, who was eight years old at the time: "From that time she scrubbed and mended and baked and sewed . . . and gossiped like a matron with the other women, and humoured the men with a tolerant smile" (p. 29).
8. (p. 14) *they were skeleton leaves, but . . . they did not come from any tree that grew in England:* That is, they are leaves from which the pulpy parts have been removed, so that only the fibrous stem structures remain. The fact that Peter Pan is dressed in skeleton leaves makes additional sense given that he is a ghost child—a boy who does not belong in the waking human world.
9. (p. 14) *he had rent the film that obscures the Neverland:* That is, he had violently torn the thin curtain that conceals the Neverland. In the first draft of the play, the island was called the Never, Never, Never Land; when the play was performed, the name changed to the Never, Never Land; in the published play it is the Never Land, and it appears as the Neverland in the novel.

Chapter II. The Shadow

1. (p. 23) *She went from bed to bed singing enchantments over them:* Here Barrie may have had in mind Shakespeare's *A Midsummer Night's Dream* (a text he refers to throughout his 1917 play *Dear Brutus*). In act 2, scene 2, Titania, the queen of the Fairies, asks her fairies to "Sing me now to sleep," and they proceed to sing spells of protection over her (which don't, as it happens, work).

Chapter III: Come Away, Come Away!

1. (p. 25) *"Wendy Moira Angela Darling":* The name Wendy existed before *Peter Pan,* but it was Barrie who made it famous. He took the name from a child who shared his mother's first name. Margaret Henley, the daughter of poet W. E. Henley, died when she was five and a half years old. Before she died, she became close to Barrie, calling him her "friendy," which she mispronounced as "wendy." Barrie's 1903 play Little Mary is the story of a girl named Moira who mothers orphan children. A daughter, Angela, was born to Gerald du Maurier (the Davies boys' uncle, who first played Hook and Mr. Darling) and his wife during the period when the play was in rehearsal. In celebration, Barrie made Angela Wendy's third name. (In the mid-1920s, when Angela was older, she played Wendy on the stage for two seasons and once crashed while flying.)
2. (p. 29) *"because she mends the pots and kettles":* Tinker Bell seems to possess a hint of Cinderella. Note that Peter has returned to the Darling house to learn the end of Cinderella's story. Yet Tinker Bell's story is nothing like that of the char-

acter from the fairy tale. Barrie plays with a similar tension between fairy tales and their distortions in his play *A Kiss for Cinderella,* which first opened at the Wyndham's Theatre in 1916.

3. (p. 33) *All was as still as salt:* Barrie also uses this phrase in his 1891 novel *The Little Minister.* It exists as a rare idiom that perhaps originates with Lot's wife in the Bible (Genesis 19:26); she is transformed into a pillar of salt when she turns back to look at the burning Sodom.
4. (p. 37) *The birds were flown:* In *The Little White Bird,* Barrie explains that all babies are birds before they become human. As baby Peter never completely stops being a bird, he is known in the book as a "Betwixt-and-Between."

Chapter IV: The Flight

1. (p. 45) *"Hook . . . Jas Hook":* Captain Hook developed from Captain Swarthy, a figure in the fantasy games played by Barrie and the Llewelyn Davies boys at Black Lake Island in Surrey during the summer of 1901. Swarthy was first immortalized in Barrie's privately printed book *The Boy Castaways of Black Lake Island* (1901), of which only two copies were produced, one lost by Arthur Llewelyn Davies, the boys' father.

Chapter V: The Island Come True

1. (p. 50) *Slightly:* The origin of this character's strange name is explained in the play when he clarifies that his mother had written "Slightly Soiled" on the pinafore he was wearing when he was lost. Therefore, he has always assumed that Slightly is his name.
2. (p. 52) *In dress he somewhat aped the attire associated with the name of Charles II:* That is, Captain Hook somewhat imitated the "Restoration" or "Cavalier" style of dress associated with the "Merry Monarch," King Charles II (ruled 1660–1685). Charles dressed and lived flamboyantly—in direct opposition to his predecessor, Lord Protector Oliver Cromwell, whose Puritan dictatorship introduced severe laws prohibiting amusements. Influenced by the style of Charles II, the late seventeenth century was a period of elaborate, foppish men's clothing.
3. (p. 52) *the ill-fated Stuarts:* The Stuart family ruled England and Scotland from 1603 through the reign of Queen Anne, who died in 1714 (except for the period of the republican Commonwealth in the 1650s). In 1649 the English Parliament tried for treason and executed one Stuart monarch, Charles I. In 1689 his grandson, James II, was dethroned and exiled for his pro-Catholic sympathies. In the eighteenth century, James II's son and grandson both unsuccessfully asserted their claims to the throne.
4. (p. 56) *"Odds bobs, hammer and tongs":* Barrie takes Hook's favorite curse from the sea ballad in Frederick Marryat's *Snarleyyow; or, The Dog Fiend* (1837).

Chapter VII: The Home under the Ground

1. (p. 70) *The couch . . . was a genuine Queen Mab, with club legs; . . . the wash stand was Pie-crust . . . but of course she lit the residence herself:* Some details here have meaning—"Queen Mab" is the queen of the fairies; "Pie-crust" means having the appearance of the crimped, raised crust of a pie—but otherwise Barrie indulges in a flight of linguistic whimsy designed to mock the pretensions of the antiques market.

Chapter VIII: The Mermaids' Lagoon

1. (p. 82) *In that supreme moment Hook did not blanch, even at the gills:* That is, Hook did not turn white, even around his chin and neck. The word "gills" also recalls the respiratory organs of most aquatic animals that breathe water to obtain oxygen, anticipating Peter's later identification of Hook with a codfish.

Chapter X: The Happy Home

1. (p. 91) *They called Peter the Great White Father:* Barrie's original title for the play *Peter Pan* when he first showed it to Charles Frohman in April 1904 was *The Great White Father*. Frohman liked everything about it except the title. By the time it was performed, the play had been retitled *Peter Pan; or, The Boy Who Would Not Grow Up*.

Chapter XI: Wendy's Story

1. (p. 101) *in half mourning:* At the time *Peter Pan* was written, "half mourning" was the third and final stage of mourning, lasting about three to six months, when people stopped wearing only black and gradually began to wear other dark or subdued colors such as gray or lavender.

Chapter XVII: When Wendy Grew Up

1. (p. 149) *"You don't feel . . . that you would like to say anything to my parents about a very sweet subject?":* Wendy wants to know if Peter would like to ask her parents whether he can someday marry her.
2. (p. 153) *Slightly married a lady of title, and so he became a lord:* This is ironic, as a woman could increase her social status by marrying a man with a title, but in fact a man had no such luck when he married a woman with a title.
3. (p. 158) *Jane is now a common grown-up, with a daughter called Margaret:* Barrie may take the name "Margaret" from that of his mother, Margaret Ogilvy.

INSPIRED BY *PETER PAN*

Film

J. M. Barrie wrote a script for a silent film version of *Peter Pan*. Though his scenario was never used, a silent *Peter Pan* appeared in 1924. Directed by Herbert Brenon, the 105-minute movie stars Betty Bronson as Peter. This version, though praised by critics, was a disappointment to Barrie. Little more than a play on celluloid, it failed to utilize the unique possibilities offered by the medium. Nevertheless, in 2002 the Library of Congress deemed it "culturally significant" and placed it in the National Film Registry for preservation. The text of Barrie's unused scenario can be found in Roger Green's *Fifty Years of Peter Pan* (1954), which traces the early history of the author's work.

Along with the Broadway musical starring Mary Martin (it opened in 1954), Walt Disney's animated musical *Peter Pan* (1953) is in part responsible for readers' continuing interest in the story. The full-length cartoon bears a fairly close resemblance to Barrie's book, although it dispenses with Peter's more sinister side. Hans Conried's voice makes Captain Hook both droll and malevolent, counterbalancing Bobby Driscoll's prankish, somewhat one-dimensional Peter Pan. This classic film is well-paced and features vivid color, abundant action and humor (including amusing slapstick), and exciting chase scenes, as well as a catchy original soundtrack.

Disney's version stood so firmly as the definitive *Peter Pan* that a reincarnation of the story did not reappear for almost forty years, until Steven Spielberg created *Hook* (1991). Spielberg's movie brazenly diverges from the famous first line of Barrie's book by representing Peter as a grown-up. Robin Williams stars as Peter Banning, a workaholic mergers-and-acquisitions lawyer who ignores his children and forgets that, as a child, he was Peter Pan. Captain Hook, played by Dustin Hoffman, kidnaps Banning's children, forcing the lawyer to travel to a cluttered Neverland that features Julia Roberts as Tinker Bell. In portraying a hero who has lost his magic, however, the film throws away the charm that makes Barrie's story so special.

Return to Never Land (2002), an animated musical sequel to Disney's 1953 production, takes place during the blitz of London during World War II. Directed by Robin Budd and Donovan Cook, the film depicts a grown-up Wendy whose daughter, Jane, doesn't believe her mother's tales of Lost Boys and flying. Captain Hook rocks Jane's complacency by kidnapping her, and Peter is forced to plan a rescue. Temple Mathews's script, written with an eye toward grade-school children, adds several new elements, such as a revised impression of Jane, who hates Never Land and finds Peter Pan foolish. But in spite of the problems that necessarily arise from filming a sequel to a powerful story, *Return to Never Land* is a witty, refreshing film. It gently satirizes all that dates the 1953 version; for example, in the 2002 movie Jane, who wants nothing to do with mothering Peter and the Lost Boys, becomes the first Lost Girl.

P. J. Hogan's intelligent, live-action *Peter Pan* (2003) is the adaptation most loyal to Barrie's book on an emotional level. While earlier film versions of the story tend to be light and campy, Hogan's *Peter Pan* captures the dark, poignant aspects of the tale, while providing an engaging, impassioned payoff. Refusing to gloss over the underlying melancholy in the novel or the pre-sexual love triangle among Peter, Wendy, and Captain Hook, the film simultaneously retains all the wonder and magic of the fantastic Neverland. Rachel Hurd-Wood steals the show as Wendy, imbuing the character with enthusiasm and a wisdom beyond her years. The beautiful and wild Jeremy Sumpter is the first boy to play a live-action Peter, and Jason Isaacs takes on dual roles as Captain Hook and Mr. Darling. Tastefully rendered computer-generated special effects give a mythical feeling to Neverland.

The star-studded *Finding Neverland* (2004), directed by Marc Foster, chronicles the fascinating story of Barrie's relationship with the Llewelyn Davies family and the premier of the play *Peter Pan; or, The Boy Who Would Not Grow Up*. Johnny Depp seems tailor-made for his role as the diminutive author, and Kate Winslet is magnificent as the widowed Sylvia Llewelyn Davies. The film takes some liberties with history; in it, Barrie meets Sylvia after her husband has died, when she already had four boys. In truth, her husband didn't die for ten years after Barrie's meeting with the family. Only three of her sons (out of five total) were alive when Barrie met them, and because Peter was still an infant at home it was George and Jack that Barrie spent his time with every day in the gardens. Nonetheless, the child actors give some of the most stunning performances in this film; particularly effective is Freddie Highmore's portrayal of Peter's fits of anger at Barrie, who he says cannot replace his dead father. Julie Christie portrays Davies's stern mother, Emma du Maurier, who disapproves of Barrie's relationship with the family. Dustin Hoffman rounds out the cast as American theater producer Charles Frohman. Based on Allan Knee's play *The Man Who Was Peter Pan* (1998), the film boasts beautiful art direction and spectacular outdoor settings, making the production a feast for both the eyes and the emotions.

George Frampton's Peter Pan Statue

Peter Pan has a real place in the national landscape of Britain. Nothing demonstrates the truth of this statement better than the statue of Peter Pan in London's Kensington Gardens; it was unveiled on May 1, 1912, near the spot where, in *The Little White Bird*, Peter disembarks from the boat fashioned from a thrush's nest. Sculptor Sir George Frampton designed the likeness after the real-life Michael Llewelyn Davies. The sculpture shows a stern, pixyish Peter playing the pipes. Bunny rabbits, squirrels, and fairies talk to one another as they climb the ornately carved pedestal on which the sprightly hero stands.

In May 1928, an identical statue was installed in Liverpool's Sefton Park, and a 19-inch miniature version is on display in the Tate Gallery in London. A well-known symbolist sculptor, Frampton also designed a monument to Queen Victoria at Leeds, a Boer War memorial in Manchester, and architectural sculptures spanning the entrance to the Victoria and Albert Museum in London.

The Wendy Craze

The charming eldest Darling child inspired scores of parents to use the name Wendy for their daughters. "Wendy" was inspired by a young friend of Barrie, Margaret Henley, who died at age five and a half. Unable to pronounce the letter "r," she used an endearment, "friendy," which sounded to Barrie like "fwendy." Saddened by the death of the child, Barrie immortalized her in his famous character. Though the name—which is related to the Welsh name Gwendydd (pronounced Gwen-deeth)—is recorded in census data (for both boys and girls) before Barrie used it, it appears only rarely. Following the production of Barrie's play and the publication of the novel, there was an explosion in the number of children named Wendy in Britain and America. The fad took hold in the 1920s and reached its peak during the 1960s and 1970s, when the Mary Martin musical was broadcast several times on television.

Other Novelists

A handful of authors have tried to assume the Barrie mantle. One of them, Gilbert Adair, is also the author of literary tributes to Thomas Mann, Lewis Carroll, and Alfred Hitchcock. His *Peter Pan and the Only Children* (1987), illustrated by Jenny Thorne, has Peter Pan trading his Neverland residence for one under the sea and finding new members for the Lost Boys among the children who tumble from ships overhead. J. Emily Somma's *After the Rain: A New Adventure for Peter Pan* (2002), illustrated by Kyle Reed, depicts an emotionally hurt Peter who feels ignored in modern times. To get even with the children who have forgotten him, Peter wishes for the world to lose its magic. In so doing he unleashes the evil Keeper, who kidnaps Tinker Bell and sends a band of soldiers to abduct Peter. With the help of three children who still believe in magic, Peter attempts to save his loyal friend while remaining free himself.

Laurie Fox's *The Lost Girls* (2004) traces the lives of five generations of Darling women visited by Peter Pan, beginning with the original Wendy. The main character, Wendy Darling Braverman, is the great-granddaughter of the first Wendy. Throughout her childhood she hears of the curse of insanity that befalls each adolescent Darling girl after a visit from Peter Pan. After her own visit, Wendy returns and marries Freeman, a man who himself avoids the trappings of adult employment and retains the mind and heart of a young boy. When it comes time for Wendy's daughter, Berry, to visit Neverland, Wendy must face difficult questions regarding motherhood, independence, self-realization, and destiny.

COMMENTS & QUESTIONS

In this section, we aim to provide the reader with an array of perspectives on the text, as well as questions that challenge those perspectives. The commentary has been culled from sources as diverse as reviews contemporaneous with the work, letters written by the author, literary criticism of later generations, and appreciations written throughout the work's history. Following the commentary, a series of questions seeks to filter J. M. Barrie's Peter Pan *through a variety of points of view and bring about a richer understanding of this enduring work.*

Comments

MAX BEERBOHM

"Peter Pan; or," adds Mr. Barrie, "The Boy Who Wouldn't Grow Up." And he himself is that boy. That child, rather; for he halted earlier than most of the men who never come to maturity—halted before the age of soldiers and steam-engines begin to dominate the soul. To remain, like Mr. Kipling, a boy, is not at all uncommon. But I know not anyone who remains, like Mr. Barrie, a child. It is this unparalleled achievement that informs so much of Mr. Barrie's later work, making it unique. This, too, surely, it is that makes Mr. Barrie the most fashionable playwright of his time.

Undoubtedly, "Peter Pan" is the best thing he has done—the thing most directly from within himself. Here, at last, we see his talent in its full maturity; for here he has stripped off from himself the last flimsy remnants of a pretence to maturity. Time was when a tiny pair of trousers peeped from under his "short-coats," and his sunny curls were parted and plastered down, and he jauntily affected the absence of a lisp, and spelt out the novels of Mr. Meredith and said he liked them very much, and even used a pipe for another purpose than that of blowing soap-bubbles. But all this while, bless his little heart, he was suffering. It would have been pleasant enough to play at being grown-up among children of his own age. It was a fearful strain to play at being grown-up among grown-up persons. But he was forced to do this, because the managers of theaters, and the publishers of books, would have been utterly dumbfounded if he had asked them to take him as he was. The public, for all its child-worship, was not yet ripe for things not written ostensibly for adults. The managers, the publishers, the public, had to be educated gradually. A stray curl or two, now and again, an infrequent soap-bubble between the fumes—that was as much as could be adventured just at first. Time passed, and mankind was lured, little by little, to the point when it could fondly accept Mr. Barrie on his own terms. The tiny trousers were slipped off, and under the toy-heap were thrust the works of Mr. Meredith. And everyone sat around, nodding and smiling to one another rather fatuously, and blessing the little heart of Mr. Barrie. All was not yet well, though—not perfectly well. By force of habit, the child occasionally gave itself the airs of an adult. There were such moments even in "Little Mary." Now, at last, we see at the Duke of York's Theater Mr. Barrie in his quiddity undiluted—the child in a state of nature, unabashed—the child, as it were, in its bath, splashing, and crowing as it splashes. . . .

For me to describe to you now in black and white the happenings in "Peter Pan" would be a thankless task. One cannot communicate the magic of a dream. People who insist on telling their dreams are among the terrors of the breakfast table. You must go to the Duke of York's, there to dream the dream for yourselves.

—from *Saturday Review* (January 7, 1905)

THE SPECTATOR

We are very grateful to Mr. J. M. Barrie for bringing Peter to closer quarters. We have known and loved him, many of us, across the footlights, but here we have him under our very eyes. It is not so much for the children among Peter's admirers that this is done. They, we feel sure, were more than content with what they had. But the "grown-ups" will welcome Mr. Barrie, and Mr. Barrie is at his best interpreting the "Never, Never Land" to them, telling them some more not only about the inhabitants of that delectable region but about Mr. and Mrs. Darling. Who will not rejoice to hear of the latter that her mind "was like tiny boxes, one within the other, that come from the puzzling East: however many you discover there is always one more?" As to Mr. Darling, we were never quite sure that Mr. Barrie was fair to him, and we are still in doubt. He behaves very handsomely in the last chapter, but then he is not permitted to have even *known* of the innermost box in Mrs. Darling's mind. On the whole we think that Mr. Barrie's attitude to him and fathers in general is that they are a necessary but unimportant part of creation. Then there is the inevitable end. Wendy grows up. Peter, for whom time does not exist, forgets to come for several years, and then, never dreaming of change, returns to find a different Wendy. Mr. Barrie knows how to do these things, but he has never done better than this—Peter sobbing on the nursery floor and Wendy, who has forgotten how to comfort him. Of course we are not left with this tragedy. Jane, Wendy's daughter, is to take her place, and so on, while children are "gay and innocent and heartless." Perhaps we feel that there could never again be quite such another as Wendy, but we are conscious that this would certainly not be Peter's point of view.

—November 10, 1911

THE ATHENÆUM

'Peter Pan' has become for the latest generation what 'Alice in Wonderland' was for a former. The foundations of Lewis Carroll's book were laid so deep that not even a generation and a half have prevailed to assail them. Elderly people still repeat tags from 'Alice,' which has passed into the traditions of the language. Will 'Peter Pan' do so? If the theme had remained embodied and embedded in the play, we should have had doubts. It is probable that the yearly expositions of Peter and Wendy and the pirates and the Neverland would have insensibly declined into exhibitions at rarer intervals, and that in time we should have had revivals on the same plan, and with the same relative frequency, as those of, say, 'Our Boys,' 'Caste,' and 'The School for Scandal.' But the translation of the fantasy into fiction has made a difference, and has more or less brought 'Peter Pan' into the competitive plane with 'Alice.' There could hardly, we must say at once, be a greater contrast of inventive and imaginative equipment. Mr. Barrie's ingenuity is as great as Lewis Carroll's, but it is exercised in another *milieu*. His notion of humour is as sharp, but less straightforward; it delights in oddities, in out-of-the-way corners, in surprises, and, it must be confessed, in sentimentalities. We experience rather a shock at the constant alternations of farce and sentiment; we are no sooner attuned to the one than the other trips it up. This is one of Mr. Barrie's methods of versatility. Some of the most delicious humour is found side by side with a rather overstrained interpretation of child-life. It is all a curious medley, but the rendering is deft and fresh beyond belief. The author's interest seems to have remained intact, as integral and sincere as that of his audience. Read, for example, the fight with the pirates, and consider if it could be improved in any way, or the conversations in the nursery, or the adventure in the lagoon. Children will enjoy this book as much as they did the play, and it will survive even the play.

—November 11, 1911

GRACE ISABEL COLBRON

Peter Pan has come to us again, Peter Pan, who was neither all a boy nor all a fairy, but something of both. He comes to us in a book which is neither a boy's book, nor a girl's book, nor a fairy book, nor anything but just a *book* which is a delight for everybody. And now that we meet him in Barrie's charming story, *Peter and Wendy*, we realise that this dainty conceit is too fairy-like to stand the necessary artificiality of the stage, too frail not to be harmed by impersonating in human shape.

The slow unfolding of the tale possible in a book, the myriad delicious details that had to be sacrificed to drama needs, surround our old friends Peter, Wendy, John, Michael, Nana the faithful nurse, the Lost Boys, the terrible Hook, the fair Tiger Lily and her Redskins, sentimental Smee, with a setting which brings them nearer to us, makes them the more human because no other human personality comes between them and us. What delight to have them in such shape that we can slip them all under the pillow at night and take them out the first thing in the morning for a stolen chat! And so many lovely new things to learn about them. Did we ever know before that Peter's greatest charm, the one which won him the hearts of all women creatures young or old, was that he had all his first teeth? And of Mrs. Darling, who walks through a few scenes in the play, a meaningless lay figure, we hear that she is in reality a lovely lady with a romantic mind and sweet mocking mouth.

—from *The Bookman* (December 1911)

Questions

1. In literature, realism is not everything. Consider the continuous popularity of *Peter Pan* from its first appearance to the present. Some deviations from realism are simply the result of bad writing; others are intentional and make a point, have meaning. What are some meaningful deviations from realism in *Peter Pan*? What meaning does flying have, for instance?

2. What is satisfying about the fantasy of a boy who never grows up? Does this conceit tap into something deep within all of us?

3. Is *Peter Pan* just for boys, or could girls enjoy it too? What is there in this tale for a girl to identify with? What is there to awaken a girl's imagination?

4. How would the ways in which a child and an adult experience *Peter Pan* differ? Can a child understand the longing for childhood in the novel as much as an adult? Can an adult sympathize with Peter's inability to grow up?

5. Critics often speak of a dark substratum in *Peter Pan*. Do you see it or feel it? If it's there, what is its source? Might incidents in Barrie's life have had something to do with it?

FOR FURTHER READING

Barrie's Other Versions of the Novel Peter Pan

The Little White Bird. London: Hodder and Stoughton, 1902.

Peter Pan in Kensington Gardens. London: Hodder and Stoughton, 1906.

Peter and Wendy. London: Hodder and Stoughton, 1911.

Biography

Chalmers, Patrick. *The Barrie Inspiration.* London: Peter Davies, 1938.

Darlington, W. A. *J. M. Barrie.* 1938. New York: Haskell House, 1974.

Darton, F. J. Harvey. *J. M. Barrie.* 1929. New York: Haskell House, 1974.

Mackail, Denis. *The Story of J. M. B.* London: Peter Davies, 1941.

J. M. Barrie and the Theater

Jack, R. D. S. *The Road to the Never Land: A Reassessment of J. M. Barrie's Dramatic Art.* Aberdeen: Aberdeen University Press, 1991.

Walbrook, H. M. *J. M. Barrie and the Theatre.* 1922. Port Washington, NY: Kennikat Press, 1969.

Criticism

Green, Roger Lancelyn. *Fifty Years of Peter Pan.* London: Peter Davies, 1954.

Hanson, Bruce K. *The Peter Pan Chronicles: The Nearly 100-Year History of the "Boy Who Wouldn't Grow Up."* Secaucus, NJ: Carol, 1993.

Rose, Jacqueline. *The Case of Peter Pan; or, The Impossibility of Children's Fiction.* London: Macmillan, 1984.

Wullschläger, Jackie. *Inventing Wonderland: The Lives and Fantasies of Lewis Carroll, Edward Lear, J. M. Barrie, Kenneth Grahame and A. A. Milne.* New York: Free Press, 1995.

Other Works Cited in the Introduction

Barrie, J. M. *Margaret Ogilvy.* New York: Charles Scribner's Sons, 1896.

———. *Peter Pan and Other Plays.* Oxford: Oxford University Press, 1995. Edited and with an introduction by Peter Hollindale. Contains *The Admirable Crichton*, *Peter Pan*, *When Wendy Grew Up*, *What Every Woman Knows*, and *Mary Rose.*

Birkin, Andrew. 1979. *J. M. Barrie and the Lost Boys.* New Haven, CT, and London: Yale University Press, 2003.

Dunbar, Janet. *J. M. Barrie: The Man Behind the Image.* Boston: Houghton Mifflin, 1970.

Geduld, Harry M. *Sir James Barrie.* New York: Twayne Publishers, 1971.

Green, Roger Lancelyn. *J. M. Barrie.* New York: Henry Z. Walck, 1961.

Robbins, Phyllis. *Maude Adams: An Intimate Portrait.* New York: Putnam, 1956.

Dead Souls	Nikolai Gogol	1-59308-092-1	$11.95
The Deerslayer	James Fenimore Cooper	1-59308-211-8	$11.95
Don Quixote	Miguel de Cervantes	1-59308-046-8	$10.95
Dracula	Bram Stoker	1-59308-114-6	$8.95
Emma	Jane Austen	1-59308-152-9	$6.95
Essays and Poems by Ralph Waldo Emerson		1-59308-076-X	$12.95
Essential Dialogues of Plato		1-59308-269-X	$12.95
The Essential Tales and Poems of Edgar Allan Poe		1-59308-064-6	$10.95
Ethan Frome and Selected Stories	Edith Wharton	1-59308-090-5	$7.95
Fairy Tales	Hans Christian Andersen	1-59308-260-6	$9.95
Far from the Madding Crowd	Thomas Hardy	1-59308-223-1	$7.95
The Federalist	Hamilton, Madison, Jay	1-59308-282-7	$10.95
Founding America: Documents from the Revolution to the Bill of Rights	Jefferson, et al.	1-59308-230-4	$13.95
Frankenstein	Mary Shelley	1-59308-115-4	$6.95
The Good Soldier	Ford Madox Ford	1-59308-268-1	$9.95
Great American Short Stories: From Hawthorne to Hemingway	Various	1-59308-086-7	$11.95
The Great Escapes: Four Slave Narratives	Various	1-59308-294-0	$6.95
Great Expectations	Charles Dickens	1-59308-116-2	$7.95
Grimm's Fairy Tales	Jacob and Wilhelm Grimm	1-59308-056-5	$10.95
Gulliver's Travels	Jonathan Swift	1-59308-132-4	$7.95
Hard Times	Charles Dickens	1-59308-156-1	$6.95
Heart of Darkness and Selected Short Fiction	Joseph Conrad	1-59308-123-5	$7.95
The History of the Peloponnesian War	Thucydides	1-59308-091-3	$12.95
The House of Mirth	Edith Wharton	1-59308-153-7	$7.95
The House of the Dead and Poor Folk	Fyodor Dostoevsky	1-59308-194-4	$9.95
The House of the Seven Gables	Nathaniel Hawthorne	1-59308-231-2	$9.95
The Hunchback of Notre Dame	Victor Hugo	1-59308-140-5	$9.95
The Idiot	Fyodor Dostoevsky	1-59308-058-1	$10.95
The Iliad	Homer	1-59308-232-0	$9.95
The Importance of Being Earnest and Four Other Plays	Oscar Wilde	1-59308-059-X	$9.95
Incidents in the Life of a Slave Girl	Harriet Jacobs	1-59308-283-5	$8.95
The Inferno	Dante Alighieri	1-59308-051-4	$10.95
The Interpretation of Dreams	Sigmund Freud	1-59308-298-3	$10.95
Ivanhoe	Sir Walter Scott	1-59308-246-0	$9.95
Jane Eyre	Charlotte Brontë	1-59308-117-0	$7.95
Journey to the Center of the Earth	Jules Verne	1-59308-252-5	$7.95
Jude the Obscure	Thomas Hardy	1-59308-035-2	$8.95
The Jungle Books	Rudyard Kipling	1-59308-109-X	$7.95
The Jungle	Upton Sinclair	1-59308-118-9	$9.95
King Solomon's Mines	H. Rider Haggard	1-59308-275-4	$9.95
Lady Chatterley's Lover	D. H. Lawrence	1-59308-239-8	$9.95
The Last of the Mohicans	James Fenimore Cooper	1-59308-137-5	$9.95
Leaves of Grass: First and "Death-bed" Editions	Walt Whitman	1-59308-083-2	$12.95
The Legend of Sleepy Hollow and Other Writings	Washington Irving	1-59308-225-8	$9.95
Les Misérables	Victor Hugo	1-59308-066-2	$11.95
Les Liaisons Dangereuses	Pierre Choderlos de Laclos	1-59308-240-1	$9.95
Little Women	Louisa May Alcott	1-59308-108-1	$7.95

(continued)

Lost Illusions	Honoré de Balzac	1-59308-315-7	$11.95
Madame Bovary	Gustave Flaubert	1-59308-052-2	$9.95
Maggie: A Girl of the Streets and Other Writings about New York	Stephen Crane	1-59308-248-7	$9.95
The Magnificent Ambersons	Booth Tarkington	1-59308-263-0	$9.95
Main Street	Sinclair Lewis	1-59308-386-6	$10.95
Man and Superman and Three Other Plays	George Bernard Shaw	1-59308-067-0	$7.95
The Man in the Iron Mask	Alexandre Dumas	1-59308-233-9	$12.95
Mansfield Park	Jane Austen	1-59308-154-5	$6.95
The Mayor of Casterbridge	Thomas Hardy	1-59308-309-2	$8.95
The Metamorphoses	Ovid	1-59308-276-2	$7.95
The Metamorphosis and Other Stories	Franz Kafka	1-59308-029-8	$9.95
Moby-Dick	Herman Melville	1-59308-018-2	$11.95
Moll Flanders	Daniel Defoe	1-59308-216-9	$9.95
My Ántonia	Willa Cather	1-59308-202-9	$6.95
My Bondage and My Freedom	Frederick Douglass	1-59308-301-7	$10.95
Narrative of Sojourner Truth		1-59308-293-2	$7.95
Narrative of the Life of Frederick Douglass, an American Slave		1-59308-041-7	$6.95
Nicholas Nickleby	Charles Dickens	1-59308-300-9	$9.95
Night and Day	Virginia Woolf	1-59308-212-6	$12.95
Nostromo	Joseph Conrad	1-59308-193-6	$11.95
Notes from Underground, The Double and Other Stories	Fyodor Dostoevsky	1-59308-124-3	$10.95
O Pioneers!	Willa Cather	1-59308-205-3	$8.95
The Odyssey	Homer	1-59308-009-3	$9.95
Of Human Bondage	W. Somerset Maugham	1-59308-238-X	$12.95
Oliver Twist	Charles Dickens	1-59308-206-1	$6.95
The Origin of Species	Charles Darwin	1-59308-077-8	$10.95
Paradise Lost	John Milton	1-59308-095-6	$9.95
The Paradiso	Dante Alighieri	1-59308-317-3	$11.95
Père Goriot	Honoré de Balzac	1-59308-285-1	$9.95
Persuasion	Jane Austen	1-59308-130-8	$5.95
Peter Pan	J. M. Barrie	1-59308-213-4	$7.95
The Phantom of the Opera	Gaston Leroux	1-59308-249-5	$8.95
The Picture of Dorian Gray	Oscar Wilde	1-59308-025-5	$6.95
The Pilgrim's Progress	John Bunyan	1-59308-254-1	$8.95
A Portrait of the Artist as a Young Man and Dubliners	James Joyce	1-59308-031-X	$8.95
The Possessed	Fyodor Dostoevsky	1-59308-250-9	$11.95
Pride and Prejudice	Jane Austen	1-59308-201-0	$6.95
The Prince and Other Writings	Niccolò Machiavelli	1-59308-060-3	$5.95
The Prince and the Pauper	Mark Twain	1-59308-218-5	$8.95
Pudd'nhead Wilson and Those Extraordinary Twins	Mark Twain	1-59308-255-X	$10.95
The Purgatorio	Dante Alighieri	1-59308-219-3	$10.95
Pygmalion and Three Other Plays	George Bernard Shaw	1-59308-078-6	$10.95
The Red Badge of Courage and Selected Short Fiction	Stephen Crane	1-59308-119-7	$6.95
Republic	Plato	1-59308-097-2	$8.95
The Return of the Native	Thomas Hardy	1-59308-220-7	$7.95
Robinson Crusoe	Daniel Defoe	1-59308-360-2	$6.95
A Room with a View	E. M. Forster	1-59308-288-6	$7.95
Scaramouche	Rafael Sabatini	1-59308-242-8	$9.95
The Scarlet Letter	Nathaniel Hawthorne	1-59308-207-X	$6.95

(continued)

The Scarlet Pimpernel	Baroness Orczy	1-59308-234-7	$8.95
The Secret Agent	Joseph Conrad	1-59308-305-X	$8.95
The Secret Garden	Frances Hodgson Burnett	1-59308-277-0	$6.95
Selected Stories of O. Henry		1-59308-042-5	$9.95
Sense and Sensibility	Jane Austen	1-59308-125-1	$5.95
Siddhartha	Hermann Hesse	1-59308-379-3	$8.95
Silas Marner and Two Short Stories	George Eliot	1-59308-251-7	$6.95
Sister Carrie	Theodore Dreiser	1-59308-226-6	$11.95
The Souls of Black Folk	W. E. B. Du Bois	1-59308-014-X	$8.95
The Strange Case of Dr. Jekyll and Mr. Hyde and Other Stories	Robert Louis Stevenson	1-59308-131-6	$6.95
Swann's Way	Marcel Proust	1-59308-295-9	$12.95
A Tale of Two Cities	Charles Dickens	1-59308-138-3	$6.95
Tarzan of the Apes	Edgar Rice Burroughs	1-59308-227-4	$8.95
Tess of d'Urbervilles	Thomas Hardy	1-59308-228-2	$8.95
This Side of Paradise	F. Scott Fitzgerald	1-59308-243-6	$9.95
Three Theban Plays	Sophocles	1-59308-235-5	$8.95
Thus Spoke Zarathustra	Friedrich Nietzsche	1-59308-278-9	$9.95
The Time Machine and The Invisible Man	H. G. Wells	1-59308-388-2	$7.95
Tom Jones	Henry Fielding	1-59308-070-0	$10.95
Treasure Island	Robert Louis Stevenson	1-59308-247-9	$6.95
The Turn of the Screw, The Aspern Papers and Two Stories	Henry James	1-59308-043-3	$5.95
Twenty Thousand Leagues Under the Sea	Jules Verne	1-59308-302-5	$8.95
Uncle Tom's Cabin	Harriet Beecher Stowe	1-59308-121-9	$7.95
Vanity Fair	William Makepeace Thackeray	1-59308-071-9	$8.95
The Varieties of Religious Experience	William James	1-59308-072-7	$11.95
Villette	Charlotte Brontë	1-59308-316-5	$10.95
The Virginian	Owen Wister	1-59308-236-3	$10.95
Walden and Civil Disobedience	Henry David Thoreau	1-59308-208-8	$8.95
War and Peace	Leo Tolstoy	1-59308-073-5	$12.95
The War of the Worlds	H. G. Wells	1-59308-362-9	$6.95
Ward No. 6 and Other Stories	Anton Chekhov	1-59308-003-4	$8.95
The Waste Land and Other Poems	T. S. Eliot	1-59308-279-7	$7.95
The Way We Live Now	Anthony Trollope	1-59308-304-1	$12.95
The Wind in the Willows	Kenneth Grahame	1-59308-265-7	$9.95
The Wings of the Dove	Henry James	1-59308-296-7	$9.95
Wives and Daughters	Elizabeth Gaskell	1-59308-257-6	$10.95
The Woman in White	Wilkie Collins	1-59308-280-0	$8.95
Women in Love	D. H. Lawrence	1-59308-258-4	$9.95
The Wonderful Wizard of Oz	L. Frank Baum	1-59308-221-5	$9.95
Wuthering Heights	Emily Brontë	1-59308-128-6	$5.95

BARNES & NOBLE CLASSICS

If you are an educator and would like to receive an
Examination or Desk Copy of a Barnes & Noble Classics edition,
please refer to Academic Resources on our website at
WWW.BN.COM/CLASSICS
or contact us at
BNCLASSICS@BN.COM

All prices are subject to change.

0116